FANTOMINA
AND OTHER WORKS

FANTOMINA
AND OTHER WORKS

Eliza Haywood

edited by Alexander Pettit,
Margaret Case Croskery, and Anna C. Patchias

broadview literary texts

National Library of Canada Cataloguing in Publication Data

Haywood, Eliza, 1693?–1756
    Fantomina and other works / Eliza Haywood ; edited by Alexander Pettit, Margaret Case Croskery, and Anna C. Patchias.

(Broadview literary texts)
Includes bibliographical references.
ISBN 1-55111-524-7

I. Pettit, Alexander, 1958– II. Croskery, Margaret Case, 1961–
III. Patchias, Anna C., 1970– IV. Title. V. Series.

PR3506.H94F35 2004   828'.508   C2003-905973-1

Broadview Press Ltd. is an independent, international publishing house, incorporated in 1985. Broadview believes in shared ownership, both with its employees and with the general public; since the year 2000 Broadview shares have traded publicly on the Toronto Venture Exchange under the symbol BDP.

We welcome comments and suggestions regarding any aspect of our publications—please feel free to contact us at the addresses below or at broadview@broadviewpress.com.

North America
PO Box 1243, Peterborough, Ontario, Canada K9J 7H5
Tel: (705) 743-8990; Fax: (705) 743-8353
email: customerservice@broadviewpress.com
3576 California Road, Orchard Park, NY, USA 14127

UK, Ireland, and continental Europe
NBN Plymbridge
Estover Road
Plymouth PL6 7PY UK
Tel: 44 (0) 1752 202 301
Fax: 44 (0) 1752 202 331
Fax Order Line: 44 (0) 1752 202 333
Customer Service: cserv@nbnplymbridge.com
Orders: orders@nbnplymbridge.com

Australia and New Zealand
UNIREPS, University of New South Wales
Sydney, NSW, 2052
Tel: 61 2 9664 0999; Fax: 61 2 9664 5420
email: info.press@unsw.edu.au
www.broadviewpress.com

Series editor: Professor L.W. Conolly
Advisory editor for this volume: Professor Eugene Benson

PRINTED IN CANADA

Contents

Acknowledgements

I would like to offer hearty and profuse thanks to my co-editors, whose intelligence, good humor, and enthusiasm made this project a great pleasure. Patrick Spedding showed characteristic generosity by sharing with me, Anna, and Margaret parts of his forthcoming *Bibliography of Eliza Haywood* (London: Pickering & Chatto) and by answering many questions about Haywood's life and work with celerity, tact, and precision. Christine Blouch kindly allowed us to use the chronology from her Broadview edition of *The History of Miss Betsy Thoughtless* (1998) as a template for our own list of Haywood's works and significant dates. Rebecca Sayers Hanson compiled the bibliography, with funding from the Department of English, University of North Texas, James T.F. Tanner, chair. Alan Fisher provided the Latin translations; Serge Soupel and Jacqueline Vanhoutte helped out with Matters French. Thanks to James Powell and Mark Pollard at Pickering & Chatto, London, for supporting the *Selected Works of Eliza Haywood* (2000-2001) and for authorizing the reprinting of three of the texts from that series. Julia Gaunce and Barbara Conolly at Broadview were consistently helpful. As always, love to Jacque, Sidney, and Emma.

A.P.

Anna C. Patchias dedicates this book to her parents, James and Christina Patchias, and her sister, Elizabeth Patchias, with gratitude for their boundless love and support; and to her husband, Patrick Keady, for his tireless efforts on behalf of this edition and his standards of editorial excellence. Margaret Case Croskery dedicates this book with deep love and gratitude to her two families, the Cases and the Croskerys; and to her husband, Patrick Croskery, who has read *Fantomina* backward more often than forward.

We would also like to thank Alex Pettit, whose mentorship sets the standard for all mentors. Our thanks too to Garrett Brown, whose advice has always been as generous as his love and support. We are also grateful to David Vander Meulen, who taught us the principles of scholarly editing at the University of Virginia; his editorial acuity and generosity of spirit continue to inspire us. The British Library, the Bodleian Library at the University of Oxford, and the Sterling Library at Yale University provided us with various editions of *Fantomina*. Mary Wootton at the Library of Congress and Lynne Farrington and John Pollack at the University of Pennsylvania's Annenberg Rare Book and Manuscript Library were helpful during our collation process. We owe a debt of gratitude to Carter Hailey for allowing us the use of his collator, the 'Comet', and to David L. Gants for teaching us how to use it. We are grateful to Bryson Clevenger at the University of Virginia's Alderman Library for his expertise and guidance. Margaret would also like to thank Charles Steele at Ohio Northern University's Heterick Memorial Library for his cheerful assistance and Kevin L. Cope for authorizing the republication in this volume of several paragraphs of an essay written for *1650–1850: Ideas, Aesthetics, and Inquiries in the Early Modern Era*.

Our debt to the guiding scholarship of Patrick Spedding and Christine Blouch is incalculable. We owe special thanks, also, to Rebecca Sayers Hanson for stellar work under grueling circumstances. Finally, thanks to everyone at Broadview Press for their support.

M.C.C.
A.C.P.

Introduction

When eighteenth-century readers thought about the novel, many of them probably thought first of one writer in particular—Eliza Haywood. As one historian of the novel points out, 'it was Eliza Haywood, more than any other native fiction writer, whose name was identified with the novel'.[1] Haywood's first novel, *Love in Excess* (1719), came out the same year that Daniel Defoe published *Robinson Crusoe*. Both novels were hugely successful. Indeed, three of the most popular British novels before 1740 were *Love in Excess*, *Robinson Crusoe*, and *Gulliver's Travels* (1726).[2] But few of Haywood's works were republished between the eighteenth century and 1963, and many modern readers of *Robinson Crusoe* and *Gulliver's Travels* have never heard of Haywood.

This raises certain questions. Why did Haywood drop out of literary history? Why are her works now undergoing substantial reassessment? And why are so many of them now being printed in widely available editions, often, like the current volume, intended in part for classroom use?

The answers to these questions are varied and complex. Certainly the fact that Haywood was an exceptionally prolific, well-known, and best-selling woman writer—at a time when female authorship was widely considered to be the literary equivalent of prostitution—goes a long way toward explaining her temporary eclipse. As a professional woman writer in a competitive and predominantly male profession, Haywood's successes brought her a certain notoriety. But her one-time deletion from the literary canon and her importance to literary studies today cannot be explained simply in terms of gender. The circumstances of Haywood's life, the history of the early eighteenth-century novel, the bias against didactic and popular literature, and Haywood's complicated experiments with genre also help explain her near-erasure and her subsequent recovery.

---

[1] Jerry C. Beasley, *Novels of the 1740s* (Athens: U of Georgia P, 1982) 162.

[2] William H. McBurney, 'Mrs. Penelope Aubin and the Early Eighteenth-Century Novel', *Huntington Library Quarterly* 20 (1957): 250.

Haywood's Life and Career

Although much is known about Haywood, many important facts about her life remain obscure. Few of her personal documents, and none of her manuscripts, have survived. It is no surprise, therefore, that until recently myths and misinformation formed the greater part of her biography. Some of these misconceptions were promulgated by Haywood's first modern biographer, George Frisbie Whicher.[1] Recent research has begun to correct the record, with salubrious results; most notably, biographical work by Christine Blouch has had a wide-ranging influence, affecting Haywood's place in literary history as well as the critical reception of her work.[2]

We do know when Haywood died (25 February 1756) and where she is buried (St. Margaret's, London). We do not know exactly when—or where—she was born. Blouch has identified two possible sets of parents for Elizabeth Fowler (Haywood's maiden name), and she has suggested a connection between one of these families and a third, well-to-do family. This conflicting information has given rise to two possible birth dates, 1689 and 1693. Blouch finds the weight of evidence inclining toward the later date (pp. xxii–xxiv).

Perhaps the most damaging misconception about Haywood devolves from the erroneous belief that she was the runaway wife of a preacher named Valentine Haywood—a theory that Whicher advanced from scanty if suggestive documentary evidence. This account ensured Haywood's early twentieth-century notoriety and endured until Blouch showed it to be inaccurate.[3] In the midst of so much mystery, one tantalizing detail remains: Haywood herself describes her marriage as 'unfortunate' and cites it as the reason that she was forced to earn a living by her pen

---

1   See Whicher, *The Life and Romances of Mrs. Eliza Haywood* (New York: Columbia UP, 1915).

2   See Blouch, 'Eliza Haywood and the Romance of Obscurity', *SEL: Studies in English Literature, 1500–1900* 31 (1991): 535–51; and 'Eliza Haywood', in *Miscellaneous Writings, 1725–43*, ed. Alexander Pettit, set 1, vol. i of *Selected Works of Eliza Haywood* (London: Pickering & Chatto, 2000) xxi–lxxxii. Except as noted, further references to Blouch are to the more recent essay.

3   Blouch, 'Eliza Haywood and the Romance of Obscurity', 538–40.

(Blouch, p. xxiv). The identity of her husband remains unclear, however, as do other circumstances of the marriage.

At least by 1715, when she appeared in a leading role on the Dublin stage, Elizabeth Fowler had begun presenting herself as Eliza Haywood. In pursuing her acting career she went against her family's wishes and against cultural bias more generally. Little is known of her roles and performances, but there is no doubt that in 1717 Haywood moved to London in an attempt to bolster her fortunes as an actress (Blouch, pp. xxvii–xxix). The venture did not last long, and by her own account—'the Stage not answering my expectations' (qtd. in Blouch, p. xxix)—she was obliged to turn to other means of support.

Haywood's decision to trade the stage for the pen was a felicitous one. *Love in Excess* went through two editions and several reissues between its publication in 1719 and its appearance in Haywood's first collected edition, *The Works of Mrs. Eliza Haywood*, in 1724. A second collected edition followed in 1725, entitled *Secret Histories, Novels, and Poems* and containing new material—such as *Fantomina: or, Love in a Maze* in volume 3—as well as reissues of previous works. Blouch reports that by 1724 Haywood had written fourteen novels, two plays, a periodical, a translation, and a short book of poems (p. xxxv). Although her pace dropped off somewhat after this initial outpouring, Haywood would continue to publish steadily throughout her life.

The particulars of Haywood's life during the 1720s are sketchy but engaging. Haywood was involved in a social 'circle' anchored by the essayist and dramatist Aaron Hill and including the playwright Susannah Centlivre and the minor poet and perennial ne'er-do-well Richard Savage. Haywood and Savage had a romantic relationship between 1720 and 1724, though the reasons it ended are unclear. Haywood's few remaining papers confirm the existence of two children, probably illegitimate; one of them may have been fathered by Savage. The other was perhaps fathered by William Hatchett, a minor playwright and actor with whom Haywood became involved after 1724 and with whom she evidently shared a domestic and professional relationship until her death (Blouch, pp. xxxii–xl).

England's preeminent poet, Alexander Pope, rather cruelly

called attention to Haywood's 'two babes of love' in *The Dunciad* (1728; bk. ii, l. 150), and some of Haywood's biographers have made strong claims about the effect on Haywood of Pope's portrayal. On the face of it, such claims seem reasonable; after all, the portrayal concludes with Haywood as the prize in a mock-heroic pissing contest between the publishers William Chetwood and Edmund Curll, the winner of which is promised 'yon Juno of majestic size, / With cow-like udders, and with ox-like eyes' (ll. 155–56). But these assessments are retrospective and based on the assumption that the publication of *The Dunciad* was connected to Haywood's relatively modest output during the 1730s. The bibliographical record speaks differently, however. Although Haywood did decrease her output, particularly of fiction, in the years following the publication of *The Dunciad*, she produced at least eight new works from 1729 to 1739—hardly a laggard's pace. She also returned to the theater. In 1729, she wrote her first play in six years; and in 1730, 1736, and 1737, she again appeared on stage, during the last year as a member of Henry Fielding's troupe at the Little Haymarket theater. Scholars continue to identify publishing ventures and projects in which Haywood was involved during and after the 1730s, and new works are now being attributed to her that add to her already extensive output during this period.

Haywood wrote two political satires during the 1730s that participated in the noisy debate about the nature of government. One of these, *The Adventures of Eovaai, Princess of Ijaveo* (written in 1736 and thus situated chronologically between 'amatory fictions' such as *Fantomina* and Haywood's later domestic novels) investigates the intersections of gender and power in social and political life. *Eovaai* is primarily a satire of Sir Robert Walpole, de facto prime minister from 1721 to 1742 and frequent butt of 'opposition' satire. But like many of Haywood's works, it is a blend of genres, merging political satire with oriental fantasy, erotic novel, imaginary voyage, and romance.

Haywood continued to engage contemporary political issues in the 1740s and 1750s, but most of her productions during this period were broader in scope. *The Female Spectator*, probably her most famous work, addresses some of the liveliest literary, political, scientific, and philosophical questions of the day. Although scholars have focused on its feminist bent—it is considered the first periodical written for women by a woman—it is much more than an exercise in ideology. Issued in twenty-four installments between April 1744 and May 1746, the work was an enormous popular and commercial success; the publisher began reissuing individual parts before the original print run had ended. The collected set went through nine editions in the next thirty years and was translated into a number of different languages. Either Haywood or her publisher (or both) must have been convinced that mentioning this work on a title page would boost sales of her other publications. Four of Haywood's subsequent works mention either *The Female Spectator* or one of its four female 'authors' on their title pages.

During the late 1740s and the 1750s, Haywood continued to write across a spectrum of genres. The fact that she was writing works on conduct such as *Epistles for the Ladies* (1748–50), *The Wife* (1755), and *The Husband* (1756) should not be taken to suggest that she had lost her taste for opposition politics. In 1749, Haywood produced an inflammatory pamphlet entitled *A Letter from H—— G——g, Esq.* This work pretended to be a letter from the 'Young Pretender', Charles Edward Stuart, whose claim to the throne had prompted the Jacobite uprising of 1745—a direct assault on the monarchy of King George II. She was arrested for publishing the pamphlet, although she was never prosecuted. In a rather different vein, Haywood in 1751 published one of the novels for which she would be best remembered, *The History of Miss Betsy Thoughtless*. This work is remarkable for its depiction of marital discord (an unusual topic for novels in Haywood's day) and for its sustained psychological scrutiny of the slow progress of a passion that both thwarts and educates its heroine.

While working in 1756 on a new weekly publication, *The Young Lady*, Haywood became ill and was forced to stop writing. She died fifteen days after reporting her illness in that periodical. Little public comment was made on her death, and none of her contemporaries ventured a biography. Indeed, according to David Erskine Baker in 1764, Haywood took steps to ensure that the details of her life would not be published: 'From a supposition of some improper liberties being taken with her [history] ... she laid a solemn injunction on a person who was well acquainted with all the particulars of it, not to communicate to any one the least circumstance relating to her'.[1] Blouch surmises that this person was William Hatchett (p. lxxxi). In any event, the injunction has cast a long shadow, although the recent successes of Blouch and others bode well for further research into Haywood's life and career.

The Eighteenth-Century Novel under Attack

The fact that many modern readers have not heard of Haywood has a great deal to do with the fact that her own early readers knew her name very well indeed. 'Mrs. Novel', as Henry Fielding dubbed her in his play *The Author's Farce* (1730), achieved her eighteenth-century notoriety partly because she was identified with a popular mode that was itself notorious. The novel's 'newness' (the word 'novel' evokes the idea of 'novelty') and its tendency to tap into rebellious instincts and question ethical and sexual mores provoked anxiety in many of Haywood's contemporaries. Pope's account perhaps suggests as much. One especially striking aspect of the novel was its tendency to portray everyday characters in familiar situations—a new tendency in fiction during the 1720s but by mid-century a defining feature of the genre. This worried the eighteenth-century pundit, Samuel Johnson, who in 1750 warned against 'the works of fiction, with which the present generation seems more particularly delighted'.[2] Johnson was particularly concerned about how the trend toward realism in the novel would affect impressionable youths. His essay was primarily a response to recent novels by Henry Fielding and Tobias Smollett, but it is nonetheless applicable to what his readers would have regarded as an upstart genre. According to Johnson, 'when an adventurer is levelled with the rest of the world ... young spectators fix their eyes upon him with closer attention, and hope by observing his behaviour and success to regulate their own practices, when they shall be engaged in the like part' (p. 176).

---

[1] Baker, *Biographia Dramatica* (1764), vol. ii, 321.

[2] Johnson, *Rambler* 4 (31 Mar. 1750), in *Samuel Johnson*, ed. Donald Greene (Oxford: Oxford UP, 1984) 175.

In other words, Johnson thought that the danger of the novel lay in the eagerness of inexperienced readers to identify too closely with characters drawn, as we would say today, 'realistically'. This development seemed curious to Johnson and many of his contemporaries, because earlier popular fictions had generally been quasi-historical 'romances': stories of knights or princes rescuing equally well-born women, fighting famous battles, and achieving impossible feats of physical prowess. In these earlier and transparently 'fictional' fictions, Johnson believed, there was no danger of readerly over-identification, because 'every transaction and sentiment was so remote from all that passes among men, that the reader was in very little danger of making any applications to himself' (p. 176). By way of contrast, many recent fictions were set in London and featured protagonists indistinguishable from people whom one might encounter on the street—*Fantomina* and *The Tea-Table: or, A Conversation between Some Polite Persons of Both Sexes*, in the present collection, are cases in point. Johnson worried that the power of such examples might be 'so great as to take possession of the memory by a kind of violence, and produce effects almost without the intervention of the will' (p. 176). Although novels are rarely the targets of such worries today, Johnson's arguments anticipate current concerns about representations of violence and sexuality on television and in music. In this age-old debate over the influence of realistic art on life, only the targeted media have changed.

Johnson's solution was to advise novelists to use fiction to inculcate virtue in young readers. Instead of favoring characters that blend good and evil, writers should create characters that advertised a plainly identifiable moral status. Johnson believed that less moral harm would result from fiction if readers identified with unequivocally 'good' characters.

Haywood was of another mind, and her representational habits would prove more indicative of future trends than those that Johnson endorsed. She argued in her introduction to *Life's Progress through the Passions; or, The Adventures of Natura* (1748) that

it ought to be considered, that if the pattern laid down before us, is so altogether angelic, as to render it impossible to be copied, emulation will be in danger of being swallowed up in an unprofitable admiration .... There never yet was any one man, in whom all the *virtues*, or all the *vices*, were summed up; for, though reason and education may go a long way toward curbing the passions, yet I believe experience will inform, even the *best* of men, that they will sometimes launch out beyond their due bounds, in spite of all the care [that] can be taken to restrain them ... (pp. 1–2)

Haywood here defends her right to create realistic 'mixed' characters in whom, as she describes it, the passions 'launch out beyond their due bounds'. In this passage, as in her early and late fiction, Haywood argues that the most interesting and instructive stories occur when passion is intensified sufficiently to overcome prudence.

Haywood's interest in characters under the stress of their own emotions positions her among the writers of her day who employed a more mediated strain of didacticism. Instead of making her characters fit prescribed moral standards of behavior, Haywood often preferred characters that broke social taboos. These stories were often not susceptible to reductive moral treatment; instead their subject was the experience of intense emotion and the 'secret springs' that motivate human behavior, as Haywood puts it in the introduction to *Life's Progress through the Passions* (p. 3). In so doing, she helped widen the subject matter of the novel both in her own time and in times to come. Haywood's preference for exploring the psyche under duress and for creating characters shaped by the power of experience (instead of by overtly didactic moral precepts) would become hallmarks of the novel as a genre.

In *Reflections on the Various Effects of Love* (1726), Haywood supposes that people in the throes of love are most likely to encounter conflicts that bring out hidden aspects of their characters. She must also have noticed that narratives structured around this belief attracted an audience eager for erotic titillation. The following passage from *The Adventures of Eovaai* is typical of Haywood's sexually charged fiction of the 1720s and 1730s. Here, the virtuous Princess Eovaai is on the verge of succumbing to an evil tyrant, Ochihatou. He invites her into his garden, where he provides every luxury he can think of to heighten her interest, including 'Rich Viands, delicious Wines, Musick, Dancing, Dalliance, and, above all, the ardent Pressures of a Man, whom if she cou'd not be said to *love*, she infinitely liked'.[1] Ultimately, Eovaai's impressive powers of reason are overmatched by her nascent sexual desires:

> After such Excitements, the Sweetness and Privacy of the Recess they were in, could not fail of inspiring her with that dissolving Softness which *Ochihatou* wished to find in her ... her shining Eyes swam in a Sea of Languor ... her Bosom heav'd more quick: a sweet Confusion reigned in every Part: the transported Lover snatch'd her to his Breast, printed unnumbered Kisses on her Lips, then held her off to feast his Eyes upon her yielding Charms: Beauties which till then he knew but in Idea, her treacherous Robes too loosly girt revealed: his eager Hands were Seconds to his Sight, and travell'd over all; while she, in gentle Sighs and faultering Accents, confessed she received a Pleasure not inferior to that she gave. (pp. 78–79)

The theme of seduction; the wealth of sensual detail; the unembarrassed observation that her heroine experiences a 'dissolving softness'; and the hovering, potentially lethal, presence of betrayal are all characteristic of Haywood's early fiction. Although tame by modern standards, in its day this description of sexual seduction—in which the heroine 'received a Pleasure not inferior to that she gave'—would have offended many readers.

And readers *were* offended, as one sees in Pope's response to Haywood, marked as it is by its emphasis on physicality ('udders ... eyes') and sexuality ('babes of love'). Unquestionably, this attack on 'Mrs. Novel' was part of a larger battle against what Pope, Johnson, and like-minded humanists perceived as the decline of literary culture. Numerous critics of the early novel

---

[1] Haywood, *The Adventures of Eovaai, Princess of Ijaveo*, ed. Earla Wilputte (Peterborough, ON: Broadview, 1999) 78.

were concerned that young women readers would become tempted by scandalous novels to indulge in amorous affairs. A periodical writer during Haywood's lifetime lumped 'Romances, Chocolate, Novels, and the like Inflamers' into his harangue against eighteenth-century British culture.[1] Novels, like chocolates, were believed to act as aphrodisiacs.

Many novels seemed deliberately to court such censure, celebrating libertine attitudes of sexual behavior that were not tolerated by the general public after the death of Charles II in 1665. Works such as Jean Barrin's(?) *Venus in the Cloister; or, the Nun in her Smock* (trans. 1724; see Appendix B, below) and John Cleland's *Memoirs of a Woman of Pleasure* (1748–49) explored an underground world of rife sexuality in which hedonism trumped conventional religious precepts. This trend toward sexual 'realism' contributed much to the novel's bad reputation.

Here it should be noted that against the backdrop of pornographic fiction, Haywood's works were in some ways quite tame: they typically mimicked acceptable moral fiction, even as they strayed beyond certain conventional boundaries. Had they been either outrageously pornographic or dully conventional, Haywood's early works would probably not have troubled critics such as Pope and Johnson. It was their melding of the moral and the erotic that made them suspect.

As the cultural climate became more conservative, Haywood changed too, toning down some of the controversial aspects of her writing in works such as *Betsy Thoughtless*. Clara Reeve, who wrote about Haywood in her literary history *The Progress of Romance* (1785), characterized Haywood's shift in tone as a personal reformation, one that stemmed from a desire to write more 'moral' books as an atonement for her early erotic works. The main character of *The Progress of Romance* declares, 'I would be the last to vindicate [Haywood's] faults, but the first to celebrate her return to virtue, and her atonement for them' (vol. i, p. 122). Reeve's account should not be taken at face value, although some critics have done just that. Until recently, the idea that Haywood's early

---

[1]   Qtd. in Geoffrey Day, *From Fiction to the Novel* (New York: Routledge & Kegan Paul, 1987) 134.

fiction is somehow more 'radical' than her later work has impeded more complex critical assessments, particularly of her later writings. There is much that is conservative in Haywood's later works, but there is also much that remained controversial. For example, the selection from *The Female Spectator* reproduced in Appendix A, below, points out a tension between the later more didactic strain in Haywood's works and the more sexually charged content of her early writings; Blouch is right to find in Haywood's later work some of her 'most ambitious experiments in genre to date' (p. lii). Indeed, as the assortment of texts in this volume reveals, one common thread throughout Haywood's oeuvre is an interest in the taboo subject of erotic passion and 'questions of sexual and social identity' (Blouch, p. lxiv).

This emphasis is one that Haywood shares with many of the better-known and more widely read novelists who have traditionally constituted the canon of eighteenth-century fiction. It is no accident, however, that most of these contemporaries chose not to associate themselves directly with the new genre. As one scholar points out, of the five male authors long deemed the 'fathers' of the British novel (Defoe, Fielding, Smollett, Samuel Richardson, and Laurence Sterne), only Smollett was willing to use the word 'novel' to describe one of his works of fiction.[1] Fielding and Richardson preferred the word 'history'. But early in the eighteenth century, 'Mrs. Novel' was intimately associated with the genre. This accounts at least in part for both her early widespread popularity and the subsequent decline in her literary-historical fortunes. As novel writers and publishers struggled to lift themselves from the scandalous milieu of the novel's early origins, writers such as Haywood who had contributed so much to the novel's early notoriety became embarrassing liabilities to a genre interested in gaining credibility.

Critical Background

Haywood is now one of the most-discussed writers, male or female, among scholars of the British eighteenth century. More

---

[1] Day, *From Fiction to the Novel*, 22; and see Smollett, *The Adventures of Ferdinand Count Fathom*, ed. Jerry C. Beasley and O M Brack, Jr. (Athens: U of Georgia P, 1988) 4.

than fifteen of her texts have been edited and published in the last fifteen years; the first substantial edition of her works appeared in six volumes in 2000 and 2001. A compendious bibliography will appear contemporaneously with this volume. *Fantomina* appears in several recent anthologies, and the first collection of critical essays on Haywood was published in 2000. To account for this phenomenon, one must consider the shift in emphasis within the academy from a purely 'literary' model of scholarship to a more expanded 'cultural' paradigm.

Scholars of the early to mid-twentieth century tended to consider Haywood (when they considered her at all) as an ill-formed precursor to maturer talents such as Defoe, Richardson, Fielding, Smollett, and Sterne. The feminist recovery effort of the 1970s, however, initiated the revival of interest in Haywood. Scholars of this period often regarded Haywood as a pioneer of feminist protest literature, in which capacity she was often grouped with a trio of female writers, whom one author of the 1720s had called 'the fair triumvirate of wit'—Aphra Behn, Delariviere Manley, and Haywood.[1]

When feminist critics began retelling the story of the novel within the traditions of domestic romance and amatory fiction, the stock of the 'fair triumvirate' rose accordingly. Ironically, this shift in scholarly interest at first caused a mild backlash against Haywood. Because her novels often punished sexually desiring women and because they did not always trumpet overtly or exclusively political agendas—many feminist critics found Haywood's depictions of female agency less powerful than Behn's and Manley's.

However, as scholars continue to reposition the parameters of literary value, Haywood becomes more central to the debate. Catherine Ingrassia, for example, argues that Haywood's novels operated much like the early stock market (which developed in Britain contemporaneously with the novel). When consumers bought a novel, or invested in stock, they could 'reinvent themselves and envisage their lives differently'.[2] William B. Warner

---

[1] James Sterling, 'To Mrs. Eliza Haywood, on Her Writings', in Haywood, *Secret Histories, Novels, and Poems* (1725), vol. i, a2.

[2] Ingrassia, *Authorship, Commerce, and Gender in Early Eighteenth-Century England: A Culture of Paper Credit* (New York: Cambridge UP, 1998) 2.

notes Haywood's involvement with early modern forms of 'private entertainment' that encouraged the reader to read for sheer enjoyment.[1] He echoes Pope when he argues that such fiction 'cannot be fixed as literary because it sustains its status as a form of entertainment and continues to feel the deforming tug of media culture' (p. 289).

Haywood, that is, generates controversy now as she did in her own time. As both Pope's attack in *The Dunciad* and recent claims that Haywood should not be regarded as a 'literary' figure demonstrate, her works have long been used as a standard against which the novel has measured itself. They are thus becoming increasingly important to a deeper understanding of the process by which we evaluate 'literary' as well as 'popular' texts.

Such new approaches to Haywood are part of what Paula R. Backscheider has described as the ongoing 'reconsideration of aesthetic standards and attention to material contexts, popular culture, and hegemonic processes' that inform the history of the novel. These processes, Backscheider suggests, 'will contribute substantially to the elucidation of Haywood's texts and her career'.[2] The reverse is no doubt true as well. The study of Haywood's work has a great deal to offer studies of the novel. If, as Backscheider claims, 'the movement in the English novel throughout the [eighteenth] century is toward the psychological, not the realistic' (p. 41), then Haywood may have shaped novelistic practice in ways that have yet to be fully understood.

Literary Background: *Fantomina* in Context

In *Fantomina*, Haywood often employs rhetorical conventions or draws on familiar literary genres to capture the experience of intense passion. For example, when, despite his vows of eternal constancy, Beauplaisir tires of the mysterious young woman who has identified herself only as 'Fantomina', the resourceful heroine

---

[1] Warner, *Licensing Entertainment: The Elevation of Novel Reading in Britain, 1684–1750* (Berkeley: U of California P, 1998) 92–93.

[2] Backscheider, 'The Story of Eliza Haywood's Novels: Caveats and Questions', in *The Passionate Fictions of Eliza Haywood: Essays on Her Life and Work* (Lexington: U of Kentucky P, 2000) 41.

does not rant and rave as a typical jilted lover might. In *The Tea-Table*, for example, Celemena gives vent to a 'sudden Rage of Temper' and issues 'Cries and Exclamations' so loudly that she can be heard from great distances (p. 96). 'Fantomina' simply pretends not to understand Beauplaisir's desire to leave her. Moreover, her reaction to this potentially devastating state of affairs contains a subtle comic send-up of standard conduct-book rhetoric. After she learns that Beauplaisir intends to leave her,

> she plainly saw it was for no other Reason, than that being tir'd of her Conversation, he was willing to be at liberty to pursue new Conquests; and wisely considering that Complaints, Tears, Swoonings, and all the Extravagancies which Women make use of in such Cases, have little Prevailance over a Heart inclin'd to rove, and only serve to render those who practise them more contemptible, by robbing them of that Beauty which alone can bring back the fugitive Lover, she resolved to take another Course .... (p. 51)

John J. Richetti observes that 'Complaints, Tears, [and] Swoonings' are the primary emotional capital in the typical 'persecuted maiden' story.[1] However, 'Fantomina' has better roles to play than that one; her next 'Course' is a turn as Celia, the innocent chambermaid. For all her donning and doffing of disguises, she never presents herself as 'persecuted'.

Eighteenth-century readers would have recognized the language of the conduct book in the heroine's idea that there is only one 'Beauty which alone can bring back the fugitive Lover' (p. 51). Conduct books often advised women to rely on the 'beauties' of feminine virtue: patience, submission, and clemency. They also counseled silence when men had extramarital affairs. According to the double standard of the day, it was expected that men would be adulterous and that women would remain constant. The popular manual *The Lady's New-Year's Gift: or, Advice to a Daughter* (1688), by George Saville, Earl of Halifax,

---

[1] Richetti, *Popular Fiction Before Richardson: Narrative Patterns 1700–1739* (Oxford: Clarendon, 1969) 208.

gives this advice to wives who are confronted with an unfaithful husband: 'Do not seem to look or hear that way: if he is a man of sense, he will reclaim himself ... [but] if he is not so, he will be provoked, but not reformed' (p. 18). 'Besides', he adds,

> modesty no less than prudence ought to restrain her; since such an undecent complaint makes a wife much more ridiculous, than the injury that provoketh her to it .... Be assured, that in these cases your discretion and silence will be the most prevailing reproof; an affected ignorance, which is seldom a virtue, is a great one here. (pp. 18–19)

Haywood herself voices these conventional sentiments in *The Wife*, but the heroine of *Fantomina* goes far beyond Halifax's advice. She does not complain; instead, she makes it impossible for Beauplaisir to break his vows to her, seducing him over and over again, changing her disguise each time.

The heroine's successive disguises also flout the conventions of a popular form of eighteenth-century fiction: the story of the seduced or persecuted maiden with which Richetti somewhat misleadingly affiliates *Fantomina*. In this type of story, a lovely and innocent woman is seduced by a remorseless libertine. Such stories were early 'tear-jerkers' and almost always ended unhappily. Often they encoded a didactic message, warning virtuous women about the consequences of relaxing their moral vigilance. *Fantomina* suggests just such a scenario, emphasizing the vulnerability, willfulness, and lack of guidance that often led the 'persecuted maiden' into trouble. The heroine 'was young, a Stranger to the World, and consequently to the Dangers of it; and having no Body in Town, at that Time, to whom she was oblig'd to be accountable for her Actions, did every Thing as her Inclinations or Humours render'd most agreeable to her' (pp. 41–42). Readers accustomed to the normal trajectory of such stories would at this point expect the heroine to become a victim of her own ignorance or willfulness. And at first, this is what seems to happen. But Haywood refuses to follow the formula.

Perhaps the most famous of all 'persecuted maiden' stories was one of the few that ended happily—Richardson's *Pamela* (1740), the story of a young servant girl whose refusal to be seduced by her young master inspires him to marry her. Like *Fantomina*, *Pamela* breaks the conventions of the genre. However, where Richardson borrows the platitudes of Christian humanism to subvert the conventions of the 'persecuted maiden' genre, Haywood looks to a more recent literary tradition: the comic drama of the late seventeenth century. Restoration comedies focused not on the tragedy of lost love and ruined virtue but on the joy and wit and danger of seduction. By importing elements of disguise, wit, and sexual freedom from Restoration comedy into a narrative that initially evokes the tragic plot of the persecuted maiden, Haywood draws attention to the fact that both genres share an interest in the process of seduction. Perhaps because Haywood refuses to choose between the two genres, *Fantomina* escapes the traditional ending of either Restoration comedy (marriage) or the 'persecuted maiden' story (typically, death or disgrace). In fact, Haywood's story almost refuses to end at all. The heroine is sent to a monastery, but her future remains undetermined. More shocking to Haywood's readers would have been the fact that the work contains no clear normative or prescriptive statement in its final pages. Instead, where the traditional moral might be expected, this story ends with a casual delight in 'an Intreague, which, considering the Time it lasted, was as full of Variety as any, perhaps, that many Ages has produced' (p. 71).

The heroine's relocation to a monastery might seem to signal the end of her sexual adventures, but another early modern literary mode—titillating stories about nuns—complicates this assumption. For example, Barrin's(?) *Venus in the Cloister* offers a risqué account of life in a convent. Haywood, like Barrin(?), Behn, and other predecessors, was not slow to exploit the topos of the attractive nun. The durability of stories about nuns may help explain why the nun's habit was one of the most popular costumes at masquerade assemblies.[1]

Overlooking this nuance, critics sometimes read the ending of *Fantomina* as defeatist and thus implicitly anti-feminist. One scholar

---

[1] See Terry Castle, *Masquerade and Civilization: The Carnivalesque in Eighteenth-Century English Culture and Fiction* (Stanford: Stanford UP, 1986) 40.

has argued, for example, that 'in the melancholy reiteration of female defeat at the hands of the fictionalizing male libertine', *Fantomina* provides only a temporary respite from the ultimate persecution necessarily awaiting the seduced maiden.[1] But *Fantomina* resists conventional categories of sexual pursuit, sexual tragedy, or sexual victory. After the heroine is raped, she refuses to become a victim. Although Beauplaisir delights in his 'Victory' (p. 46), it is obvious that the heroine has engineered her own seduction. Eventually, when Beauplaisir discovers the heroine's true identity (as, notably, the reader never does), he leaves the house 'more confus'd than ever he had known in his whole Life' (p. 71).

Haywood's readers, too, might be confused by the ending of this story. If it focuses our attention on the power of passion to create and mask identity, it also highlights the difficulties of defining exactly what happens during the process of seduction. It does not reduce this process to conventional or predictable stories, nor does it villainize men at the expense of women who can only play the role of victims. Instead, *Fantomina* confronts the complicated dynamics of seduction that change from scene to scene and from disguise to disguise.

Generic Diversity in Haywood's Works

Haywood wrote more than seventy works, including periodicals; conduct books; translations from the French; plays (musical, comical, tragic); political satires; and collections of letters. Moreover, as the preceding discussion of *Fantomina* demonstrates, within individual works she often combines the conventions of different genres.

That so many of Haywood's works incorporate a number of different genres often makes them difficult to classify, particularly for modern readers. The works in this collection are loosely representative of four different genres, but a closer look at each reveals their hybridity. For example, *Fantomina* is a short piece of fiction while *Love-Letters on All Occasions* is a collection of letters

---

[1]   Ros Ballaster, *Seductive Forms: Women's Amatory Fiction from 1684 to 1740* (New York: Oxford UP, 1992) 192.

or stories told by way of letters. However, *Fantomina* contains several letters; and *Love-Letters on All Occasions* incorporates many short stories, one of which, the account of Theano and Elismonda, is half as long as *Fantomina* itself. *The Tea-Table* contains an amatory novel in miniature—the story of Beraldus and Celemena—that resembles many of Haywood's erotic fictions of the 1720s and 1730s.

In her generic heterogeneity Haywood was a product of her cultural moment. The eighteenth century popularized hybrid forms such as the periodical, which contained everything from letters to philosophical and moral essays; and the miscellany, collections of diverse works, usually by different authors. Despite these historical conditions, it can be argued that Haywood pushed generic boundaries more than most writers did. For example, *The Tea-Table*, *Reflections on the Various Effects of Love*, and *Love-Letters on All Occasions* present themselves as didactic, thereby participating in the well-established tradition of conduct literature. But upon closer inspection, it is evident that these works do more than simply replicate conventional precepts of conduct. Instead, all three raise provocative questions about the nature of sexuality, identity, and morality.

In *The Tea-Table*, five men and women converse at the home of their elegant hostess, Amiana, on topics such as the nature of love, the importance of exerting reason to control the passions, and the usefulness of various codes of behavior. Differing views are expressed within the group, which includes Amiana, the lovely Brilliante, an unnamed female narrator, and two young gentlemen, Dorinthus and Philetus. Other characters enter and exit the scene, but at the heart of the work is the entertaining dialogue of the five protagonists, all of whom are paragons of good breeding and sound morality as well as witty and intelligent conversationalists.

Importantly, the *tête-à-tête* is not as harmonious as it first appears. The friends disagree about certain topics, and they leave many of their debates unresolved. One significant example occurs in their final discussion, which is interrupted by the sudden arrival of an interloper. Having heard Brilliante recite the story of Beraldus and Celemena—a 'Manuscript Novel' with an 'excellent Moral'

(p. 86)—the company engages in a spirited debate about the beauties and dangers of romantic desire. The 'Manuscript Novel', full of love, betrayal, and death, ostensibly illustrates the vicissitudes of life but ultimately makes a powerful statement about the dangers of misplaced love and unguarded passion. The discussants, however, do not all read the piece in the same way. Philetus finds it admirable, exclaiming that 'these kind of Writings are not so trifling as by many people they are thought.—Nor are they design'd, as some imagine, for *Amusement* only, but *Instruction* also' (p. 104). Philetus, that is, attempts to reconcile the 'Novel' to the sorts of moral concerns that Johnson would later express. Amiana employs a proto-Johnsonian argument against the work when she argues that authors should present only stories of virtuous and faithful lovers and not tales of lust and betrayal: 'if I were of Counsel with the Writers of such Books, I shou'd advise 'em to chuse only such—For, methinks, to read of Villainy so ... monstrous as that we have just now heard ... gives too great a Shock to the Soul, and poysons the rest of the Entertainment' (p. 104). Brilliante attempts to rebut this position when she asserts that 'sometimes 'tis necessary ... to be reminded that there have been Men so base ... especially when we suffer what little share of Reason we have to be debilitated by Passion ... we stand in need of all the Helps we can procure' (p. 104). Philetus agrees that most of these books contain 'Morals, which if well observed would be of no small Service to those that read 'em' (pp. 104–5). Were it not for the book-ending interruption, we assume, the debate would continue. As it is, Haywood leaves the central question unanswered.

Of course the discussion of Beraldus and Celemena is in essence a discussion of Haywood's own narrative tendencies in the 1720s, specifically her interest in the nature of sexual desire and the conflict between reason and passion. One of the questions that *Fantomina* suggests concerns the degree to which individuals are in control of the experience of love and the extent to which society can judge the actions of a person who is motivated by passion. Such issues are also central to *Reflections on the Various Effects of Love*, which explores the myriad experiences of love, 'illustrated with a great many Examples of the *good* and *bad* Consequences of that Passion', as the title page explains. The examples are culled from a variety of sources, including the 'best Ancient and Modern Histories'. One source is Nahum Tate's *A Present for the Ladies: Being an Historical Account of Several Illustrious Persons of the Female Sex* (1692), part of which is excerpted in Appendix C, below. Haywood follows Tate by invoking a convention familiar in literature since the Medieval period: the use of 'exempla', fictional stories or anecdotes that illustrate a moral precept. But, as usual, Haywood opts for amalgamation rather than imitation. In any given story, she is likely to forego exemplary representation in favor of a contrasting mode, for example the *roman à clef*, or 'secret history', in which the secrets of contemporary figures are passed off, often transparently, as fictional. Sometimes a 'key' was sold separately or appended to a secret history in order to help readers correlate fictional and private identities. The most famous of these secret histories is perhaps Delariviere Manley's *The New Atalantis* (1709). Some of Haywood's first readers may have read *Reflections on the Various Effects of Love* as a secret history of this sort, the more so as a key to the work was advertised in 1727 as part of a new edition. No copies of this edition seem to have survived, however.

Modern readers may want to consider the ways in which the stories and exempla of *Reflections on the Various Effects of Love* raise enduring questions about the nature of romantic and sexual passion and the limitations of human reason. In *Reflections on the Various Effects of Love*, Haywood interrupts what appears to be a philosophical disquisition to tell the story of Sophiana and Aranthus. While this story might be read as an exemplum, the emotional predicaments of the characters quickly outpace any overt didacticism. Because Sophiana cannot discipline her passion, Aranthus jilts her, chastising her 'Wildness' and 'ill Conduct' and telling the desperate girl that she must 'learn if possible to be discreet' (pp. 140–41). According to eighteenth-century convention, Sophiana had indeed exceeded the bounds of female decorum, and yet the narrator maintains a degree of sympathy towards Sophiana's plight even while criticizing her misconduct. Perhaps the story is meant to illustrate the limitations of prescriptive didacticism, especially where matters of the heart are concerned. The story becomes more bizarre as Sophiana's behavior grows more desperate: she disguises herself as a lower-class merchant woman to gain access to her estranged lover's house. But unlike the resourceful disguises of the heroine in *Fantomina*, Sophiana's ploy fails, and the narrator implies that her fate will not be a happy one.

Maintaining sympathy for those ruined by the excesses of passion, the narrator ultimately concludes that 'the Instability of a very young Person's Affection' (p. 151) is largely to blame in Sophiana's case. This interpretation of her conduct is unorthodox at a time when women were expected to remain virginal until marriage and even to decline to express affection for a man before he had made a formal declaration of love. And here some similarities to *Fantomina* emerge. Although both these narratives are in some way didactic, their force resides in the emotional participation of the reader in the plight of the characters. When Haywood invites moral consideration for those women who have become 'fallen' victims of their own sexual desires, she tempers didactic convention with a plea for a greater understanding of the overwhelming power of love. This generosity is characteristic of her work.

Reflections on the Various Effects of Love comments as well on the question of the relative capabilities of men and women to experience love. For example, the narrator avers that women love more deeply and constantly than men because of intrinsic differences and because of women's narrower spheres of experience:

> only consider with how much greater Force that Passion influences the Minds of Women, than it can boast on those of a contrary Sex, whose Natures being more rough and obdurate, are not capable of receiving those deep Impressions which for the most Part are so destructive to the softer Specie.—The other may Love with Vehemence, but then it is neither so tender nor so lasting a Flame ... A Woman, where she loves, has no Reserve; she profusely gives her all, has no Regard for any Thing, but obliging the Person she affects, and lavishes her whole Soul.—But Man, more wisely, keeps a Part of his for other Views, he still has an Eye to Interest and Ambition! (pp. 114-15)

This question of who loves longest and most deeply concerned many writers from the medieval period to Haywood's time and beyond. In Jane Austen's final novel, *Persuasion* (1818), Anne Elliot defends her sex's capacity to love: "'We certainly do not forget you, so soon as you forget us'", the heroine asserts; "'we live at home, quiet, confined, and our feelings prey upon us.'" Men are not forced to live such narrow lives, she avers: "'You have always a profession, pursuits, business of some sort or other, to take you back into the world immediately, and continual occupation and change soon weaken impressions.'" But Anne cites an intrinsic difference between the sexes when she insists that men's feelings are 'strong[er]' and more fleeting than women's, and that women's are hardier and more 'tender' than men's: "'All the privilege I claim for my own sex (it is not a very enviable one, you need not covet it) is that of loving longest when existence or when hope is gone.'"[1]

This is one of the most memorable moments in English literature, for while the heroine is speaking of someone else, she is also implicitly referring to her own experiences. Indeed, the similarities between the two passages—Haywood's and Austen's—are striking. And while *Reflections on the Various Effects of Love* is not a novel in the modern sense, it can be argued that Haywood's generic experiments affected the course that the novel would take towards greater emotional depth and psychological realism.

Haywood explores the experiences of love and loss again in *Love-Letters on All Occasions*. The work includes many joyful letters that celebrate the beauties of faithful love, but more often Haywood is interested in the precariousness of desire, particularly for women. Most of the stories comprise only one or two letters; and most are left unfinished—as such, there is no linear plot in this work. The one exception is the correspondence of Theano and Elismonda, which requires twenty-four letters (over one-third of the work) to trace the progress of a love affair from its consummation to the reunion of the lovers after an enforced separation. While readers are able to participate vicariously in the progress of the relationship, the work resists closure; we are not

---

[1]   Austen, *Persuasion*, in *'Northanger Abbey' and 'Persuasion'*, ed. R.W. Chapman (London: Oxford UP, 1952) 232–35.

told whether Theano and Elismonda plan to marry, and we do not witness their reunion. We are simply told in the last letter of Theano's impending arrival. It is the intensity of their feelings for one another—and the doubts and fears that those feelings create—that becomes the subject of their correspondence and the object of the reader's attention.

Clearly, it is not plot that drives this work, but rather the disparate experiences of a range of individuals. Given that writers of eighteenth-century fiction were only beginning to experiment with the linear plot, and given the prevalence of philosophic treatises during this period, this generic mixture is not so strange. One of the striking and forward-seeing features of *Love-Letters on All Occasions*, however, is the work's often jagged cross-referentiality among superficially discrete letters.

Letter XXXVII, for example, discusses the issue of love at first sight; the pleading lover, Dorimenus, defends himself against Erminia's skepticism, insisting on the emotional validity of his instantaneous love for her. He asks why she would 'suppose that there is a Necessity for [her] to be seen more than once, to make [her] be ador'd?' Then, accusing her of being 'Blind to [her] own Loveliness', he begs to be allowed to visit her in order to formally declare his passion (p. 207). The reader never encounters the woman's response, however; the 'exchange' comprises only one letter. The next and more intricate letter provides an interesting counterpoint. Amythea has rejected Rosander because he had loved someone before her, and he writes to defend himself against the charge of fickleness. Of his former lover, he says, 'a young and unexperienc'd Heart is set on Fire by the least spark of Beauty'; and, when this happens, 'we immediately *like*, and ... imagine what we feel at that Time, *Love*' (p. 208). Such a sudden onset of emotions should be suspect, he concludes, given 'how widely different are all those wandring Flames, from the solid glow of serious Inclination' (p. 208). Rosander's dismissal of love at first sight, however, contrasts with the previous letter, in which Dorimenus claims that '[if] Beauty be properly compar'd to Lightning, why should the sudden Influence of yours be doubted?' (p. 207).

With whose point of view should the reader sympathize, and is there a moral to glean from either letter? Rosander ends his missive by insisting that his passion is 'inspir'd, assisted, and ... continued by my Reason' (p. 209); but the role of 'Reason' in the affairs of the heart remains open to question. Haywood often juxtaposes such opposing points of views in this work; and her readers are thus, like the fictional characters themselves, often left to guess at the truth-value behind declarations of love. Moreover, Haywood's interest in the direct juxtaposition of opposing points of view anticipates one of the narrative devices in Richardson's novel *Clarissa* (1747–48).

A lack of closure, evident here as in *The Tea-Table* and *Fantomina*, testifies to Haywood's interest in the type of love story that both invites and resists critical and didactic judgment. As the four works in this volume show, during a period of social and literary transition, Haywood's writings embraced the complexities of human experience, both structurally and thematically. In order better to reflect a multitude of human experience, Haywood took risks as an author, experimenting with generic forms and perspectival shifts, all the while successfully negotiating the competitive and ever-changing literary marketplace. Far from exploiting the same formula over and over, as some of her detractors have charged, Haywood's writings create a comprehensive matrix for exploring the complexities of seduction, of love, and of passion, outside any single conventional paradigm.

M.C.C.
A.C.P.

Eliza Haywood: A Brief Chronology

[Attributions and dates of publication derive primarily from Patrick Spedding, *A Bibliography of Eliza Haywood* (London: Pickering & Chatto, forthcoming). For biographical data, we have generally favored Christine Blouch, 'Eliza Haywood', in Haywood, *Miscellaneous Writings, 1725–43*, ed. Alexander Pettit (London: Pickering & Chatto, 2000) xxi–lxxxii.]

1693?   Born Elizabeth Fowler in London.

1714   Having apparently separated from a husband, EH begins an apprenticeship at the Theatre Royal in Smock Alley, Dublin; appears under her own name in Thomas Shadwell's adaptation of Shakespeare's *Timon of Athens*.

1717   Appears in John Banks's *The Unhappy Favourite* at Lincoln's Inn Fields, London.

1719   Around this time EH becomes part of Aaron Hill's literary 'circle' and meets the feckless writer Richard Savage, with whom she becomes intimate.
Love in Excess; or, The Fatal Enquiry (parts 1 and 2).

1720   *Letters from a Lady of Quality to a Chevalier* (by Edmé Boursault; trans. from the French by EH), with 'A Discourse Concerning Writings of this Nature'.
Love in Excess (part 3).

1721   *The Fair Captive* (EH in the cast at Lincoln's Inn Fields).

1722   *The British Recluse: or, The Secret History of Cleomira, Suppos'd Dead.*
The Injur'd Husband; or, The Mistaken Resentment.

1723   *Idalia: or, The Unfortunate Mistress.*
Lasselia; or, The Self-Abandon'd.
The Rash Resolve: or, The Untimely Discovery.
A Wife to Be Lett.

1724   Ends relationship with Savage.
The Arragonian Queen: A Secret History.
Bath Intrigues; in Four Letters to a Friend in London.

La Belle Assemblée; or, The Adventures of Six Days (by
Madeleine d'Angélique Poisson de Gomez [Mme.
de Gomez]; trans. from the French by EH).
The Fatal Secret: or, Constancy in Distress.
The Masqueraders; or, Fatal Curiosity (part 1).
*Memoirs of a Certain Island Adjacent to the Kingdom of
Utopia* (vol. 1).
Memoirs of the Baron de Brosse.
Poems on Several Occasions (in vol. 4 of *The Works of
Mrs. Eliza Haywood*).
*A Spy upon the Conjurer: or, A Collection of Surprising
Stories, with Names, Places, and Particular
Circumstances Relating to Mr. Duncan Campbell.*
The Surprise; or, Constancy Rewarded.
*The Works of Mrs. Eliza Haywood; Consisting of
Novels, Letters, Poems, and Plays* (4 vols.).

1725　Around this time EH begins a personal and
professional relationship with the playwright and
actor William Hatchett, with whom she may have
been involved until the time of her death.
*The Dumb Projector: Being a Surprizing Account of a
Trip to Holland Made by Mr. Duncan Campbell.*
Fantomina: or, Love in a Maze (in vol. 3 of *Secret
Histories, Novels, and Poems*).
The Fatal Fondness; or, Love Its Own Opposer.
The Force of Nature; or, The Lucky Disappointment (in
vol. 4 of *Secret Histories, Novels, and Poems*).
*The Lady's Philosopher's Stone; or, The Caprices of Love
and Destiny* (by Louis Adrien Du Perron de
Castera; trans. from the French by EH).
Mary Stuart, Queen of Scots.
The Masqueraders (part 2).
*Memoirs of a Certain Island Adjacent to the Kingdom of
Utopia* (vol. 2).
Secret Histories, Novels, and Poems (4 vols.).
*The Tea-Table: or, A Conversation between Some Polite
Persons of Both Sexes.*
The Unequal Conflict; or, Nature Triumphant.

1726   *The City Jilt; or, The Alderman Turn'd Beau.*

Cleomelia: or, The Generous Mistress, with *The Lucky Rape: or, Fate the Best Disposer* and *The Capricious Lover: or, No Trifling with a Woman.*

The Distress'd Orphan, or Love in a Mad-house.

The Double Marriage: or, The Fatal Release.

Letters from the Palace of Fame.

The Mercenary Lover: or, The Unfortunate Heiresses.

Reflections on the Various Effects of Love.

The Secret History of the Present Intrigues of the Court of Caramania.

The Tea-Table ... Part the Second.

1727   *The Fruitless Enquiry.*

The Life of Madam de Villesache.

Love in its Variety: Being a Collection of Select Novels (by Matteo Bandello; trans. from the Spanish by EH).

The Perplex'd Duchess; or, Treachery Rewarded.

Philidore and Placentia: or, L'Amour Trop Delicat.

1728   Ridiculed in Alexander Pope's *Dunciad.*

The Agreeable Caledonian: or, Memoirs of Signiora di Morella (part 1).

The City Widow: or, Love in a Butt.

The Disguis'd Prince; or, The Beautiful Parisian (part 1; by Sieur de Préchac or Mme. de Villedieu; trans. from the French by EH).

Irish Artifice; or, The History of Clarina (in *The Female Dunciad*).

The Padlock; or, No Guard without Virtue (in *The Mercenary Lover*, 3rd ed.).

Persecuted Virtue; or, The Cruel Lover.

1729   *The Agreeable Caledonian* (part 2).

The Disguis'd Prince (part 2).

The Fair Hebrew; or, A True, but Secret History of Two Jewish Ladies, Who Lately Resided in London.

Frederick, Duke of Brunswick-Lunenburgh.

1730   Appears in Hatchett's *Rival Father* at the Little Haymarket theater, London; portrayed as

'Mrs. Novel' in Henry Fielding's *Author's Farce* at the same theater.

Love-Letters on All Occasions.

1733   *The Opera of Operas; or Tom Thumb the Great* (by EH and Hatchett, music by John Frederick Lampe).

1734   *L'Entretien des Beaux Esprits, Being the Sequel to La Belle Assemblée* (by Madeleine d'Angélique Poisson de Gomez [Mme. de Gomez]; trans. from the French by EH).

1735   *The Dramatic Historiographer: or, The British Theatre Delineated.*

1736   Appears in her own adaptation of *Arden of Feversham* at the Little Haymarket.

A Companion to the Theatre: or, A Key to the Play (reissue of *The Dramatic Historiographer*).

The Adventures of Eovaai, Princess of Ijaveo.

1737   Active in Fielding's troupe at the Little Haymarket, appearing in Hatchett's *Rehearsal of Kings* and Fielding's *Historical Register for the Year 1736* and *Eurydice Hiss'd*. Her career as an actress ends when the government shuts down the playhouse.

1740   *The Unfortunate Princess, or, The Ambitious Statesman* (reissue of *The Adventures of Eovaai*).

1741   *Anti-Pamela: or, Feign'd Innocence Detected.*

1742   Around this time EH opens a bookselling and printing business in Covent Garden, London; in some form, it may have operated until 1749 or later.

The Virtuous Villager, or, Virgin's Victory (by Charles de Fieux de Mouhy [Chevalier de Mouhy]; trans. from the French by EH).

1743   *A Present for a Servant-Maid: or, The Sure Means of Gaining Love and Esteem.*

1744   *The Fortunate Foundlings.*

The Female Spectator (books 1–8).

1745   *The Female Spectator* (books 9–20).

1746   *The Female Spectator* (books 21–24).

The Parrot.

1747 *A Companion to the Theatre* (2 vols.; vol. 1: reissue of
      The Dramatic Historiographer).

      Memoirs of a Man of Honour (by Antoine François
      Prévost d'Exiles [Abbé Prévost]; trans. from the
      French by EH).

1748 *Epistles for the Ladies* (parts 1–3).

      *Life's Progress through the Passions: or, The Adventures
      of Natura.*

1749 Arrested for writing and publishing *A Letter from
      H—— G——g, Esq.*, a fictional letter from
      Charles Edward Stuart, the pretender to the
      British throne and leader of the failed Rebellion
      of 1745. (EH was not prosecuted.)

      Dalinda: or, The Double Marriage.

      Epistles for the Ladies (parts 4–6).

      A Letter from H—— G——g, Esq.

1750 *Epistles for the Ladies* (parts 7–12).

1751 *The History of Miss Betsy Thoughtless.*

1752 *The History of Jemmy and Jenny Jessamy.*

1754 *The Invisible Spy.*

1755 *The Wife.*

1756 Dies 25 February in London; buried 3 March at St.
      Margaret's, Westminster.

      The Husband.

      The Young Lady.

1768 *Clementina; or, The History of an Italian Lady* (reissue
      of *The Agreeable Caledonian*).

1788 *The History of Leonora Meadowson.*

A Note on the Texts

The texts in this volume are based on first editions. Margaret Case Croskery and Anna C. Patchias prepared the text of *Fantomina* from the copy of volume 3 of Haywood's *Secret Histories, Novels, and Poems* (4 vols., 1725, misleadingly labeled 'second edition') held by the Sterling Memorial Library at Yale University (shelfmark IK H336 C725 B). Collation against the following copies of *Secret Histories* revealed no substantive or accidental differences: Annenberg Rare Book and Manuscript Library, University of Pennsylvania (shelfmark PR 3506 H94 A6 1725); Bodleian Library, University of Oxford (shelfmark Harding M239); and British Library (shelfmark 12614 C14). *Fantomina* did not appear independently of *Secret Histories* (that is, in more than one edition) in the eighteenth century. Alexander Pettit prepared the texts of *The Tea-Table* (1725), *Reflections on the Various Effects of Love* (1726), and *Love-Letters on All Occasions* (1730) using photoreproductions of the copies held by the Mills Memorial Library at McMaster University (shelf-marks B14517, 'disb[ound]', and B13532, respectively) and checking passages against the original volumes as necessary. No manuscriptal record of any of the four works has survived.

The texts of *The Tea-Table*, *Reflections on the Various Effects of Love*, and *Love-Letters on All Occasions* originally appeared in Haywood, *Miscellaneous Writings, 1725–43* (ed. Pettit [London: Pickering & Chatto, 2000]). All four of the present texts were edited in conformity with the principles outlined in that volume (see 'Textual Introduction', pp. 275–79). Specifically, we have retained word-forms, regardless of their lexical correctness, that research suggests are likely to represent Haywood's usual practice. Grammatical infelicities stand unless they seem to have resulted from a printer's error or an error in a lost manuscript. We have eliminated bulky display capitals and regularized words originally set in a mix of full capitals and lower case characters at the beginning of epistles and other sections; these words are now set in full capitals, in accordance with the tendency of the original texts. Most of the numerous strings of hyphens characteristic of the early editions appear herein as short dashes; longer dashes indicate elisions in poetry. We have corrected several obvious errors of commission (for example, 'P. S,' becomes 'P. S.') and omission (for example, in a heading, 'LETTER XXI' becomes 'LETTER XXI.').

The first editions have also dictated our use of roman and italic type and small capitals. As some of the foregoing comments will have suggested, however, we have not attempted to replicate the physical appearance of the original texts. For example, epistles have been reformatted and regularized for the present texts, and a table of contents from the first edition of *Love-Letters on All Occasions* has been omitted from this edition.

FANTOMINA:
OR, LOVE IN A MAZE

In Love the Victors from the Vanquish'd fly.
They fly that wound, and they pursue that dye.

WALLER.[1]

A YOUNG Lady of distinguished Birth, Beauty, Wit, and Spirit,
happened to be in a Box[2] one Night at the Playhouse; where,
though there were a great Number of celebrated Toasts,[3] she
perceived several Gentlemen extremely pleased themselves with
entertaining a Woman who sat in a Corner of the Pit, and, by
her Air and Manner of receiving them, might easily be known
to be one of those who come there for no other Purpose, than
to create Acquaintance with as many as seem desirous of it. She
could not help testifying her Contempt of Men, who, regardless
either of the Play, or Circle,[4] threw away their Time in such a
Manner, to some Ladies that sat by her: But they, either less
surprised by being more accustomed to such Sights, than she
who had been bred for the most Part in the Country, or not of
a Disposition to consider any Thing very deeply, took but little
Notice of it. She still thought of it, however; and the longer she
reflected on it, the greater was her Wonder, that Men, some of
whom she knew were accounted to have Wit, should have Tastes
so very depraved.—This excited a Curiosity in her to know in
what Manner these Creatures were address'd:—She was young,
a Stranger to the World, and consequently to the Dangers of it;
and having no Body in Town, at that Time, to whom she was
oblig'd to be accountable for her Actions, did in every Thing as

---

1   The lines, from Edmund Waller, 'To A.H., of the Different Successes of Their Loves'
    (1645), ll. 27–28, appear on the original title page. For a reproduction of that page,
    see *Popular Fiction by Women, 1660–1730: An Anthology*, ed. Paula R. Backscheider and
    John J. Richetti (New York: Oxford UP, 1996) 226.
2   Private compartment.
3   Beautiful women (toasted over drinks by men).
4   That is, dress circle; the lower gallery, with the most expensive seats.

her Inclinations or Humours[1] render'd most agreeable to her: Therefore thought it not in the least a Fault to put in practice a little Whim which came immediately into her Head, to dress herself as near as she cou'd in the Fashion of those Women who make sale of their Favours, and set herself in the Way of being accosted as such a one, having at that Time no other Aim, than the Gratification of an innocent Curiosity.—She no sooner design'd this Frolick, than she put it in Execution; and muffling her Hoods over her Face, went the next Night into the Gallery-Box,[2] and practising as much as she had observ'd, at that Distance, the Behaviour of that Woman, was not long before she found her Disguise had answer'd the Ends she wore it for:—A Crowd of Purchasers of all Degrees and Capacities were in a Moment gather'd about her, each endeavouring to out-bid the other, in offering her a Price for her Embraces.—She listen'd to 'em all, and was not a little diverted in her Mind at the Disappointment she shou'd give to so many, each of which thought himself secure of gaining her.—She was told by 'em all, that she was the most lovely Woman in the World; and some cry'd, *Gad, she is mighty like my fine Lady Such-a-one,*—naming her own Name. She was naturally vain, and receiv'd no small Pleasure in hearing herself prais'd, tho' in the Person of another, and a suppos'd Prostitute; but she dispatch'd as soon as she cou'd all that had hitherto attack'd her, when she saw the accomplish'd *Beauplaisir* was making his Way thro' the Crowd as fast as he was able, to reach the Bench she sat on. She had often seen him in the Drawing-Room, had talk'd with him; but then her Quality and reputed Virtue kept him from using her with that Freedom she now expected he wou'd do, and had discover'd something in him, which had made her often think she shou'd not be displeas'd, if he wou'd abate some Part of his Reserve.—Now was the Time to have her Wishes answer'd:—He look'd in her Face, and fancy'd, as many others had done, that she very much resembled that Lady whom she really was; but the vast Disparity there appear'd between their Characters, prevented him from

---

[1] Temperament.
[2] Box in the higher and less expensive gallery.

entertaining even the most distant Thought that they cou'd be the same.—He address'd her at first with the usual Salutations of her pretended Profession, as, *Are you engag'd, Madam?—Will you permit me to wait on you home after the Play?—By Heaven, you are a fine Girl!—How long have you us'd this House?*—And such like Questions; but perceiving she had a Turn of Wit, and a genteel Manner in her Raillery,[1] beyond what is frequently to be found among those Wretches, who are for the most part Gentlewomen but by Necessity, few of 'em having had an Education suitable to what they affect to appear, he chang'd the Form of his Conversation, and shew'd[2] her it was not because he understood no better, that he had made use of Expressions so little polite.— In fine,[3] they were infinitely charm'd with each other: He was transported[4] to find so much Beauty and Wit in a Woman, who he doubted not but on very easy Terms he might enjoy; and she found a vast deal of Pleasure in conversing with him in this free and unrestrain'd Manner. They pass'd their Time all the Play with an equal Satisfaction; but when it was over, she found herself involv'd in a Difficulty, which before never enter'd into her Head, but which she knew not well how to get over.—The Passion he profess'd for her, was not of that humble Nature which can be content with distant Adorations:—He resolv'd not to part from her without the Gratifications of those Desires she had inspir'd; and presuming on the Liberties which her suppos'd Function allow'd of, told her she must either go with him to some convenient House of his procuring, or permit him to wait on her to her own Lodgings.—Never had she been in such a *Dilemma:* Three or four Times did she open her Mouth to confess her real Quality;[5] but the Influence of her ill Stars prevented it, by putting an Excuse into her Head, which did the Business as well, and at the same Time did not take from her the Power of seeing and entertaining him a second Time with the same Freedom she had done this.—She told him, she was under

---

1   Banter.
2   That is, showed.
3   In short.
4   Enraptured.
5   High social status.

Obligations to a Man who maintain'd her, and whom she durst not disappoint, having promis'd to meet him that Night at a House hard by.[1]—This Story so like what those Ladies sometimes tell, was not at all suspected by *Beauplaisir*, and assuring her he wou'd be far from doing her a Prejudice, desir'd that in return for the Pain he shou'd suffer in being depriv'd of her Company that Night, that she wou'd order her Affairs, so as not to render him unhappy the next. She gave a solemn Promise to be in the same Box on the Morrow Evening; and they took Leave of each other; he to the Tavern to drown the Remembrance of his Disappointment; she in a Hackney-Chair[2] hurry'd home to indulge Contemplation on the Frolick she had taken, designing nothing less on her first Reflections, than to keep the Promise she had made him, and hugging herself with Joy, that she had the good Luck to come off undiscover'd.

BUT these Cogitations[3] were but of a short Continuance, they vanish'd with the Hurry of her Spirits, and were succeeded by others vastly different and ruinous:—All the Charms of *Beauplaisir* came fresh into her Mind; she languish'd, she almost dy'd for another Opportunity of conversing with him; and not all the Admonitions of her Discretion were effectual to oblige her to deny laying hold of that which offer'd itself the next Night.—She depended on the Strength of her Virtue, to bear her safe thro' Tryals more dangerous than she apprehended this to be, and never having been address'd by him as Lady,—was resolv'd to receive his Devoirs as a Town-Mistress,[4] imagining a world of Satisfaction to herself in engaging him in the Character of such a one, and in observing the Surprise he would be in to find himself refused by a Woman, who he supposed granted her Favours without Exception.—Strange and unaccountable were the Whimsies she was possess'd of,—wild and incoherent her Desires,—unfix'd and undetermin'd her Resolutions, but in that of seeing *Beauplaisir* in the Manner she had lately done. As for her Proceedings with him, or how a second Time to escape him,

---

[1] Near by.
[2] That is, chair; a one-seated vehicle for hire, carried on poles.
[3] Thoughts.
[4] To receive his addresses as a prostitute would.

without discovering who she was, she cou'd neither assure herself, nor whether or not in the last Extremity she wou'd do so.—Bent, however, on meeting him, whatever shou'd be the Consequence, she went out some Hours before the Time of going to the Playhouse, and took Lodgings in a House not very far from it, intending, that if he shou'd insist on passing some Part of the Night with her, to carry him there, thinking she might with more Security to her Honour entertain him at a Place where she was Mistress, than at any of his own chusing.

THE appointed Hour being arriv'd, she had the Satisfaction to find his Love in his Assiduity:[1] He was there before her; and nothing cou'd be more tender than the Manner in which he accosted her: But from the first Moment she came in, to that of the Play being done, he continued to assure her no Consideration shou'd prevail with him to part from her again, as she had done the Night before; and she rejoic'd to think she had taken that Precaution of providing herself with a Lodging, to which she thought she might invite him, without running any Risque, either of her Virtue or Reputation.—Having told him she wou'd admit of his accompanying her home, he seem'd perfectly satisfy'd; and leading her to the Place, which was not above twenty Houses distant, wou'd have order'd a Collation[2] to be brought after them. But she wou'd not permit it, telling him she was not one of those who suffer'd themselves to be treated at their own Lodgings; and as soon she was come in, sent a Servant, belonging to the House, to provide a very handsome Supper, and Wine, and every Thing was serv'd to Table in a Manner which shew'd the Director neither wanted[3] Money, nor was ignorant how it shou'd be laid out.

THIS Proceeding, though it did not take from him the Opinion that she was what she appeared to be, yet it gave him Thoughts of her, which he had not before.—He believ'd her a *Mistress*, but believ'd her to be one of a superior Rank, and began to imagine the Possession of her would be much more Expensive

---

[1] Perseverance.
[2] Light meal.
[3] Lacked.

than at first he had expected: But not being of a Humour to grudge any Thing for his Pleasures, he gave himself no farther Trouble, than what were occasioned by Fears of not having Money enough to reach her Price, about him.

SUPPER being over, which was intermixed with a vast deal of amorous Conversation, he began to explain himself more than he had done; and both by his Words and Behaviour let her know, he would not be denied that Happiness the Freedoms she allow'd had made him hope.—It was in vain; she would have retracted the Encouragement she had given:—In vain she endeavoured to delay, till the next Meeting, the fulfilling of his Wishes:—She had now gone too far to retreat:—*He* was bold;—he was resolute: *She* fearful,—confus'd, altogether unprepar'd to resist in such Encounters, and rendered more so, by the extreme Liking she had to him.—Shock'd, however, at the Apprehension of really losing her Honour, she struggled all she could, and was just going to reveal the whole Secret of her Name and Quality, when the Thoughts of the Liberty he had taken with her, and those he still continued to prosecute, prevented her, with representing the Danger of being expos'd, and the whole Affair made a Theme for publick Ridicule.—Thus much, indeed, she told him, that she was a Virgin, and had assumed this Manner of Behaviour only to engage him. But that he little regarded, or if he had, would have been far from obliging him to desist;—nay, in the present burning Eagerness of Desire, 'tis probable, that had he been acquainted both with who and what she really was, the Knowledge of her Birth would not have influenc'd him with Respect sufficient to have curb'd the wild Exuberance of his luxurious[1] Wishes, or made him in that longing,—that impatient Moment, change the Form of his Addresses. In fine, she was undone; and he gain'd a Victory, so highly rapturous, that had he known over whom, scarce could he have triumphed more. Her Tears, however, and the Distraction she appeared in, after the ruinous Extasy was past, as it heighten'd his Wonder, so it abated his Satisfaction:—He could not imagine for what Reason a Woman, who, if she intended not to be a *Mistress*, had counterfeited the Part of one,

---

[1] Lascivious.

and taken so much Pains to engage him, should lament a Consequence which she could not but expect, and till the last Test, seem'd inclinable to grant; and was both surpris'd and troubled at the Mystery.—He omitted nothing that he thought might make her easy; and still retaining an Opinion that the Hope of Interest[1] had been the chief Motive which had led her to act in the Manner she had done, and believing that she might know so little of him, as to suppose, now she had nothing left to give, he might not make that Recompence she expected for her Favours: To put her out of that Pain, he pulled out of his Pocket a Purse of Gold, entreating her to accept of that as an Earnest of what he intended to do for her; assuring her, with ten thousand Protestations, that he would spare nothing, which his whole Estate could purchase, to procure her Content and Happiness. This Treatment made her quite forget the Part she had assum'd, and throwing it from her with an Air of Disdain, Is this a Reward (*said she*) for Condescentions,[2] such as I have yeilded to?—Can all the Wealth you are possess'd of, make a Reparation for my Loss of Honour?—Oh! no, I am undone beyond the Power of Heaven itself to help me!—She uttered many more such Exclamations; which the amaz'd *Beauplaisir* heard without being able to reply to, till by Degrees sinking from that Rage of Temper, her Eyes resumed their softning Glances, and guessing at the Consternation he was in, No, my dear *Beauplaisir*, (*added she*,) your Love alone can compensate for the Shame you have involved me in; be you sincere and constant, and I hereafter shall, perhaps, be satisfy'd with my Fate, and forgive myself the Folly that betray'd me to you.

BEAUPLAISIR thought he could not have a better Opportunity than these Words gave him of enquiring who she was, and wherefore she had feigned herself to be of a Profession which he was now convinc'd she was not; and after he had made her a thousand Vows of an Affection, as inviolable and ardent[3] as she could wish to find in him, entreated she would inform him by what Means his Happiness had been brought about, and also to whom

---

[1]   Profit.
[2]   Acts of attentiveness to one's social inferiors.
[3]   Passionate.

he was indebted for the Bliss he had enjoy'd.—Some Remains of yet unextinguished Modesty, and Sense of Shame, made her blush exceedingly at this Demand; but recollecting herself in a little Time, she told him so much of the Truth, as to what related to the Frolick she had taken of satisfying her Curiosity in what Manner *Mistresses*, of the Sort she appeared to be, were treated by those who addressed them; but forbore discovering her true Name and Quality, for the Reasons she had done before, resolving, if he boasted of this Affair, he should not have it in his Power to touch her Character: She therefore said she was the Daughter of a Country Gentleman, who was come to Town to buy Cloaths, and that she was call'd *Fantomina*. He had no Reason to distrust the Truth of this Story, and was therefore satisfy'd with it; but did not doubt by the Beginning of her Conduct, but that in the End she would be in Reality, the Thing she so artfully had counterfeited; and had good Nature enough to pity the Misfortunes he imagin'd would be her Lot: But to tell her so, or offer his Advice in that Point was not his Business, at least, as yet.

THEY parted not till towards Morning; and she oblig'd him to a willing Vow of visiting her the next Day at Three in the Afternoon. It was too late for her to go home that Night, therefore contented herself with lying there. In the Morning she sent for the Woman of the House to come up to her; and easily perceiving, by her Manner, that she was a Woman who might be influenced by Gifts, made her a Present of a Couple of Broad Pieces,[1] and desir'd her, that if the Gentleman, who had been there the Night before, should ask any Questions concerning her, that he should be told, she was lately come out of the Country, had lodg'd there about a Fortnight,[2] and that her Name was *Fantomina*. I shall (*also added she*) lie but seldom here; nor, indeed, ever come but in those Times when I expect to meet him: I would, therefore, have you order it so, that he may think I am but just gone out, if he should happen by any Accident to call when I am not here; for I would not, for the World, have him

---

[1] Coins worth twenty shillings, or one pound, each, a substantial sum for a prostitute but not for a gentlewoman.

[2] Two weeks.

imagine I do not constantly lodge here. The Landlady assur'd her she would do every Thing as she desired, and gave her to understand she wanted not the Gift of Secrecy.

EVERY Thing being ordered at this Home for the Security of her Reputation, she repaired to the other, where she easily excused to an unsuspecting Aunt, with whom she boarded, her having been abroad all Night, saying, she went with a Gentleman and his Lady in a Barge, to a little Country Seat[1] of theirs up the River, all of them designing to return the same Evening; but that one of the Bargemen happ'ning to be taken ill on the sudden, and no other Waterman to be got that Night, they were oblig'd to tarry till Morning. Thus did this Lady's Wit and Vivacity assist her in all, but where it was most needful.—She had Discernment to foresee, and avoid all those Ills which might attend the Loss of her *Reputation*, but was wholly blind to those of the Ruin of her *Virtue*; and having managed her Affairs so as to secure the *one*, grew perfectly easy with the Remembrance, she had forfeited the *other*.—The more she reflected on the Merits of *Beauplaisir*, the more she excused herself for what she had done; and the Prospect of that continued Bliss she expected to share with him, took from her all Remorse for having engaged in an Affair which promised her so much Satisfaction, and in which she found not the least Danger of Misfortune.—If he is really (*said she, to herself*) the faithful, the constant Lover he has sworn to be, how charming will be our Amour?—And if he should be false, grow satiated, like other Men, I shall but, at the worst, have the private Vexation of knowing I have lost him;—the Intreague being a Secret, my Disgrace will be so too:—I shall hear no Whispers as I pass,—She is Forsaken:—The odious Word *Forsaken* will never wound my Ears; nor will my Wrongs excite either the Mirth or Pity of the talking World:—It will not be even in the Power of my Undoer himself to triumph over me; and while he laughs at, and perhaps despises the fond, the yeilding *Fantomina*, he will revere and esteem the virtuous, the reserv'd Lady.—In this Manner did she applaud her own Conduct, and exult with the Imagination that she had more Prudence than all her Sex beside. And it must be confessed, indeed,

---

[1]   Residence.

that she preserved an OEconomy[1] in the management of this Intreague, beyond what almost any Woman but herself ever did: In the first Place, by making no Person in the World a Confident in it; and in the next, in concealing from *Beauplaisir* himself the Knowledge who she was; for though she met him three or four Days in a Week, at that Lodging she had taken for that Purpose, yet as much as he employ'd her Time and Thoughts, she was never miss'd from any Assembly she had been accustomed to frequent.— The Business of her Love has engross'd her till Six in the Evening, and before Seven she has been dress'd in a different Habit,[2] and in another Place.—Slippers, and a Night-Gown loosely flowing, has been the Garb in which he has left the languishing *Fantomina*;— Lac'd, and adorn'd with all the Blaze of Jewels, has he, in less than an Hour after, beheld at the Royal Chapel, the Palace Gardens, Drawing-Room, Opera, or Play, the Haughty Awe-inspiring Lady.—A thousand Times has he stood amaz'd at the prodigious Likeness between his little Mistress, and this Court Beauty; but was still as far from imagining they were the same, as he was the first Hour he had accosted her in the Playhouse, though it is not impossible, but that her Resemblance to this celebrated Lady, might keep his Inclination alive something longer than otherwise they would have been; and that it was to the Thoughts of this (as he supposed) unenjoy'd Charmer, she ow'd in great measure the Vigour of his latter Caresses.

BUT he varied not so much from his Sex as to be able to prolong Desire, to any great Length after Possession: The rifled Charms of *Fantomina* soon lost their Poinancy,[3] and grew tasteless and insipid; and when the Season of the Year inviting the Company to the *Bath*,[4] she offer'd to accompany him, he made an Excuse to go without her. She easily perceiv'd his Coldness, and the Reason why he pretended her going would be incon-venient, and endur'd as much from the Discovery as any of her Sex could do: She dissembled it, however, before him, and took her

---

1 Discretion.
2 Outfit.
3 That is, poignancy; intensity.
4 Resort town where people of fashion summered, known for its medicinal waters and its social opportunities.

Leave of him with the Shew of no other Concern than his Absence occasion'd: But this she did to take from him all Suspicion of her following him, as she intended, and had already laid a Scheme for.—From her first finding out that he design'd to leave her behind, she plainly saw it was for no other Reason, than that being tir'd of her Conversation, he was willing to be at liberty to pursue new Conquests; and wisely considering that Complaints,[1] Tears, Swoonings, and all the Extravagancies which Women make use of in such Cases, have little Prevailance over a Heart inclin'd to rove, and only serve to render those who practise them more contemptible, by robbing them of that Beauty which alone can bring back the fugitive Lover, she resolved to take another Course; and remembring the Height of Transport[2] she enjoyed when the agreeable *Beauplaisir* kneel'd at her Feet, imploring her first Favours, she long'd to prove[3] the same again. Not but a Woman of her Beauty and Accomplishments might have beheld a Thousand in that Condition *Beauplaisir* had been; but with her Sex's Modesty, she had not also thrown off another Virtue equally valuable, tho' generally unfortunate, *Constancy:* She loved *Beauplaisir;* it was only he whose Solicitations[4] could give her Pleasure; and had she seen the whole Species despairing, dying for her sake, it might, perhaps, have been a Satisfaction to her Pride, but none to her more tender Inclination.—Her Design was once more to engage him, to hear him sigh, to see him languish, to feel the strenuous Pressures of his eager Arms, to be compelled, to be sweetly forc'd to what she wished with equal Ardour,[5] was what she wanted, and what she had form'd a Stratagem[6] to obtain, in which she promis'd herself Success.

SHE no sooner heard he had left the Town, than making a Pretence to her Aunt, that she was going to visit a Relation in the Country, went towards *Bath*, attended but by two Servants, who she found Reasons to quarrel with on the Road and discharg'd:

---

[1] Sorrowful utterances.
[2] Ecstasy.
[3] Experience.
[4] Entreaties.
[5] Passion.
[6] Scheme.

Clothing herself in a Habit she had brought with her, she forsook the Coach, and went into a Waggon, in which Equipage she arriv'd at *Bath*.[1] The Dress she was in, was a round-ear'd Cap, a short Red Petticoat, and a little Jacket of Grey Stuff;[2] all the rest of her Accoutrements were answerable to these, and join'd with a broad Country Dialect, a rude[3] unpolish'd Air, which she, having been bred in these Parts, knew very well how to imitate, with her Hair and Eye-brows black'd, made it impossible for her to be known, or taken for any other than what she seem'd. Thus disguis'd did she offer herself to Service in the House where *Beauplaisir* lodg'd, having made it her Business to find out immediately where he was. Notwithstanding this Metamorphosis she was still extremely pretty; and the Mistress of the House happening at that Time to want a Maid, was very glad of the Opportunity of taking her. She was presently receiv'd into the Family; and had a Post in it, (such as she would have chose, had she been left at her Liberty,) that of making the Gentlemen's Beds, getting them their Breakfasts, and waiting on them in their Chambers. Fortune in this Exploit was extremely on her side; there were no others of the Male-Sex in the House, than an old Gentleman, who had lost the Use of his Limbs with the Rheumatism, and had come thither for the Benefit of the Waters, and her belov'd *Beauplaisir;* so that she was in no Apprehensions of any Amorous Violence, but where she wish'd to find it. Nor were her Designs disappointed: He was fir'd with the first Sight of her; and tho' he did not presently take any farther Notice of her, than giving her two or three hearty Kisses, yet she, who now understood that Language but too well, easily saw they were the Prelude to more substantial Joys.—Coming the next Morning to bring his

---

1   Fantomina swaps a middling public vehicle for an inferior one, used by travelers without servants; 'equipage' is ironic, denoting a fine private carriage with servants.

2   According to Backscheider and Richetti, 'the cap was shaped to curve around the face to the ears or below … this style was usually associated with the country and often worn under a hat by women working outdoors. Some women tied the skirt ["petticoat"] up on both sides to display their decorative or embroidered petticoats, which, when short, revealed their ankles and some leg. Jackets were close fitting, buttoned tightly at the waist, and deep cut, which emphasized the woman's shape and also revealed the front of her dress or cleavage. Stuff was a fashionable wool fabric' (*Fantomina*, in *Popular Fiction by Women*, 234, n. 8).

3   Rough.

Chocolate, as he had order'd, he catch'd her by the pretty Leg, which the Shortness of her Petticoat did not in the least oppose; then pulling her gently to him, ask'd her, how long she had been at Service?—How many Sweethearts she had? If she had ever been in Love? and many other such Questions, befitting one of the Degree she appear'd to be: All which she answer'd with such seeming Innocence, as more enflam'd the amorous Heart of him who talk'd to her. He compelled her to sit in his Lap; and gazing on her blushing Beauties, which, if possible, receiv'd Addition from her plain and rural Dress, he soon lost the Power of containing himself.—His wild Desires burst out in all his Words and Actions; he call'd her little Angel, Cherubim, swore he must enjoy her, though Death were to be the Consequence, devour'd her Lips, her Breasts with greedy Kisses, held to his burning Bosom her half-yielding, half-reluctant Body, nor suffer'd her to get loose, till he had ravaged all, and glutted each rapacious Sense with the sweet Beauties of the pretty *Celia*, for that was the Name she bore in this second Expedition.— Generous as Liberality itself to all who gave him Joy this way, he gave her a handsome Sum of Gold, which she durst not now refuse, for fear of creating some Mistrust, and losing the Heart she so lately had regain'd; therefore taking it with an humble Curtesy,[1] and a well counterfeited Shew of Surprise and Joy, cry'd, O Law, Sir! what must I do for all this? He laughed at her Simplicity, and kissing her again, tho' less fervently than he had done before, bad her not be out of the Way when he came home at Night. She promis'd she would not, and very obediently kept her Word.

His Stay at *Bath* exceeded not a Month; but in that Time his suppos'd Country Lass had persecuted him so much with her Fondness, that in spite of the Eagerness with which he first enjoy'd her, he was at last grown more weary of her, than he had been of *Fantomina*; which she perceiving, would not be troublesome, but quitting her Service, remained privately in the Town till she heard he was on his Return; and in that Time provided herself of another Disguise to carry on a third Plot, which her inventing Brain had furnished her with, once more to renew his twice-decay'd Ardours. The Dress she had order'd to be made, was

---

[1] That is, curtsy.

such as Widows wear in their first Mourning, which, together with the most afflicted and penitential Countenance that ever was seen, was no small Alteration to her who us'd to seem all Gaiety.—To add to this, her Hair, which she was accustom'd to wear very loose, both when *Fantomina* and *Celia*, was now ty'd back so strait, and her Pinners[1] coming so very forward, that there was none of it to be seen. In fine, her Habit and her Air were so much chang'd, that she was not more difficult to be known in the rude Country *Girl*, than she was now in the sorrowful *Widow*.

SHE knew that *Beauplaisir* came alone in his Chariot[2] to the *Bath*, and in the Time of her being Servant in the House where he lodg'd, heard nothing of any Body that was to accompany him to *London*, and hop'd he wou'd return in the same Manner he had gone: She therefore hir'd Horses and a Man to attend her to an Inn about ten Miles on this side *Bath*, where having discharg'd them, she waited till the Chariot should come by: which when it did, and she saw that he was alone in it, she call'd to him that drove it to stop a Moment, and going to the Door saluted the Master with these Words:

THE Distress'd and Wretched, Sir, (*said she,*) never fail to excite Compassion in a generous Mind; and I hope I am not deceiv'd in my Opinion that yours is such:—You have the Appearance of a Gentleman, and cannot, when you hear my Story, refuse that Assistance which is in your Power to give to an unhappy Woman, who without it, may be render'd the most miserable of all created Beings.

IT would not be very easy to represent the Surprise, so odd an Address created in the Mind of him to whom it was made.—She had not the Appearance of one who wanted Charity; and what other Favour she requir'd he cou'd not conceive: But telling her, she might command any Thing in his Power, gave her Encouragement to declare herself in this Manner: You may judge, (*resumed she,*) by the melancholy Garb I am in, that I have lately lost all that ought to be valuable to Womankind; but it is impossible for you to guess the Greatness of my Misfortune, unless you had

---

1   Cap, or the hanging flaps thereof, worn by women of high social standing.
2   Lightweight four-wheeled carriage with seats in the back only.

known my Husband, who was Master of every Perfection to endear him to a Wife's Affections.—But, notwithstanding, I look on myself as the most unhappy of my Sex in out-living him, I must so far obey the Dictates of my Discretion, as to take care of the little Fortune he left behind him, which being in the Hands of a Brother of his in *London*, will be all carry'd off to *Holland*, where he is going to settle; if I reach not the Town before he leaves it, I am undone for ever.—To which End I left *Bristol*, the Place where we liv'd, hoping to get a Place in the Stage at *Bath*, but they were all taken up before I came; and being, by a Hurt I got in a Fall, render'd incapable of travelling any long Journey on Horseback, I have no Way to go to *London*, and must be inevitably ruin'd in the Loss of all I have on Earth, without you have good Nature enough to admit me to take Part of your Chariot.

HERE the feigned Widow ended her sorrowful Tale, which had been several Times interrupted by a Parenthesis of Sighs and Groans; and *Beauplaisir*, with a complaisant and tender Air, assur'd her of his Readiness to serve her in Things of much greater Consequence than what she desir'd of him; and told her, it would be an Impossibility of denying a Place in his Chariot to a Lady, who he could not behold without yielding one in his Heart. She answered the Compliments he made her but with Tears, which seem'd to stream in such abundance from her Eyes, that she could not keep her Handkerchief from her Face one Moment. Being come into the Chariot, *Beauplaisir* said a thousand handsome Things to perswade her from giving way to so violent a Grief, which, he told her, would not only be destructive to her Beauty, but likewise her Health. But all his Endeavours for Consolement appear'd ineffectual, and he began to think he should have but a dull Journey, in the Company of one who seem'd so obstinately devoted to the Memory of her dead Husband, that there was no getting a Word from her on any other Theme:—But bethinking himself of the celebrated Story of the *Ephesian* Matron,[1] it came into his Head to make Tryal, she who seem'd equally susceptible of *Sorrow*, might

---

[1] The story originates in Petronius (d. AD 65; see *Satyricon*, 'Eumolpus', 111–12) and had been adapted in 1659 by Sir Walter Charlton. In it, a woman famous for her chastity has sex with a soldier whom she encounters while mourning by the tomb of her recently deceased husband.

not also be so too of *Love*; and having began a Discourse on almost every other Topick, and finding her still incapable of answering, resolv'd to put it to the Proof, if this would have no more Effect to rouze her sleeping Spirits:—With a gay Air, therefore, though accompany'd with the greatest Modesty and Respect, he turned the Conversation, as though without Design, on that Joy-giving Passion, and soon discover'd that was indeed the Subject she was best pleas'd to be entertained with; for on his giving her a Hint to begin upon, never any Tongue run more voluble[1] than hers, on the prodigious Power it had to influence the Souls of those possess'd of it, to Actions even the most distant from their Intentions, Principles, or Humours.—From that she pass'd to a Description of the Happiness of mutual Affection;—the unspeakable Extasy of those who meet with equal Ardency;[2] and represented it in Colours so lively, and disclos'd by the Gestures with which her Words were accompany'd, and the Accent of her Voice so true a Feeling of what she said, that *Beauplaisir*, without being as stupid, as he was really the contrary, could not avoid perceiving there were Seeds of Fire, not yet extinguish'd, in this fair Widow's Soul, which wanted but the kindling Breath of tender Sighs to light into a Blaze.—He now thought himself as fortunate, as some Moments before he had the Reverse; and doubted not, but, that before they parted, he should find a Way to dry the Tears of this lovely Mourner, to the Satisfaction of them both. He did not, however, offer, as he had done to *Fantomina* and *Celia* to urge his Passion directly to her, but by a thousand little softning Artifices, which he well knew how to use, gave her leave to guess he was enamour'd. When they came to the Inn where they were to lie, he declar'd himself somewhat more freely, and perceiving she did not resent it past Forgiveness, grew more encroaching still;—He now took the Liberty of kissing away her Tears, and catching the Sighs as they issued from her Lips; telling her if Grief was infectious, he was resolv'd to have his Share; protesting he would gladly exchange Passions with her, and be content to bear her Load of *Sorrow*, if she would as willingly ease the Burden of his *Love*.—She said little in answer to the strenuous

---

[1]   Fluently.
[2]   Passion.

Pressures with which at last he ventur'd to enfold her, but not thinking it Decent, for the Character she had assum'd, to yeild so suddenly, and unable to deny both his and her own Inclinations, she counterfeited a fainting, and fell motionless upon his Breast.— He had no great Notion that she was in a real Fit, and the Room they supp'd in happening to have a Bed in it, he took her in his Arms and laid her on it, believing, that whatever her Distemper was, that was the most proper Place to convey her to.—He laid himself down by her, and endeavour'd to bring her to herself; and she was too grateful to her kind Physician at her returning Sense, to remove from the Posture he had put her in, without his Leave.

IT may, perhaps, seem strange that *Beauplaisir* should in such near Intimacies continue still deceiv'd: I know there are Men who will swear it is an Impossibility, and that no Disguise could hinder them from knowing a Woman they had once enjoy'd. In answer to these Scruples, I can only say, that besides the Alteration which the Change of Dress made in her, she was so admirably skill'd in the Art of feigning, that she had the Power of putting on almost what Face she pleas'd, and knew so exactly how to form her Behaviour to the Character she represented, that all the Comedians at both Playhouses[1] are infinitely short of her Performances: She could vary her very Glances, tune her Voice to Accents the most different imaginable from those in which she spoke when she appear'd herself.—These Aids from Nature, join'd to the Wiles of Art, and the Distance between the Places where the imagin'd *Fantomina* and *Celia* were, might very well prevent his having any Thought that they were the same, or that the fair *Widow* was either of them: It never so much as enter'd his Head, and though he did fancy he observed in the Face of the latter, Features which were not alto-gether unknown to him, yet he could not recollect when or where he had known them;—and being told by her, that from her Birth, she had never remov'd from *Bristol*, a Place where he never was, he rejected the Belief of having seen her, and suppos'd his Mind had been deluded by an Idea of some other, whom she might have a Resemblance of.

---

[1] Actors in the comedies staged by the licensed theaters at Drury Lane and Covent Garden, London.

THEY pass'd the Time of their Journey in as much Happiness as the most luxurious Gratification of wild Desires could make them; and when they came to the End of it, parted not without a mutual Promise of seeing each other often.—He told her to what Place she should direct a Letter to him; and she assur'd him she would send to let him know where to come to her, as soon as she was fixed in Lodgings.

SHE kept her Promise; and charm'd with the Continuance of his eager Fondness,[1] went not home, but into private Lodgings, whence she wrote to him to visit her the first Opportunity, and enquire for the Widow *Bloomer*.—She had no sooner dispatched this Billet, than she repair'd to the House where she had lodg'd as *Fantomina*, charging the People if *Beauplaisir* should come there, not to let him know she had been out of Town. From thence she wrote to him, in a different Hand, a long Letter of Complaint, that he had been so cruel in not sending one Letter to her all the Time he had been absent, entreated to see him, and concluded with subscribing herself his unalterably Affectionate *Fantomina*. She received in one Day Answers to both these. The first contain'd these Lines:

To the Charming Mrs. BLOOMER.

IT would be impossible, my Angel! for me to express the thousandth Part of that Infinity of Transport, the Sight of your dear Letter gave me.—Never was Woman form'd to charm like you: Never did any look like you,—write like you,—bless like you;—nor did ever Man adore as I do.—Since Yesterday we parted, I have seem'd a Body without a Soul; and had you not by this inspiring Billet, gave me new Life, I know not what by To-morrow I should have been.—I will be with you this Evening about Five:—O, 'tis an Age till then!—But the cursed Formalities of Duty oblige me to Dine with my Lord—who never rises from Table till that Hour;—therefore Adieu till then sweet lovely Mistress of the Soul and all the Faculties of
> Your most faithful,
> BEAUPLAISIR.

---

[1] Foolish infatuation.

THE other was in this Manner:

To the Lovely FANTOMINA.

IF you were half so sensible as you ought of your own Power of charming, you would be assur'd, that to be unfaithful or unkind to you, would be among the Things that are in their very Natures Impossibilities.—It was my Misfortune, not my Fault, that you were not persecuted every Post with a Declaration of my unchanging Passion; but I had unluckily forgot the Name of the Woman at whose House you are, and knew not how to form a Direction that it might come safe to your Hands.—And, indeed, the Reflection how you might misconstrue my Silence, brought me to Town some Weeks sooner than I intended—If you knew how I have languish'd to renew those Blessings I am permitted to enjoy in your Society, you would rather pity than condemn

Your ever faithful,

BEAUPLAISIR.

P.S. I fear I cannot see you till To-morrow; some Business has unluckily fallen out that will engross my Hours till then.—Once more, my Dear, Adieu.

TRAYTOR! (*cry'd she,*) as soon as she had read them, 'tis thus our silly, fond, believing Sex are serv'd when they put Faith in Man: So had I been deceiv'd and cheated, had I like the rest believ'd, and sat down mourning in Absence, and vainly waiting recover'd Tendernesses.—How do some Women (*continued she*) make their Life a Hell, burning in fruitless Expectations, and dreaming out their Days in Hopes and Fears, then wake at last to all the Horror of Dispair?—But I have outwitted even the most Subtle of the deceiving Kind, and while he thinks to fool me, is himself the only beguiled Person.

SHE made herself, most certainly, extremely happy in the Reflection on the Success of her Stratagems; and while the Knowledge of his Inconstancy and Levity[1] of Nature kept her from having that real Tenderness for him she would else have had, she found the Means of gratifying the Inclination she had for his agreeable Person, in as full a Manner as she could wish.

---

[1] Lack of seriousness.

She had all the Sweets of Love, but as yet had tasted none of the Gall,[1] and was in a State of Contentment, which might be envy'd by the more Delicate.

WHEN the expected Hour arriv'd, she found that her Lover had lost no part of the Fervency[2] with which he had parted from her; but when the next Day she receiv'd him as *Fantomina*, she perceiv'd a prodigious Difference; which led her again into Reflections on the Unaccountableness of Men's Fancies, who still prefer the last Conquest, only because it is the last.—Here was an evident Proof of it; for there could not be a Difference in Merit, because they were the same Person; but the Widow *Bloomer* was a more new Acquaintance than *Fantomina*, and therefore esteem'd more valuable. This, indeed, must be said of *Beauplaisir*, that he had a greater Share of good Nature than most of his Sex, who, for the most part, when they are weary of an Intreague, break it entirely off, without any Regard to the Despair of the abandon'd Nymph.[3] Though he retain'd no more than a bare Pity and Complaisance for *Fantomina*, yet believing she lov'd him to an Excess, would not entirely forsake her, though the Continuance of his Visits was now become rather a Penance than a Pleasure.

THE Widow *Bloomer* triumph'd some Time longer over the Heart of this Inconstant, but at length her Sway was at an End, and she sunk in this Character, to the same Degree of Tastelesness,[4] as she had done before in that of *Fantomina* and *Celia*.—She presently perceiv'd it, but bore it as she had always done; it being but what she expected, she had prepar'd herself for it, and had another Project in *embrio*, which she soon ripen'd into Action. She did not, indeed, compleat it altogether so suddenly as she had done the others, by reason there must be Persons employ'd in it; and the Aversion she had to any *Confidents* in her Affairs, and the Caution with which she had hitherto acted, and which she was still determin'd to continue, made it very difficult for her to find a Way without breaking thro' that Resolution to

---

1   Bitterness.
2   Passion.
3   Usually, young virgin; here the use is either ironic or more general.
4   Dullness.

compass what she wish'd.—She got over the Difficulty at last, however, by proceeding in a Manner, if possible, more extraordinary than all her former Behaviour:—Muffling herself up in her Hood one Day, she went into the Park about the Hour when there are a great many necessitous Gentlemen, who think themselves above doing what they call little Things for a Maintenance, walking in the *Mall*,[1] to take a *Camelion* Treat, and fill their Stomachs with Air instead of Meat.[2] Two of those, who by their Physiognomy[3] she thought most proper for her Purpose, she beckon'd to come to her; and taking them into a Walk more remote from Company, began to communicate the Business she had with them in these Words: I am sensible, Gentlemen, (*said she,*) that, through the Blindness of Fortune, and Partiality of the World, Merit frequently goes unrewarded, and that those of the best Pretentions[4] meet with the least Encouragement:—I ask your Pardon, (*continued she,*) perceiving they seem'd surpris'd, if I am mistaken in the Notion, that you two may, perhaps, be of the Number of those who have Reason to complain of the Injustice of Fate; but if you are such as I take you for, have a Proposal to make you, which may be of some little Advantage to you. Neither of them made any immediate Answer, but appear'd bury'd in Consideration for some Moments. At length, We should, doubtless, Madam, (*said one of them,*) willingly come into any Measures to oblige you, provided they are such as may bring us into no Danger, either as to our Persons or Reputations. That which I require of you, (*resumed she,*) has nothing in it criminal: All that I desire is *Secrecy* in what you are intrusted, and to disguise yourselves in such a Manner as you cannot be known, if hereafter seen by the Person on whom you are to impose.—In fine, the Business is only an innocent Frolick, but if blaz'd abroad, might be taken for too great a Freedom in me:—Therefore, if you resolve to assist me, here are five Pieces to drink my Health, and assure you, that I have not discours'd you on an Affair, I design not to proceed in; and when it is accomplish'd fifty more lie ready for your

---

[1] Fashionable pedestrian concourse in St. James's Park, London.
[2] The chameleon was believed to live on air.
[3] Facial appearance.
[4] Claims (here, to merit).

Acceptance. These Words, and, above all, the Money, which was a Sum which, 'tis probable, they had not seen of a long Time, made them immediately assent to all she desir'd, and press for the Beginning of their Employment: But Things were not yet ripe for Execution; and she told them, that the next Day they should be let into the Secret, charging them to meet her in the same Place at an Hour she appointed. 'Tis hard to say, which of these Parties went away best pleas'd; *they*, that Fortune had sent them so unexpected a Windfall; or *she*, that she had found Persons, who appeared so well qualified to serve her.

INDEFATIGABLE in the Pursuit of whatsoever her Humour was bent upon, she had no sooner left her new-engag'd Emissaries, than she went in search of a House for the compleating her Project.—She pitch'd on one very large, and magnificently furnished, which she hir'd by the Week, giving them the Money before-hand, to prevent any Inquiries. The next Day she repaired to the Park, where she met the punctual 'Squires of low Degree; and ordering them to follow her to the House she had taken, told them they must condescend to appear like Servants, and gave each of them a very rich Livery.[1] Then writing a Letter to *Beauplaisir*, in a Character vastly different from either of those she had made use of, as *Fantomina*, or the fair Widow *Bloomer*, order'd one of them to deliver it into his own Hands, to bring back an Answer, and to be careful that he sifted out nothing of the Truth.—I do not fear, (*said she*,) that you should discover to him who I am, because that is a Secret, of which you yourselves are ignorant; but I would have you be so careful in your Replies, that he may not think the Concealment springs from any other Reasons than your great Integrity to your Trust.—Seem therefore to know my whole Affairs; and let your refusing to make him Partaker in the Secret, appear to be only the Effect of your Zeal for my Interest and Reputation. Promises of entire Fidelity on the one side, and Reward on the other, being past, the Messenger made what haste he could to the House of *Beauplaisir*; and being there told where he might find him, perform'd exactly the Injunction that had been given him. But never Astonishment

---

[1] Uniform.

exceeding that which *Beauplaisir* felt at the reading this Billet, in which he found these Lines:

To the All-conquering BEAUPLAISIR.

I IMAGINE not that 'tis a new Thing to you, to be told, you are the greatest Charm in Nature to our Sex: I shall therefore, not to fill up my Letter with any impertinent Praises on your Wit or Person, only tell you, that I am infinite in Love with both, and if you have a Heart not too deeply engag'd, should think myself the happiest of my Sex in being capable of inspiring it with some Tenderness.——There is but one Thing in my Power to refuse you, which is the Knowledge of my Name, which believing the Sight of my Face will render no Secret, you must not take it ill that I conceal from you.——The Bearer of this is a Person I can trust; send by him your Answer; but endeavour not to dive into the Meaning of this Mystery, which will be impossible for you to unravel, and at the same Time very much disoblige me:——But that you may be in no Apprehensions of being impos'd on by a Woman unworthy of your Regard, I will venture to assure you, the first and greatest Men in the Kingdom, would think themselves blest to have that Influence over me you have, though unknown to yourself acquir'd.——But I need not go about to raise your Curiosity, by giving you any Idea of what my Person is; if you think fit to be satisfied, resolve to visit me To-morrow about Three in the Afternoon; and though my Face is hid, you shall not want sufficient Demonstration, that she who takes these unusual Measures to commence a Friendship with you, is neither Old, nor Deform'd. Till then I am,

Yours,
INCOGNITA.

HE had scarce come to the Conclusion, before he ask'd the Person who brought it, from what Place he came;——the Name of the Lady he serv'd;——if she were a Wife, or Widow, and several other Questions directly opposite to the Directions of the Letter; but Silence would have avail'd him as much as did all those Testimonies of Curiosity: No *Italian Bravo*,[1] employ'd in a Business of the like Nature, perform'd his Office with more Artifice;[2] and the impatient Enquirer was

---

[1] Hired thug.
[2] Cunning.

convinc'd, that nothing but doing as he was desir'd, could give him any Light into the Character of the Woman who declar'd so violent a Passion for him; and little fearing any Consequence which could ensue from such an Encounter, resolv'd to rest satisfy'd till he was inform'd of every Thing from herself, not imagining this *Incognita* varied so much from the Generality of her Sex, as to be able to refuse the Knowledge of any Thing to the Man she lov'd with that Transcendency of Passion she profess'd, and which his many Successes with the Ladies gave him Encouragement enough to believe. He therefore took Pen and Paper, and answer'd her Letter in Terms tender enough for a Man who had never seen the Person to whom he wrote. The Words were as follows:

To the Obliging and Witty INCOGNITA.

THOUGH to tell me I am happy enough to be lik'd by a Woman, such, as by your Manner of Writing, I imagine you to be, is an Honour which I can never sufficiently acknowledge, yet I know not how I am able to content myself with admiring the Wonders of your Wit alone: I am certain, a Soul like yours must shine in your Eyes with a Vivacity, which must bless all they look on.—I shall, however, endeavour to restrain myself in those Bounds you are pleas'd to set me, till by the Knowledge of my inviolable Fidelity, I may be thought worthy of gazing on that Heaven I am now but to enjoy in Contemplation.—You need not doubt my glad Compliance with your obliging Summons: There is a Charm in your Lines, which gives too sweet an Idea of their lovely Author to be resisted.—I am all impatient for the blissful Moment, which is to throw me at your Feet, and give me an Opportunity of convincing you that I am,

Your everlasting Slave,
BEAUPLAISIR.

NOTHING could be more pleas'd than she, to whom it was directed, at the Receipt of this Letter; but when she was told how inquisitive he had been concerning her Character and Circumstances, she could not forbear laughing heartily to think of the Tricks she had play'd him, and applauding her own Strength of Genius, and Force of Resolution, which by such unthought-of Ways could triumph over her Lover's Inconstancy, and render that very Temper, which to other Women is the greatest Curse, a Means to make herself more bless'd.—Had he been faithful to me, (*said she, to herself,*) either as *Fantomina*, or *Celia*, or the Widow *Bloomer*, the most violent Passion, if it does not change its Object, in Time will wither: Possession naturally abates the Vigour of Desire, and I should have had, at best, but a cold, insipid, husband-like Lover in my Arms; but by these Arts of passing on him as a new Mistress whenever the Ardour, which alone makes Love a Blessing, begins to diminish, for the former one, I have him always raving, wild, impatient, longing, dying.—O that all neglected Wives, and fond abandon'd Nymphs would take this Method!—Men would be caught in their own Snare, and have no Cause to scorn our easy, weeping, wailing Sex! Thus did she pride herself as if secure she never should have any Reason to repent the present Gaiety of her Humour. The Hour drawing near in which he was to come, she dress'd herself in as magnificent a Manner, as if she were to be that Night at a Ball at Court, endeavouring to repair the want of those Beauties which the Vizard[1] should conceal, by setting forth the others with the greatest Care and Exactness. Her fine Shape, and Air, and Neck, appear'd to great Advantage; and by that which was to be seen of her, one might believe the rest to be perfectly agreeable. *Beauplaisir* was prodigiously charm'd, as well with her Appearance, as with the Manner she entertain'd him: But though he was wild with Impatience for the Sight of a Face which belong'd to so exquisite a Body, yet he would not immediately press for it, believing before he left her he should easily obtain that Satisfaction.—A noble Collation being over, he began to sue for[2] the Performance of her Promise of granting every Thing he could ask, excepting the Sight of her Face, and Knowledge of her Name. It would have been a ridiculous Piece of Affectation in her to have seem'd coy in complying with what she herself had been the first in desiring: She yeilded without even a Shew of Reluctance: And if there be any true Felicity in an Amour such as theirs, both here enjoy'd it to the full. But not in the Height of all their mutual Raptures, could he prevail on her to satisfy his Curiosity with the

---

[1] Mask worn at a masquerade ball.
[2] To press (her) for.

Sight of her Face: She told him that she hop'd he knew so much of her, as might serve to convince him, she was not unworthy of his tenderest Regard; and if he cou'd not content himself with that which she was willing to reveal, and which was the Conditions of their meeting, dear as he was to her, she would rather part with him for ever, than consent to gratify an Inquisitiveness, which, in her Opinion, had no Business with his Love. It was in vain that he endeavour'd to make her sensible of her Mistake; and that this Restraint was the greatest Enemy imaginable to the Happiness of them both: She was not to be perswaded, and he was oblig'd to desist his Solicitations, though determin'd in his Mind to compass what he so ardently desir'd, before he left the House. He then turned the Discourse wholly on the Violence of the Passion he had for her; and express'd the greatest Discontent in the World at the Apprehensions of being separated;—swore he could dwell for ever in her Arms, and with such an undeniable Earnestness pressed to be permitted to tarry with her the whole Night, that had she been less charm'd with his renew'd Eagerness of Desire, she scarce would have had the Power of refusing him; but in granting this Request, she was not without a Thought that he had another Reason for making it besides the Extremity of his Passion, and had it immediately in her Head how to disappoint him.

THE Hours of Repose being arriv'd, he begg'd she would retire to her Chamber; to which she consented, but oblig'd him to go to Bed first; which he did not much oppose, because he suppos'd she would not lie in her Mask, and doubted not but the Morning's Dawn would bring the wish'd Discovery.—The two imagin'd Servants usher'd him to his new Lodging; where he lay some Moments in all the Perplexity imaginable at the Oddness of this Adventure. But she suffer'd not these Cogitations to be of any long Continuance: She came, but came in the Dark; which being no more than he expected by the former Part of her Proceedings, he said nothing of; but as much Satisfaction as he found in her Embraces, nothing ever long'd for the Approach of Day with more Impatience than he did. At last it came; but how great was his Disappointment, when by the Noises he heard in the Street, the Hurry of the Coaches, and the Crys of Penny-

Merchants,[1] he was convinc'd it was Night no where but with him? He was still in the same Darkness as before; for she had taken care to blind the Windows in such a manner, that not the least Chink was left to let in Day.—He complain'd of her Behaviour in Terms that she would not have been able to resist yielding to, if she had not been certain it would have been the Ruin of her Passion:—She, therefore, answered him only as she had done before; and getting out of the Bed from him, flew out of the Room with too much Swiftness for him to have overtaken her, if he had attempted it. The Moment she left him, the two Attendants enter'd the Chamber, and plucking down the Implements which had skreen'd him from the Knowledge of that which he so much desir'd to find out, restored his Eyes once more to Day:—They attended to assist him in Dressing, brought him Tea, and by their Obsequiousness, let him see there was but one Thing which the Mistress of them would not gladly oblige him in.—He was so much out of Humour, however, at the Disappointment of his Curiosity, that he resolv'd never to make a second Visit.—Finding her in an outer Room, he made no Scruple of expressing the Sense he had of the little Trust she reposed in him, and at last plainly told her, he could not submit to receive Obligations from a Lady, who thought him uncapable of keeping a Secret, which she made no Difficulty of letting her Servants into.—He resented,—he once more entreated,—he said all that Man could do, to prevail on her to unfold the Mystery; but all his Adjurations[2] were fruitless; and he went out of the House determin'd never to re-enter it, till she should pay the Price of his Company with the Discovery of her Face and Circumstances.—She suffer'd him to go with this Resolution, and doubted not but he would recede from it, when he reflected on the happy Moments they had pass'd together; but if he did not, she comforted herself with the Design of forming some other Stratagem, with which to impose on him a fourth Time.

SHE kept the House, and her Gentlemen-Equipage for about a Fortnight, in which Time she continu'd to write to him as

---

[1]   Street merchants selling cheap goods.
[2]   Entreaties.

Fantomina and the Widow *Bloomer*, and received the Visits he sometimes made to each; but his Behaviour to both was grown so cold, that she began to grow as weary of receiving his now insipid Caresses as he was of offering them: She was beginning to think in what Manner she should drop these two Characters, when the sudden Arrival of her Mother, who had been some Time in a foreign Country, oblig'd her to put an immediate Stop to the Course of her whimsical Adventures.—That Lady, who was severely virtuous, did not approve of many Things she had been told of the Conduct of her Daughter; and though it was not in the Power of any Person in the World to inform her of the Truth of what she had been guilty of, yet she heard enough to make her keep her afterwards in a Restraint, little agreeable to her Humour, and the Liberties to which she had been accustomed.

BUT this Confinement was not the greatest Part of the Trouble of this now afflicted Lady: She found the Consequences of her amorous Follies would be, without almost a Miracle, impossible to be concealed:—She was with Child; and though she would easily have found Means to have skreen'd even this from the Knowledge of the World, had she been at liberty to have acted with the same unquestionable Authority over herself, as she did before the coming of her Mother, yet now all her Invention was at a Loss for a Stratagem to impose on a Woman of her Penetration:—By eating little, lacing prodigious strait, and the Advantage of a great Hoop-Petticoat, however, her Bigness was not taken notice of, and, perhaps, she would not have been suspected till the Time of her going into the Country, where her Mother design'd to send her, and from whence she intended to make her escape to some Place where she might be deliver'd with Secrecy, if the Time of it had not happen'd much sooner than she expected.—A Ball being at Court, the good old Lady was willing she should partake of the Diversion of it as a Farewel to the Town.—It was there she was seiz'd with those Pangs, which none in her Condition are exempt from:—She could not conceal the sudden Rack[1] which all at once invaded her; or had her Tongue been mute, her wildly rolling Eyes, the Distortion of her Features, and the Convulsions which shook her

---

[1]   Loosely, jolt.

whole Frame, in spite of her, would have reveal'd she labour'd under some terrible Shock of Nature.—Every Body was surpris'd, every Body was concern'd, but few guessed at the Occasion.—Her Mother griev'd beyond Expression, doubted not but she was struck with the Hand of Death; and order'd her to be carried Home in a Chair, while herself follow'd in another.—A Physician was immediately sent for: But he presently perceiving what was her Distemper, call'd the old Lady aside, and told her, it was not a Doctor of his Sex, but one of her own, her Daughter stood in need of.—Never was Astonishment and Horror greater than that which seiz'd the Soul of this afflicted Parent at these Words: She could not for a Time believe the Truth of what she heard; but he insisting on it, and conjuring her to send for a Midwife, she was at length convinc'd of it.—All the Pity and Tenderness she had been for some Moment before possess'd of, now vanish'd, and were succeeded by an adequate Shame and Indignation:—She flew to the Bed where her Daughter was lying, and telling her what she had been inform'd of, and which she was now far from doubting, commanded her to reveal the Name of the Person whose Insinuations had drawn her to this Dishonour.—It was a great while before she could be brought to confess any Thing, and much longer before she could be prevailed on to name the Man whom she so fatally had lov'd; but the Rack of Nature growing more fierce, and the enraged old Lady protesting no Help should be afforded her while she persisted in her Obstinacy, she, with great Difficulty and Hesitation in her Speech, at last pronounc'd the Name of *Beauplaisir*. She had no sooner satisfy'd her weeping Mother, than that sorrowful Lady sent Messengers at the same Time, for a Midwife, and for that Gentleman who had occasion'd the other's being wanted.—He happen'd by Accident to be at home, and immediately obey'd the Summons, though prodigiously surpris'd what Business a Lady so much a Stranger to him could have to impart.—But how much greater was his Amazement, when taking him into her Closet, she there acquainted him with her Daughter's Misfortune, of the Discovery she had made, and how far he was concern'd in it?—All the Idea one can form of wild Astonishment, was mean to what he felt:—He assur'd her, that the young Lady her Daughter was a Person whom he had never, more than at a

Distance, admir'd:—That he had indeed, spoke to her in publick Company, but that he never had a Thought which tended to her Dishonour.—His Denials, if possible, added to the Indignation she was before enflam'd with:—She had no longer Patience; and carrying him into the Chamber, where she was just deliver'd of a fine Girl, cry'd out, I will not be impos'd on: The Truth by one of you shall be reveal'd.—*Beauplaisir* being brought to the Bed-side, was beginning to address himself to the Lady in it, to beg she would clear the Mistake her Mother was involv'd in; when she, covering herself with the Cloaths, and ready to die a second Time with the inward Agitations of her Soul, shriek'd out, Oh, I am undone!—I cannot live, and bear this Shame!—But the old Lady believing that now or never was the Time to dive into the Bottom of this Mystery, forcing her to rear her Head, told her, she should not hope to Escape the Scrutiny of a Parent she had dishonour'd in such a Manner, and pointing to *Beauplaisir*, Is this the Gentleman, (*said she,*) to whom you owe your Ruin? or have you deceiv'd me by a fictitious Tale? Oh! no, (*resum'd the trembling Creature,*) he is, indeed, the innocent Cause of my Undoing:—Promise me your Pardon, (*continued she,*) and I will relate the Means. Here she ceas'd, expecting what she would reply, which, on hearing *Beauplaisir* cry out, What mean you, Madam? I your Undoing, who never harbour'd the least Design on you in my Life, she did in these Words, Though the Injury you have done your Family, (*said she,*) is of a Nature which cannot justly hope Forgiveness, yet be assur'd, I shall much sooner excuse you when satisfied of the Truth, than while I am kept in a Suspence, if possible, as vexatious as the Crime[1] itself is to me. Encouraged by this she related the whole Truth. And 'tis difficult to determine, if *Beauplaisir*, or the Lady, were most surpris'd at what they heard; he, that he should have been blinded so often by her Artifices; or she, that so young a Creature should have the Skill to make use of them. Both sat for some Time in a profound Resvery;[2] till at length she broke it first in these Words: Pardon, Sir, (*said she,*) the Trouble I have given you: I must confess it was with a Design to oblige you to repair the supposed Injury you had done this

---

[1] Morally odious act.
[2] That is, reverie.

unfortunate Girl, by marrying her, but now I know not what to say:—The Blame is wholly her's, and I have nothing to request further of you, than that you will not divulge the distracted Folly she has been guilty of.—He answered her in Terms perfectly polite; but made no Offer of that which, perhaps, she expected, though could not, now inform'd of her Daughter's Proceedings, demand. He assured her, however, that if she would commit the new-born Lady to his Care, he would discharge it faithfully. But neither of them would consent to that; and he took his Leave, full of Cogitations, more confus'd than ever he had known in his whole Life. He continued to visit there, to enquire after her Health every Day; but the old Lady perceiving there was nothing likely to ensue from these Civilities, but, perhaps, a Renewing of the Crime, she entreated him to refrain; and as soon as her Daughter was in a Condition, sent her to a Monastery in *France*, the Abbess of which had been her particular Friend. And thus ended an Intreague, which, considering the Time it lasted, was as full of Variety as any, perhaps, that many Ages has produced.

THE TEA-TABLE:
OR, A CONVERSATION BETWEEN SOME POLITE PERSONS OF BOTH SEXES

The Heavens have Clouds, and Spots are in the Moon,
A faultless Virtue's to be found in none.

Howard's Indian Queen.[1]

Advertisement.

THE World is so apt to pick Meanings out of every thing, especially if there be the least Room for Censure or Ridicule, that I think my self obliged to acquaint my Reader, that I have no View to any particular Persons, or Families in the Characters contained in the following Sheets.——The Design of them being only to expose those little Foibles which disgrace Humanity, and render those who are guilty of them incapable of receiving that Admiration and Respect, which their other good Qualities and Accomplishments would else merit from the World. If I succeed in my Aim so far as to influence but one Person to correct any of these Solecisms in Humour,[2] I shall think my self happy; and if I fail, have yet this Comfort, that it is less my Fault than my Misfortune.

WHERE have the Curious an Opportunity of informing themselves of the Intrigues of the Town, like that they enjoy over a TEA-TABLE,[3] on a Lady's *Visiting-Day?*——Can the Love-sick *Maid,* the Wanton *Wife,* or Amorous *Widow,* be guilty of the least false Step which falls not under the Observance of these *Criticks* in Fame?——Can the seemingly Uxorious *Husband,* who in all Company extols the Merit of his *Wife,* and talks of nothing but their mutual Fondness, keep from the prying Eyes of this Cabal, his Amour with her *Chamber-maid* undiscover'd?——Can the new wedded *Bride,*

---

[1] The lines, from Sir Robert Howard and John Dryden, *The Indian Queen* (1665), III. i. 151–52, appear on the original title page. For a digitally enhanced facsimile of that page, see Haywood, *Miscellaneous Writings, 1725–1743,* ed. Alexander Pettit (London: Pickering & Chatto, 2000) 3.

[2] Quirks.

[3] 'Tea-table' had the gossipy connotation then that 'coffee-klatsch' would have later.

trembling and blushing at the approach of Night, prevent the inquisitive Fleerers[1] from examining her past Conduct; and if her Modesty be real, or affected?—Can the *Beau*, with a splendid Equipage[2] and no Estate, pass here without the most strict Scrutiny into the Means by which his Grandeur is supported!—is the false Hair, fine Cosmetick, or any other Assistant to Beauty, laid on with so much Art, that the Rival *Belle* cannot distinguish it from Natural?—In fine, is there any Irregularity in Conduct, any Indecorum in Behaviour or Dress, any Defect in Beauty, which is not here fully expatiated on?[3]—Scandal, and Ridicule seem here to reign with uncontested Sway, and but rarely suffer the Intrusion of any other Themes.—Sometimes, indeed, it does happen that more useful Topicks make the Conversation, but it is so scarce, and so little approv'd of by the Generality of the persons who compose those Assemblies, that I never found Wit and good Humour in fashion among them, except at AMIANA's: That Lady is possess'd of so much Sweetness of Disposition herself, that she endeavours all she can to inspire the same in others; and one cannot, without being guilty of Ill-manners to her, maintain any Argument, in her Company, to the Prejudice of an absent Person.—None can be Master of a *Virtue* which she does not *Magnifie*; a *Fault*, which she does not carefully *Conceal*, or if too obvious, shadow it over by enhancing the Value of some Perfection.—She excuses the *Whims* of the *Virtuoso*[4] on the account of his Philosophy;—the Vanity of the *Poet* for the sake of his good Verses;—the Severity of the *Prude* in respect to that Virtue she assumes;—and the Affectation of the *Coquette*, for the Diversion she affords the Company. She endeavours, 'tis certain, to select her Assembly out of such of her Acquaintance, as will not put her to the Blush to defend, but if any such do force themselves among them, it is in the manner already represented she behaves.

I was sometime ago introduc'd, by a particular Friend, to the Acquaintance of this admirable Lady, we went too early to find

---

1 Gossips.

2 Fine carriage, with servants, or perhaps personal accoutrements more generally.

3 Discussed in detail.

4 Dilettante, for example an amateur scientist or scholar ('philosopher'). The type is commonly ridiculed in late seventeenth- and eighteenth-century satire.

much Company there, tho' it was that Day on which none who appear well are refused Admittance; but those who were with her hapned all of them to be Persons of a very elegant Taste: We had just began to enter into a Conversation, which wou'd have been very Entertaining, when a Titled *Coxcomb*[1] came into the Room, and with an Inundation of Impertinence put a Stop to every Current of good Sense.—He had been that Morning at the Rehearsal of a New Play, and the whole Company were teiz'd for full three Quarters of an Hour, with his ridiculous Remarks on the Scenery, the Plot, the Diction;[2] the *Poet*, it seems, had not consulted him in the Affair, and he was resolved to Damn it, at least in the Opinion of those to whom his *Quality* gave a Sanction to his *Judgment*. Had any Person been inclin'd to take the Part of either the Work or Author, it had been impossible, without being possess'd of an equal Share both of Assurance and Volubility,[3] to introduce one Word of Contradiction, and 'tis probable he wou'd have run on in the manner he had begun much longer, if five or six fine Ladies had not on a sudden encreas'd the Assembly, and oblig'd him to break off to pay his Compliments to them. This wou'd have been a very great Ease to the Company, if one of these fair Visiters had not been of a Disposition to render herself as much or more troublesome.—She was no sooner seated, than she began to complain of a most terrible Headake, rolled her Eyes wildly round the Room, wreath'd her Neck, and distorted a Face which Nature had made extremely lovely, into such Looks of Anguish, that one could never have imagin'd, without being assur'd it was so, that she should do it thro' Choice. I was beginning to express some part of the Concern her supposed Disorder had rais'd in me, when a Lady who sat near me, whisper'd me that it was all Affectation, and that she never appeared in any publick Assembly, without pretending to fall into these Fits.—She fancies, added my fair Informer, that it gives her an Air of Delicacy; and having little in her Conversation or Person capable of attracting any extraordinary Devoirs,[4] hopes to find that compassionate Notice for her

---

[1]   Aristocratic fop or fool; another familiar butt of satire in the period.
[2]   Not only the choice of words, but also their delivery.
[3]   Fluency.
[4]   Acts of respect.

Distemper,[1] which neither her indifferent Circumstances, nor the Misfortune she has lately met with in being forsaken by the Knight, has the Power to raise. These last Words were accompanied with so malicious a Look and Accent, that however blamable I thought the Foible of the other, I could not judge with less Severity on this.—I made but little Answer, being unwilling either to affront, or to say any thing which might look like an Encouragement of a Temper so pernicious to Society; and not being desirous of hearing any more of the same Nature, I rose, and, retiring to a distant Window, fell into a deep Musing, mixed with a Wonder at the indulged Follies of a Sex, which, but for themselves, might be held in equal Estimation with the other.—Were every Woman, said I to my self, but half as zealous in correcting the little Vanities of her own Humour, as she is in exposing those of her Acquaintance, they would be as preferable to Men in *Understanding*, as they are allow'd to be in *Beauty*. What I had just observ'd of these two Ladies, bringing to my Mind a thousand other whimsical Passages of the same kind, which I had remark'd among some of those I had convers'd with, I became so lost in Thought, that for a good while I was altogether ignorant of what was said or done in the Room; and might perhaps have continued in that *Resvery*[2] much longer than I did, if the agreeable AMIANA had not called to me, desiring me to join Company, and at the same time, the Person who did me the Favour of introducing me, pluck'd me by the Sleeve, reminding me that the little Impertinencies of those who visited her, ought not to make me forget what was due to a Lady of her Quality and Merits. I could do no less than apologize in the best manner I was able, for the Rudeness I had been guilty of; which being done, I resum'd my Seat, and saw with no small Satisfaction, that the Counterfeit indispos'd, and the Lady who had found Fault with her, and betray'd her to me, were both gone, and, as I was afterwards inform'd, went in the same Coach,[3] and with all the Appearance of the greatest Friendship on both sides. I had not sat long before, to add to my

---

[1]   Illness.
[2]   That is, reverie.
[3]   Large carriage.

Contentment, Lord *Critick* also took his Leave, and those that now remain'd were all of them either People of real *Wisdom*, or had *Wit* sufficient to enable them to conceal that Deficiency, and render their Conversation agreeable on such Subjects of Entertainment, as would not discover a Defect in Judgment; and indeed, a Person who knows how to hold his Tongue in Matters, which to discourse of must be a Disadvantage to him, cannot, I think, properly be said to want[1] Wisdom; I know not if to avoid (in a manner which may not seem as if we did so) all Speech of that which is above our Capacity to talk judiciously of, be not as great an Argument of good Sense, as to be able to declaim on it with the utmost Oratory:[2] It has ever been allow'd, that to know one's self is the most valuable Part of Knowledge, and if so, these prudent *Chusers* of Conversation merit more Applause than the World is sensible of; and though they desire not to *receive*, nor are *paid* any, find their own Account in the Practice of this silent Virtue.

OUR Company was now happily reduced to five; the Lady of the House; PHILETUS, a Gentleman than whom there is scarce to be found one Master of more Accomplishments, a greater Capacity, or a Taste more refin'd and polite; he is just arriv'd at those Years, which look back with Shame on the Inadvertencies of Youth, and far from those which threaten a Decay of Vigour and Understanding. He can be grave without Austerity, a Plain-dealer without Bluntness, facetious without derogating from that Majesty of Sentiment and Behaviour which is necessary to command Veneration; in fine, there is in him nothing wanting[3] that one would wish to find in a Lover, a Husband, a Brother, a Companion, or a Friend. The third Person was BRILLIANTE, by some distinguished by the Title of the *Lovely*, by others the *Witty*; 'tis certain indeed that she so well deserves both, that it is difficult to determine in which she most out-shines the Generality of her Sex. DORINTHUS, that Friend on whose Account I was admitted, to do him Justice, has few Equals for fine Sense; and he, with my self, made up the Number of this little Company.

---

[1] Lack.

[2] Loosely, rhetorical sophistication; 'to declaim' is to speak in an impassioned style.

[3] Lacking, absent.

HAPPENING to speak of the Passions, PHILETUS said something in Defence of that which is called *Love*; endeavouring, as much as was consistent with Justice, to excuse the Errors committed by those influenced by it. Methinks, said he, there is nothing so cruel as to condemn a Person for what is unavoidable. Ought any one to be blam'd for Actions, which are not only impossible to be shun'd, but also such as the very Person guilty of 'em knows not that he is so, till the Cause which enforced him to commit them is no more?—*Love*, as it differs from all the other Passions in its Consequences, does so too in the Manner by which it first gains Entrance in the Soul, and after wholly engrosses all the Faculties of it.—*Ambition*, that lawless Thirst of Power which inspires in some Mens Breasts such unwarrantable Designs, we easily perceive the Approaches of, by those restless Wishes which rob our Nights of Sleep, and Days of Ease, whenever we chance to see a Person greater than our selves.—*Revenge* is known by a thousand corroding, galling Symptoms.—Even *Anger*, sudden as it is, gives some little Warnings of its coming Power.—All these bring with them a Train of Furies,[1] and, by the Mind guarded by Virtue and by Prudence, may be repell'd: Even Nature trembles at them, joins her Force to drive them back, and but with Pain submits to act what they inspire.—Not so all-soothing *Love* presents it self; what can be more pleasing than the first kindling of that tender Flame!—When new Desires play round the gently throbbing Heart, thrill through each swelling Vein, and make us all o'er Pulse!—With what unspeakable Delight we gaze upon the darling[2] Object!—With what sweet Hopes do we beguile her Absence!—The soft Inchantment steals upon us ere we are aware!—o'erwhelms the Senses with a Tide of Extasy, and we are lost before we see the Danger!—Then all Attempts are fruitless.—Vainly we strive to raise our sinking Reason, the Current flows too strong, and with a Force which only can be felt, drives us to Actions, such as one must be guilty of to pardon. Though nothing, said DORINTHUS, perceiving he had done, can be more plain than that you have experienced, to a very great degree, the Power

---

[1] Fierce and vengeful.
[2] Beloved.

you can so well describe, yet I think there may be something added to that you have alledged: Which is, that True *Reason* being utterly depos'd, the sweet Deceiver, *Love*, usurps his Seat, and appears to our deluded Imagination the same.—Guilty in *Fact*, but innocent in *Design*, while we obey the one, we believe we are following the Dictates of the other; the very wildest of our Wishes seem inspir'd by *Reason*, a Prospect of unutterable Joy opens it self to ravish'd Fancy,[1] and we think (if Lovers have the Power to think) 'twould be the highest Proof of Madness or Stupidity not to attempt to make that Heaven our own. Well have you argued, Gentlemen! replied the charming BRILLIANTE, in Vindication of your selves: A View of Pleasure in the Gratification of your Wishes, join'd with the Pride of having it in your Power to subdue, are powerful Motives to excite your Prosecutions.—No Ruin of Character, no Loss of Fame, glare in your Face, and stop the Progress of your Passion.—*Religion* is all that can defend you from the joint Assaults of Love, and Vanity, and Nature.—But 'tis not so with us; a thousand different, dread Ideas strike us with Horror at but a Thought of giving up our Honour.—When Woman falls a Prey to the rapacious Wishes of her too dear Undoer, she falls without Excuse, without even Pity for the Ruin her Inadvertency has brought upon her.—So truly has a late celebrated *Poet* made JANE SHORE complain on this Occasion, that methinks it shou'd be a Warning to the whole Sex.[2]

> *Such is the Fate unhappy Women find,*
> *And such the Curse entail'd upon our Kind,*
> *That Man, the lawless Libertine, may rove*
> *Free, and unquestion'd, thro' the Wilds of Love:*
> *While Woman, Sense and Nature's easy Fool,*
> *If poor weak Woman swerves from Virtue's Rule,*
> *If strongly charm'd she leave the thorny Way,*
> *And in the softer Paths of Pleasure stray;*

---

[1]   Enraptured imagination; 'to ravish' also means 'to rape'.

[2]   The 'poet' is the playwright Nicholas Rowe (1674–1718), whose *Tragedy of Jane Shore* (1714) recounts the life of the low-born mistress to Edward IV and to Thomas Grey, Marquess of Dorset. Shore died in poverty, *c.* 1527, after having endured imprisonment and other humiliations. The quotation is from *Jane Shore*, I. ii. 181–93.

Ruin ensues, Reproach, and endless Shame,
And one false Step entirely damns her Fame:
In vain with Tears the Loss she may deplore,
In vain look back to what she was before,
She sets, like Stars that fall, to rise no more.

Your Quotation is extremely just, my Dear! said AMIANA, and I would have every Woman imprint it in her Mind, that, when prest too closely by the ador'd Pursuer, and perhaps too by her own secret Inclination, she may remember, that she but shares the Joy, while the Remorse, the Grief, the Shame, and the Heart-rending Care is all her own.—The proud Triumpher having gain'd his Conquest, forgets the Difficulties by which it was attain'd.—His soft Professions—his Vows—the counterfeited Agonies, all the innumerable Artifices[1] which pleaded in his Behalf, and join'd to seduce the too believing Maid, are now no more remember'd, and cold Indifference is the best of what succeeds Possession. Nay, rejoin'd BRILLIANTE, even when Desire is highest, and mutual Ardour promises the utmost Felicity[2] which that Passion can afford, even then we are but blest by Halves,—our Sweets are mingled with Bitters, and the most seeming happy Lover is a real Wretch, as the *French* Poet says,

In vain soft Ease the Love-tost Heart pursues,
  Ev'n in Possession of the long-sought Joy
We rob the bounteous God of half his Dues,
  And future Fears the present Bliss destroy.[3]

How mad then, continu'd that beautiful Lady, must be a Woman to run her self into such certain Miseries, for an uncertain, wavering, short, and imperfect Happiness.—It is, methinks, a Failing which, in spite of all that these Gentlemen have alledged in its Defence, is so vastly contrary to Reason, good Sense, and even the first great Law of Nature, Self-preservation, that, did not

---

[1] Cunning actions.
[2] That is, when mutual passion promises the utmost happiness.
[3] The lines also appear in Haywood's *Love-Letters on All Occasions* (1730), with minor variations; they, or the translation, are perhaps by Haywood.

too many Instances confirm the Knowledge, one shou'd scarce believe any Infatuation forcible enough to oblige us to be guilty of it. There is a Tenderness, reply'd AMIANA, in the Nature of our Sex, which will not suffer us to see another in Pain, without feeling a double Portion of it our selves.—And when we see the Person, whom we think the most perfect of his kind, dying at our Feet, and are by his Insinuations made to believe that nothing but our Compassion can relieve his Miseries, Virtue but faintly makes Resistance, and soon, too soon her Admonitions are entirely rejected, as more severe than is consistent with Humanity.—As elegantly as PHILETUS has described the Passion of Love, 'tis evident, by the prodigious Risque we run of losing every thing which ought to be dear or valuable to us, that our Sex, when we are really possess'd of it, give Proofs of our Sensibility to a much greater Excess than theirs. I have a Copy of Verses in my Pocket,[1] which were wrote by a young Lady of my particular Acquaintance, in the time when she was in Possession of all those Pleasures which are to be found in Love.—I am certain none here can guess at the Person.—I will therefore read them to you, to shew[2] the Extravagance which that Passion inspires. She had no sooner spoke these Words, than she took the Paper out of her Pocket, and, with the most agreeable Voice and Manner in the World, read these Lines.

XIMENE fearing to be forsaken by PALEMON,
desires he would kill her.

If by my Words my Soul cou'd be express'd,
You will not wonder at my fond Request:
But in Compassion with my Wish partake,
'Tis kinder far to Kill, than to Forsake.
'Tis not Long Life, but glorious Death renowns
The Hero's Honour, and the Martyr crowns:
Lawrels acquir'd in Youth, in Age decay;
Or, by Superior Force, are torn away

---

[1] Pocketbook.
[2] That is, show.

To deck some *New-made, hated, Favourite's Brow,*
Who on the noble Ruin great does grow.
A happy End *is still the wise Man's Prayer,*
Death is a safe, a sure Retreat from Care.
Shou'd I live longer I may lose your Love,
And all the Hells of Desperation prove![1]
But now to Dye—now, in my Joys high Noon,
Ere the cold Evening of Contempt comes on,
Were to dye Bless'd; and baffle cruel Fate,
Which, envious, watches close to change my State.
Nay more, to dye for Thee! *and by* Thee *too!*
Wou'd all my Rivals Happiness out-do:
My Love would live for ever in thy Mind,
And I shou'd pity those I left behind.
To have those Eyes, dear Heaven-dress'd Orbs of Light!
Convey soft Pity to expiring Sight!
That Voice! whose every melting Note inspires
Dissolving Languishments, and warm Desires,
Tun'd to kind, mournful, Murm'rings at my Pain,
Wou'd give a Pride which Life cou'd never gain!
Haste then!—the Joys of Passion to refine,
Let through my Breast thy glitt'ring Weapon shine,
Dispel my Fears, and keep me ever thine!

I look on the Inspiration of these Verses, said PHILETUS, to be
rather owing to the Extravagance of the Lady's own Temper, than
to the Passion with which she seems animated:—There is a
Restlessness in the Nature of some People, which compels them
to postpone their Misfortunes, and will never suffer them to be
at Peace.—I cou'd instance many Examples, but there is one
which I can aver for Truth to prove the Reality of what I have
alledg'd, and which I believe will not be disagreeable to the
Company to hear.

EVERY body having assur'd him, that they should listen with
Pleasure to any Relation he should be pleas'd to make, he
resumed his Discourse in these or the like Words:

---

[1]   Experience.

ARABELLA, said he, was one of the most lovely Women I have seen, nor did her Wit and Humour render her *Conversation* less pleasing to the *Ear*, than the Charms of her *Person* were to the *Eye*.—She was born in *London*, always liv'd in it, and was of a Rank which made her be Visited by the Politest of both Sexes.— She behaved herself amidst the Temptations of a Court, and the Flatteries of her Admirers, in a manner which obliged every Body to look on her as a most accomplish'd Pattern of Modesty and Regularity: I was for some time a pretty near Witness of her Conduct, and indeed it would have puzzled the most enviously curious Eye to have discover'd the least Defect, either in her innate Principles, or outward Deportment.[1]—Among the Number of those who sought her in Marriage, was Mr. WORTHY; it must be confess'd he was a Gentleman every way deserving her, but so perhaps were some others who were less fortunate: She became enamour'd of him, however; not all her Moderation could defend her from his Charms: and when the mischievous little Deity once enter'd into her Breast, all his Attendants, Hope, Fear, Distrust, restless Wishes, disorder'd Joy, and causeless Grief, rush after him: She grew immediately another Creature; and as before her Conversation was Affable, Sweet, and Entertaining, she now became Dull, Reserved, and sometimes Peevish.—A Disagreement hapning between their Parents on the Account of a Jointure[2] to be made her, the Marriage seem'd to be broke off.—WORTHY desisted Visiting her, and she gave her self up wholly to Despair.—'Tis impossible for Words to express the Calamity of her Condition.—I have seen her in Agonies which one would think were impossible to be sustain'd with Life. But not to spin my Story to a tedious length; after three Years Separation, WORTHY'S Father (prevailed on by the incessant Importunities of his Son) consented to do whatever was required by hers;—Writings were drawn, and the wish'd-for Knot was ty'd, to the unspeakable Satisfaction of the new-wedded Pair.—I waited on her a few Days after to congratulate the happy Event;—but how was I amaz'd, when instead of the Gaiety of a

---

[1] Conduct.
[2] The portion of an estate reserved for the wife after the decease of the husband.

Bride, adorn'd with Blushes, and beautified with Smiles, I found her rather an Object of Condolence: a gloomy Melancholy sat upon her Brow!—her lovely Eyes were swell'd with Tears!—her Voice faulter'd, and sometimes was wholly stopp'd with Sighs!— I cou'd not presently find Words to express the Concern she gave me, nor the secret Rage I conceiv'd against the Ingratitude or Falshood of a Husband whom she had so tenderly Lov'd, and suffer'd so much for; for I cou'd impute the Sorrows I beheld her in, to no other Cause than his ill Treatment: But when I had got so far leave of my Surprize, as to be able to talk with her, and take notice of her Answers, I fell into a much greater one, at the Unaccountableness of her *Caprice*,[1] than I had been before at the Sight of her Disorders.—She told me that she thought her self on the Summit of all humane Felicity!—possest of a Happiness so immense!—such a Profusion of accumulated Blessings! that she was certain they could not be of long Continuance: and then (said she weeping) how shall I support so dreadful a Fall? It was in vain for me to represent how little Likelihood there was of her Fears ever coming to pass.—The *Chimera*[2] every Day gain'd Ground in her distemper'd Imagination; till at last, by fancying herself too happy, she became compleatly miserable, and made her Husband and every body about her so too, by her uneasy and discontented Humour.—She wou'd lye awake whole Nights, counting over in her Mind how many Accidents might happen that cou'd possibly lessen WORTHY's Esteem of her, which always concluded in a sort of an assured Belief that in Time it would be so one way or other. All his Endearments served only to increase her Malady; and the more he endeavour'd to *give* her Comfort, the less she was capable of *receiving* it.—Thus did she languish for many Months, in a continual Waste of Spirits, and dyed without the least visible Sign of any Bodily Indisposition.

THO' few *Wives* Sin this way, continued PHILETUS, yet there are a great many of both Sexes, who by the Formation of Imaginary Ills disquiet themselves to a very great degree: and, indeed, most People are wretched more by the Fears of what

---

[1]   Capriciousness; irrational behavior.
[2]   Delusion.

may come, than what they endure at present. It proceeds from a Discontentedness of Disposition, which we ought by no means to indulge; because, in the first place such a Habit of Mind is the direct Opposite to *Religion* (which commands not only an entire Resignation to the Divine Power in every thing, but an Implicite Dependance on him also for all we desire, or think a Blessing;) and *Secondly*, a manifest Contradiction to good Sense; for who, with the right use of that, wou'd lose the Enjoyment of a *present Comfort*, to lament a *Misfortune* only in *Supposition*; which ten to one never comes to pass, or we live to see if it does.—I grant, one sometimes meets with Tryals in this World, which justly may be accounted Fiery ones, but then one shou'd consider that Fortitude[1] is the most Heroick Virtue a Mortal can possibly arrive at, and the greater our Misfortunes are, the greater Opportunity we have, in nobly bearing them, to make the Courage and Eminency of our Souls conspicuous.

BESIDE, pursued this agreeable Declaimer, to make one easy under the most heavy Load of Affliction, we need, methinks, but reflect on the Vicissitude[2] of all humane Affairs: *Fortune* is a fickle Goddess, and the longer we have suffer'd by her *Frowns*, we may believe our selves, in all probability, the nearer being profited by her *Smiles:* and if at last we shou'd find that our Hopes have deceiv'd us, and all our glittering Expectations vanish into Air; pray what have we lost by the agreeable Delusion, but so much Time from Woe?—What reason then have we to repent having given way to it?—Who, if he might be allowed his Wish, wou'd not chuse to Dream rather of a *Garden* than a *Wilderness?*—a *Palace* than a *Prison?* And since Man's Life is little better than a Dream, we may be glad to lay hold on any innocent Means to render it as delightful as we can, and to secure us from the Horrors of Despondency.

PHILETUS received the Thanks of the Company, both for the History, and those useful Reflections he had made on it: After which, Nothing, said BRILLIANTE, can be more certain than that People who really meet with no Misfortunes in Life, make to themselves Woes more terrible than all that Fortune cou'd inflict

---

1 Moral strength.
2 Variability.

on them.—And since we have insensibly[1] fallen from the particular Passions, to the Temper in general, I will read you a
Manuscript Novel which I put into my Pocket with a Design to
entertain AMIANA with, when her Company was gone; but as it
contains some Variety for the Shortness of it, and also an excellent Moral for the Subject, it will not I imagine seem tedious in
Reading to any here. She had scarce concluded these Words,
when every Mouth was open to entreat she wou'd favour them
with it; which she immediately began to do, and it was with a
vast deal of Pleasure that we listned to the following Pages.

BERALDUS and CELEMENA: OR, *The Punishment of Mutability.*[2] A NOVEL.

ONE of the most accomplish'd Princes of the Empire having
an Aversion to Marriage, had, by a Lady of no mean Rank, a
Daughter of such exquisite Beauty that it was almost impossible
for any body to see her without regarding her with a sort of
Parental Affection.—As she encreas'd in Years she did also in the
Power of Charming, and it seem'd as if Nature had taken pains
to make her double Reparation for the Misfortune of her Birth,
by rendring her above Contempt by the extraordinary Graces of
her Person.—The Prince her Father, by reason of some
Accidents in Life, had reduc'd his Estate to so low an Ebb that
he had scarce sufficient to keep his Title in Countenance.[3]—He
had it not in his Power to provide for this young Beauty in the
manner he wish'd, and it was with the most tender Concern he
beheld her.—She was arriv'd at the Age of Fourteen, when the
Duke *de* GUERRE, touch'd with the Melancholy he saw him in,
took the Privilege of their long Friendship to enquire the Cause,
which the Prince made no Scruple of revealing to him. The
Duke, who was a Father himself, cou'd not forbear acknowledging the Justice of his Grief, and truly pity'd both him and the
young Lady. Reflecting on the Affair, it came into his Mind to

---

1 Imperceptibly.
2 Changefulness.
3 Loosely, good repute.

recommend her to the Service of the Princess of *Parma*,[1] with whom he had great Interest,[2] as having been her General for several Years, and fought with such Success her Battles, that he was look'd on as invincible.—Never was a Woman fam'd for more Perfections than that excellent Princess, and he knew if CELEMENA (for that was the Name of this lovely Unfortunate) were once received into her Family, it must be wholly her own Fault if she were not in a State rather to be envy'd than pity'd: He soon communicated his Sentiments to the Prince, who receiv'd his Offer with all the Gratitude of a transported[3] Father, long anxious for the Welfare of a beloved Child, and now certain of the utmost Happiness his Soul cou'd wish.—He was perfectly acquainted with the Virtues of that Princess, and doubted not but that CELEMENA wou'd not only be blest under her Care, but also profit so much by her Example, as to deserve the Felicity her Favour wou'd bestow.—The Duke soon let him see he meant to do as he had promis'd; and, having some Business which in a little Time requir'd his Return to *Parma*, hasten'd his Departure; and every thing being provided by the Prince to equip CELEMENA in a manner befitting the Honour she was going to enjoy, took leave of her with Pleasure, hoping to see her again in a short Time with infinitely more Satisfaction.

THE Duke was not at all deceiv'd in his Expectation of this young Lady's Reception.—The Knowledge to whom she owed her Birth, the being presented by the Hand of so great a Favourite, and her own Beauty and Accomplishments, made her be look'd on by the Princess in a manner which created the Envy of all the Maids of Honour, some of whom being of the best Blood in the Kingdom, thought it a Disdain to be rank'd with a Lady, who, though she was greatly born, was yet illegitimate, and notwithstanding her Charms, was a Foreigner.—But the Ill-nature of those who were her Equals in Condition, had not the Power to prejudice her.—She who was their common Mistress gave her many Marks of her distinguished Favour; and as the others had only their

---

[1] The capital of the duchy of Parma (1545–1731), in northern Italy.
[2] Influence.
[3] Enraptured.

Months of Attendance, she was kept ever under her Eye, and indeed regarded with a Tenderness which visibly demonstrated that it was rather owing to the Love she had for her, than any Decorum of State, she so little suffer'd her from her Presence.

IN all the Pleasures of an undisturbed Tranquility did she pass her Hours in the Court of *Parma*, till *Love*, that sweet Destroyer, that stealing Poyson of a Woman's Peace, diffus'd it self through all the Veins of the unexperienc'd Maid.—Among the Number of those who pretended to adore her, was BERALDUS, a young Gentleman of but a small Fortune; but Master of so many outward Charms, that had his Soul been at all worthy of the Case in which it was inshrin'd, she wou'd have had no Reason to repent the Tenderness she had for him.—But, alas! there was not the least Agreement between them.—All his *Softness* was centred in his *Eyes;*—all his *Sincerity* in his *Words.*—His *Heart* disavow'd the Tenderness of his *Professions*, was unaffected, trifling, changeable, and when provok'd to Anger, most cruel and malicious.—Poor CELEMENA! yet little skill'd in the destructive Artifices of undoing Man, and charm'd even to a degree of Doatage with his exterior Graces, believed all that the too lovely BERALDUS said; it was not in her Thoughts that he that spoke and look'd with so much Fondness, cou'd ever bring himself to act with Neglect or Cruelty: The Confidence she had in him made her as little careful in concealing her own Passion, as she was in searching into the Validity of his; she confess'd without Reserve the Tenderness she had for him, indulg'd him in all the Liberties that Modesty wou'd allow; and at last (as what will not a violent Passion, and the continued Importunities of the darling Object, transport one to!) permitted him to transgress those Bounds:—He obtain'd of the believing Maid all she had to give:—Triumph'd in all those Joys which ought only to have been the Reward of the most pure Affection, and which might have made a real Lover blest.—But this inconstant Rover, the Victory once gain'd, despis'd the too easy Conquest.— Her Innocence, her Beauty, her Tenderness, served only to make him place the greater Value on himself for the Condescensions[1] he had the Power to influence her to make him.—In *publick* she became the Subject of his *Mirth*, and in *private* of his *Contempt.*—That little

---

[1]   Acts of attentiveness to one's social inferiors.

Regard which *Love*, especially in a young Heart, leaves for Reputation, together with his Vanity, soon made the Affair between them the common Talk; and as she was greatly envied, there wanted not a Number to represent, in the worst Colours, her late Conduct to the Princess; who, though she did not immediately give Credit to all that was told her concerning this too-faulty Fair,[1] yet she cou'd not help condemning her Mismanagement, in doing any thing which might give her Enemies an Opportunity of censuring her Behaviour: She was extremely concern'd to find that it was past doubt that she had entertain'd BERALDUS in Quality of a Lover, who, setting aside the known Inconstancy of his Humour, was not in Circumstances to make her happy in a Husband.—That good Lady sent for CELEMENA into her Closet,[2] and having a little prepar'd her for what she was about to say by a thousand kind Expressions, testifying the Care she had for her Happiness, represented to her, in the mildest Terms that cou'd be, how blameable she had been in listening to any Declarations of Love, without having first acquainted her; and then proceeded to inform her with how much Severity her Conduct had been treated.—The guilty Fair, conscious of the Justice of this Reproof, hung down her Head, by her Blushes and her Silence testifying some Part of the Confusion she was in; but the Horrors, the Remorse, the Shame, which at that Instant work'd in her secret Soul, were little visible to the Princess, 'till growing too violent, too outragious for Suppression, they operated so fiercely on the vital Spirits, that every Faculty lost at once its Use, and down fell the unhappy Prey of Passion swooning on the Floor.—The Princess, half-angry with her self for having said any thing to occasion such a Disorder, and half afraid that more than she had said, or indeed, before, had imagin'd, of the Accusation, had but too just a Foundation, grew extremely troubled; but that not hindering her from doing what was necessary for the Recovery of CELEMENA, she rung her Bell for Help.—Attendants presently coming in, that wretched Lady not coming to herself immediately was carry'd to her own Apartment, where many Applications were made before she shew'd any Signs of Life; and, at her Return of Sense, appear'd

---

[1]   Woman or girl.
[2]   Private room.

so wild, and so perplexed, that though none of those about her were able to guess at the Cause, yet it was very plain, that it had been from some very terrible Agitation of the *Mind* that the Disorder of the *Body* had proceeded.

THE Princess was all this while in a very deep *Resvery*; she not only lov'd CELEMENA, for her personal Accomplishments, but also look'd on her as an Orphan entirely committed to her Charge, having neither Parent, Relation, nor Friend near her, to whom she cou'd apply for Advice in any Affair, nor fly to for Protection if injur'd; she thought it therefore her Duty to take Care of her: and both by what she had been told, and the Confusion she now saw CELEMENA in, being fully convinc'd that something more than Complaisance[1] had pass'd between her and BERALDUS, resolv'd to know the Truth, and preserve that friendless Innocent, if possible, from Ruin. She therefore sent for BERALDUS privately to come to her; 'tis probable that he was little pleas'd with the Summons, having heard of CELEMENA's Indisposition, and guessing the Truth of what had occasion'd it; but the Command was too absolute not to be obey'd.—He waited on her in her Closet, as she had commanded, where, having dismiss'd her Attendants, she began to question him about that afflicted Lady; but he, who had before determin'd how to behave, in case he shou'd be examin'd, made such Replies as were not at all satisfactory to her, till she, exerting her Authority, and putting on an Air full of Austerity, told him she wou'd not be trifled with, that the Welfare of CELEMENA was very dear to her, and that she shou'd find a way to resent the needless Reserve with which he behaved: He then, with a most unparalell'd Impudence assur'd her, that he had no Views in that Lady, that he never address'd her but with the Civility of an ordinary Acquaintance.—Had not the least Notion of Love for her.— That tho' he confess'd her extreamly deserving, yet she was not a Beauty of that kind which cou'd make any Impression on him— and that in reality his Affections were engaged elsewhere.—To all this he swore with the greatest Solemnity, and confirmed what he said with Imprecations too terrible to be disbelieved by one who was herself so great a Friend to Truth.—She made him

---

[1] Loosely, a courteous but innocent exchange.

however but a short Reply, and having nothing farther to say to him, dismiss'd him from her Presence with only this Menace, Look BERALDUS, said she, that you have not dissembled[1] with a PRINCESS, who wants neither the Will nor Power to punish the Affront.

IT gave him no small Trouble, when he was out of the Presence, and had liberty to reflect on this Affair, in what manner he should behave. He easily foresaw that if CELEMENA shou'd betray the Truth, he shou'd either be compelled to marry her, or submit to some Punishment for the Offence he had been guilty of.—The first of these was dreadful to his Imagination, he cou'd not bear the Thoughts of making a Woman whom he had enjoy'd, his Wife; besides, he knew she had no other Fortune than her Dependance on the Princess; and the supreme Reason of all was, that he had in good earnest lately entred into an Engagement with another, whom he loved as much as it was in the Power of a Man so wavering to love.—At present, however, she was the reigning Mistress of his Soul, and in this, tho' in this alone, he had told no Falshood to the Princess. However defi-cient he might be in the other Parts of Wit, no Man that ever liv'd had a better Invention, nor was more expert in the Art of Dissimulation[2] than he was; the first of these furnish'd him with a Stratagem[3] to secure himself from any further Attacks of the kind he had lately met with, and the other to carry it on to the total Ruin of the too credulous CELEMENA.

HE had no sooner laid the Scheme, than assuming a Countenance[4] all Tenderness and Softness, he went to the Apartment of CELEMENA, and counterfeiting the greatest Concern imaginable for the Disorder he heard she had been in, entreated her to reveal the Cause, which with her usual Frankness of Behaviour she immediately did, not keeping from him the least Word the Princess had said to her.—I fear'd, said he, the Truth; she is determin'd, I perceive, (tho' for what Cause I dare not tell you) to prevent any farther Progress of our

---

[1]   Been dishonest.
[2]   Hypocrisy.
[3]   Scheme.
[4]   Facial expression.

Affections.—Our only way therefore to secure ourselves to each other for the future, is to be more wary than we have hitherto been.—To feign a *Hatred* for each other, is, my Angel, (continued he) the sole Expedient that is left us to preserve our *Love* from being made the Victim of her cruel Resolution. It is natural to believe CELEMENA could not hear so surprizing a Piece of News without an Impatience to know the Meaning of it; and hastily asking him for what Cause the Princess refus'd her Consent to their mutual Passion—I have already told you, answer'd he, that it springs from what I dare not name; and perhaps, pursued he, with a well-acted Air of Modesty, you wou'd believe me the vainest Creature in the World to Imagine.—Nor shou'd I, had I not received Proofs too plain to suffer me to doubt it. What other Explanation cou'd CELEMENA make of this Expression, than that the Princess had herself entertained a Passion for BERALDUS; and there being nothing in the World more natural than for one to believe every body must like what we admire, not all the Virtues of that Princess, nor the Tenderness which every Action shew'd she bore to her Husband, cou'd defend her in the Opinion of CELEMENA from the Suggestions of her Jealousy.—The Care she had express'd for her, and the Advice she had given her of chusing an Object more worthy of her Affections than BERALDUS, seem'd now all Artifice, and the Product of a jealous Envy of her Happiness in being beloved by him.—She fail'd not to communicate the Conjectures his Words had rais'd in her, and while he was overjoy'd to find her so readily fall into the Snare he had prepar'd for her, pretended the greatest Perplexity, lest by some unguarded Word he had betray'd a Secret which ought to be most dear and precious to a Man of Honour.—It is not, cry'd he, the Power she has to prejudice me either in my Life or Fortune, that I dread, but I confess I tremble when I reflect on the Baseness I must appear guilty of in revealing the Foible of a Lady that loves me, and whose Tenderness I should have reason to be proud of, did not the more prevailing Charms of my for ever dear, for ever adorable CELEMENA, make me look on all her Sex beside as worthless Nothings. The Reader will easily believe it was with Words full of Transport the deceived CELEMENA returned so seemingly fond a Declaration, and after having assur'd him that the Secret never shou'd escape her Lips, begun to advise with him what was best to be done for the Conservation of their Happiness; it is, answer'd he, hastily, as I have already told you, my Dear, utterly to deny we see each other with Lovers Eyes.—I have already perform'd the cruel Task.—My unwilling Tongue has renounc'd the Dictates of my Heart, and protested against the Charms of CELEMENA; she must also do so too, or the Jealousy of this too powerful Foe will find some Means to sever us for ever. She, who always found invincible Reason in every thing he said, readily acquiesced, and assur'd him that when next spoke to by the Princess on that Affair, she wou'd utterly deny it. But, said the artful Villain, (when he had brought her thus far) there is yet another Danger, which if we do not get over, all the Asseverations[1] which both of us can make will only serve but more to expose us to her Fury.—Guessing perhaps (continued he with a Sigh, and Air all languishing) by my faultring Accents, and the Reluctance which I fear was too perceivable in my Eyes and Voice, when I wou'd have aim'd to seem indifferent of CELEMENA's Charms, that all I said was Dissimulation, she told me there was a way to know if I spoke Truth; it presently struck into my Mind, that under some Pretence or other, which she may easily find, she has a Design to search your Cabinet[2] for Letters, which, if she does, there are undeniable Proofs both of my unceasing Passion, and your kind Return.—What might not her jealous Rage at such a Discovery incite her to!—How miserable might not the Power she has over us make both!—Do not torment your self, my dear BERALDUS! interrupted the believing Fair, with such a needless Apprehension.—I will this Instant ease you of that Fear, by returning all I have of yours; or, precious as these Tokens of your Affection are, burn 'em before your Face.— They will, rejoin'd he, be no more safe in my Possession than in yours; let us then, said he, destroy 'em—let no Evidences of our mutual Tenderness remain, but those indelible ones written in our Hearts, and which I hope no Time, or Chance, or Malice,

---

[1]   Assertions.
[2]   Safe-box.

shall ever have the Power to erace.—The Answer she made to these Words was no other than obeying the Purport of 'em.— She went immediately to her Closet, and bringing out all the Letters she had receiv'd from him in their Time of Courtship, gave 'em one by one into his Hand, which, as fast as he took, were committed to the Flames.—He staid not long with her after, having obtain'd the End for which he came, excusing his sudden Departure, by saying, if it were known they had a private Conversation[1] it might undo all the Measures that cou'd be taken. Poor CELEMENA had an implicite Faith in every thing that came from him, and yielded a ready Obedience to all he seem'd to approve, not in the least suspecting the Misery she was now entring into, and fully contented with the Promise he made her at parting, never to rest till he had found some Means to be separated no more.

HE had been but a few Moments gone before the Princess enter'd the Chamber of CELEMENA; she had not been perfectly satisfy'd with the Assurances which had been made her by BERALDUS, in Contradiction of what the whole Court had, at Times, inform'd her of, and was resolv'd to know the Certainty from her, who alone had the Power of affording it, and whose Interest it was to hide nothing from her.—She prest that unhappy Creature with so kind an Earnestness to let her into the whole Affair, that had she been told by any other than BERALDUS, nay had the united Voice of the whole World, join'd to the Testimony of Angels, endeavour'd to persuade her that it was owing to any other Motives than her Care and Affection for her, she appear'd so zealous, she wou'd have rejected the Information as false and scandalous; but her ador'd BERALDUS had said 'twas otherwise, and that was enough to make her assur'd of its being so.—He was all Truth—all Honour—all Tenderness, and must not be question'd.—The more Softness and Good-nature that excellent Princess made use of in her Efforts to draw the Secret from her, the more she fancy'd herself convinc'd it was Design and Artifice, and with the greater Zeal she still deny'd ever having been address'd to by BERALDUS in the manner represented: And

---

[1]   The word denotes sexual congress as well as oral discourse.

so exactly did she obey the Injunction he had laid on her, that the Princess, who expected no Disguise from one so young and unexperienced, was at last won to believe as she wou'd have her.

THUS did this unthinking, unsuspecting Lady join in the Deceit against her self, and aid the Ruin of her own Hopes; yet pleas'd with the Delusion, imagining herself most Politick,[1] when in reality she was most fool'd and cheated.—But alas! she had but a little, a very little time allowed by Fate for the Continuance of this happy Ignorance.—Too soon the cruel Curtain was drawn away, and all the black and horrid Scene of Villany appear'd to View.—A few Days after the burning of the Letters, hapning to be alone in a little Summer-house in the Palace-Garden, indulging Contemplation on her dear BERALDUS; she fancy'd she heard something near her which sounded like the Accents of his Voice, and putting her Ear as near as she cou'd to the Place whence the Sound seem'd to proceed, she soon distinguish'd that it was he indeed, and to her great Confusion heard him speak these Words,—Why (said he, with that undoing Softness in his Voice, which had been so ravishing to her that now listned to it, but with Agonies which only can be felt) Why shou'd you so often give me Hopes of Happiness, yet still delay me the Possession!—Can any thing be more favourable than this present Moment.—What hinders me now to seize that Treasure I so long have languish'd for, and you have so kindly promis'd?— The Person to whom these Words were address'd spoke too low for the distracted[2] CELEMENA to be able to know either the Voice or the Sense of her Reply; but presently after she heard him rejoyn, O pride not in the Torture of a Heart that loves you, that adores you, that but for you never felt one tender Wish, nor never can cease to be your Slave.—By Heaven (continued he with greater Eagerness) I taste more Delight, more Extacy in being permitted but to touch your Hand, than all the united Charms of your whole Sex beside cou'd give even in the highest Enjoyment.—This was too much for our unfortunate Listner to hear, and restrain the struggling Emotions of her o'erburthen'd

---

[1] Judicious.
[2] Deranged.

Soul.—She cou'd not help crying out in the most bitter Anguish,—O Villain! Monster! No, I am convinc'd thou never knew'st what 'tis to love sincerely, but thou hast feign'd the Passion as artfully as now thou dost.—The sudden Rage of Temper which had extorted from her this Exclamation, occasion'd its being uttered with so much Vehemence that BERALDUS and his new Charmer being in the very next Room in the same Summer-house, heard her with more Ease than she had done the Expressions which let her into the Secret of his Falshood, and had rais'd her to so unusual a height of Fury.—Neither the treacherous Lover nor surprised Rival were willing to give an Ocular Demonstration of their being together in that manner, and therefore hasted down another Pair of Stairs which led 'em into a Terras which had no Communication with that part of the Garden through which CELEMENA had pass'd.—The Noise they made in going down, made that now desolate and despairing Lady know which way they took to escape her Pursuit and Reproaches, but from a Window which over-look'd the Terras she follow'd them with her Eyes, and by the Dress and Air, tho' she saw not her Face, presently knew her Rival to be LAMIRA, one who had been grac'd with the Title of Maid of Honour to the Princess, But who having for some Years been too careless of her Behaviour to merit the Continuance of that Favour, had been discharg'd. Where is the Pen that can describe that vast Variety of mingled Passions, which all at once now seiz'd the Bosom of the abandon'd CELEMENA!—Where is the Soul that can conceive her Sufferings!—Horror and Rage for the first Moments were the most prevailing Agitations; but Grief, Disdain, and Shame, soon took their Turn, and rack'd her with a strange Vicissitude of Torment.—She now saw his Falshood, her own Credulity[1] and Ruin with open Eyes.—She reflected on the past, and trembled for the future Consequences of her fond[2] Belief.—She might be call'd a little World of Woe, where all the different kinds of Wretchedness, which plague the Slaves of

---

[1] Gullibility.
[2] Foolishly infatuated.

Passion, were here summ'd up, and congregated: each in its horrid Power, and striving to out-vye each other in inflicting Torture on the divided Soul.—She had not presently the Relief of Tears, and her wild Griefs, deny'd that most natural and less painful way of venting themselves, burst out in Cries and Exclamations so loud, so violent, that the Princess accompany'd by several of the Court hapning to be that instant coming into the Garden, heard her tho' it were at a pretty good distance.— 'Tis not to be doubted, by what has been already remark'd of the Goodness of that Princess, but that she went up immediately to her; where, in her present Agony of Soul, she revealed all that she so long and so careful had kept secret, not concealing the minutest Circumstance of BERALDUS's Baseness, even to his impudent accusing the Princess of a criminal[1] Passion for him.—That prudent Lady listen'd to that Part of her Relation with greater Signs of Disdain than Anger; but assur'd the afflicted CELEMENA, she should have ample Justice done her for the Wrong she had received. BERALDUS, who little imagin'd the gentle CELEMENA could be so far transported as to oblige her to unravel the Mystery by which had deluded her, was thinking in what manner he shou'd a second time deceive her, and render her own Ears even more suspected than his Words, when some of his Friends, who were present at the Confession of CELEMENA, came to him with their Advice that he should retire, till the first Gust of the Princess's Anger being blown over, they might, without Danger of incurring her Displeasure, intercede in his Behalf.— This was News which did indeed alarm him; he cou'd never have expected it from the accustomed Softness of CELEMENA's Disposition, and knowing little of the real Force of Love himself, seem'd amaz'd that it could so far alter the very Natures of the Persons possest with it.—He fancy'd not his Case, however, so bad as those who counselled him to fly were of Opinion, there was nothing he so much feared as the Odium he had thrown on the Princess; yet the Success he had met in many Affairs where Hypocrisy and Impudence were prevailing Advocates, made him not despair but he should, some way or other, evade the

---

[1] Immoral.

Punishment of this last base Action, as he had already done many others of as black a Dye.—He could not consent to leave the Court, his whole Dependence being on a small Post he had there, and some Friends whom he expected would promote him, nor could he immediately resolve in what manner he shou'd answer to the Misdemeanours he was told wou'd be laid to his Charge.—He was in this Dilemma when the Princess's Guards seiz'd him, and brought him before some of the Nobility appointed for his Judges.—At first he appear'd very much confus'd; but that Fiend, which prompted him to the committing such Actions, had not yet forsaken him, this once more he assisted his Votary,[1] and was very near enabling him to get the better of his fair Accuser. He still persisted in his Denials of ever having made any Pretensions[2] of Love to CELEMENA; said that he must confess that Lady had given him some Hints she shou'd receive a Declaration of that kind from him with Pleasure; but that he had never seem'd to understand her, for which Neglect he imagin'd she had contriv'd this Plot to ruin him. This gain'd but little Credit with those that heard it.—It appear'd very improbable that a Lady of CELEMENA'S Modesty and reserv'd Behaviour cou'd bring herself to offer Love, or that a Man, known to be of so amorous a Disposition as BERALDUS, shou'd refuse her if she did: And some of them cry'd out to him, to speak no more of that Affair; for what he alledged was so little of a piece with the rest of the Behaviour of either of them, that if he had no better Arguments to bring in the Vindication of his Innocence, it were as well for him to confess himself guilty of all was laid to his Charge. I know not, my Lords, said he, how far the Charms of CELEMENA may have prejudiced you in her Favour, else, methinks, there is nothing more easy than to perceive this wild Accusation is the Effect of Frenzy.—Had I ever professed any thing of that Passion she pretends, wou'd there have been no Evidences against me but herself? Is it reasonable to imagine an Intreague, such as she mentions, cou'd be carry'd on without some Letters passing between the Persons concerned in

---

[1] Disciple.
[2] Declarations.

it?—I am ready to confess all she charges me with, if she can produce but one Line under my Hand, signifying I ever had a Design on her.—But I dare challenge all the Inhabitants of *Parma* to bring one Proof against me of this kind;—To our excellent Princess I must also appeal, who, examining me herself on the Affair which brings me now before you, I made no scruple of avowing my Passion for another, and declaring I never had for that Lady any thing beyond Indifference. And to whom then, cry'd one of the Judges of this Contest, have your Vows been address'd? I acknowledge the Question in any other Cause had been unfair, and what you justly might refuse to answer; but as the only Means to invalidate the Evidence of CELEMENA, is to prove you have, before that Time she mentions, paid Courtship to another; if there be such a Person, you wou'd do well to convince us of it. Nothing cou'd be more fortunate for BERALDUS than this Motion.—He did not doubt but LAMIRA would be highly satisfy'd to have the Passion he had profess'd for her declared in the Presence of so many illustrious Witnesses, and therefore immediately named her as the Lady of his Affections;— a Shout of Laughter and Astonishment ran at these Words through all the young Part of the Assembly; but the graver among them thought it too improbable that a Man of so much Cunning and Penetration[1] as BERALDUS was esteem'd, shou'd think it so great a Hardship to be compell'd to marry CELEMENA; yet avow a Wish of that kind in favour of LAMIRA, a Woman as far inferior to her in Beauty, as she was in Reputation.—They were in a little Dispute among themselves in what manner to judge of this Affair, when the Prince of *Parma*, who, with the Princess, had sat all this Time only as a Spectator, started from his Chair, and mingling with the Lords, I will my self, said he, decide this Business.—All of them giving way with humble Reverence, he seated himself in the middle; and, after some little Conversation with two or three of the Principal, order'd LAMIRA should be brought before him. As soon as she appear'd, he demanded of her if BERALDUS had ever made any Profession of Love to her; to which she readily answering in the affirmative, And are you

---

[1]   Insight.

willing to marry him? rejoin'd he. An Interrogatory[1] of this kind fill'd her with too much Astonishment to permit her to reply: it had been in Terms very contrary to those of Marriage BERALDUS had sollicited her; and not being able to dive into the Design of a Demand she so little expected, cou'd not presently resolve in what manner it was most proper for her to behave. The Prince, having a pretty near Conjecture to the Truth of the whole Matter, bid her be bold, and speak her Inclinations; for, said he, on the Word of a Prince, if you consent to be his Wife, it shall not be in his Choice to refuse making you so.—Surpriz'd as she was, the Offer appeared too much to her Advantage to be rejected, and she answer'd in these, or the like Terms: That since his Highness desir'd it might be so, she was ready to comply. But with what Words is there a Possibility of representing the Confusion, the Perplexity, the secret Rage, which seized the Soul of BERALDUS? the Motives which had render'd the Thoughts of Marriage with CELEMENA disagreeable were, because she was not in Possession of a Fortune sufficient to gratify his Ambition, and because he had enjoy'd her; and now to be compell'd to be the Husband of one who had as little Share of the former, and a much less Share of Honour and Reputation, was a severer Penalty than he cou'd have imagin'd for the Crime[2] he had been guilty of.—The Passion he had for this Lady, and that ardent[3] Desire he had express'd for the Possession of her, when CELEMENA happen'd to be Witness of their Conversation, was, in the Thought that she must be his Wife, extinct, and he began to look on her already with Loathing and Detestation.—He was at his very Wit's End, knew not which way to evade a Sentence which was so terrible to be submitted to, and when he attempted to urge any thing to procure the Delay of the Ceremony; as that his present Circumstances not agreeing with his Desires, he should but make a Person miserable whom he wish'd rather to render the happiest of her Sex, and such like Arguments; they were deliver'd with so stammering an Accent, and expressed with so much Disorder, that it confirm'd the Prince he had determin'd

---

[1]   Question.
[2]   Morally odious act.
[3]   Passionate.

rightly in the Cause, and that there could not be a more fit Punishment assign'd for his Perfidiousness[1] and Ingratitude; therefore, putting an End to all the Speeches he was about to make, he commanded one of his own Chaplains to attend, and oblig'd him to marry her that Moment. The Ceremony perform'd: This, said the Prince, is but one Part of that Justice your Behaviour demands.—The Favour you have done the Princess deserves some Acknowledgment.—You must therefore, with that Woman who is now your Wife, leave *Parma* for ever; if ever you are known to set your Feet again on this forbidden Ground, Death is the Welcome you must expect to find. It was in vain that both BERALDUS and his new-wedded Bride petition'd to have their Doom revoked, or that the former entreated that, since he must be banish'd, he might not be compell'd to take her with him. The Prince rose from his Seat the Moment he had given this Decree, which being prodigiously applauded by the whole Assembly, the Sentenc'd were order'd into Confinement, till a Ship[2] should be provided for sending 'em away.—As the Guards were carrying them out of the Hall, CELEMENA, who by some busy Person had been inform'd of what was done, and misinterpreting the Prince's View in enforcing this Marriage, ran raving into the thickest of the Nobility, crying out, Is this the Favour I expected!—Is this the Justice I hop'd from this August Assembly!—O how does LAMIRA merit to be preferr'd to CELEMENA!—If in the false BERALDUS's Eyes she seems more lovely, does she so in yours also, that you dispose my Right, and, to make her happy, doom me to everlasting Ruin!—Her Words, and the Distraction which appeared in her Countenance, with the wild Confusion of her unregarded Dress, fill'd every Beholder with the utmost Compassion.—The Prince and Princess were both of 'em beginning to give her all the Consolation which Friendship could afford, when, turning hastily toward the Door where BERALDUS was going out, she saw LAMIRA with him.—The sudden Sight of that hated Face, and

---

[1] Deceitfulness.

[2] The Po River runs through the former duchy of Parma, although its gulf is on Italy's east coast, far from Genoa, where Beraldus will settle. Haywood follows convention in placing geography at the service of mood, effect, or plot.

the Knowledge that she was now in Possession of that Title which she thought her Due, and had paid so dear a Price for, heighten'd the Distraction she before was in to so violent a Degree, that, snatching a Partizan[1] from one of the nearest Guards, she ran to her with so fatal a Speed, that it was to be wonder'd that, in so great a Surprize, any of them were quick enough to prevent her from sending that envy'd Rival out of the World. Disappointed in her Revenge, as in her Love, never was Madness more outragious than hers: In her present Condition, Advice or Consolation was in vain, and tho' the Princess extremely pitied her, she was oblig'd to have her forc'd out of the Hall, and carry'd to her own Apartment, where she remained a long Time wholly incapable of Reason.

BERALDUS and his Bride had not been many Hours in the Prison, before the latter was taken very ill; a Physician being permitted her, he soon found her Condition such as stood in need of help from one of her own Sex.—In fine, it was a Midwife was wanted; she was soon after deliver'd, tho' with great danger of her Life, of an Abortion,[2] which it was thought was occasion'd by the Fright CELEMENA had put her in.—This confirming the Character which had long been given her, and heightning the Punishment of the unworthy BERALDUS, gave a great deal of Diversion to the whole Court. As soon as she was in a Condition of Travelling they were both sent away, pursuant to the Prince's Sentence. Poor CELEMENA recover'd not the use of Reason for a long time, but when she did, entreated to be sent to a Monastery, where she lingred out a few Years of Life in wasting Sorrow, which threatned her with a Dissolution long before it came; Fate not permitting her to leave the World till she had seen her Injuries in full reveng'd: BERALDUS, hating his Wife with a perfect Hatred, never rested till he had contrived the means to get rid of her, which he at last accomplished by a Cup of Poyson.—The horrid Fact was immediately discovered, and he suffer'd for it a shameful Death at *Genoa*, where he had liv'd a mean and obscure Life for about two Years. The News soon arriv'd at *Parma*, and was by the Princess immediately sent to

---

[1]   Spear with a long handle and lateral projections along the blade.
[2]   Dead fetus.

CELEMENA, who blessing the Justice of Providence, expir'd soon after, as tho' she had no longer Business with the World.

THUS is *Heaven* sometimes pleas'd to give a Proof of its Abhorrence of such Crimes as Falshood and Ingratitude in the Affairs of *Love*, which because the *Law* has provided no Punishment for, are look'd on by the *World* only as Matters of Sport and Ridicule: But let not the guilty Heart triumph in Security, a Time may come

When the deceiving Ruiner shall find,
That Vows once made, of whatsoever kind,
Are Registred in Heaven, and cannot cease to bind.[1]

I thank you, my Dear! (said AMIANA, perceiving she had done) in the behalf of the Company, since I dare swear there are none here who have not thought themselves well entertain'd.—But notwithstanding the Pains you have taken to oblige us, and that there are some lively Strokes of Passion in the Story, I cannot help saying that I think the Character of CELEMENA faulty.—She yields, in my Opinion, with too much Ease, to create that Pity for her Misfortunes, which otherwise they cou'd not fail of exciting.—I wou'd have all Women have a better Excuse for such an Excess of Passion, than meerly the agreeable Person of a Man.—If there were no Measures to be taken to secure ones self of his Affection, there are certainly to discover if he has Wit, Honour, and Good-nature; and she that can love where these encourage not, her Expectations receive an Impression which from the very first can promise nothing but Misery and Contempt. But you forget, Madam, answer'd PHILETUS, that if the Ladies always made use of their Penetration, and chose for their Favourites only such as were worthy of them, there wou'd be no such thing as Woes in *Love*; to be possess'd of that Passion wou'd be the highest Felicity a Mortal cou'd arrive at, and to devote ones whole Soul to it rather a *Merit* than the contrary. PHILETUS is beyond all dispute in the right, added DORINTHUS; Pity wou'd be a Passion which the equally loving, equally deserving Pair, would have no need of.—

---

[1]   The lines are unidentified and were perhaps written by Haywood.

Mournful MELPOMENE[1] wou'd cease to be invok'd.—*Complaints*[2] no more wou'd be the *Muses* Theme.—*Panegyrick*[3] wou'd be the sole Business of the *Poet's* Quill.—*Satyr* grow out of Fashion, and all the Histories[4] for *Novels* lost. I cannot own the Justice of what you say, reply'd AMIANA; there are doubtless many Misfortunes to be found in Love, even where both Parties are perfectly sincere, which may afford Theme enough to gratify an Author's Genius, and if I were of Counsel with the Writers of such Books, I shou'd advise 'em to chuse only such—For, methinks, to read of Villany so gross,[5] so monstrous as that we have just now heard in the Character of BERALDUS, gives too great a Shock to the Soul, and poysons the rest of the Entertainment. But yet sometimes 'tis necessary, said BRILLIANTE, to be reminded that there have been Men so base; our Sex is of it self so weak, especially when we suffer what little share of Reason we have to be debilitated by Passion, that we stand in need of all the Helps we can procure, to defend us from becoming the Victim of our own Softness. I am so far of your Mind, Madam, answer'd DORINTHUS, that these kind of Stories are of great use to persuade the Ladies to make use of that Penetration which AMIANA just now recommended. I wou'd have Beauty the Reward of Merit, not fall the Prey of Villany and Deceit; and if a Woman, when she reads of such a Fate as CELEMENA'S, will but give her self leave to reflect how very possible it is that the Man she is most inclin'd to favour, may be a BERALDUS, it will certainly make her inspect into his Behaviour with a Care and Watchfulness which cannot fail of discovering the *True* Affection from the *Counterfeit*. In my Mind, therefore, rejoyn'd PHILETUS, these kind of Writings are not so trifling as by many People they are thought.—Nor are they design'd, as some imagine, for *Amusement* only, but *Instruction* also, most of them containing Morals, which if well observed would be of no small

---

[1]   One of the nine muses, daughters of Zeus and Mnemosyne who inspired practitioners of the various arts. Classical writers set the precedent for using the muses interchangeably.

[2]   Sorrowful utterances.

[3]   The literature of praise, often flattery.

[4]   Plots.

[5]   Blatant.

Service to those that read 'em.——Certainly if the Passions are well represented, and the Frailties to which Humane Nature is incident, and cannot avoid falling into, of one kind or another, it cannot fail to rouze the sleeping Conscience of the guilty Reader to a just Remorse for what is *past*, and an Endeavour at last of Amendment for the *future*.——Those who wou'd, perhaps, be impatient of Reproof when given them by a Parent, a Guardian, or a Friend, listen calmly to it when instill'd this way.——Tho' the Follies we find expos'd are our own, we hear of them without Anger, because related in the Character of another, and reap all the Benefit of the Admonition, without the Shame of having receiv'd it.——But, methinks, pursued he, there is little occasion of Defence for writing of *Novels*, the very Authority of those great Names which adorn the Title-Pages of some large Volumes of them, is a sufficient Recommendation; and we cannot believe that the celebrated Madam D'ANOIS, Monsieurs BANDELL, SCUDERY, SEGRAIS, BONAVENTURE Des PERRIERS,[1] and many other learned Writers, would have been at the Expence of so much Time and Pains, only for the Pleasure of inventing a Fiction, or relating a Tale.——No, they had other Views.——They had an Eye to the Humours of the Age they liv'd in, and knew that Morals, meerly as Morals, wou'd obtain but slight Regard: to inspire Notions, therefore, which are necessary to reform the Manners, they found it most proper to cloath Instruction with Delight.——And 'tis most certain that when Precepts[2] are convey'd this way, they steal themselves into the Soul, and work the wish'd Effect, almost insensibly, to the Person who receives them.——We become virtuous ere we are aware, and by admiring the great Examples which in the Narrative appear so amiable, are led to an Endeavour of imitating them.

---

1   European fiction-writers Madame d'Aulnoy, i.e., Marie-Catherine Le Jumel de Barneville, comtesse d'Aulnoy (1650?–1705); Matteo Bandello (1485–1561); Georges de Scudery (1601–67); Jean Regnauld de Segrais (1624–1701); and Bonaventure des Periers (1500?–44?). De Scudery's name appeared on the title pages of *Artamène, ou le grand Cyrus* (10 vols., 1649–53) and *Clélie* (10 vols., 1654–60), by his sister Madeleine, who had been established as author of these works by the eighteenth century. Segrais's name appeared on *Zayde* (1670), a *roman héroïque* in the tradition of Madeleine de Scudery, on which Segrais collaborated with Madame de Lafeyette.

2   Instructions concerning moral conduct.

HE was about to add something more; but was prevented by the coming in of a Lady in a new Suit of Cloaths.—Her Appearance put an End to the Conversation we were upon, and it turn'd immediately on Dress.—Every body in the Room were ask'd how they lik'd her Fancy in the choice of her *Brocade*,[1] the Manner of its being made, the Air of the Sleeve.—I believe it took up little less than an Hour, to answer to the Interrogatories she made on each particular Part of it.—From that she fell into a most learned Dissertation[2] on Dress in general, condemning one Lady for wearing Red, another for being seen in Blue, a third for affecting Yellow.—One had her Petticoats too scanty, another was as extravagant in the Fullness of them; some had them too short, some too long. Lady BELLAIR discovered an unbecoming Assurance in exposing her bare Neck, because it was the only handsome thing about her. Lady PRUDENCE, to conceal the Deformity of hers, sweated in *July* under the Weight of a Scarf and half-a-dozen Handkerchiefs.[3]—In fine, she took abundance of Pains to prove, that no body had any Understanding in the Elegancies of Dress but herself;—and whoever had a Mind to be perfect in that Art might have listen'd to her with Pleasure. But as neither PHILETUS, BRILLIANTE, DORINTHUS, nor my self, had any Ambition to excell that way, we rose to take our Leave. The obliging AMIANA easily perceiving the Reason of our Departure, follow'd us to the Door; and, with a most becoming Smile, I will not, said she, press for the Continuance of your agreeable Society at this Time, but beg to be favour'd with it to Morrow about Tea-drinking Time, I have something to shew you, which I fancy will be entertaining. PHILETUS was the first that answered, Though nothing can be added to the Pleasure with which you inspire all you make happy in your Company, yet, to make Amends for the little I am able to return, I will also bring a small Piece of Ingenuity along with me. After this we all made our Compliments, and took an unwilling Leave, impatient for the Time when we were to re-enjoy that Satisfaction we had so lately quitted.

---

[1] Fine fabric with a raised pattern.
[2] Loosely, speech.
[3] Neckerchief.

REFLECTIONS ON THE VARIOUS
EFFECTS OF LOVE

Love is not Sin, but where 'tis sinful Love.[1]

THO' there is no Passion more universally spoken of than *Love*,
yet none appears so little understood: Those who have pretended
to give us any Definition of it, seem, methinks, as widely different from the Truth, as they are from one another in their Idea's.
The Unsuccessful (in their Wishes) term it, the most destructive
of any the Soul is capable of entertaining; they ransack History
for Examples of unhappy Lovers, and ascribe all the Misfortunes
of their Lives to their having been so.—Others, more prosperous, accuse their Antagonists of Prophaneness, and undertake to
prove, that the greatest and noblest Actions that ever have been
done in the World, owed their Birth only to the Incitements of
this Passion, and wholly of the Opinion of that Poet, who says,

Love kindles all the Soul with Honour's Fire,
To make the Lover worthy his Desire.[2]

They seem to place it among those Rays of Excellence with
which the Celestial Being illuminates the Minds of those design'd
for Wonders: Both impute infinitely more to its Influence, than
ever was simply in its Power of performing, either in *Good* or *Ill*.
A third Sort there are, who, having never felt the Force of it,
believe the Passion nothing but a Name, the Chimera of a distemper'd Imagination,[3] and will neither admit of it as an Excuse for
any *Inadvertency*, to which they see some of its Votaries[4] led, nor
allow it the Honour of having contributed to the *Improvements*
which they behold in others: But to judge in this Manner, one

---

1 The line, from John Dryden, *Don Sebastian* (1690), II. i. 575, appears on the original
   title page. For a digitally enhanced facsimile of that page, see Haywood, *Miscellaneous
   Writings, 1725–1743*, ed. Alexander Pettit (London: Pickering & Chatto, 2000) 77.
2 The lines are unidentified and were perhaps written by Haywood.
3 Delusion fostered by mental imbalance.
4 Disciples.

must, in my Opinion, be either stupidly *insensible*,[1] or barbarously *brutal*,[2] incapable of being rouz'd by any Emotions; or the whole Soul, engross'd by rougher Passions, have left no Room for the Approaches of Tenderness: Not but that there are some People, who having liv'd a long Time without feeling any Symptoms of that Passion, laugh at the Effects they see of it in others; yet owing their Indifference neither to Unsusceptibility[3] nor ill Nature, cannot imagine, that there is any Thing in it more than Invention, and join with the *Insensibles* and *Brutals* in censuring, and ridiculing all the Arguments which the Attestors of its Force have laid down, either to *allure*, or *fright* Mankind from enrolling themselves among the List of Lovers. But when one of these happens to change his Mind, and by the Influence of some prevailing Charms is at last compell'd to own the Power he has so long despis'd, how unhappy is his State! as a Punishment for his former Unbelief, a Gaul-dipt Arrow festers in his Heart; none of the *Sweets*, but all the *Bitterness* of *Desire* he tastes; asham'd of recanting his long publish'd Errors, and hopeless of Favour from the resenting God, in silent sad despair he sighs away the Remnant of his Days, consuming in the smother'd Flame, and like the famous *Niabod*, the Astrologer of *Padua*, who having foretold that he should dye on such a Day, took Poison to verify his own Prediction.[4] The obstinate Enamorato[5] chuses to fall a Sacrifice to the hidden Impulse, rather than acknowledge it, dying at once its *Martyr* and *Opposer*. But as the Fate of Persons of this Disposition is of Consequence only to themselves, and the Occasion of it being conceal'd, contributes nothing in Favour of those who have written either in the Praise, or Condemnation of that Passion which now employs my Pen, I shall forbear any further Remarks on them, and pursuing my first Design, enquire into the Justice of those Reasons made use of by the contradicting Parties, to demonstrate the Verity[6] of their different Assertions.

---

1 Incapable of feeling.
2 Animal-like.
3 Emotional sluggishness.
4 The mathematician Valentinus Nabod, or Naibod, in fact died in 1593, thirty-three years after the publication of his work on Ptolemy, *Enarratio Elementorum Astrologiae*.
5 Lover.
6 Truth.

When we behold a Person, who for a long Time has been careless of his Studies, neglectful of improving himself, and in fine, wholly devoted to his looser Pleasures, on his hap'ning into the Acquaintance of some Woman, equally adorn'd with Beauty and with Virtue, with whom he falls passionately in Love on a sudden, relinquish his former Follies, and become the Reverse of what he was; with how vast an Appearance of Reason do we believe the Change is owing to his Passion, and how readily concur with the Sentiments of those, who declare themselves the greatest Favourers of it: Or, when on the contrary, we find a Man reputed wise and virtuous, forfeit that Character, and degenerate into Acts of Folly and Injustice, to gratify the Pride or Caprice[1] of some fair Triumpher, who boasts no other Merit than her Beauty, how apt are we to lay the Fault on Love! and how agree to curse a Softness, which seems so pernicious to all the nobler Sentiments of the Soul!—Who can forbear condemning that fatal Tenderness, which transported[2] *Ninus* King of the *Assyrians*, first to make *Semiramis*, a Maid of mean[3] Extraction, the Partner of his Throne and Bed, and after to put into her Hands a Power, which she made use of for his own Destruction?[4]—With how much Horror do we consider the Violence of those Emotions which agitated the Breast of *Philip* I. of *France*, who being married to *Bertha*, a Lady of great Virtue, divorc'd himself from her, and gave the Title of Queen to *Bertrade de Monfert*, having barbarously put to Death her Husband the *Count* of *Anjou*, one of the best and bravest Men of his Time.[5]—Can any one unshock'd read that Passage in History which relates, How *Crispus* the Son of *Constantine* the

---

[1]   Capriciousness; irrational behavior.
[2]   Inspired.
[3]   Lowly.
[4]   Semiramis (fl. *c.* 808 BC), or Sammuramat, often synonymous with power, beauty, and sexual appetite, may have married her son Ninyas after the death of her husband, the Assyrian Shamshi Adad V, in 812 BC. In a source from which Haywood draws several times in this work, Nahum Tate lists Semiramis among women who 'became their Armour as well as their Robes' (*A Present for the Ladies: Being an Historical Account of Several Illustrious Persons of the Female Sex,* 73).
[5]   Philippe I (1052–1108) divorced Berthe of Holland and, in 1092, abducted and wed Bertrade de Montfort, married at the time to Foulques le Réchin, count of Anjou. The exploit prompted Pope Urban II to excommunicate Philippe, who in fact died one year before the man Haywood says he murdered.

Great, burning with incestuous Fires, attempted the Honour of his own Fathers Wife; by which dreadful Accident that glorious Emperor, tho' cover'd with Lawrells,[1] and deservedly the Admiration of the whole wond'ring World, was for a long Time perplex'd with home-bred Jarrs,[2] and at last compell'd to deprive himself of an Heir, who till his Fall from Virtue he look'd on as the supremest of his Blessings.[3]—How dreadful were the Effects of those wild Desires which reign'd in the Soul of *Ogna-Sancha*, Countess of *Castile!* This Lady being in Love with *Abdellraizer*, a Moorish Prince, endeavour'd the Murder of her only Son *Sanchogracia*, fearing he wou'd prevent her Marriage; but her Design being discover'd, and also her Hope disappointed by the Banishment of *Abdellraizer*, she swallowed Poison, and testify'd, that where such furious Wishes are suffer'd to preside, neither the Dictates of Religion, Morality, or even Nature, are of any Force.[4]—Who does not lament the unhappy Consequences of *Helen's* Rape, or the fatal Intreague of *Mark Antony* and *Cleopatra!* the one, involv'd all the Princes of *Greece* in a ten Years War, in which unnumber'd Lives were lost, *Troy* was destroy'd, and a whole Nation perish'd: The other, cost the greatest, bravest Man of the then living World, his Fame, his Peace of Mind, his Honours, and at last his Life.[5]—But wherefore shou'd we go so far for Instances of this Kind? the present Age, and our own Experience presents us with too many: Among the Great what is more common, than to see a Husband contemning the Embraces of the Partner of his Bed and Dignity, forfeit every Thing that ought to be valuable, for the polluted Joys, which some fair pros-

---

1   Bay leaves, here symbolizing military prowess.

2   Domestic quarrels.

3   Constantine I ('the Great') executed his eldest son, Crispus, and his own wife, Fausta, in 326; officially, the charge was treason.

4   The referent may be Queen-Regent Toda of Pamplona-Navarre (fl. *c.*925), wife (thus, 'ogna' or 'doña') of Sancho Garcés I, mother of García Sánches I and grandmother of Sancho Garcés II. Following her husband's death in 925, Toda put her territories under the protection of her husband's former enemy, the heroic Umayyad ruler 'Abd al-Rahmān III.

5   The abduction of Menelaüs's wife, Helen, initiated the Trojan War, as recounted in Homer's *Iliad* (*c.*8th century BC) and other sources; the Roman general Mark Antony (83[?]–30 BC) and his lover Cleopatra, Queen of Egypt (69–30 BC) are immortalized in Shakespeare's *Antony and Cleopatra* (1606) and elsewhere.

titute, abandon'd to all Sense of Shame, gladly consents to yield.—
How frequently do we see Wives, by the Benevolence of Fortune,
plac'd in a Station which gives them a glorious Opportunity of
becoming shining Patterns[1] to the rest, quit all the Advantages
they enjoy for the pursuit of lawless Love, and wholly govern'd
by their wild Desires, grow fond of Infamy, and triumph in
Disgrace.—How many high-born Maids, forgetful of their own,
and Houses Honour, resign themselves a Prey to the loose Wishes
of some upstart Wretch, who conquers but to insult, and makes
his Boast of having the power of ruining.—Numerous are they
of both Sexes, who are undone by unequal Marriages; but much
more numerous those, especially of the softer and more believing Kind, who wanting[2] even that Sanction, sacrifice their All to
their blind Passion for some worthless Object. How is it possible
then, say the Foes of Love, to know and to reflect on these Things,
without being convinc'd that the Soul ought to guard itself against
the Assaults of Tenderness, more than from any other Emotion
whatsoever?

When one thinks no farther, one shall, indeed, be of that
Opinion; but when one considers that there are no Proofs of the
Misfortunes and Vices it occasions, but what may be equaliz'd by
as strong ones of a contrary Effect. He that wou'd go about to
decide the Contest in Favour of either opposite, wou'd find his
Judgment extremely at a Loss, and at last be oblig'd to leave the
Question undetermin'd.

What a noble Idea does the Example of *Artemisa*, Queen of
Caria, give us of that Passion, which in her was not to be
vanquish'd by Death. Those pale and ghastly Looks, which the
King of Terrors imprints on every Victim of his Power, render'd
not *Mausolus* less dear to his constant Wife. With the same
unequal'd Tenderness she regarded him dead as living; left not his
cold Corps a Moment, till he was interr'd, and then built a
Monument for him, which is esteem'd one of the Wonders of the
World, and from which all famous Sepulchres[3] have since taken
their Name; that Testimony of her Affection finish'd, as if she had

---

[1]   Examples.
[2]   Lacking.
[3]   Tombs, implicitly elaborate.

no longer Business for Life, she resign'd her Breath with Pleasure, and hasted to meet her dear-lov'd Consort in another World.[1]— With what Fortitude that Passion inspires a noble Mind, is evident from the Example of *Paulina*, the Wife of *Seneca:* That Heroick Lady, when her Husband was condemn'd to Death by the Tyrant *Nero*, caus'd her own Veins to be open'd, that she might dye with him; and tho' the Emperor, touch'd with so uncommon a Proof of Constancy and Magnanimity, prevented her Design, and commanded his own Physicians on Pain of Death to cure her voluntary Wounds; the ghost-like Paleness thenceforward of her bloodless Cheeks, was a lasting Testimony of her Courage and Affection.[2]—How great an Assistant *Love* is to *Wit*, especially to the Improvement of the Genius in *Poetry*. The *Romans* acknowledg'd in the Works of *Sulpitia*, who in the Time of the Emperor *Domitian* wrote many elegant Pieces; but that for which she was most celebrated, was the History of her Amours with him, who afterwards became her Husband *Celænus*.[3]—*Sappho* the *Lesbian* Boast, was to her Softness indebted for her Fame.[4]—The Charms of *Corrinna* had long since been bury'd in Oblivion, had not Love immortaliz'd her Song.[5]—The tender and never-dying Strains of *Ovid* confess the Refinements which this Passion made, and the Power of *Julia's* Eyes.[6]—*English Aphrara* had been less admir'd, had Love less influenc'd her Muse.[7]—*Sidney* and *Sidley* were oblig'd

---

[1] Artemisia was sister and wife to Mausolus; she built the Mausoleum at Halicarnassus in his memory, *c.*353 BC. Tate claims that Artemesia 'drank the Ashes of her Husband', then died (*A Present for the Ladies*, 52).

[2] Seneca and Paulina took their own lives in AD 65, after Seneca was implicated in a plot against the emperor Nero. Haywood's account incorporates wording from Tate, *A Present for the Ladies*, pp. 41–42, and from *The Annals and History of C. Cornelius Tacitus*, 2nd ed. (1716), bk. ii, 414.

[3] Sulpicia (fl. *c.*25 BC) wrote love poems for Cerinthus. Tate mentions her in *A Present for the Ladies*, 53.

[4] A commonplace about the lyric poet Sappho of Lesbia (b. *c.*650 BC).

[5] Corinna is celebrated throughout Ovid's *Amores* (*c.*20 BC).

[6] Ovid may have had an adulterous liaison with Julia Minor, daughter or granddaughter of Augustus Caesar, or may have played a role in one of her many affairs. Augustus banished Ovid and Julia, separately, in AD 8. Ovid never explicitly wrote about Julia; but see Aphra Behn, 'Ovid to Julia: A Letter' (1685): "Twas *Julia's* brighter Eyes my soul alone / With everlasting gust, could feed upon' (ll. 41–42).

[7] Aphra Behn (1640–89), amatory poet, playwright, fiction writer, and translator; here, 'muse' connotes 'source of inspiration'.

to the Inspiration of the melting God, which in all Ages has been a Friend to Verse.[1]

Countless are the Examples of both the good and ill Effects of this Passion, when animated by it, and encourag'd by the Hope of obtaining his Desire, with how much Ardour[2] does the *Soldier* fight! or the *Poet* apply himself to write! nothing appears too dangerous or Difficult! It infuses a generous Emulation[3] through the Mind, and will not suffer the Person possest of it to rest till he arrives at Excellence, and becomes worthy of the Joy he aims at. As the incomparable *Spencer* says:

> Love fir'd his noble Soul to brave Atchievements
> And generous Thirst of Fame.————[4]

But then again to what opposite Extremes does it transport some People! how does it stifle all the Suggestions of Religion, Morality, Honour, Piety, and every human Virtue! and urge the Soul to Acts, the most impious and horrible to Nature, for the Accomplishment of its Desires! How then is it possible, when one considers *Love* meerly as *Love*, without any further Regard than to the Quality of that Passion in itself, to judge whither it has contributed most to the Advantage or Disservice of Mankind? The deepest Penetration will never be able to fathom the hidden Mistery, Learning cannot explode it: Inferences drawn from History or Experience will but more puzzle us in the fruitless Search, and still the Question will remain unanswerable! To what Purpose then, my Reader will be apt to think, is this Discourse? To which I reply, That the Reason of those Contradictions which we see in the Consequences of the same Passion, is only because we imagine it of much greater Force than in Reality it can boast; and this which has so much the Appearance of an Enigma, be very easily solv'd, if People wou'd

---

[1] Sir Philip Sidney (1554–86), poet, and Sir Charles Sedley (1639?–1701), poet and playwright.

[2] Passion.

[3] Loosely, desire for improvement.

[4] The lines are not by Edmund Spenser (c.1552–99), although the theme and wording recall his *Astrophel* (1595), ll. 67–72.

once be persuaded to go the right Way for an Explanation: Let us take away a little of that almighty Power which we ascribe to *Love*, and allow something more to *Nature* and those Inclinations born with us, and we shall immediately reconcile the seeming Impossibility. *Love*, like the Grape's potent Juice, but heightens *Nature*, and makes the conceal'd Sparks of Good, or Ill, blaze out, and show themselves to the wond'ring World! It gives an Energy to our Wishes, a Vigour to our Understanding, and *adds* to the *Violence* of our Desires, but *alters* not the *Bent* of them.

The Explanation of LOVE.

WHEN in the Soul the Seeds of Virtue lye,
Love does the Want of native Warmth supply:
Soon they spring up in living Acts of Fame,
And justly glorify their Patron's Name!
But, when it actuates a vicious Mind,
Rapes! Murders! Incest! common Crimes we find.
No Precepts[1] can its lawless Flames asswage,
Nor stop the Course of its impetuous Rage:
Boldly o'er every Boundary it flys,
And all the Powers of Heaven and Earth defys!
Then whatsoe'er the Consequences show,
We not to *Love*, but our *own* Nature owe:
Love but improves the Sentiments it finds,
And tho' it *raises*, cannot *change* our Minds.

Love in itself cannot be consider'd either as a Virtue, or a Vice; it often, indeed, excites to both, but never changes the one to the other; there must be some secret Propensity in the Soul, tho' perhaps long (by the Prejudice of Education or some other Motive) conceal'd, on which this Passion must work, and create Consequences, which without that Aid, it would be impossible to bring to pass.

To prove the Truth of this Assertion, one need, methinks, only consider with how much greater Force that Passion influences

---

[1] Instructions concerning moral conduct.

the Minds of Women, than it can boast on those of a contrary Sex, whose Natures being more rough and obdurate, are not capable of receiving those deep Impressions which for the most Part are so destructive to the softer Specie.[1]—The other may Love with Vehemence, but then it is neither so tender nor so last-ing a Flame, and seldom does it carry them any farther than a Self-gratification; the Good of the Object they pretend to admire, being what they very rarely consult.—A Woman, where she loves, has no Reserve; she profusely gives her all, has no Regard to any Thing, but obliging the Person she affects, and lavishes her whole Soul.—But Man, more wisely, keeps a Part of his for other Views, he has still an Eye to Interest[2] and Ambition! As a certain Lady, who, 'tis to be suppos'd, has experienc'd what she writes, somewhere affirms:

> Women no Bounds can to their Passion set;
> Love and Discretion in our Sex ne'er met.
> Men may a cold Indifference, Prudence call,
> But we to Madness doat, or not at all.[3]

Not but there are some Exceptions to this general Rule, there have been Men, and still are some who think nothing too great a Price to purchase the Gratification of their Desires, nor to reward the Tenderness which makes them happy; and to that End will run the greatest Hazards in Fortune, Life, and Reputation: And there are also some Women, whose Pride, Ambition, or Revenge, has influenc'd them to Actions the very Reverse of Disinterestedness;[4] but when any Instances of this kind happen, the Sexes seem to have exchang'd Natures, and both to be the Contradiction of themselves.

As the Softness therefore of Womenkind renders them more liable to the Impressions of that Passion, and joins with it in influencing them to the Inadvertencies they too frequently fall into; so in a Mind prone to Constancy, Avarice, Cruelty, or any

---

[1] Loosely, group, here meaning women.
[2] Profit.
[3] The lines are unidentified and were perhaps written by Haywood.
[4] The state of being unmotivated by desire for profit.

otherVice, *Love* becomes an Abettor of the Crimes[1] they act: Or, in one addicted to Virtue, encreases the Value of it, and makes the illustrious Beams shine forth with greater Brightness:

> *Love*, when ill treated, in a worthy Mind,
> From patient Suffering may some Glory find:
> Who unresenting, can his Injuries bear,
> Does a new Merit gain by his Dispair.
> But when it mingles with a vicious Soul,
> Unnumber'd Ills appear without Controul!
> Each daring Sin its horrid Form displays!
> And the wild Will, destroys a thousand Ways.

The Power of *Love* being, as I have already said, no more than to enliven and make bold the Inclination, must certainly derive its Nature from the Mansion in which it dwells, and varies in its Effects according to the Disposition to which it joins itself. *Broom*, an old *English* Poet,[2] in one of his Plays gives, in my Opinion, a very good Description of this Passion, when he terms it:

> In *Heaven*, all *Angel!* and in *Hell* all *Fiend!*

And another Author of greater Reputation, and much more modern Date, joins in the same Sentiments, which, with a vast deal of Elegance, he expresses in these Lines:

> *Love*, various Minds does variously inspire,
> He stirs in gentle Natures gentle Fire,
> Like that of Incense on the Altar laid:
> But raging Flames tempestuous Souls invade,
> This Way and that th'impetuous torrent flows,
> With Pride it mounts, and with Revenge it glows.[3]

---

1 Morally odious acts; sins.

2 Haywood presumably intends to attribute the subsequent line to the playwright Richard Brome (*c.*1590–1653), but its source is uncertain.

3 Dryden, *Tyrannick Love* (1670), II. i. 292–97.

But since I have, contrary to my Design, stumbled on some Quotations of Poetry, I think it will not be amiss to present the Reader with a Copy of Verses, which never yet were publish'd, and were occasion'd by the different Effects of the Passion I am treating of, in the Hearts of two Ladies, who were both in Love with the same Man, and had been both render'd unhappy by his Ingratitude and Perjury. It was written by a Person perfectly acquainted with the whole Affair, and who assumes the Character of one of those concern'd in it.

Celia and Evandra.

WITHIN a dismal Shade, where nothing grew,
But mournful Willow and the baleful Yew,
Despairing *Celia*, that once lovely Maid,
Stretch'd at her Length, on the cold Earth was laid.
Her Garments torn, her panting Bosom bare,
Her Eyes half drown'd in Tears, and in the Air,
Was madly toss'd her loose dishevell'd Hair.
When after many a Sigh and piteous Groan,
She to relentless Heaven thus made her Moan,
Why was I destin'd to so hard a Fate,
Of all my Sex the most unfortunate?
Thus to be tortur'd with successless Love,
And endless Miseries which round me move!
When will my poor distracted[1] Heart find Rest,
Must I be ever! ever thus opprest!
No Glimpse of Hope, no dawning Joy appears,
Not one kind Glance to dissipate my Fears,
Or stop the Source of never ceasing Tears!
Let mellancholly Bards who write of Miserie,
A Pattern take and copy't out by me!
See here the truest Emblem of Despair,
Of pining Discontent, and endless Care!
Oh *Lysimour!* ungrateful *Lysimour!* said she,
What have I done—

---

[1] Deranged.

Or rather, what have I not done for thee!
But here she stop'd, and at that Name
Vollies of Sighs from her heav'd Bosom came;
So quick they flew, and with such Vehemence,
One wou'd have thought her Soul had issu'd thence:
'Till almost strangled with the swelling Grief,
She in loud Outcrys vainly sought Relief.
Like one distracted the wild Wood ran round,
While cruel Thorns her cruel Flesh did wound;
Th'opposing Trees her Ornaments did tear,
And every Bush was proud to catch her Hair.
At last, half breathless, tir'd with fruitless Rage,
A Flood of Tears the Passion did asswage:
She knelt, and thus did Justice of the gods implore,
To grant Revenge on perjur'd *Lysimour.*
Find out some Way, she cry'd, ye Powers divine!
To plague his Soul, as he has tortur'd mine:
Let him burn inward with consuming Fires!
Like me, unhoping, waste in vain Desires!
Like me abhor the Day that gave him Birth!
Like me distracted grovel on the Earth!
Blast him with Lightnings in Youth's prideful Joy,
And with Deformity his Charms destroy!
Some sudden Mark of your just Vengeance show
That the Contemners of your Power may know
You can both see and punish Crimes below!
    I had no Patience longer to forbear
But rushing forth disturb'd the guilty Prayer,
And with an angry Look disturb'd the mournful Fair:
Behold, fond Maid! said I, and blush to see
Thy Rival's Love and Generosity.
Like you, by *Lysimour* I am betray'd,
Alike by his Deceits unhappy made:
Greater than yours my Wrongs appear, yet still,
Methinks, I love too well, to wish him Ill:
My Passion does a nobler Aim pursue,
You but his *Heart*, I wou'd his *Soul* subdue!
And by my long and patient Suffering prove

That I alone am worthy of his Love!
You can no Pleasure, but when with him, know;
But I am happy when I hear he's so:
His Wishes far above my own I prize,
And for his Sake Self-int'rest can despise!
And since my Image has forsook his Breast,
Exil'd from thence for a more charming Guest,
May she be kind, to his Desires comply,
And study for his Good as much as I.
May choicest Blessings be her Virgin Dowr,[1]
Live long in Peace with her lov'd *Lysimour*,
And lest Remorse of Injuries to me,
Shou'd damp his Bliss, may I forgotten be,
And never enter in his Memory.
May no disturbing Care his Peace molest,
But be of all he can desire possest,
And then *Evandra* will be truly blest.

There is nothing more certain than that some Women, when instigated by this Passion, and disappointed in their Aim, want only the Power of inflicting most dreadful Kinds of Revenge on the Authors of their Misfortune; nor have any Regard to what themselves may suffer in the Attempt, either as to Reputation or Interest; nay, wou'd even hazard Life, rather than lose the Means of retaliating an Injury in this tender Part. A certain great Lady of this Age having had an Intreague with a young Gentleman, of whom she was passionately fond, perceiving his Ardours began to derogate[2] from their accustom'd Warmth, and in a little Time to sink into an entire Indifference, try'd first all the Arts she was Mistress of, to recover the decaying Fire, but all being unsuccessful, she had Recourse to Threats, and with an unparalell'd Assurance told him, That if he discontinu'd giving her those Proofs of his Affection she had been us'd to receive from him, she wou'd not only relate all that had pass'd between them to her Lord, but also cause him to be sued for bastardizing a noble

---

[1] That is, dowry.
[2] Lessen in force.

Family, and that she herself wou'd appear in Court an Evidence against him: A Menace of this Nature was scarce to be credited, and the Lover was so far from being terrify'd by it, that he only made it an Excuse for breaking totally: But he was soon after convinc'd she meant really to do as she had said: He receiv'd a Letter from a Lawyer, which gave him an Account, that he had Orders to prosecute him, on the Trespass before-mention'd. The Spark having a good Estate, and knowing well the Severity of the Law in such Cases, was glad to solicit a Pardon from the offended Fair; and make what Retributions she was pleas'd to think a sufficient Attonement for the Wrong he had done her: Being compell'd now to act the Deceiver's Part, and feign a Tenderness he was far from feeling, till the Inconstancy of the Lady's own Humour reliev'd his Vexation; and by her making Choice of a new Favourite, left him at Liberty to pursue his Inclinations, which long before had been elsewhere devoted. Another of equal Quality, and much the same Degree in Vice, meeting that Fate which all Women must expect, when to gratify their Passion they make a Sacrifice of their Honour, that of being slighted and forsaken, turn'd her whole Soul to Fury, meditating nothing but Revenge, apply'd to a Person reputed to have Skill in Negromancy:[1] From him she receiv'd an Image made in Wax, on which she was to practise several Sorts of Cruelties; the pretended Sorcerer having impos'd so far on her Credulity, as to make her believe, that the Person whom she hated, by Simpathy, shou'd be sensible of all those Torments his lifeless Effigy was not capable of feeling. 'Tis hardly to be imagin'd, how many various Ways her Invention furnish'd her with, of inflicting Punishment on this Proxy of her Revenge, sometimes she held it to the Fire, till ready just to melt, then plung'd it into Water, crying as she did it, *Thus may the perjur'd Villain burn and freeze, the two great Opposites of Nature join to give him Pain, till with the mingled Anguish he runs mad.*—Sometimes wou'd she turn, and wreathe, and twist the supple Form into a thousand Shapes, dislocating in Imagination every Limb.—Sometimes she stuck it all o'er from Head to Foot with Pins; at others, stab it in the Eyes with her Penknife, and gash

---

[1]   That is, necromancy; magic.

it in those Parts which in a living Body are most tender.—'Tis certain, that had the real Person sustain'd but one half of what his Image suffer'd, Death had reliev'd him from the other. This satisfy'd however, the Impatience of her Resentment; and the Magician was greatly to be commended, in preventing her by this innocent Piece of Enchantment, from having Recourse to Means more hurtful: At the same Time that he gave her the Image, he privately sent the Gentleman an Account of what had happen'd, and desir'd he wou'd keep himself conceal'd for some Time; which he complying with, the Lady doubted not but the Spells had taken Effect, nor discover'd she the Imposition, till the Impression of a new Idea had put the former entirely out of her Head, and she had no longer Leisure for Revenge.

When *Love* finds Entrance in a Mind, such as these Ladies were possest of, it becomes indeed a most vile and wicked Passion, and its Effects are dreadful to Earth, and detestable to Heaven, and when it takes Possession of a Heart all Gentleness and Softness, it then grows fatal to itself.—Woman shou'd, therefore, but with the utmost Caution entertain it; not all the Dictates of Religion, Reason, Virtue, Interest or Fame, being seldom of sufficient Force to combat with that more prevailing Tenderness, which seems inherent to the very Nature of her Sex: Besides, there is something so very pleasant in the first Approaches of that Passion, when new Desires play round the Heart, and thrill the swelling Veins, and fill deluded Fancy with a thousand gay Ideas of future Happiness, that there had need be a greater Strength of Judgment than is usually to be found in a female Mind, to defend it from giving Way to the ruinous Delight, which when once enter'd, I need not say how difficult to be repell'd. A Woman of Wit when thus ensnar'd, is infinitely more unhappy than one of a less distinguishing Capacity, because she sees and knows the Dangers into which she is about to plunge herself, yet withal finds them unavoidable, with open Eyes she gazes on the vast Abyss where her dear Peace of Mind is already lost, and which also threatens the Destruction of her Fame, her Honour, and all that is valuable, yet is still blind to every Path that might guide her from the impending Mischiefs.—This Reflection puts me in mind of some Copies of Verses written by one of my particular

Acquaintance, and who had so good an Opinion of my Sincerity and Secrecy, as to make me the Confident of the tenderest and most ardent[1] Passion, certainly, that ever Woman was possest of. I have them still by me in Manuscript, and as the Names are feign'd, and the real Persons cannot easily be guess'd at, I believe it will be no Breach of that Trust reposed in me, to insert them: The first was written when she had yielded to become a Partner in her own Ruin, and on some Occasion oblig'd to be absent from him, and appears to be the Overflowings of a Mind full of Love, and the most perfect Tenderness.

Climene to *Mirtillo*.
EPISTLE the First.

THIS to *Mirtillo* does *Climene* send,
The fondest Lover and the truest Friend,
Wishing you all the Pleasures you can prove,[2]
When absent from the Nymph[3] you say you love.
Tho' cruel Fate debars me from thy Sight,
It cannot take away the Power to write,
By Letters we some Pleasure may impart,
And the Pen speak the Language of the Heart.
A Time will come when we again shall meet,
And, undisturb'd, our former Joys repeat:
Nor let a jealous Thought make sad thy Mind,
Climene can to none but thee prove kind.
The happy Hours we have together past,
Give sweet Reflections which will ever last:
Each rapt'rous Thought such Ecstasy doth give,
I scarcely cou'd when with thee more receive.
Sure never any Pair were blest as we,
When in my Bower retir'd you liv'd with me,
From Noise, and the great World's Contention free.
Soon as *Aurora's* Beams brought forth the Morn,

---

1   Literally, burning.
2   Experience.
3   Young virgin.

We'd leave our Beds, and to the Grove adjourn,
Together rang'd the Fields and Gardens round,
Where, when we some delicious Fruit had found,
Of all the Choicest we depriv'd the Tree,
I gave the best to you, and you to me.
Then on some Carpet by kind Nature spread,
Our weary Bodies were supinely laid;
While the melodious Choiristers o'th'Grove,[1]
Sang tuneful Praises to almighty Love;
To th'utmost Pitch stretching their little Throats,
In soft harmonious tho' unskilful Notes,
Hov'ring around our Heads aloud declar'd,
The happy State which mutual Lovers shar'd:
Thus blest we were and envy'd not the gods,
The Pleasures of Cœlestial Abodes.
But now those dear transporting Hours are past,
They gave a Joy too exquisite to last.
Thou absent, I all Conversation shun,
And wander round the Meadows all alone,
No Company can please, now thou art gone.
Here in the Solitude this Shade affords,
I sit, and think o'er all thy tender Words:
They all are register'd in my Memory,
Nothing of thine can e'er forgotten be.
Thy Name is all the Musick I wou'd hear,
Thy Name is all that can delight my Ear;
Unpleasing all Discourses seem to me,
Unless they're sweeten'd with some Talk of thee!
The very Birds, methinks, thy Absence moan,
And warble out—*Oh is* Mirtillo *gone!*
And well they may their Master's Loss deplore,
The Pipe that rais'd their Notes they hear no more!

    Hard by the Grove a well-spread Oak there grows
Under the Shadow of whose friendly Boughs
We've sat whole Hours and pleasing Stories told,
Of constant Lovers, and their Faith extol'd.

---

[1] Birds.

That Place you more than any did frequent,
Both for the Solitude and Shade it lent.
A thousand Times a-Day I kiss that Tree,
Which was so happy to be lov'd by thee!
Warm'd by my Heat I think it more does thrive,
Renews its Youth, and spite of Time will live.
Its monstruous Roots are grown to that Extent,
They scorn to be in Earth's dark Prison pent;
But rending forcibly the hollow Ground,
Rear up their Heads and with green Moss is crown'd.
Oh! that our Love might flourish as that does,
And renew'd Scenes of Joy once more disclose.

On finding herself totally abandon'd by him, her despairing
Muse thus pour'd forth her Complaints:[1]

Climene to *Mirtillo.*
EPISTLE the Second.

IS this your Promise, base ungrateful Man!
That e'er the Sun had twice his Circle ran,
You wou'd return; did you not strictly swear,
Nothing shou'd hold you any longer there?
Seven tedious Days has vain Expectance born,
Yet do I still thy cruel Absence mourn.
Each Morning early as the Sun I rose,
For racing Thoughts chac'd away soft Repose;
To the adjacent Hills I madly fly,
Hoping from thence my long-lost Love to spy.
A thousand Times my Confident I sent,
Who back return'd as mournful as she went;
In Vain she looks, you shun the hated Place
Where poor *Climene* may behold your Face.
But now, too late, the cursed Cause I know
From which Scorn, and this Neglect does grow;
Serapion's Daughter is your only Joy,

---

[1] Sorrowful utterances.

There all your Hours with Pleasure you employ.
Fond Man! what is it you can see in her,
Which makes you, before mine, her Charms prefer?
She never yet did any Heart subdue,
And slighted is by every Swain but you:
But she has Money—that's the Thing you prize,
The golden Object charms your greedy Eyes.
All Imperfections in her Wealth are lost,
She seems most fair, that can most Riches boast.
Mean, sordid Soul! not so *Climene* prov'd,
When scorning Greatness, only thou wert lov'd,
Philander, Damon, Strephon, left for Thee!
Who a base Mettal dost prefer to me;
Oh Indignation! I cou'd tear my Breast!
For harbouring such a false unworthy Guest.
I, once the Pride and Glory of the Plain,
Am now the Jest of every vulgar Swain,
Who scornfully pass by, and laughing say,
Will not Mirtillo *visit you to Day.*
Curst be the Day in which I first saw Light!
Curst be the Day which brought thee to my Sight!
But doubly curst for ever may that Prove
In which I first confess'd my fatal Love!
Skip, skip it o'er, bright Planet of the World!
Let it be ever in Confusion hurl'd!
Let not the Skies the smallest Glory wear,
But all the Heavens in sable Hue appear!
Let all the Infants who that Day are born,
Be by the Midwives Hands in Pieces torn!
Lest living longer they shou'd chance to be
As lost, as wretched, and undone as me!
Wou'd I'd been bred in some fierce Tyger's Den,
'Tis safer to converse with Beasts than Men:
Whatever they had done, yet still 'twould be
A milder Fate than what I've found from thee.

Too many Companions in her Misfortunes has *Climene*; countless are the Number of these fair Complainers, and tho' there are

but few, whom reading, Experience, or Example, have not warn'd of the Danger to which they are subjected, there are yet fewer, who at all Times have Power to defend themselves from Love and Nature, those joint betrayers of the Sex. There have been many Instances of Women who have chose Death rather than Dishonour, and flown for Shelter to the Grave to shun the Embraces of even the Man they lov'd; but rarely shall we find one who liv'd and dy'd in a happy Insensibility. Mr. *Tate* in his Historical Vindication of the Female Sex,[1] mentions a Lady as an Heroick Pattern of Fortitude and Chastity: 'A certain Duke of *Tuscany*', says he, 'was so extremely avaricious, that he deny'd to his Son, one of the most accomplish'd Princes of his Time, that Allowance which was necessary to support his Quality in any tollerable Degree: An old *Count* of the same Territory was possest of a very plentiful Fortune, and a most beautiful young Wife, who became so not out of Choice, but meerly in Obedience to the positive Commands of her Parents. The *Count* having been married to her some Time, and despairing of Issue, thought he cou'd not better employ his Wealth than in supplying the Wants of the foremention'd Prince: He therefore not only made him very great Presents, but also entreated he wou'd honour him so far as to permit him to make him his adopted. The Prince readily accepted so obliging and beneficial an Offer, and hereupon being frequently entertain'd at his House, in a small Time became passionately enamour'd of the Lady: Former Successes with the Fair embolden'd him to make known his Wishes, which with an Appearance of the utmost Indignation, she severely reprov'd;[2] but finding him not discourag'd, and that there was no Cessation of his Importunities, she solemnly protested, that if he did not desist, she wou'd acquaint her Lord with what, till then, she thought proper to conceal. On this final Answer, the Prince, to divert the Uneasiness of a fruitless Passion, betook himself to Travel, whence he return'd not in several Years: But absence not having been able to extinguish his former Flame, the first Thing he did at his Arrival in *Tuscany*, was to enquire after the ador'd Object of his Affections,

---

1   The subsequent passage is adapted from Tate, *A Present for the Ladies*, 48–50.
2   Expressed disapproval of.

and being told that she had long been sick of a languishing Disease, and was believ'd to be now at the Point of Death. He ran immediately to her House, and fearing he should come too late to find her living, prest abruptly to her Chamber, the Attendants withdrawing to some little Distance, as imagining by the Disorder which appear'd in his Countenance,[1] that he had something to communicate; he threw himself on his Knees by her Bed-side, and was beginning to express his Concern for the Condition in which she was, in the most tender and endearing Terms imaginable. She had before been speechless for some Hours, but the Surprize which the Sight of him occasion'd, recover'd her so much Breath, as to enable her to utter softly these Words: *I dye for you*, said she, *too charming Prince! which I have now confest, because I have therewith spoke my last.* Having spoke this, she fetch'd a deep Sigh and immediately expir'd; leaving him who heard her in the most terrible Agonies of Astonishment and Grief, that ever Heart endur'd.'

It must be confest that this Lady gave an extraordinary Proof of Virtue, but her Behaviour makes good my Argument, that to the Softness of her Nature she was indebted for those Sufferings, which at last brought on her Fate, had she not been possest with an equal Share of Virtue, it had transported her to the most criminal[2] Tenderness; but influenc'd by both, the one prevented her from forfeiting her Honour, and the other from a Possibility of living in so severe a Self-denial.

Having thus, I flatter myself, made it undeniably evident, that the Inadvertencies which *Women*, when guilty of, impute to the Force of Love, are in great Measure occasion'd by their own Tenderness of Nature, I think it will be easy to prove, That that Passion has the same Effect on *Men* of the same Disposition, and that it is but an *Incentive*, not a *Guide* or *Controller* of those Actions, which either *glorify* or *disgrace* the Name of it.

Was it *Love* or the Extravagance and Rashness of his own Humour, which influenc'd *Alexander* the Great, to set the famous City *Persepolis* on Fire, when *Thais* the Courtizan entreated it?[3]—

---

[1] Facial expression.
[2] Immoral.
[3] Accounts of the involvement of the prostitute Thaïs in the burning of Persepolis by Alexander the Great in 330 BC appear in various classical sources.

Cou'd *Love*, without a Cruelty of Nature joined with it, have prevail'd so far on *Lewis* Marquiss of *Thuringia*, as to transport him to the Murder of *Frederick* I. Duke of *Saxony*, that he might with the greater Freedom have the Enjoyment of his Wife?[1]—Was it *Love*, or a wild Impatience incident to his Disposition, which made *Florez* Duke of *Brabant*, become the Ravisher[2] of *Erminia*, when a few Days was design'd to make him the lawful Possessor of her Beauties?[3]— Is it possible that Passion, in a Soul not wholly abandon'd by all Sentiments of Honour and Modesty, shou'd have the Power of compelling *Berenice* the Daughter of *Aggripa*, to forsake her Husband's Bed, for the incestuous one of her own Brother; with whom she liv'd publickly, seeming to glory in her own Shame?[4]— Did *Eleanor* Queen of *England* testify in other Things so great an Affection to her Husband *Henry* II. that we may impute to *Love* rather than *Revenge*, the inhuman Murder of the beautiful *Rosamonde?*[5]—Shall we ascribe to *Love*, or to a certain Enviousness of Disposition, that strange Action committed by the Wife of *Fergus* King of *Scotland?* This Princess finding herself in the Pangs of Death, and having some Reason to imagine a Lady of her Train wou'd soon succeed her in her Bed and Throne, entreated her Husband to come near her, under the Pretence of taking her last Farewel, which assoon as he did, she drew a Dagger, which she had conceal'd in the Bed for that Purpose, and stabbing him to the Heart, cry'd out at the same Time, *Now I am sure no other will possess thee.*[6]—Was it not more

---

1   The referent is perhaps Ludwig (or Louis, or Lewis) II, landgrave of Thuringia from 1140 to 1172 and husband to the half-sister of Emperor Frederick I (1152–90). Both he and his son, Ludwig III, had troubled relations with Frederick, who died, however, by drowning, while at war.

2   Rapist.

3   No 'Florez' was duke of Brabant during the duchy's period of existence, 1190–1430.

4   Berenice (b. AD 28), daughter of Herod, or Agrippa I, lived incestuously with her brother, Agrippa II, before and during her marriage to the king of Cilicia. Paul defends himself before her ('Bernice') and Agrippa in Acts 25.13–26.30.

5   Eleanor of Aquitaine (1122?–1204) married Henry of Anjou, later Henry II of England, after the nullification of her marriage to Louis VII of France. The first of many lurid accounts of Eleanor's putative murder of Henry's mistress Rosamund de Clifford (d. 1176?) appeared in *Croniques de London* (*c*.1350).

6   A typically lurid account of the death of 'Fergus III', a rough chronological, if not historical, equivalent to Fergus, son of Eochaid (d. 780?). Seventeenth- and eighteenth-century accounts differ in certain respects; but in all of them, Fergus is killed by his wife, Ethiola, who confesses and then commits suicide to escape public punishment.

owing to her Ambition and Desire of Rule, that *Cartesmunda*, Queen of the ancient *Britons*, forsook her Husband and sided with the *Romans*, when they invaded his Dominions, than to the Passion she had for their General, who had promis'd her, that if he overcame by her Means, he wou'd engage the Emperor *Claudius* to permit her to reign alone?[1]—It wou'd be needless to recount the various Mischiefs which in all Ages have been acted under the Sanction of *Love*; but, methinks, the very Plurality of the Objects which some of those who lay their greatest Faults to that Passion, have pretended to admire, is a sufficient Demonstration that they are instigated only by a brutal Inclination.

'Tis a Question I have often heard disputed, whether there is a Possibility or not, of loving, to any great Degree of Passion, more than once; and the Arguments which are generally brought *Pro* and *Con* on that Subject, seem both, in my Opinion, as different from Nature as those I have endeavour'd to refute.—And I think the very explaining what the Quality of *Love* is, may also serve for an Answer to these Cavalists,[2] for if it takes Possession of a Soul compos'd of Constancy, the Affection will be so too, if of one irresolute and changeable, the Passion must be the same. There are others too, who pretend to fix a Time for Loving; some will have it to be at one Age, some at another. I have heard many with a great deal of Confidence affirm, that there is no such Thing as being sincerely touch'd with that Passion, but at the Time when we are just beginning to know what it is the Name of it implies; but I never hear any Discourse of this Kind, without believing that the Person who makes it, is yet to learn the Nature of the Thing he pretends to define.—Had this Passion, like the Planets, a settled Hour for reigning, all who take upon them the Charge of educating Youth, wou'd certainly provide against the Danger, and seclude their Pupils from the Sight of all desire-inspiring Objects, till the Season for being charm'd with them was past. I

---

[1] Cartesmunda (fl. *c.*AD 60), or Cartimandua, queen of the Brigantes, cooperated with the Roman governor Aulus Plautius after the invasion of the emperor Claudius, *c.*43; she relied on Roman support during her wars of the 60s against her husband, Venutius. Her reputation was further tarnished by her divorce from Venutius and her tryst with his armor-bearer, Vellocatus. Tate mentions her in *A Present for the Ladies*, 76.

[2] Disputants.

have somewhere read a Story of a *Persian* Monarch, who by his Conduct appears to have been of this Opinion.[1]

This Prince had for many Years no Issue, and being extremely desirous to have an Heir of his own Body, on his earnest Supplications to the gods, at last he obtain'd his wishes in the Birth of a Son; so unexpected a Blessing made him more than ordinary Sollicitous for the Education of the Child, and his future Fortunes; and having sent to the Astrologers for an exact Calculation of his Nativity, they return'd him Answer, That he must beware of *Love*. The King imagining there was no Possibility of being overcome by that Passion but in Youth, order'd a Cell to be cut in a deep Rock, where he was immur'd till the Age of 20; in all these Years being secluded from the Light either of Sun or Moon, or any Part of this great and beautiful Creation, but an old Tutor who continu'd constantly with him, instructing him in all the Liberal Sciences,[2] and presenting to him those necessary Supports of Life, without which he cou'd not subsist, and which were convey'd through a Hole, the young Prince not being permitted to see even any of the Attendants who brought him either Food or Rayment.[3] Among the Number of those Precepts the Learn'd Tutor endeavour'd to infuse in him, was to take Care of *Love*, and to have an Aversion for the Female Sex in general, making him believe that they were all Fiends, and permitted by Heaven to wander up and down the Earth, only to try the Constancy of Man; that those who yielded to the sweet Temptations of their Tongues and Eyes, were certain of Misery, but those who cou'd resist the sweet Temptation, were sure to obtain Happiness and Glory. The Time being expir'd which put an End to his Father's Apprehensions, he was allow'd to come into open Day. They brought before him a Dog, a Horse, a Lion, with several other Creatures, of which he had been told, but knew not how to distinguish them; He express'd some Pleasure at the Sight of Objects so strange to him, and

---

[1]   The subsequent passage is adapted from Tate, *A Present for the Ladies*, 5–7; see Appendix C.

[2]   Historically, grammar, logic, rhetoric, arithmetic, geometry, music, and astronomy; more broadly, the curriculum required properly to educate a gentleman.

[3]   Clothing.

asking their several Names, suffer'd them to be remov'd without any further Notice; they likewise show'd him Gold, Silver and Jewels of various Kinds, which he survey'd with as little Regard; The King at length commanded certain Virgins richly attir'd, and of the most exquisite Beauty, to come into his Presence, whom he no sooner beheld, but with a strange Alacrity and Transport[1] in his Countenance and Voice, he demanded what kind of Creatures they were, by what Names they were call'd, and to what Use created. His Tutor immediately reply'd, *These are those evil Spirits of whom I have so often warn'd you, the great Seducers and Destroyers of Mankind.* To which the Prince warmly made Answer, *If you have Angels then make much of them your self, good Tutor, but give me the Society of these pretty Devils.*

My Author gives no farther Account, but 'tis highly probable, if the Story be Fact, that the King was disappointed in his Aim, and convinc'd that *Love* is not confin'd to Years.

I confess, indeed, that in Youth, when the Spirits are just beginning to exert themselves, and Judgment has not well fix'd its Empire in the Mind, the Heart with greater Readiness receives the Impression of any Passion, than afterwards; But then it is no more than a fleeting Idea, and liable to be banish'd thence by the next pleasing Image.—We are generally of Age to possess an Estate, before we are of Age to know how to make the best Use of it; much less to guide our Passion in the Choice of an Object worthy of inspiring it; which Error afterward discover'd, brings on Shame and Repentance, and soon we nauseat[2] what before we lov'd. A Person of my Acquaintance, who is accounted to have a perfect understanding in Nature, says, that *a young Heart is like Tinder, apt to take Fire from the least Spark of Beauty*; but also maintains, *that it is a Flame extinguish'd with the same Ease with which 'twas kindled, whereas that of riper Years, if it less fiercely blazes, has a more lasting and substantial Glow.* Nothing can be more certain, than that till Experience has made us wise, we know as little of ourselves as of the World.—How many Examples do we daily see of young People in *Love*, who have sworn not to survive

---

[1] Cheerfulness and ecstasy.
[2] Are nauseated by.

the Loss of Hope; on every little Quarrel or Jealousy of the darling Object, are ready to lay violent Hands on their own Lives; and by their extravagant Behaviour make one, indeed, believe their Condition the most truly pityable that can be; yet in a very little Time after, perhaps without any Provocation, they take a sudden disgust, avoid the Sight of what they lately with so much Eagerness pursu'd, and seem to wonder at the Infatuation they were guilty of, in admiring what now they look on disagreeable. I shall instance one, which tho' of an Adventure extraordinary enough in its Kind, to make it be taken for fabulous, I can aver for Truth, having been an Eye-witness of some of the most remarkable Passages.

Sophiana, a Maid of Quality, not exceeding 16 Years of Age, and equal in Beauty to any that yet grac'd the Ring, or Circle,[1] was address'd in the most passionate Manner by *Aranthus*, a Gentleman of Birth and Fortune, which, join'd to the Charms of his Person, than which, few Men have more; made her in a little Time listen to him with Pleasure, and soon after become enamour'd of him to that violent Degree, that she cou'd not conceal it from the View of the whole World; she grew the most restless Creature that ever was, she cou'd think of nothing but *Aranthus*, talk of nothing but *Aranthus*, in whatever Company she was, his Name was perpetually in her Mouth; his Wit, his Beauty, his good humour, were the eternal Themes with which she entertain'd every Body that came to visit her; He seem'd so wholly to engross her Soul, that she not only forgot that Decorum due to her Sex and Birth, but also grew Remiss in her Devoirs[2] to those, whom it was her Interest as well as Duty to make it her Study to oblige; for having no Dowry but her personal Perfections, and the Honour of being descended from a Heroe, whose brave Actions have fill'd all *Europe* with his Fame; Her whole Dependance was on the Favour of a certain great and good Lady, to whose Care she was recommended.—She had behav'd with such Prudence and Sweetness of Disposition, that she justly became extremely dear to her Patroness, till her unhappy

---

[1] The Ring was the popular equestrian pathway in Hyde Park, London; the circle, or 'dress circle', is the lower gallery in a theater, with the most expensive seats.

[2] Acts of respect.

Passion for the too lovely *Aranthus* made her deaf to all Considerations but those of pleasing him, and chang'd her Conduct to the very Reverse of what it had been. When most her Company or Attendance was expected in the Drawing-room, she was shut up in her closet with him, from whom she wou'd by no Means be persuaded to remove, tho' frequently sent to; and when gently admonish'd[1] of her Error, answer'd in so peevish and disobliging a Manner, that she forfeited all the Respect which had before been paid her; yet still was she regardless, still insensible of every Thing but the Dictates of her ungovernable Passion. Blest in her Amour, Interest and Fame were of no Moment to her Peace, and she proceeded to such extravagant Lengths, and at last grew guilty of such Irregularities, and indeed, indecent Fondnesses, even in Publick, that she fell into the utmost Contempt, and her Society no longer coveted but shun'd. Lost in the Esteem of the rest of the World, she soon became cheap also in the Opinion of him for whose Sake she had suffer'd so unhappy a Change in her Affairs and Reputation. Either satiated with her too easy yielding, or charm'd with the more prevailing Graces of some new Object, which of them is uncertain, but the Ardors he had profess'd for *Sophiana* cool'd on a sudden; he visited her but seldom, and when he did, appear'd far different from what he was, Desire no more play'd in his languid[2] Eyes, nor did his Tongue press for repeated Confirmations of her Love. Tho' little of Discretion this unhappy Beauty had to boast, she had however an infinite deal of Wit and Penetration, whenever she pleas'd to make use of it; and these Faculties render'd her the more wretched, by an immediate and poynant[3] Intelligence of the Misfortune her Inadvertency had brought upon her. She accus'd him of Ingratitude and Unconstancy, represented to him the Disadvantages which his Acquaintance had been to her, and finding that all she said had but little Effect, and that every Day rather increased his Indifference, than flatter'd her with any Hopes of its abating, Love and Rage burning with equal Violence in her impatient Soul, made her

---

[1] Made mindful.
[2] Apathetic.
[3] That is, poignant; emotionally painful.

proceed to Threatnings and Revilings,[1] she reproach'd him in the most bitter Terms, and call'd him every Name of Ill, that her wild Passion cou'd invent, vowing Revenge, and that nothing but his Life should expiate for his broken Faith. Nothing cou'd be more pleasing to a Man who desir'd to break off, than such a Behaviour. He had now a Pretence for quarelling, which the Continuance of her Softness never wou'd have given him; and tho' he very well knew that to the Extremity of her Love, the Extremity of the Indignation she profest, was owing, yet he took the Opportunity it afforded of telling her, that he was satisfy'd she grew weary of his Addresses, and that he had so great a Regard to her Happiness, as no more to disturb her with the Sight of a Person she no longer lov'd.—Having said this, he took a hasty Leave, nor wou'd turn back, tho' her Woman ran after him to the Door entreating him to return, assuring him that her Mistress was fallen into a Swoon. The Force of so many different Emotions had indeed thrown this wretched Lady into the Condition her Servant had told him; She was not but with great Difficulty recover'd, and when with much ado she regain'd the Use of Speech and Motion, it was but to exercise the one in Curses and Exclamations of the most terrible Despair, and the other to endeavour to revenge on herself the Injuries she had receiv'd from *Aranthus*, had she not been withheld by Force, she had certainly in this Tempest of her Thoughts laid violent Hands on her own Life; but by Degrees being brought to a something greater Degree of Moderation, she contented herself with venting the Anguish of her Soul in writing to him; but in what Terms she shou'd do it, she was for a long Time consulting, sometimes she thought it best to attempt to sooth him by renew'd Endearments, and supplicate his Return; at others, she disdain'd the mean[2] Submission, and was determin'd to have Recourse only to Upbraidings.—This Irresolution occasion'd a great waste of Tears and Paper, and for many Hours the Conflict between Love and Pride made her become a Chaos of Confusion, yielding to both by Turns, yet giving the absolute Victory to neither.—At last, she suffer'd her Pen to reveal the Force of both,

---

[1] Abusive speech.
[2] Groveling.

accordingly as the Dictates of each prevail'd that Moment above the other. The Contents of her Letter were as follows.

To the Most Ungrateful, Most Perjur'd,
but Most Lovely of his Sex, The Ruinous *Aranthus*.

WHAT can be more plain, than that my Life being no longer of any Moment to your Happiness, you wish my Death to be eas'd of my Reproach! Nothing else cou'd have induc'd you to treat me in so barbarous a Manner.—But I am now convinc'd that Grief has not the Power to kill, nor will I, wretched as I am, obey the Dictates of that, or my Despair, so far, as to seek in the Grave, that Quiet which is deny'd me here; No, tho' lost to every Hope of my desiring Soul,—tho' more miserable, more accurst, than Words can find a Name for; yet I will live a lasting Monument of thy Ingratitude,—a Dagger or a Bowel of Poyson wou'd put a Period[1] to the Anguish I sustain, and to which all that is represented of Futurity is but mean, but soon the Memory of my Wrongs wou'd be forgotten, and with myself buried in Oblivion.—O! grant me then, good Heaven, a Length of Days, while I unceasing persecute the false, the base *Aranthus*, that vile Betrayer of my Youth and Innocence.—Good God, cou'd I have believ'd I ever shou'd have Cause to call you so! Had any other Kind of Misery befallen me I cou'd have born it; had I been struck blind, or lame, had Poverty with all its worst Effects overtook me, pity'd by *Thee*, those Ills had lost their Name, nor cost my Soul one pang.—*Fate*, but through *Thee*, had not the Power to reach me.—O why then dost thou use me so?—Why take a barbarous Pleasure in tormenting the Heart that doats upon thee?—even savage Creatures, and Brutes[2] the fiercest, and most untameable by Nature, are fond and gentle where they are belov'd; all but Man, the Lord of the Creation, discover some Sparks of Gratitude in their Composition; Fool that I was, and too assisting to my own Undoing, I thought thy Temper different from the rest of thy deceiving Sex, and as infinitely surpassing them in the Virtues of the Mind, as, still I must acknowledge

---

[1]   End.
[2]   Animals.

thee, in bodily Perfections.—O' what wou'd I give to be still thus deluded, to hear thy soft enchanting Tongue protest eternal Truth, to taste the balmy Sighs of Pain-mix'd Pleasure, and feel the Tremblings of unsated Love shooting through every Pulse, and panting in thy Heart.—But whither am I going? to what a shameful Confession does my uncautious Tenderness transport me!—Confusion on the guilty Scene of ruinous Delight—'tis hateful to Remembrance, and I cou'd curse my self and thee, and even those Principles which told me I did Ill, yet were too weak to hinder me from sinning.—If Love be criminal, how monstruously guilty have I been!—But wherefore do I question it? O too, too sure it is, and Heaven to revenge the Preference my sacrilegious Thoughts gave thee, thus punishes me with thy Infidelity.—What will become of me? my Brain is rack'd to Madness, wild Horror reigns through every Part, and all my Soul is Hell! O thou most lov'd, and yet most hated of Mankind! either return and once more bless me with renew'd Affection, or be more cruelly kind, and do that for me which I want Resolution to do for my self, put an End to the Wretchedness thou hast occasion'd, and send from the World,

The Miserable

Sophiana.

P.S. If the Incoherence and Distraction[1] of these Lines make you think the Writer of them incapable of Conversation, be so just to your own Merits and my Passion as to know, that as my Disorders spring only from your want of Tenderness, they wou'd vanish on the least Appearance of recovering it.—Let me know what I am to expect, for to whatever Extreams my Rage may have transported me, contrary to the natural Softness of my Soul, I own I cannot, will not live without you.

The Messenger by whom this was sent, return'd immediately with an Account, that *Aranthus* was gone out of Town, nor was expected home in some Days. *Sophiana's* Impatience wou'd not permit her to remain unsatisfy'd so long, she therefore order'd the same Person whom she had entrusted with the Care of the Letter,

---

[1]   Derangement.

to make a strict Enquiry to what Place he was gone, and follow him with all Speed.—The Contents of that Letter, said she, are of the greatest Consequence, and on his Answer depends more than my Life.—I charge you to overtake him wheresoever he be gone, take Post, no Money shall be wanting to defray the Charges of thy Journey, nor to reward thy Diligence. The Fellow thus encourag'd, assur'd her he wou'd travel round the World rather than return without seeing him: And having receiv'd from her an Earnest of his future Gratification, departed to make good his Promise.

He was no sooner gone, than she began to make Reflections on what she had written, and soothing more and more, as Hope grew stronger in her, repented the Severity of some of the Expressions she had made use of, and wish'd she had testify'd her Desires of a Reconciliation in Terms more tender.—Sometimes she flatter'd herself with the Imagination he had but affected an Indifference to make a Trial of her Temper; at others, she believ'd his Heart entirely estrang'd, and that all she said wou'd be ineffectual to touch him with any Regret.—There is nothing more uneasy to be born than Suspence, and hers was of that restless Nature, that it was with all the Difficulty in the World she was persuaded either to eat or sleep till the Return of her Messenger; which she doubted not but wou'd bring the Certainty of her yet undetermin'd Fate. Sleep was, however, more favourable to her than she expected, and after passing some Hours in disturb'd Meditations, her Disquiets at last gave Place to the god of Silence and Repose, who not only gave a Cessation to the Torments she had endur'd while waking, but also entertain'd Imagination with some Ideas, which cou'd not be but pleasing in a superlative Degree, since they inspir'd her to write the following Description.

The DREAM.

WHY did the Day its hateful Beams disclose?
Or, why wak'd I so soon, so soon arose?
Kind Sleep presented me immortal Joys,
And brought *Aranthus* to my ravish'd[1] Eyes.

---

[1] Enraptured.

Close to my Bed the faithless Wand'rer came,
And did a thousand sweet Excuses frame.
To his cold Heart the far-fled god return'd,
Repentant seem'd, and his long Absence mourn'd.
I, fill'd with Ecstasies too high, too great!
For Eloquence itself to imitate,
With silent Raptures snatch'd him to my Breast,
And fierce Embraces more than Words exprest!
Such Transports ours, as when from Sight remov'd
The *Paphian* Queen with soft *Adonis* prov'd.[1]
O' that each Thought cou'd the like Vision frame,
Sure I wak'd then, and now, 'tis now I dream!
Why must my Cares, my racking Tortures stay,
And why my Joys fleet with the Night away?
Alas! how weak's my Judgment, and how poor
Who call Death Sleep, but on a longer Score,
For I did ne'er so truly live before.
Oh that the Night cou'd have for ever stay'd,
Oh too, too soon its fading Glories fled;
When, lovelier far than was the fairest Day,
The Shield of Night to painted Rays gave Way,
And on her Wings bore her and all my Joys away!

Between the Waverings of Hope and Fear did her poor Heart suffer itself to be tormented, till the Return of the Messenger she had sent to *Aranthus*, brought her the sad Certainty of her Fate. That cruel Man receiv'd her Letter with a Countenance which testify'd how little it was welcome: And after having read it slightly over, told the Person who deliver'd it to him, That it requir'd no Answer. But notwithstanding, the Fellow, faithful to his Trust, entreated him to write, and was so earnest in pressing him to do so, that the other with an angry Voice, bad him begone, or he wou'd cause him to be us'd in the Manner his Impertinence deserv'd. Finding it impossible to prevail on him, he came back

---

[1] Aphrodite, a goddess of erotic love who had many worshippers in the Cypriot city of Paphos, fell in love with the beautiful youth Adonis. Haywood invokes the version of the myth in which Persephone angers Aphrodite by keeping the boy from her.

with a heavy Heart to *Sophiana*, giving her a full Account of the ill Success of his Journey. Convinc'd now, that there was no retrieving this inconstant Heart, one wou'd have thought she shou'd rather have endeavour'd to forget him, than make herself more wretched by continuing Efforts, which her own Reason had told her were but vain: Yet so little was she capable, in this Distraction of Mind, to judge what it was she ought, or was best for her to do, that wholly abandoning herself to the wild Sallies of her ungovernable Passion, she resolv'd to see him, let the Consequence be what it wou'd:—To that End she hir'd a Coach and Six,[1] to carry her to the Place where he was; and partly by Entreaties, and partly by Gifts, having persuaded the same Man to go with her, stopp'd a little short of the House, and sent him to *Aranthus*, while she waited in the Coach the Success of this second Billet.

To the detestably Ungrateful Aranthus.

IF there be nothing to be fear'd from the Resentment of an injur'd Woman, do you not tremble when you reflect on the Indignities you have offer'd Heaven, by whom you have a thousand Times so falsly sworn eternal Love, eternal Truth to me?—Thou Monster of Deceit, Hypocrisy, Arrogance, Cruelty, and every horrid Crime which Justice ever punish'd with severest Vengeance! Was it not enough to ruin and forsake me, Devil-like to be at once the Abettor and Tormentor of my Guilt, but you must also insult and glory in it.—To refuse an Answer to my Letter, and affront me in the Person of my Messenger, is such a Compound of Impudence, Ingratitude and Rudeness, as nothing but *Aranthus* cou'd be guilty of.—But think not I will tamely bear it, nor that you shall for ever skreen your self from the Reproaches of my Tongue and Eyes.—I am determin'd to see you, and am come thus far to meet you; I will now be satisfy'd with no Answer but from your own Mouth. Come to me immediately, or I will order the Coach to drive to the House where you are.—Your dissembled[2] Tenderness made me throw off all Considerations of Interest and Virtue, and your Barbarity has

---

[1] Large carriage, drawn by six horses.
[2] Pretended.

since made me deaf to all that Shame can urge, I have now no Sense of any Thing but my Rage, and those unexampl'd Wrongs which have occasion'd it, and render'd me incapable of subscribing my self by any other Name than,

The Distracted and Undone
Sophiana.

The Messenger not coming back in a considerable Time, made her imagine that either *Aranthus* was not to be found, or else that he detain'd him for some Reason she cou'd not approve, and following the Dictates of her Impatience, was just about ordering the Coachman to go to the House, when his Return prevented her: But instead of *Aranthus*, he deliver'd her a Letter from him, in which she found these Lines:

To Sophiana.

YOUR late Behaviour leaves me no other Room to doubt if you are in Reality distracted or not, but your confessing that you are so, which Persons in that Condition seldom believe themselves.—I regard the Wildness of your Accusations no farther, than to be sorry for the Misfortunes to which your own ill Conduct, not my Inconstancy has reduc'd you. I dare appeal to all who make a Jest of our Amour, whither they owe the Information of it to me or to your self.—'Tis a great Pity, that a Lady, in other Things deserving enough of Esteem, shou'd forfeit all the Advantages which Nature gave her, by giving Way to Passions so unbecoming, and am still so much your Friend, as to advise you to bridle them for the Future, by which Means, perhaps, you may retrieve your Character in the World.—As for complying with your Request of seeing you, I think it altogether improper, especially at this Time: Here are a great deal of Company, and among them the suspicious *Marramour*, who wou'd not fail to send a Spy after me, if I shou'd go out of the House. Believe me, it is your own Reputation and Peace of Mind that I chiefly consult, when I endeavour to persuade you to an entire Forgetfulness of him, who, tho' he ceases to entitle himself your Lover, will always be

Your real Well-wisher
Aranthus.

P.S. After what I have said I hope you will not think of coming any farther, which wou'd not only more expose what is already too much the publick Chat, but also oblige me, in the Vindication of my own Honour to treat you, in a Manner vastly different from what I desire to do. Farewell. Learn if possible to be discreet.

With what Emotions the Breast of this unhappy Lady was agitated at reading Admonitions[1] so insolent in him who gave them, I need not inform any who will give themselves the Trouble to consider Nature even in the meanest Person, much more how it must operate in a Woman of *Sophiana's* Birth and Quality, and who had been accustom'd to receive only Admiration. She wou'd have had as little Regard to his Menaces, as he had testify'd for her Complaints, had it not been for the Fear of being seen by *Marramour*, she had made no Scruple of going to the House, and venting before all the Company some Part of the Fury she was possest of: Nor wou'd she perhaps have been restrain'd by his telling her that Lady was there, if the Messenger who she had sent with her Letter, and had waited in the Hall for his Answer, had not confirm'd the Truth of what he wrote, and assur'd her that he saw her Servants, whom he knew by their Livery.[2] *Marramour* was a Person who hated *Sophiana* on the Account of her superior Beauty, and being highly in Favour with that great Lady, on whom both had their Dependance, this unhappy Victim of Desire, obey'd so far the Caution of her ungrateful Lover, as not to give her Enemy so considerable an Advantage over her, as the Opportunity of reporting such an Adventure wou'd have been: And without much struggling with the opposing Passions of her Soul, at last prevail'd on herself to give Command to the Coachman to turn back. In her Return from this unlucky Progress, she had not only the Disorders of her mind to cope with: it being at a Season of the Year when the Roads are generally bad, the Coach overturn'd, and she receiv'd a Hurt in her Right-Arm in the Fall, which for several Days

---

[1]   Warnings.
[2]   Uniforms.

confin'd her to her Bed. This Accident, tho' it prevented her from writing any more Epistles to *Aranthus*, did not keep her from sending Messages to him, assoon as she heard he was in Town; to all which he reply'd in the same Manner as he had done before, and at length threaten'd the Person who brought them with so much Severity, that not all she cou'd say or promise, cou'd engage him to go any more.

Resolute to obtain the unprofitable Satisfaction of upbraiding, in Person, the Author of her Ruin, the Moment she found herself in a Condition, she went herself to visit him at his own House; being told by his Servant that he was not at home, she went a second Time, and at an Hour in which she very well knew he was not us'd to be abroad, but meeting the same Answer as before, she doubted not but he had order'd himself to be deny'd, and no longer being able to preserve the least Regard to Decorum, wou'd have prest into the House in Search of him, which the Servant opposing, confirm'd her in what she had conjectur'd, and kindled such a Wild-fire of Indignation in her Soul, that she flew upon the Fellow, and continu'd cursing and reviling him, spitting in his Face and buffeting him with her Hands, till some other of his fellow Servants hearing a Noise, came to his Assistance: He not in the least attempting to defend himself, either prevented from doing so by Surprize, or the Pity he had for her, as believing she had too just a Cause for Desperation. It was with some Difficulty the enrag'd Amazon[1] was oblig'd to quit her Hold, and put by Force into her Chair. And tho' it was with all the Shame imaginable that her cooler Thoughts, when she came home, presented to her the Idea[2] of her Behaviour, yet it did not at all abate the Resolution she had taken of seeing *Aranthus* some Way or other: And beginning to think it wou'd be impossible in her own Shape, it came into her Head to endeavour it in Disguise. Her ill Genius bent to compleat her Miseries, furnish'd Invention with a Stratagem,[3] which she no sooner thought on, than she put in Practice; she provided herself of a Habit much the same as those Women wear

---

[1]   Female warrior.
[2]   Standard of perfection.
[3]   Scheme.

who have no better Business than to frequent Butchers Stalls, and carry Meat to the Houses of those that buy it; her small and delicate Feet seem'd now lost in a Pair of great flat-sol'd Shoes,— instead of a Hoop[1] 4 Yards in Circumference, and a long Train, in whose capacious Sweep *Cupid* her little Lap-dog, was us'd to fold himself, a short and scanty Petticoat of red Serge,[2] but ill defended her shivering Limbs from the cold nipping Air;—her fine Hair tuck'd up under a coarse Doulass Cap[3] and great Straw-Hat, over-shadowing the Majesty of her Awe-inspiring Brow; how little probable was it, that any who beheld her should distinguish *Sophiana*, the Court Bell, and general Toast of all the Young and Gay.

Thus equipt, she went on Foot to the Street where the cruel *Aranthus* had his Habitation, and sitting down on the Threshold of a Door just opposite to his, where having the Opportunity of observing all that pass'd, she waited not long before she saw his Chair[4] come to the Door, into which he soon went, the Street being pretty narrow, she heard to what Place the Men were order'd to carry him, and follow'd with as much hast as her Legs, little accustom'd to travelling in that Manner, wou'd bear her.

The Sight of him giving a fresh Alarm to her Indignation, and all her Spirits being hurried between Love and Rage, she had no Leisure to reflect on what might probably be the Catastrophe of so wild an Undertaking, but wholly depending on her Disguise, she went boldly to the House which he had just enter'd, and knocking at the Door, desir'd to be brought to the Presence of *Aranthus*. The Person to whom she made this Demand, seem'd strangely surpriz'd that a Creature of her Appearance cou'd have any Business with one of *Aranthus*'s Rank, which was not to be communicated to him by a third Person, and after a little Hesitation, told her, that he would call a Servant of that Gentleman's, to whom she might impart what she had to say. No, answer'd she, you may spare your self that Trouble, the Affair which brings me here is not proper to be heard by any Ears but his, nor

---

1   Hoop skirt.
2   Skirt (not, here, underskirt) made of an inexpensive woolen fabric.
3   A cap of dowlas, a coarse linen.
4   One-seated vehicle for hire, carried on poles.

will I reveal it to any other. In Spite of the mean Habit[1] she had on, there was something so graceful and commanding in the Accent of her Voice, and the Air with which she deliver'd these Words, that the Fellow cou'd not keep himself from being influenc'd by them, and tho' half asham'd, and fearful of incurring the Displeasure of *Aranthus* by obeying her, yet he did so, and at the same Time told him, that he could not help believing there was something very extraordinary both in the Adventure and the Woman: The ready Apprehension of *Aranthus*, join'd to the Knowledge of her Despair, immediately made him guess at the Truth, and happening to be in a low Parlour next the Street, he look'd through the Window, and alter'd as she was by her Dress, confirm'd himself that his Conjectures were true, and that it was indeed *Sophiana* who had Recourse to this Stratagem to obtain an Interview; but that barbarous Man resolving to disappoint her, told the Fellow, who acquainted him with her Desire of speaking to him, that she was only a poor lunatick Wretch, who was accustom'd to follow him from Place to Place, in Hope of getting Money from him, and bad him turn her from the Door, and if she should grow troublesome or noisy, as, said he, sometimes either her Distemper[2] or her Impudence will make her, send for an Officer of Justice, and let her be taken away by Force and dispos'd of according to his Pleasure. The Servant who made no Doubt of the Truth of this, return'd to her, and at first in gentle Terms, desir'd she would leave the Door, but she refusing to do so, and repeating her Demands of speaking to *Aranthus*, he began to grow more rude: What, said he, we should have a fine Time of it, if such as you should be admitted to Gentlemen.—You look, indeed, as if you were a Companion for *Aranthus*. Whatever I am, cry'd she, ready to burst with Passion, I must and will see him, nor shall you nor all the World prevent me. In speaking these Words, she push'd into the Entry so suddenly, that the Fellow had not Time to oppose her; and had proceeded farther, if he had not call'd to some others of the Family, bawling out as loud as he was able, that there was a Mad-woman got into the House: The Passage, at this Exclamation,

---

[1] Outfit.
[2] Illness.

was immediately fill'd with Persons of both Sexes, who came running not only out of several Rooms in the House, but also from the Street, the Door being still open. Every Body being possest, from the Fellows Words, that she was a Lunatick, join'd a Helping-hand to force her from the Place, which she too weak, alas! to struggle with such boisterous Opposers, was soon compell'd to quit.—The wild Confusion which appear'd in her Face at such inhuman Treatment, confirmed what *Aranthus* had said of her Condition: And the Boys in the Street having got the Hint, cry'd out, There was a Mad-woman: And before she could get from the Door, there was a Mob about her, through which it was as impossible for her to pass, as she had found it to get Shelter in that House from whose inhospitable Gate she had lately been thrust.—One pluck'd her by the Arm, another by the Petticoats, a third pull'd off her Hat, and her Hair falling about her Shoulders, exposed her lovely Face to the View of this unpolish'd Crowd, who, instead of paying that Respect her Beauty merited, had a thousand scurrillous[1] Jests upon her, and the imaginary Disease which had subjected her to their Derision.[2] Nothing is more strange, than that the Agonies of her Mind, join'd with this ill Usage, had not, indeed, deprived her of her Senses, but she seemed in this Distress, which she had brought upon herself, to retain more Presence of Mind than she had sometimes been able to do in Cases infinitely less shocking.—She answered the Scoffs with which they hooted her along, only with Entreaties that they would let her go; but finding that all she could say to that End, was vain, and not knowing where to take Shelter from the present Persecution, which would not more expose her for the Future, when her Misfortune should be blazed abroad, she took a sudden Thought, of making towards the Water-side, and throwing herself in, before her rude[3] Attendants could have any Suspicion of her Design; beginning now to have a true Sense of the contemptible Estate to which her Folly had reduced her, and judging it better to dye concealed in this Disguise, than have it known what she had suffered while she

---

[1] Obscene.
[2] Mockery.
[3] Rough.

wore it. Pursuant to this Design, she turned down a Street which led to the River, and which having a little low Wall at the End of it, she fancied she could easily throw herself over, and become past all Relief or Pity, before any Boats could reach her: But Heaven was pleased to disappoint her Purpose; as she was passing by, a Gentleman, who had that Moment alighted from his Chariot,[1] and was going into a Shop, stop'd at the Door seeing a Crowd of People, (for still as she went her promiscuous Equipage[2] encreased) he no sooner cast his Eyes upon her than he knew her, in Spite of all the Disadvantages of Dress and Confusion. The Surprize he was in, did not hinder him from doing what was proper: He presently found from what Supposition the Insults with which they treated her proceeded, tho' he could not guess for what Reason she had made herself subject to it, and stepping in among the thickest of[3] this disorderly Rout, who all gave back at the Appearance of a Gentleman, I know you, Madam, said he, tho' I will not seem to do so at present,—but run, continued he, into that House, I will engage you shall have Protection there. As he spoke this, he pointed to the Door where the Chariot waited, and which had just before been open'd to give him Entrance: As much determined as she had been on Death, this seemed of the two a better rescue, and without much Hesitation she took his Advice; who no sooner saw her enter than he followed, and shutting the Door after him, deprived those cruel Insulters over her Misery, of their barbarous Pleasure, and also prevented the Persons belonging to that House where she had flown for Shelter, from treating her with any Rudeness, as else 'tis probable they would have done, in the Condition and Appearance she then was. I will not ask, said he to her, the Meaning of so strange a Metamorphosis, as that I see in you, it may perhaps encrease your Disorders; I shall therefore testify more of the Friend to convoy you to some Place, where you may throw off a Shape so unworthy of *Sophiana*, and recover at once your former Form and Composure of Mind. O never, cried she, bursting into Tears, never must I hope to enjoy the latter,—Eternal Shame!—Eternal Horror!

---

1   Lightweight four-wheeled carriage with seats in the back only.
2   Disorderly mob.
3   In the midst of.

are only now my Portion.[1]—But since your generous Care extends to such a Wretch, uncapable even of acknowledging, as I ought, the Obligation, I beg that you will order a Hackney-coach,[2] my own Apartment is the only Place where I can indulge the Anguish of my Soul, and give the labouring Passions Vent. There was sufficient Reason for him to believe she was not at this Time fit for Conversation, and therefore instead of replying to what she said, called to his Servant, that her Commands might be obey'd, which being done, he asked if she wou'd permit him to attend her; but she desired he would omit that Ceremony, and order'd the Coach to drive home, where let us leave her, at present the most wretched and forlorn Creature on Earth, and see to whom it was she was indebted for the Deliverance from that publick Shame she had subjected herself to bear.

His Name is *Martius*, a Man of Birth and Fortune, and a very great Courtier. He had for a long Time been inspired with a very violent Passion for the lovely *Sophiana*, but her known Affection for *Aranthus* prevented him from declaring it: He made no doubt but her Despair proceeded from his Ingratitude, and blessed his own good Stars for making him the Instrument of delivering her from the Hands of her Persecutors. He was not without Hopes, That that Service, joined with the other's Unkindness, might work an Alteration in her Sentiments to the Advantage of his Desires, and resolved to make her sensible of them the first Opportunity.

The next Day he went to visit her, under the Pretence of enquiring after her Health: The Fatigue she had endured had added to the Agonies of her Mind so great a Disorder of Body, that she was little fit for Company; the Obligation she had to him, however, would not suffer her to let him depart without seeing him; she ordered he should be admitted, but her Indisposition making the Ceremony of entertaining him perceivably Troublesome, he staid but a short Time, after having obtained her Leave to wait on her when Company would be less disagreeable.

He was happy enough in the several Visits he afterwards made her, as to perceive that every Time he came, her Inquietudes were

---

[1] Fate.
[2] Four-wheeled, six-seated vehicle for hire.

visibly abated; the Lustre of her Eyes again broke forth with usual Brightness, and her Cheeks resum'd their Bloom. Tho' he had never yet absolutely declared himself her Lover, he had given her many Hints to think that he was so; and the easy Freedom with which she continued to receive him, was a sufficient Encouragement for him to explain what 'twas he aim'd at in his Assiduities;[1] and finding her alone one Evening, and in a perfect good Humour, he no longer deferred revealing his Passion; to which, if she listened not with a visible Satisfaction, yet it was with an Air, which denoted neither Anger nor Dislike; in fine, her Behaviour was such, as made him not greatly doubt if he should in Time be able to triumph over all the Tenderness she bore *Aranthus:* And soon did he find Matter for his growing Hopes to feed upon, the more he spoke of his Desires, the less she seemed to be offended with them, was never weary of his Conversation, nor ever seemed displeased, but when Business, or a prior Engagement with some other Company obliged him to make his Stay but short.

In the mean Time the whole Adventure of *Sophiana's* Misfortune came to the Ears of that great Lady, on whom she had her Dependance, who having a real Tenderness for her, sent for her, and having gently reproved her ill Conduct, told her, that she thought it highly improper she should continue in a Place, where nothing was at the Present talk'd on so much as her Mismanagement, and that she had provided for her in the Country, at the House of a Person, who would study to oblige her, and where she should want nothing to make her Retirement as pleasant as possible.—Time, said this generous Benefactoress, wears every Thing away; in a few Years the Memory of the whole Affair will be lost, Absence will also contribute to the Cure of your unhappy Passion, and we may have you again, both with more Ease to your self, and less Disadvantage to the Reputation of those who continue to profess a Friendship for you. Nothing could be more shocking to the Desires of *Sophiana* than this Proposal; she made use of all the Arguments she was Mistress of, to persuade the other, that there was no Occasion for this voluntary Banishment;

---

[1] Perseverance.

but the other, who imagined her Unwillingness to quit the Town, was because *Aranthus* was in it, and believing she would render herself yet more ridiculous on his Account, than yet she had done, if possible, was not to be prevail'd with to recede from the Resolution she had taken, of sending her away; and express'd herself on that Head in so positive a Manner, that as averse as *Sophiana* was, she durst make no further Objections, and took her Leave, with a Promise to comply, assoon as Things could be got ready for her Departure.

Now did this unhappy Creature think herself more undone than ever, the Agonies she sustained on the first Discovery of *Aranthus*'s Cruelty and Falshood, were not more terrible, than those which seiz'd her Soul at the Thoughts of being separated from *Martius*; she was now a second Time become the Slave of Love, and no less devoted to this, than to her former Passion: She had never yet reveal'd, but now no longer able to forbear, the Moment she came home, she sat down to her Escritore[1] and writ him the following Billet.

To the most Worthy Martius.

IF the Passion you have for me be in any degree suitable to your Professions, what I have to acquaint you with, will fill your Breast with the most poynant Anguish.—O *Martius!* I must shortly lose the Power of rewarding your generous Affection, and never will you see the unfortunate *Sophiana* more.—perhaps my Eyes may have betray'd what now my Grief sufficiently reveals; and you are not, till now, ignorant that I have not been ungrateful to a Flame, which I believe, because I wish it, to be sincere!— But what avails, you'll say, this late Confession? the Knowledge how much I share in your Misfortune will but add to it, yet cannot I consent to quit the World without telling you, that you are the dearest Thing in it, and that to be separated from you, is the worst of Deaths to

Sophiana.

P.S. Let me see you, while Fate permits us the Power, a few Days deprives me of that Hope.

---

[1] Writing desk.

The Surprize he was in at the Receipt of this, would not allow him Patience to answer it any otherwise, than by his Presence; he flew immediately to her Lodgings, where being inform'd of the Cause of this intended Separation, he secretly rejoic'd at it, as thinking nothing could happen more favourable to his Design: Nor was he flatter'd with a fictitious Hope: On his making use of some few Arguments to back his Entreaties, she consented to be his in the Manner he desir'd, rather than remove from him: The Consequences of which were a second Blot on her Reputation, infinitely more unpardonable than the first; a total Quarrel with her Patroness, who on her refusing to leave the Town, would never see her more; and being reduced, to be oblig'd for the Means of Subsistance, to the Man on whom she would wish only to confer Favours; which last Article one would imagine, imbitter all the Sweets of Love, yet so little does she regard either that or the Censure of the World, that she means not to Aim at Secresy in any Part of the Affair between them. If Love alone can make a Woman happy, she has indeed no Reason as yet to think herself the contrary.—That Winter of Indifference and Neglect, which rarely, if ever, fails to succeed the sultry Summer of too fierce Desire in Man's unconstant Heart, is not yet arriv'd: And so felicious[1] does she think her present State, that she for ever expressing herself in Praise of the Passion which brought her to it, among many other Things of her composing on this Subject, the following Couplets fell into my Hands, which seem to be too feeling not to be natural.

On LOVE.

LET surly Anchorites,[2] past Sense of Joy,
Their rugged Wits maliciously employ
In vile Invectives[3] on the Heav'nly Boy;
But I, Oh Love! thy zealous Votary am:
And boldly own, nay glory in the Flame!

---

[1] Fortunate.
[2] Hermits.
[3] Denunciations.

Thou only canst on Earth true Joys dispence,
Lighten the Mind and elevate the Sense:
The most exalted Bliss the Soul can prove
Is in thy transport found, Almighty Love!
When Fates opposing Storms our Labours meet
This softens all and makes our Toyls seem sweet:
In this successful, we may dare the rest,
Who thrives in Love can be by Nought opprest.
Some will Reflections on thy Godhead[1] make,
And tell what they have suffer'd for thy sake
Of an ungrateful Fair, whose haughty Pride
Has to their Service just Returns deny'd:
But let those Fools, for so I must esteem
Those whom thy pleasing Pains a Torment deem,
Be answer'd thus, Love is its own Reward,
And of it self can Happiness afford;
For those who in their Wish can't prosperous be
May glory in unshaken Constancy.

This Lady's Behaviour is, I think, sufficient to convince any one of the Instability of a very young Person's Affection, for tho' the Ingratitude of her former Admirer was a justifiable Reason for converting all the Love she had for him into an equal degree of Hate, yet it was none for transferring it to another Object; to have despis'd *Aranthus* wou'd have render'd her Praise-worthy, but so suddenly to become devoted to *Martius* is certainly so great a Proof of Levity[2] as nothing can excuse. 'Tis true, that there are People from whose riper Years one might expect a more Maturity of Judgment, who err in the very same Manner with *Sophiana*, but it is no Argument that because some are Inconstant in their Humour their whole Life-time, that those who are now Patterns of Stability were always so.—No, in the Dawn of Inclination, when first Desire begins to spring, there is always a kind of wandring and uncertain Fire which plays about the Heart, and blazes at the sight of every agreeable object long

---

[1]   Divine nature.
[2]   Lack of seriousness.

before it is fix'd to one, and can be call'd no more than the Harbinger[1] of real Passion: I appeal to those most fix'd in their Devoirs, if they have not felt some of the Waverings I speak of, and imagin'd themselves in Love many times before they became so in earnest. We are told by the late Mr. *Dryden* of justly celebrated Memory,[2] that

> The Cause of Love can never be assign'd,
> 'Tis in no Face, but in the Lover's Mind.

The Mind must therefore first be settled before the Passion can be so, and how long that remains unfix'd our own Experience may inform us; a Boy who is to be put out to an Apprenticeship cannot determine tho' it be left to his own Choice, what Trade to chuse, sometimes he likes one, sometimes another, and is at last oblig'd to be directed by his Parents, or the Vanity of his Inclinations wou'd be of equal Hindrance to each other, and he apply himself in Reality to none, even so it is in Love, and it wou'd be as strange to find a Person under Twenty know his own Mind in that Case, as it wou'd be shameful for one of Thirty not to do it.

I am not however of that Opinion, that a Person can Love but once. Death may deprive us of the first Object, and methinks there is nothing so terrible in the Passion, that we shou'd be deterr'd from entertaining it a second Time, nor do I see any Reason why an unworthy Treatment shou'd not unloose the Bonds of Passion, and leave the Heart free for an Idea more deserving of Admittance; but this to a Person that has lov'd sincerely, cannot easily be effected; they cannot, like *Sophiana*, pass suddenly from one Passion to another, many a bitter Pang, restless Days, and sleepless Nights must it cost, before such an Alteration can be brought about; and perhaps he that most attempts it, after all that he can do will but find his Labour lost: So difficult is it to vanquish a real Tenderness! or chase from the Mind Ideas which have once afforded us so

---

[1] Forerunner.

[2] Haywood drew heavily on the work of the former poet laureate John Dryden (1631–1700) throughout her career. The subsequent couplet is from *Tyrannick Love*, III. i. 122–23.

much Delight! Hence it is that Women, when they love with that Kind of Passion of which I am speaking, generally love for ever: They have not Strength enough of Mind to repel the sweet Remora's[1] which past Pleasures yield,—they re-enjoy them in Imagination, as *Ovid* makes the Nymph *Ænone* to say of *Paris*:

Every dear Word of thine to Mind I call,
For they who truly love remember all.[2]

Besides, wanting the Avocatives of Baseness,[3] or those Amusements which a Variety of Company affords the other Sex, they have more Leisure, as well as more Desire to indulge their Thoughts, and sooth deluded Fancy: Thus do they, self-deceiv'd, supply Fuel to the unceasing Fire which consumes their Peace, and rarely is extinguish'd but by Death.

What can be more wretched than *Amasia*, Daughter to one of the chiefest Nobility, and once the Pride of her illustrious Race, does she not languish out her Days in irksome Solitude, while a thousand noble Youths languish for the Blessing of her Presence, and envy the happier Swains who tend the rural Flocks: She lov'd, and was some Time belov'd by *Hermius*, but all her Stock of Charms being too weak to defend his Heart against the more prevailing Attractions of Wealth, a Widow bore away the Prize, and triumph'd over the Beauties of her fair unhappy Rival.

Love is therefore, for many Reasons, dangerous to the softer Sex; they cannot arm themselves too much against it, and for whatever Delights it affords to the Successful few, it pays a double Portion of Wretchedness to the numerous Unfortunate,— Insensibility, is, with all the Deficiencies imputed to it, a State of Ease and Tranquility; and I cannot think that Woman prudent who, if she can avoid it, quits a certain *good* for the Prospect of an uncertain *better*. That Heaven which Lovers talk so much of, is indeed, too much a real Heaven to be frequently found on Earth; and for one Example of two Persons, who with equal

---

[1] Obstacles; the usage here is irregular.
[2] A paraphrase from Ovid, *Heroides*, V, along the lines of Aphra Behn's 'Paraphrase on Oenone to Paris' (1680).
[3] Lacking distractions of a worldly sort (for example, commercial, social, or sexual).

Ardour and equal Tenderness regard each other, we shall find ten thousand of the contrary,—even among those, whose Choice seem'd wholly guided by Inclination. We shall not see many, whom either an unrestrain'd Enjoyment does not satiate, or some darling Foible, from which, not the most perfect are exempt, does not disgust, and make them say with *Morat* in the Play, that

Marriage is but the Pleasure of a Day,
The Mettal's base, the Gilding worn away.[1]

There are some Men who seem to have so strange a Taste in their Amours, that one can scarce impute the Choice they make to any thing but Fate. Various are the Instances one might bring of this Nature, but one, which I had an Account of from a Person perfectly acquainted with the whole Affair, shall suffice at this Time. *Hibonio*, a Person of the first Rank in the Kingdom of *Norbania*, is descended from a Family which deriv'd their Nobility from as brave and singular an Action, as History can Produce. The Story is much after this Manner: A certain Enemy having landed with a powerful Army, had over-run great Part of the Country, before any necessary Preparations cou'd be made for Defence: They committed the most terrible Outrages, sparing not the Lives of even Women and Children sucking at their Breasts. The Prince was not wanting in his Endeavours to repel the Force of these cruel Invaders, and having gather'd together as great a Number of Men as the Time would permit, march'd against them; but the Foe, flush'd with the Success they had already obtain'd, and knowing themselves much the Superior in Strength, the Leaders of them, to secure the Valour of their Men, gave out among themselves, that no Man must hope to return to the Camp but as a Conqueror. They attack'd the *Norbanians* with such Fury, that both Wings were broken, and fled, and the main Body very much disorder'd: All was likely to be on the Rout, when it seem'd as if Heaven had done a Miracle in their Behalf: A Countryman, who, with his two Sons, had at a Distance observ'd great Part of the Action, on a sudden, animated with something that had the

---

1   Dryden, *Aureng-Zebe* (1676), IV. i. 248–49.

Appearance of more than mortal Courage, flew into the thickest of the Danger; by their Example inspiring a new Vigour in their drooping Countrymen, the Battle was restor'd with double Fierceness, and contrary to all Expectation, or almost Hope, the *Norbanians* had the Victory; which being wholly owing to the Fortitude and Bravery of this gallant Farmer and his Sons, the Prince acknowledg'd, by bestowing on him immediate Honours, and possessions to countenance the Titles he conferr'd on him. Of this Family have descended many great and worthy Men, who have distinguish'd themselves in as brave, tho' less remarkable Actions, as that which first rank'd them with the Nobles: The present Heir of the Estate and Title, was as promising a Youth as ever appear'd on the Stage of the World, he became an early proficient in all commendable Qualifications, when arriv'd to Manhood he appear'd no less fortunate than deserving, and obtain'd in Marriage the beautiful *Harmonia*, Daughter to one of the chief of the Nobility in a Neighbouring Nation, and a Lady in whom 'tis difficult to distinguish if her Wit, Good Humour, Piety or Virtue be most Praise-worthy. Never did *Hymen* shower Blessings more refin'd and delicate, than on these equally loving, equally meritorious Pair: For ten whole Years did they live together in a perfect Amity, in which time six lovely Daughters, and four fine Sons were the Product of their Marriage Joys. Who would not now believe that such a Happiness was compleat, that such a Love was not establish'd on a Foundation too sure to be shaken, even by the most prevailing Charms. But alas! what Security for any thing on this side Death! 'tis the End alone which proves us truly blest. *Hibonio* being, on some Business, oblig'd to go to that Country where *Harmonia* receiv'd her Birth, Millions of Tears and fond Endearments past between them before they could resolve to part, but that prudent Lady, suffering her Regard for her little ones to overcome the Softness of her Passion, would not consent to leave them, tho' to accompany a Husband she so sincerely lov'd, and as she expected he would not tarry long, chose rather to sustain the Pangs of a short Absence, than abandon them to the Care of any but her self, or occasion the Expences which cannot be avoided when Ladies Travel, looking on every unnecessary Charge as an Injury to her numerous Family.

But fatal to her future Peace was this Frugality, her Presence, and the Love he had then for her, might probably have hinder'd him from falling into those Errors he afterwards committed. Happening into the Company of some young *Debauchées*,[1] they carry'd him, being pretty warm with Wine, to the House of one of the most noted Bawds in the Kingdom, where every one chusing for himself a *fille de joye*,[2] the Woman who fell to his share was one of the least lovely, but most artful in the shameful Trade of any who practic'd it: He found such Charms in her Conversation, as made him Visit her again the next Day, and approving of her Company as much when sober, as when the Strength of the Liquor had o'erpower'd his Understanding, after he had engag'd her Promise of Fidelity to him, he remov'd her from that place, and took a Lodging for her in a very pleasant Part of the Town, never missing going to her every Night, but he had not continued this amorous Conversation above a Fortnight, before he found the ill Effects of it in a pernicious Disease, frequently experienced by those who run the Risque of it, in the Search of those polluted Pleasures. Yet this, which one should think, might have been sufficient, not only to have made him abandon the Wretch who had inflicted it on him, but also to make him forever after shun all of the same Profession, had no Effect on him, to alter him from that Course of Life in which he now enter'd: She had corrupted his very Principles, debauch'd his Soul, and as before his Acquaintance were only among the Wise and Virtuous, he now delighted in those which profest themselves most the contrary, and not only forgave this Creature, whom I shall call by the Name of *Putania*,[3] but became so fond of her, that he scarce ever suffer'd her out of his Sight; he remov'd her to another Lodging, on purpose that she might be nearer to the Court, where he at that time had an Apartment, and rarely din'd or supp'd without her; but being discover'd in this Intrigue, and fearing the reproaches of *Harmonia*'s Kindred, he plac'd her with a Sister she had of the same Disposition as her self. About this time

---

[1] Libertines.

[2] Prostitute.

[3] Playing on the French *putain* (prostitute).

his Father dy'd, leaving him in Possession of a very great Title and plentiful Estate, which he no sooner was inform'd of, than he ordered the same Preparations of Mourning to be made for *Putania*, as those his Lady desir'd for her self. Thinking now that his Presence might be needful in *Norbania*, he took leave of this Criminal Partner of his Pleasures in the most tender manner imaginable, leaving with her a sufficient Sum of Money to maintain her till his Return, which he promis'd should be as speedy as possible: But in his Journey he was overtaken by a Misfortune which put a Stop to the Progress of it: His old Distemper return'd upon him with almost as great Violence as at the first, and he was oblig'd to tarry at a Place where there happen'd to be an eminent Physician who made a Cure of him, but not so perfectly but that he was oblig'd to go to a City some Miles out of his Way, which is famous for its purging Waters;[1] staying there some time, it seem'd as if with one Virtue he had shaken off another, and that he was not only now become a Libertine, but Coward too; having behaved himself in an unhandsome manner to a Gentleman, satisfaction was demanded of him in that way which Men of Honour make use of, when they imagine themselves injur'd by each other; but instead of accepting the Challenge, *Hibonio* took Post-Horses and immediately made off, prosecuting his Journey to *Norbania* with all possible Expedition. At his Arrival there, he return'd with fictitious Pretences of Business, which he said had occasion'd his long Stay, the true Endearments his tender Wife receiv'd him with, and after having settled his Affairs, began to express a Dissatisfaction of living in *Norbania* tho' it were the Place of his Birth, on which his Lady, willing in all things to oblige him, readily compell'd to quit it. Unhappy Lady, little did she guess at the Attractions he had in another Place; but soon did she find a sad Change in his Behaviour, he was scarce ever at home with her, he us'd to dine and sup constantly with *Putania*, go to Bed with her about 10, rise from her about 3, and then retire cold and regardless to the Embraces of his Wife.

Putania in the mean time, tho' Partner of the Fortune, and sole Engrosser of the Affections of this infatuated Nobleman, could not

---

[1] Water allegedly with medicinal properties, for drinking and immersion.

forget her former manner of Life, and having been accustomed to subsist by Variety of Embraces, now took a Pleasure in that, which before she was compell'd to by Necessity; one she admitted for his Wit, another for his fine Shape and Air, a third for his Complexion, in fine all who had any Perfections, or that she imagin'd had any. One of these Enamoratoes having been appointed to pass the Night with her, and by the Noble Lord's being there before, oblig'd to retire, that when turning away he saw the more happy *Hibonio* sitting in the Window, with the object of their common Desires, he took up a Stone, and hurl'd it with such Violence, that it was very near knocking his Lordship's Brains out. This alarm occasion'd his removing her from that Place, and being resolv'd to hinder all future Interruptions if possible, he took a House for her, furnish'd it in a very handsome manner, and hired Servants to attend her; yet was not all this sufficient to excite this Wretch to any Sentiments of Gratitude or Constancy: With the same Artifice[1] with which he treated his Lady on her Account, did she deceive him, and having an Intrigue with a Person, whom at that time she preferr'd to all Mankind beside, she went away with him, leaving *Hibonio* to mourn the Loss of his Mistress, and regret his ill-plac'd Favours.

Who wou'd not have imagin'd, that this Usage should indeed have open'd his long blinded Eyes, and made him see how little Truth or Justice there is to be expected from a Creature who has thrown off all Regard to her self: 'Tis possible, that for some Moments he reflected as he ought on this Adventure, but happening one Day, as he was passing through a Street, to meet her by Accident, the sight of her intirely banish'd all the Resolutions he had taken against her; she wept, and pretended she had been false to him, not through Inclination but Compulsion, entreated his Forgiveness, and made a thousand Vows never to Love but him: He readily believ'd all she said, went with her immediately, and provided her a Lodging, where he tarry'd with her the whole Night, grew fonder of her than before, and swore that if she continu'd true to him, he wou'd Marry her if his Wife dy'd, as he hop'd to Heaven she would in a little time, for she was then lying sick of the Small Pox, and given over by the Physicians. 'Tis not

---

[1] Cunning.

impossible, considering the Infatuation he was under, but that he might have been as good as his Word; but Providence was pleas'd to disappoint the Ambition of this abandon'd Creature, the good Lady recover'd, which as soon as she heard of, and that there was no Hope of her being rais'd to that Dignity, she elop'd a second time with the before mention'd Spark.

Impossible, one would imagine, it must be, that after this repeated Proof of the highest Baseness, she could be thought on by *Hibonio* but with the utmost Detestation, yet so prevailing to him were the Endearments of her Embraces, that rather than not partake of them at all, he could be contented to share them with others: He searched the whole Town for her like a Man distracted, and finding his Endeavours vain, at last bethought him of a Woman he had often seen with her, the Wife of a mean Tradesman, who sat behind the Counter more for Show than Profit, having formerly made greater Advantages of her Person than any other Goods in her Shop; but Age, that implacable Enemy of Beauty, having ruin'd her Commerce that way, she humbly and industriously got her living, by procuring those Pleasures she was no longer capable of enjoying her self. To her he had Recourse, entreating she would once more bring him to the Sight of his dear *Putania*, assuring her of his Gratitude for so great a Piece of Service, and at the same time giving her a Purse of Gold, this Reverend, Well-wisher to Intrigue promis'd him her Assistance, and in a few Days compleated the Happiness he so much desired.

The Excuse she now made for having abandon'd him was, that she was married, but professing still the extremest Tenderness for him, offer'd to quit her Husband and live again with him, he clasp'd her in his Arms, quite transported with this Excess of Goodness, as he call'd it, and Swore his Life and Fortune should be ever wholly at her Devotion. Every thing being agreed on between them, he took another House for her, and liv'd entirely with her, concealing his Quality, and calling himself by a Name very different from that of *Hibonio:* His Wife and Family believing him to be in the Country, he having taken a solemn Leave of them, under the Pretence of going to pass some time with a certain Duke, something related to him.

Now was he in full, and for some time sole Possession of all that he esteem'd Felicitous,[1] but Heaven suffers not a Tranquility, so Criminal as was his, to be of any long Duration, that Person, whom among all her numerous Gallants,[2] she pretended was her Husband, having found out where she liv'd, came one Night, and had like to have surpriz'd them in Bed; on which, they having scarce time to get on their Cloaths, made their Escape at one Door, while he was entring at another, with infinite Fatigue, it being too late to get either Coach or Chair; the Lord with his dear purchas'd Treasure arriv'd at last at a *Bagnio*,[3] where being receiv'd, they took some few Hours repose, after which, the former of them went home, pretending he was that Moment come to Town; but she continuing still to have a greater Inclination to the other than to her Noble Cully,[4] instead of waiting till he should return to her at Night, as he had promis'd, and she had no need to doubt: She sent an Account to the Spark at what Place she was, desiring him to come and take her thence, and express'd the greatest Concern, that she had been compell'd to give him so great a Disappointment the Night before; he obey'd the Summons, and she went with him to the House, tarrying with him about four or five Days, in which time it was agreed between them, that she should perswade her Lord to let her go to the Country to pass the Summer Season; she manag'd the Matter so effectually, that he hir'd a Coach and Servant to attend her in her Journey.

More of this in our next.[5]

---

1 Happy.
2 Fashionable, pleasure-seeking gentlemen.
3 Brothel.
4 Dupe.
5 A sequel was advertised and presumably printed, but no copies seem to have survived.

LOVE-LETTERS ON ALL OCCASIONS

> *Pleasure with Sorrow, Peace with War allay'd,*
> *Liberty fetter'd, Hope by Fear dismay'd,*
> *Imbitter'd Honey, Earnest mix'd with Play,*
> *Are, Love! the Emblems of thy sov'reign Sway.*[1]

To the HONOURABLE
Mrs. WALPOLE,
Relict of the HONOURABLE
GALFRIDUS WALPOLE, Esq;[2]

MADAM,

AS I look on Flattery to be the meanest Vice of the Soul, and
in reality rather an Affront than Compliment to the Person so
Address'd, I have ever most carefully avoided Dedicating the little
I have wrote, but to such whose Worth exceeds all I am able to say
in the Praise of it, chusing sooner to discover my *inability* of doing
Justice to Merit, than injure my *Sincerity* in Unduly ascribing it.

THOSE possest of the greatest Virtues are always least pleas'd
with the repetition of them; and in Persons of an elevated Station
are too Conspicuous to stand in need of a Panegyrick:[3] the
World is sensible of them by the Advantages it receives by them;
and their very Names are an Elogy[4] of themselves.

IN Entreating the Sanction of Yours, Madam! I am, therefore,
excus'd from following the common Method of Dedications;[5]
for who is there so much a stranger to *Fame* as to be unacquainted
with what a graceful Sweetness you have adorn'd every Stage of
Life thro' which you have passed? The unaffected innocence of

---

[1] The lines, which appear on the original title page, are unidentified and were perhaps
written by Haywood. For a digitally enhanced facsimile of that page, see Haywood,
Miscellaneous Writings, 1725–1743, ed. Alexander Pettit (London: Pickering & Chatto,
2000) 127.

[2] The dedicatee is Cornelia Hays Walpole, widow ('relict') of Galfridus (d. 1726),
brother to de facto prime minister Sir Robert Walpole (1676–1745).

[3] Praise, connoting flattery.

[4] That is, eulogy; an expression of praise.

[5] Dedications in the period were often transparent attempts at flattery.

your *Virgin* State, the endearing softness of your *Matrimonial* one, and the inviolable integrity of your *Widowhood*, even while your Charms are at the height, and surrounded with a Crown of Admirers, devoting Yourself wholly to the Memory of that Dear, and Worthy Partner of your Vows, and continuing to be a *Wife* after Death has made him cease to be a *Husband*, justly render You the subject of every one's Admiration, and Applause. Nor are those shining Branches of your Character ever mentioned without adding the *Tender Mother*, the *Indulgent Mistress*, the *Faithful Friend*, and the inimitable Pattern of *Affability* and *Sweetness of Disposition* towards all.

'TIS this last, and in my Opinion, equally Beautiful Qualification, Madam! that silences the Tongue of Envy, which the more scrutinous[1] to discover something to blemish your Perfections, becomes insensibly the more charm'd, till it is wholly lost in Transport[2] and Surprize! 'Tis this, that, softning the severity of your other Virtues, makes us *Love*, what else we only should *Revere*!

VIRTUE is represented by the most amiable Figure that *Art* can paint, to the End that we may be *allured* by her *Smiles* to an Obedience of her Precepts,[3] not *aw'd* into it by her *Frowns*; and it is thus, Madam! *Nature* has made her shine in You; giving you such Charms of Form and Behaviour, as make all, who wish to please, endeavour to be good in the Hope that they may look like You!

BUT I forget that the *greater* your *desert*, the *less worthy* your Protection is the mean Oblation I now offer to it, and should rather Apologize for the *Presumption*, than the *Zeal* of this Address: But here also I find myself unequal to the Task, and shall only beg leave to remind you the Sacrifice of the *Heart* is acceptable to the *True Divinity*, when the most pompous *Exterior* Homage is rejected: and, as the *Widow's Mite* was infinitely more precious than the Treasures of *Ananias*,[4] I flatter myself this Trifle may be permitted a place in your Closet, and that the Ambition

---

1 Loosely, eager.
2 Ecstasy.
3 Instructions concerning moral conduct.
4 In Mark 12.41–44 and Luke 21.1–4, a poor widow gives 'two mites', or a lowly farthing, to Jesus, who declares that she has given more than others; in Acts 5.1–11, Ananias withholds money from Peter.

of Entertaining you may atone for whatever Deficiencies may be found either in that, or its Author, who is,

With the greatest Respect and Veneration,

MADAM,

Your most humble, most Obedient,
And most Faithfully devoted Servant,

Eliza Haywood.

LETTER I.

Darian *to* Climene,
On her Undertaking to prove there could be no Love
without Jealousy.

HOW much Occasion have you for that all-powerful Wit you are Mistress of, for the maintaining an Argument so contradictory to Reason and good Sense?—Can I love you, most adorable *Climene!* without assuring myself that you are worthy of the Passion I profess? How can you believe me when I say I think you adorn'd with every Heavenly Virtue; yet, at the same Time accuse you with the blackest Crimes[1] which can deprave Humanity, Inconstancy and Deceit? Have you not a thousand Times sworn to me, that I was in Possession of your Heart? And shall I suspect you guilty of Perjury and Falshood? But you tell me, that if I lov'd you with that Height of Passion, you would wish to inspire, I should be eternally in Apprehensions of losing you, tremble even at my own Shadow, going in the dark to your Apartment, lest it should be that of a Rival, hoping to share the same Degree of Happiness; watch your very look, and if I chanc'd but even to imagine you cast one too favourable on any other, show my Resentment to the Man so favoured, by immediately drawing my Sword; then, fearful of offending you, drop the Point, and, presenting you with the Hilt, beg you on my Knees to plunge it in my Breast, or ease me of the Pain of Doubt!—Why, really, my dear *Climene!* this is a fine sort of Romantick[2] Behaviour; but I can

---

[1]   Morally odious acts, as well as illegal ones.
[2]   Extravagant.

scarce believe the Woman who knows what 'tis to feel a sincere Affection, would wish to find it in the Man she loves.—'Tis a Proof of Vanity and Coquetry to the last Degree, and as valuable as I think your Charms, you must never expect I will purchase the maintaining the Happiness you now allow me to enjoy at the Expense of my Understanding, or Peace of Mind.—In the Days of Courtship, 'tis certain, I endured as much Anxiety as you now desire to see me in; but consider that the Circumstance is entirely altered, you might then without a Crime have made Choice, among the Number who ador'd you, of some other than *Darian*; but having given yourself to me, not without testifying a Mutability[1] of Mind, which would cure my Passion, quit me. We are now in a Situation which leaves no Room for Jealousy, and I should be the most unjust and unreasonable Man on Earth to be guilty of it without a Cause; as you would be the most ungrateful and perjur'd of Women to do any Thing which should forfeit the Esteem I have for you, and which only yourself can diminish.— Continue therefore, my Angel, to bless your faithful *Darian*, and by maintaining that Conduct, which at first engaged my Affection, preserve it: Be assured, that nothing can equal the Satisfaction of believing one's self beloved by a Woman of Honour; nor that no personal Perfections are capable to hold the Heart which is once convinced, the more lasting Beauties of the Mind are wanting.[2] Charming as you are, and lovely, even beyond all that can be conceiv'd of Loveliness; 'Tis your Tenderness, your Constancy, your Integrity, which endears you to my Soul, and could I be capable of suspecting you guilty of a Breach of any of these, all your exterior Graces would lose their usual Lustre, I should think of you no otherwise than of a fine Picture, a curious[3] Statue, perfectly beautiful at the first, but marr'd by some malicious Hand, and Pity would succeed Desire.—But I am too well acquainted with your good Sense to believe you wish in earnest I should be that Coxcomb[4] you, last Night, described; such I am certain, you have seen, and have despis'd, and will not make myself wretched by

---

[1] Changefulness.
[2] Lacking.
[3] Unusual.
[4] Fop, fool.

imagining it would not give you some Pain to find me less deserving of your Affections, than you have been pleas'd to think I was.— Of this be certain, that I love you with the most sincere and unchangeable Passion that ever was.—That I esteem your Love the supreamest Blessing of my Life; that no Act of mine shall ever forfeit it; and that I am, and ever will be, no less your Adorer, for being

Your favoured Servant
DARIAN.

LETTER II.

PHYLETUS *to* DELIA.
On Tenderness.

NEVER did I find you swerve so much from Reason and from Nature, as in the Contents of your last, otherwise obliging Billet.[1] You seem, my Dearest, to mistake the Theme you argue on, and confound *Tenderness*, with its very opposite. *Fondness*[2] is a mean and childish Passion, or at best but the Effect of Fancy, which seldom is of long Duration, especially for the same Object; but *Tenderness* has in it the very Essence both of Love and Friendship, and cannot be felt without the most sincere Esteem, nor will find Room but in a soft and generous Soul. This Passion, or rather this Virtue, may be demonstrated, as well in absence as when present, our Impatience for an Interview, our Assiduities[3] in Writing, our Cares for the Welfare of the darling[4] Object, make it known. *Fondness* is still accompanied with *Desire*, and when one is satisfied, the other degenerates into Indifference; but *Tenderness* is the Sublimity of *Friendship*, blended with that Love which the exterior Beauties inspire, and will continue even when the Difference of Sexes is forgot.—*Fondness* is what we may feel for divers[5] Objects, as occasionally they present themselves

---

[1] Letter.
[2] Foolish infatuation.
[3] Perseverance.
[4] Beloved.
[5] That is, diverse.

to our View; *Tenderness* is confin'd to one, and, where it is real, is as immutable as it is particular. Is it, my dearest *Delia!* when I kiss you with a raging Eagerness, when I clasp you to my Bosom with a strenuous and almost painful Force, that I am most Tender? No, these are the Effects of that wild Rapidity of Passion that fires me for the Enjoyment of your Charms, and were I to give you no other Proofs of my Sincerity, it might justly enough be taken for Self-gratification: But 'tis when my working Mind is labouring for your Interest, when, neglecting those Affairs which are immediately my own, all my Thoughts are taken up with yours, when studious for your Happiness alone, I prove it makes the best of mine, and that nothing relating to myself *only* is capable of giving me a Moment's Joy or Grief. Is it not the most refined Affection to devote my whole Soul so entirely to you, that I have neither the Power nor Inclination to afford Room for any other Idea of what Kind soever?—Nature, 'tis true, cannot support unceasing Rapture, there must be a Relaxation, some little Respite for the scattered Spirits to collect themselves, or Life must be destroyed. Yet even in those Moments when I am least able to testify the abundant Tenderness I have for you, by exterior Signs, it works as strongly in my Breast as ever. Accuse me not, therefore, of Coldness, Indifference, or Satiety,[1] 'tis impossible for me ever to love you less than I have done, and I do still, nor can any Man love you more. Even that *Fondness*, which you seem so greatly to be pleas'd with, I feel, in as immense a Degree as you could wish, or mortal is capable of conceiving; but then I would not have you rank that Branch of Passion equal with the more lasting one of *Tenderness*, nor imagine that when the *one* seems a little to recede from its first Vigour, the *other* is at all diminish'd. The former, my adorable *Delia*, may be compared to that uncertain and momentary Blaze which arises from kindled Stubble, the latter to the constant Glow of a Furnace.—Cease then to suspect that eternal Fire your Charms have lighted in my Breast can ever decrease.—Banish such Sentiments as Enemies to your own Repose,[2] and most unjust

---

[1] Complete gratification.
[2] Tranquillity.

to me.—Be assured the vital Heat which actuates my Frame must be extinguish'd with that other, and that I must not be at all, when I give over to be,

My loveliest, dearest, and

most charming DELIA's

faithfully devoted and

passionately Tender

PHYLETUS.

LETTER III.

The unfortunate MYRTILLA *to the forgetful* SARPEDON.

IS it then possible that Man can be so base? Are you resolved to prove, that all that has been invented of the Ingratitude and Perjury of your Sex falls short of the Reality in you? And was there none among believing Woman-kind but *Myrtilla* to be made the Sacrifice of your betraying Vows, and counterfeited Ardors?[1]—Good God! How can you, dare you, treat me in this Manner? Think you I want a Soul to resent it? To be five Days without seeing me, ill-suited with those vehement Professions you have made of an everlasting Passion; but not to write to me in all this Time is beyond all Excuse! Nay, shows you wish not to attempt one!—I am grown now so low in your Opinion, I seem not worth the Pains of Deceiving, and am left at Liberty to judge as I please of your Ingratitude, and my Undoing! Inconstant, barbarous Man! How am I altered since you so deeply swore, no Charms would have the Power to make you forget mine?—That I was all of Excellent that Woman-kind could boast, and that Life was less dear to you than my Affection?—You lov'd me once, 'tis certain, every Word, every Action, every Look was a Proof of the most raging Passion, when despairing to obtain the Reward which I, alass! too soon bestowed! Oh how vastly different in your Sex are Love and Friendship? the latter, ashamed to be too much obliged, endeavours still to repay what it receives; the former flies the Giver, and

---

[1] Passion.

having acquired its Wish, contemns the Bounty!—Oh! Flame, destructive to itself, which looks bright at Distance, and sparkles for a while, but soon is lost in Air, and leaves only a darkning Smoak behind! Yet how monstrous is it to Reason and Reflection, that Love should beget Hate? That no longer than Indifference in our Sex subsists, Desire can live in yours? 'Tis not yet one poor Month since, deceived by your fictitious Vows, I yielded up my Honour, and am already abandoned to Despair and Shame, cruel Requital for such Love as mine!—But think not I will tamely bear it; No, by my Wrongs, I will not! For you I am lost to all this World calls dear, perhaps, too ruin'd in all my Hopes of a future one, and having nothing now to fear, wish but to see myself revenged!—You have a Wife but too justly suspicious of your Conduct, she shall be inform'd of all, not one Tittle shall pass untold, I value not what shall become of me, but shall rather pride myself in being expos'd, when I consider, that by being so, I inflict the worst of Punishments on you, domestick Jars,[1] and the unceasing Clamour of a Tongue, who wants but a Pretence to become the Plague of your Life, and which you must be doom'd to hear, or, flying from it, fly at the same Time from what you truly adore with as violent an Ardency[2] as you once feign'd to have for me, your Grandeur, and the Homage of the inferior World!—Be assured, I am extreme in all my Passions, and as I have scrupled nothing to gratify that of my Love, I shall as little hesitate to do what my Revenge demands!—Clear yourself, therefore, if there be a possibility of it, convince me that you are not the thankless and the perjured Wretch your late Behaviour has made you seem, restore me to that Repose you have too long disturbed, and yourself to the Arms and Heart of her who, in spite of her Indignation, still wishes with the utmost Warmth to continue

Your truly devoted
and most faithful
MYRTILLA.

---

1   Quarrels.
2   Passion.

LETTER IV.

IF you had not, indeed, Charms infinitely superior to any of your Sex, the natural Uneasiness of your Temper would render you most disagreeable: There is nothing so much absolves the Breach of Trust as to be eternally suspected; where there is a real Cause of Doubt, Complaints, such as yours, are far from working the Effect they aim at; but as I am perfectly innocent of the Crime you accuse me of, it gives me a Disquiet scarce to be born, and I am tempted to make use of my utmost Efforts to love you less, that I might, with more Patience, endure the Reproaches you throw on me.—Does an Absence of a few Days, which also I can easily make appear to have been enforced, deserve those cruel Epithets[1] you treat me with? Or, because I am some Moments happy in your Embraces, is there a Necessity that all my others must be disturbed by your unjust Upbraidings? No, too Tyranick and insulting Beauty! As constant Grating will in Time wear away the hardest Stone, so will repeated Jars break the Harmony of the strictest Friendship.—'Tis impossible to esteem what continually gives us Pain, and when once Esteem is fled, you have too much good Sense not to know, Love will not long remain.—You are offended that I have not wrote to apologize for the Necessity of my Absence; but how unjust is it to condemn without being well convinced there is a Cause for it? What appears to you a Crime is in reality a Virtue, and the highest and most refined Proof of the Respect I bear you.— The Servant who used to be employed in conveying to you the tender Meanings of my Soul, lies now at the Point of Death, and there is not a Person in the World to whom I dare commit so great a Trust as your Reputation. Were I that ungrateful, that perjured Wretch you say, how easy were it for me to deceive you?—The false ones of our Sex find it no Difficulty to continue the Profession, when the Passion is no more; and were that I feel for you extinguished in me, Shame, for such a Mutability, would make me, perhaps, disguise it by Pretences which true Affection disdains

---

[1] Loosely, insults.

to have Recourse to.—Be assured, 'tis with the utmost Sincerity I love you, nor can any Thing but yourself make me think on you with less Tenderness. Cease then to be unjust, either to your excelling Charms, or my Admiration of them, and destroy not, with your own Repose,[1] a Passion which else will be inviolable.—If I am really dear to you, how greatly will you hereafter repent to see that Extremity of Fondness with which I have regarded you, converted only to a cold Pity that you were of a Disposition which I fain would, but could not persevere to support the Effects of.— In fine, all-lovely as you are, the Charms of your Person will not always compensate for the Caprices[2] of your Mind; and though I should account it an infinite Misfortune to be deprived of the Bliss your Kindness affords; yet will I rather resolve to tear myself away than pay so dear a Price, as my whole Peace, to preserve it.—I grieve to find you sway'd by your Passion to Menaces so extravagant, and which certainly you must know too much of my Soul to imagine I regard.—Let me hear no more of Reproaches or Complaints. I conjure[3] you, if you have indeed any sincere Affection for me, or wish to maintain it in him, who desires nothing more than to continue

Your faithful Adorer
SARPEDON.

LETTER V.

The Transported ANEXANDER *to his adorable and lovely* BARETTA,
on her consenting to meet him.

HOW difficult did I find it to express the Agonies of my Despair? when, doubtful if my Services would ever have the Power to move your Soul; but how much more impossible is it to make you sensible of the Extacy with which I received the rapturous Promise of your Condescention![4]—My Heart labours

---

1 Inactivity.
2 Capriciousness; irrationality.
3 Implore.
4 Attentiveness to one's social inferiors.

beneath the over-powering Joy, and pants to unload its Weight of Tenderness; but Oh! there are no Words to represent what it is I feel!—The vast *Idea*[1] overswels Description, and bears down Thought!—Good Heaven! Is it then at last permitted me to hope, nay, to be assured, by your own divine Confession, that I am so happy as to be lov'd by *Baretta*?—Am I this Night to clasp the Charmer in my Arms, to press her Bosom, to feed on those Angelick Lips, and riot on all the ravishing Sweets[2] of kind consenting Beauty?—Yes, Yes, these Blessings are decreed for the fortunate, the adoring, the constant *Anexander.*—The loveliest of Women is ordained to reward the most faithful of Men; for such I am, and glory more in that Perfection, than I could do in being Lord of the Universe, since Love, and only such a Love as mine, can merit the Enjoyment of the Divine *Baretta.*—Why then, O lovely and everlasting Mistress of my Soul! do you tell me you expect ten thousand Vows for the Security of my future Constancy?—Is there Satiety in the Joys of Heaven?—Can he who is admitted to celestial Pleasures send the least distant Wish to Earth again! No, Charmer, no, your own inimitable Beauties are your best Assurance, and might, methinks, make you certain, that it is impossible to love you once, without doing so always.— Besides, it is easy for you to judge by the *Past*, what the *future* will be.—By my Assiduities to please you, my patient enduring, even your utmost Cruelties, my Perseverance in Affection when I had least Hope of any Reward, the Agonies of a long Despair, and all the burning, bleeding, Pangs, which moved you at last to Pity, you may imagine with how much Diligence I shall endeavour to preserve a Blessing so difficult to be attained, and which has cost my restless Heart so many wretched Hours. But why do I go about to demonstrate what you cannot be ignorant of.—You are, you must be sensible that I love you with an Infinity of Passion, with a Tenderness unspeakable, not to be equaliz'd, nor diminish'd.—All I have done, all I have suffered hitherto, are proofs of it, and may assure you, that what I shall hereafter do,

---

1 The essential or 'Platonic' form of an object (here, the 'idea' of Baretta, as distinct from her physical self).
2 Enjoy all the enchanting pleasures.

will more confirm what you already have so much Reason to believe.—Banish, therefore, I beseech you, sweet Distruster, all anxious Suspicions from your Breast; let soft Ideas only swell up that dear Mansion, and give a Loose to Bliss.—Believe that nothing can be more true than these Words of the Poet:

> *In vain soft Ease the Love-tost Mind pursues:*
> *Even in Possession of the long-wish'd Joy,*
> *We rob the bounteous God of half his Dues,*
> *And future Fears the present Bliss destroy!* [1]

What Heaven, and Love, and Nature, then continues to give us, let us not frustrate by Reserve or Doubt.—Know yourself, your own unequal'd Power of charming, and you will then know me for
Your unalterable Slave
ANEXANDER.

LETTER VI.

SYLVANDER *to* JANTHE *in Absence.*
HOW cruelly do you ascribe that to my Choice, which is the very Extremity of my ill Fate! Can you believe I have a Soul or Sense, yet suspect me capable of wilfully depriving myself of those ravishing Delights your Conversation affords.—No, my for-ever lovely, for-ever adorable *Janthe*! This is among the Things which are in their very Natures impossible. When divided from you, methinks, I want Part of myself.—You are the Soul to my Body, and tho' I retain the Power of Motion, yet is it not much more than may be seen in Images actuated by Clockwork.— Thought I have none, and though I have been compelled to this tedious Absence of five Days, on purpose to compleat some Business, yet how unfit I am for it, you may guess, when I shall acquaint you, that the Affair stands just as it did. Heaven! How

---

[1] The lines also appear in Haywood's *Tea-Table* (1725), with minor variations, where Haywood introduces them as the work of 'the *French* Poet'. The lines, or the translation, are perhaps by Haywood.

incompatible are Love and Reason? A Person unacquainted with the Force of that prevailing Passion would perhaps answer, that my Impatience to return to you again, should have made me doubly assiduous to dispatch the Impediment which held me from you.—So indeed, I thought to do at taking leave, but found the Vanity of the Attempt, and, that there was a Necessity to be near you, even to be able to tell you, how vehemently I adore you.—I shall leave the Conduct of my Affairs to Heads less taken up than mine, and hasten to those Arms, where perfect Happiness is only to be found.—Let dull and stupid[1] Souls, ignorant of the Joys of Love, place their Felicity[2] in Wealth and Grandeur, mine disdains all meaner Pleasures than *Janthe*. Nor will I live another Day debarred from her Divine Presence; expect, therefore, at the usual Place, to Morrow Evening the

Impatient and faithful
SYLVANDER.

LETTER VII.

STREPHON *to* DALINDA,
On her forbidding him to speak of Love.

GREAT as your Power is, O most Divine *Dalinda*! I wish it were even greater still, and that while your Commands awe me into Silence, you could also deprive me of Reflection.—Madness were a Blessing when compared to the Agonies of Thought.— Long, too-cruel Beauty, long have you known me to be the Vassal of your Charms, and took Pleasure to behold the humble Love which trembled in my Eyes, but dare not venture through my Lips, till that unhappy Hour in which you chid it thence at once, and bad me be dumb[3] upon that Theme for ever.—Oh, God! On the Penalty of seeing you no more.—If so far unworthy to be ranked among the Number of those, who are permitted to tell you they adore, why did you not, in Pity, check the Infant-flame

---

[1] Unfeeling or unthinking.
[2] Happiness.
[3] Silent.

before it was grown too mighty for Control? Convinced of my Demerit by your early Scorn, Absence and Time perhaps might have relieved me: But you, alass! cherish'd my fond Imagination, heaped Favours on me, received my frequent Visits, talked to me with all the Freedom of a perfect Friendship, let me into all the amazing Wonders of your Wit and Beauty, and secured your Victory e're you let me know to how severe a Conqueror I had resign'd my Peace.——Lovely Tyrant! Can you defend this Treatment, is it conformable to that matchless Generosity, demonstrated in every other Action of your Life?——No, when you consider, you will repent, and soft Compassion overwhelm whatever Pride or Reserve may alledge against me!——In the mean Time, impute not this Epistle as an Aggravation of my Fault, I beseech you.——You bad my Tongue be silent, but forbad not my Pen, nor Eyes: the Complainings of the latter are not in my Power to restrain, and if the former seem too great a Presumption, pardon it on the Score of the Torments which enforce it.—— Despair is the Word made use of to describe what it is the Damned endure, and sure severer Anguish is not to be invented, nor inflicted.——Oh! there are Books, which teach the Theory of all the Passions, would you but study mine for one short Hour, certain I am, it would be my last of Misery, your gentle Nature would dissolve in Floods of Pity, and once more lift me up to Hope, and your Forgiveness.——But why need I wish you to have recourse to Rules? Reflect but on your self, your own resistless Charms, and you will then know, it is impossible to see you without loving, or forbearing to tell you so, nor will it then be difficult to guess how dreadful it is still to be doom'd to languish, to burn with an unextinguishable Desire, yet know that Desire is vain.——'Tis by this Means alone you can conceive the Pangs of my distracted[1] Soul, and be wrought to compassionate

The most Faithful,
tho' Despairing,
STREPHON.

---

[1] Deranged.

LETTER VIII.

Alexis *to* Serinda,
excusing his Jealousy.

HOW unjust are you, Oh, in all Things else most divine *Serinda!* to accuse me of the Want of that, which, the being possess'd with an Excess of, occasions all my Faults?—Were you the Mistress but of ordinary Charms, or did I love you with a moderate Passion, I could not offend you in the Manner I do.—It is not your Virtue, but my own Merits I suspect.—I know my self incapable of deserving so rich a Treasure as your Heart, and tremble least your Judgment should one Day get the better of your Fancy, and recall the Gift your lavish Bounty gave.—Do I not see you daily surrounded with the great and gay?—Grandeur, alas! has Charms for too many of your Sex, and those who feel not half my Tenderness may, perhaps, have the Art to express it in more moving Terms.—Could I therefore hear, without being ready to go mad with Apprehension, the vast Offers of the wealthy *Cleander,* or the elegant Encomiums on your Beauty by the amorous *Myrtillo;*—and Oh! to what a Height might not Jealousy be allowed to rise, at seeing you smile at what they say, and still continue to admit their Visits!—You tell me, that you behave in this Manner but to divert yourself, and never thought the Declarations of either worth a serious Thought, I flatter my self you speak sincerely, and that *Alexis* is still as blest as ever in your dear Favour; but yet, *Serinda,* 'tis dangerous trifling with Men of their Character:—Your Reputation, if not your Virtue, is exposed to the utmost Danger; and can I love you as I ought, without expressing my Concern? No, by Heaven! so sincere is my Friendship, exclusive of my other more warm and tender Passion, that were I abandon'd by you, depriv'd for ever of all those Joys you made me hope should be as lasting as our Lives, still would I counsel you against Plurality of Adorers.—It is not only the Terror of Despair for myself, I feel, I am also influenced by my Regard for your Honour and Repose, and if sometimes I utter my Sentiments with more Vehemence than becomes the Humility of Love, impute that Error to the Ardency and Zeal of my Passion, and *pardon*, at least, what, could you see into my Soul, you could not but *approve.*—Were my whole Fortune at Stake, my Life in Danger, I might with Patience wait the Event, but the least Shadow which threatens me with the Loss of you, blows up my Reason! 'Tis insupportable to Thought, and I am all Distraction! I then wish I had never seen your Beauties, and never had tasted Joys, which, the bare Apprehension of being depriv'd of, proves so great a Torment.—Nay, I am sometimes prophane enough to endeavour to love you less, to conquer the strong Impression of your Charms, and be as inconstant as I think you are;—but, alas! with infant Arms I wage War with the Skies, and aim to scale *Olympus:*[1] I sink, I die beneath the unequal Power of your ravishing Idea; and when I think to call you false, ungrateful, perjur'd, something within me stops the half-form'd Words, and turns to *Praises* what I meant *Invectives:*[2] My own Demerit rises to my View, and represents me the most thankless Wretch alive.—Then my rash Rage recoils upon myself, and Horrors nameless, numberless, croud on my repenting Soul.—O *Serinda!* what you call my Crime is the severest of my Misfortunes, and if I am guilty sometimes of disturbing your Repose, I break my own entirely, and suffer far more than you would wish.—Pity then the Agonies of my bleeding Heart, and cease to do any thing which may, tho' but for a Moment, give me Cause to think I am less bless'd in your Affection, than I have been.—I dare not promise to offend no more, 'till you have assur'd me you will no more tempt the Impatience of a Love so tender and so ardent[3] as mine, by encouraging Pretences to my Prejudice. Too dearly I prize the Heaven of your Embraces, to bear with Moderation the Fears of partaking them with another; much less can I support the least distant Probability of being depriv'd of them.—Oh! therefore, if it be true that you indeed think me worthy of your Love, allay[4] not a Blessing so immense by Doubts and Fears, but comfort, forgive, and revive the

Adoring, and
Passionately-devoted
ALEXIS.

---

[1] In Greek mythology, the mountain on which the gods dwelled.
[2] Denunciations.
[3] Passionate.
[4] Weaken, repress.

LETTER IX.

ARISTUS *to the haughty* PANTHEA.

AT length my Heart has broke its Chain, and I disdain the Servitude I have so long laboured under; I could have remained your *Lover* for a long Eternity, but a few Months convinced me, how ill I could endure to be your *Slave*.—A little Submission, I confess, is expected from our Sex to yours, but then you should take Care not to tyrannize too far, or make use of the Power we give you over Us to exact any Thing of us, which may debase the Dignity of Manhood.—Remember, that if we yield, it is *Love* alone makes us do so, and, whenever we find *Love* ceases to be the Inspirer of your Commands, we cease also to obey.—'Tis not because you continue to be *fair*, that we must continue always to adore, some Condescention is necessary on your Side, or Passion, still on the Rack[1] to please, will grow weary at length on ours.—'Tis shameful to Remembrance, when I reflect, how much I have made your Will my Study.—How I watch'd the Motion of your Eyes, and squar'd my every Action by their Glances; I came not, went not, spake not, look'd not, but with a View of pleasing you;—yet, all my Cares were fruitless:—You could not, or you would not Smile on my Endeavours, and seemed to think my Submissions were my Duty.—Vain-glorious[2] Beauty! Who but myself made you the Disposer of my Destiny? What but my fond Passion gave you Authority to treat me in this Manner? If you thought me unworthy of your Heart, why did you not confess it? Why accept my Services, if determined not to recompense them? To have rejected my Pretensions[3] had been generous, and I should have esteemed you for it, but to encourage them, only to fill up the Train of your Admirers, is base; and shows an Insolence of Nature as little becoming her that practises it, as him who, after the Discovery of it, persists to love.—All the Favours I now wish to receive from you, is, that you will return my Letters, those shameful Testimonies of my past Folly, and cease to imagine I ever can degenerate into the Wretch

---

[1] Suffering.
[2] Full of unwarranted pride.
[3] Overtures; loosely, advances.

I was.—Forget me, as I resolve to do you, your Beauty and your Pride shall henceforth be Things indifferent to me: And if I chance to look on any other Woman with the Eyes of Love, it shall be one, whose Wisdom and good Nature enhances the Merit of her Charms, and knows how to value the Affection of

ARISTUS.

LETTER X.

PANTHEA *to the vain* ARISTUS.

TO convince you, how entirely free I am from that Pride or Vain-glory you accuse me of, I sincerely rejoice to be eas'd of Importunities, which, if I ever encouraged, it was only owing to an Excess of that good Nature, which you say I want.—Believe me, *Aristus*, it never was in your Power to oblige me half so much as now you assure me, you will think of me no more: I cannot promise you to do the same by you, because the most trifling things will sometimes come into our Heads; but, I am certain, I may venture to say, that I shall always chuse to employ my Mind with Contemplations of more Consequence.—I return, according to your Desire, all the Letters I received from you, and am so little picqued at being forsaken, that I wish you may send the Copies of them to some Lady, who may have more Consideration of your great Merits, than the

Insensible[1] PANTHEA.

LETTER XI.

The repenting ARISTUS *to the too cruel, but most adorable* PANTHEA.

IF Madness silences the Sentence of the Law, and from the guilty Neck turns the remorseless Ax, *Panthea* must be more rigorous than either, not to forgive the Fault my rash ungoverned Passion caus'd.—Oh, could you know what it is to Love, and to Despair, you would not blame, but pity me!—Too well, alass! are you

---

[1]   Incapable of feeling.

acquainted with your Charms, and the Effect they have on me, to imagine I could renounce their Power; but wild with hopeless Wishes, I blasphemed the Heaven I was denied to enjoy, and seemed to scorn what was above my Reach.—What shall I say, or how attone the Crime of my Presumption, my audacious Boldness? I fear that all I have done, or still can do, will be too little, and I must depend wholly on your Mercy.—To that then, the most darling Attribute of the Deity, permit me to address, and once more accept me for your Votary.[1]—Believe my Penitence is sincere, and that before you received that Evidence of my Guilt, I almost curst my Hand for writing it.—Never did a Heart experience like mine, the Extremes of Love, Grief, and Rage; were your Beauties of an ordinary Kind, or did I regard them with a moderate Passion, I should not have offended in the Manner I have done; even that which is most my Fault, proves most my Love, and in the utmost Fury of my Despair, you may perceive yourself as much the Mistress of my Soul, as in the humblest of my Submissions.—Oh! therefore, let the Cause extenuate[2] the Crime, and if my Faith and Constancy merit not the glorious Recompence they aim at, let, at least, my Sufferings excite your Compassion. This, in the present Situation of my Affairs, is all I dare Petition for, and this I should be almost certain of obtaining, could you but be brought to believe the real Miseries I labour under: Not all your natural Haughtiness, your Reserve, nor the little Tendency you have to Love, would be able to defend you from melting into a soft Concern for what I feel, nay, I am half tempted to flatter myself with an Imagination you would put a Period[3] to the Woes you pitied, and raise me to a Condition as greatly to be envied, as that I am now in, is the contrary.—But with what vain Delusions do I feast fond Fancy!— O Love, What airy Castles do thy Votaries build!—Are these, alass! Ideas for a Wretch like me, who, by one fatal Rashness, has destroyed all that esteem my long and constant Services has aim'd to inspire.—Can I, who have defied, nay impiously affected to contemn your Charms, hope ever to enjoy them? No, I confess,

---

[1]   Disciple.
[2]   Lessen the severity of.
[3]   End.

that it is with Justice now you drive me to Despair, nor will I call you cruel more.—See with what strange Vicissitudes[1] of different Agitations Passion wracks me, and judge how terrible those Disorders must be, which will not suffer me to be composed, even while I am endeavouring to excuse my Crime.—All I have to hope is, that the irregularity of this Epistle will testify the Sincerity of it, and that you will believe, that if my Perturbations[2] were less violent, I could have been better able to have expressed the Affliction I am in to have incurred your just Displeasure, or the Ardency with which I languish to prove myself as before,

The Divine PANTHEA'S
Eternal Adorer,
ARISTUS.

P.S. *I find it impossible to live without seeing you, let therefore, the Return of my Messenger bring me your Permission to throw myself at your Feet, or in a short Time I shall not be in a Condition to entreat it.*

LETTER XII.

PANTHEA *to* ARISTUS.

I AM so very indifferent to the Love of your Sex, that I can easily forgive the Assurances you gave me of renouncing all Thoughts of it. I know not if your last Letter has so much Claim to my Pardon.—I am a Stranger to the Passion you speak of, and the Demonstrations you would give me of it, therefore will have but little Effect on me. The less you trouble me with any Discourses of that Kind, the more I shall be pleased with your Society, and if, as you say, you desire nothing so much as to oblige me, show it in taking no farther Notice of what has past: 'Tis on that Condition alone I consent to admit your Visits, and subscribe myself

Your Well-wisher
PANTHEA.

---

[1]   Variation.
[2]   Agitation.

LETTER XIII.

THEANO *to* ELISMONDA
On having obtained the last Favour.

WERE there a Possibility for the Raptures of your Condescention to know allay,[1] the cold Reserve with which you received my Visit this Morning would have given it me: Or were I not assured that my Tenderness, and the unchangeable Sincerity of my Soul, would hereafter convince you, that, in making me happy, you had not acted contrary to Reason, I should almost repine at[2] my own Bliss, and rather wish you had continued cruel, than repent your Kindness. Believe me, my most dear *Elismonda!* that it is with a Passion vastly different from what I ever felt for any other Woman that I regard you.—The Desires to which my Heart has been accustomed tended but to Enjoyment, and there found a Period: But here, Oh God! Even in the most extatick Moment of Delights, when all dissolved, and melting in my Arms, you yielded Joys which Sense could hardly bear, I had but half been blest, had not the Truth, the Zeal, the Delicacy of my Love, made me conscious I was not altogether unworthy of the Bounty, and that it would be lasting as it was great. Why then was that Divine Softness, which last Night smiled with such Beneficence upon me, this Morning changed to sullen Frowns, and Looks of coy Indifference? 'Tis true, there were Witnesses of our Behaviour, and my impatient Tongue was compelled to Silence on the darling Theme; yet were the struggling Meanings of my Soul intelligible enough in my Eyes, had you vouchsafed to observe them.—But oh! all kindly Notice was withdrawn, and, tho' I watch'd each Glance, not one enlivening Ray broke out upon me to gladden Hope, but all obscured, like the Sun's Beams behind a clouded Sky: What cruel Demon, envious of my Joys, has had the Power over *Elismonda's* Mind, to work her to so sudden an Alteration? what Dreams of my Inconstancy, or Want of Ardor, has mimick Fancy[3] represented, while Reason

---

[1] Diminution.
[2] Regard with discontent.
[3] Frenzied imagination.

slept, and I was absent, to chase them from her gentle Thoughts?—Oh! cease, thou Life of my Desires! thou best and dearest Aim of my Hopes! to be unjust, or to thy own Deserts, or my unbounded Love.—Think thou hast blest a Man, whose only Ambition is to please thee, who neither ever can, or will swerve in the least Degree, from his first Fervency[1] of Passion, and who, by Fate and Inclination, is decreed

His Lovely ELISMONDA's
entirely devoted Slave,
THEANO.

P.S. *I beg an immediate Answer, But oh! my Dearest! let your Pen speak kinder than your Eyes have done this Day, and inform me, if I may hope the Blessing of seeing you this Evening.—I have been too happy, not to burn with the extremest Impatience for a Repetition of it, which only can assure me of the Continuance of your Affection, or afford me the Means to give you Proofs of mine.—For a short time, therefore, adieu, my Soul's only Joy.*

LETTER XIV.

ELISMONDA *to* THEANO,
in Answer to the former.

HAVING, by my late Behaviour, forfeited all the little Pretensions I once had to your Esteem, you must certainly be the most generous Man alive, to continue the Professions of it.— Too just an Admiration have I for your Virtues, and too fixed a Tenderness for your Person, to repent having given myself to one so infinitely deserving: But, oh! my dear *Theano!* the *Manner* of my yielding admits of no Excuse, and leaves not the least Room to hope I can maintain any Place in a Heart fill'd only with the most noble and refin'd Idea's.—Heavens! on your first Request to grant what ought to have been the Reward of Years unceasing Pressures, and prov'd Constancy!—What can you think of me?—or rather, what is there of weak, or vile, that you may not think of me?— Shame, and Confusion overwhelm my Soul, and the most dread

---

[1] Heat.

Despair alarms Reflection, and tells me, 'tis impossible you can love what seems so unworthy to be lov'd.—How severely have I condemn'd in others that very Error I have now fallen into myself! and can neither merit nor expect Compassion, whatever Misfortune shall ensue.—Yet were there a Window to my Soul, and every secret Movement there exposed to view, not one unchaste Desire, or wanton Thought, would rise to my Disgrace; *guilty* in Fact, but *innocent* in Intent: I stand indeed an Instance of my Sex's *Weakness*, but not *Immodesty*. From the first Moment that I saw, I lik'd you; that *Liking*, by Degrees, grew up to *Love*; but still that Love was pure, and circumscrib'd within those Bounds which Friendship sets.—Heaven knows how free from any Wish, a Foe to Virtue, I accompany'd you to that fatal Garden, which soon after became the Scene of my Undoing.—How unsuspicious of your Design I suffer'd you to entertain me there, 'till falling Darkness dispers'd the Company, and the still Solitude of the silent Night encourag'd you to make an Attempt, by Day my Blushes might have oblig'd you to desist!—Oh! what was the Disorder of my Spirits in that Moment! the extreme Tenderness my Soul had long harbour'd for you, disarm'd my Indignation; I had not Courage to *resent*, and my Surprize render'd me unable to make use of any Arguments, that might have been of Force to *perswade*; quite power-less, and depriv'd, by these destructive Passions, of all Means of Defence, I suffer'd every Encroachment your rapacious Love could make, 'till it had all obtain'd, and I was wholly lost!—Oh, *Theano*! dear, lovely Conqueror! judge this Action as it is, and think not more meanly of the Victory, because acquir'd with Facility;[1]— believe that 'twas decreed for you alone; nor could even you, all-charming as you are, so soon have triumph'd, unaided by such powerful Allies.—You know I have some Fortitude,[2] and, in other Things, some Share of Reason also; think then how abundant that Love must be, which could at once destroy all Considerations but those inspir'd by itself; and let that Love plead in my Vindication.— The restless Hours I have pass'd this Night, the Tears I have shed, the bitter Agonies of my tumultuously-beating Heart, and that

---

[1] Ease.
[2] Moral strength.

heavy Melancholy you observed in me this Morning, were all, I confess, less owing to my Remorse, for having been guilty of an Action, which both the Laws of Heaven and Earth set down as criminal, than to my Fears that I had done what might render me cheap and contemptible to you.——Blest in your Affection, all the Proofs I am able to give of that exhaustless Store, which fills my Breast for you, I shall account my *Glory*, not my *Shame*.——A Visit from you this Evening about Six, confirming the kind, the ravishing Assurances your Letter gave, will, I hope, dissipate the Anxieties I labour under.——I will take Care to rid myself of all impertinent Interrupters, and be at Liberty to tell the dear Engrosser of my Soul, how much, and how truly I am his,

ELISMONDA.

LETTER XV.

THEANO to ELISMONDA.

NOTHING but those immortal Transports you last Night vouchsafed to bless me with, could have convinc'd me it was in Nature to have known a Joy more exquisite, than what I felt at the Receipt of your obliging Letter.——How immensely happy am I, to find my Love of so much Consequence to your Peace! and that the Melancholy I complain'd of in your Looks proceeded from so tender, tho' so unjust a Cause.——Absolve yourself, my Dear! and banish all Suggestions injurious to my Love and Gratitude.—— Long, tho' silently, have I ador'd you, and forbore to tell you so, only because I knew you were divinely stor'd with Arguments unanswerable; but by the Proofs of the most fervent and constant Passion that ever was, the Endeavours we make to ingratiate ourselves into the Affection of the Darling-Object, while in pursuit of what we wish, may justly be suspected, considering the indeed too general Instability of our Sex, but must be allowed real, when we have no more to obtain. It was, therefore, this Method I took to demonstrate a Sincerity, as uncommon as the Merits which inspir'd it. The Surprize my sudden Boldness gave you, can be atton'd for, but by the Assiduities of my whole future Life; and such they shall be, as will, I am certain, engage a pleas'd

Forgiveness.—In the mean time, permit, I conjure you, the sweet Serenity of mutual Love to reign alone in that soft lovely Bosom; too much already disquieted with causeless Doubts; and believe it, as it is, an utter Impossibility that my faithful Soul can ever cease to own you, as its dear and only Mistress, and Dictatress of its every Wish and Sentiment.—I send this Billet, not only to beguile some Part of the Time, 'till the appointed, long'd-for Hour, when I shall re-enjoy the sole Blessing, for which I desire Life, but also to prepare my adorable *Elismonda* to receive, with a firm Assurance of his Love and Honour, the

Happy THEANO.

LETTER XVI.

ELISMONDA *to* THEANO.

HOW impossible is it to have perfect Happiness! our supreamest Pleasures are blended with Disquiet, and Gall[1] is ever mingled with the Sweets of Life. I had but just begun to taste the Joys rewarded Passion yields; but just establish'd in my Breast that Tranquillity you have so long wish'd to settle, when a sudden, and unthought-of Interruption tears me from your Embraces, and inflicts the inseparable Racks of Doubt. How fatal Absence may be to our Loves! *Armida*, who you know I am oblig'd, by an unavoidable Necessity, to continue with some Time, having received some late Slights from her Favourite *Berillus*, is grown envious of my Happiness in the approved Faith and Tenderness of my dear *Theano*, and cannot bear to see me in the assur'd Possession of a Joy she now despairs of obtaining. Her haughty Soul, torn with the Pangs of jealous and neglected Love, wishes to make the Misery contagious, and seeks its Repose[2] only in destroying that of others. A thousand Stratagems[3] has her cruel Malice made use of to fill me with Suspicions of your Truth. Not a Word you speak that will endure two Interpretations, but she wrests to your Prejudice.—Scarce a Look you give me, but she endeavours to make appear either

---

[1] Bitterness.
[2] Endpoint.
[3] Schemes.

deceiving, or contemptuous: But finding I have not so little Penetration as to be seduced by her Artifices,[1] she now throws off the Mask at once, avows her Hatred to you, and will no longer admit your Visits: She has sworn to treat you with the utmost Rudeness, if you again attempt to enter her forbidden Gates; and, in spite of the Secrets which a reasonable Person would imagine must put her infinitely more in my Power, than I can possibly be in hers, has given me some Hints, that if I continue any Correspondence with you, she will expose me to the utmost Censures of the ill-judging World.—A Woman, whose distracted Passions, such as fill her Breasts, renders regardless of her own Character, will make no Scruple to ruin that of another's, when it affords but the least Shadow of a self-Gratification.—I know her too well not to believe her *Actions* will even exceed her *Words*, and I must either avoid giving her the Opportunity, or resolve to suffer all that the most consummate Envy and Malice can invent. The Caution with which you have always behaved, convinces me that my Reputation is too dear to you, to permit you to desire I should do any to hazard it; and I am certain have given too substantial Proofs of the Ardency of my Affection, not to make you know my Inclination has no Part in this Separation.—Oh, *Theano*, never has my Soul endur'd a Shock more severe, to be depriv'd of your dear Presence, as for some Days I must be, is of it self scarce supportable! But when I reflect that from seeing me seldom, you may by Degrees be brought to an Indifference whether you see me at all, I cannot contain my Senses, Despair and Jealousy rend my tormented Breast, and *Armida* has her cruel Wish.—Write to me, advise me, comfort me, I have found a faithful Messenger who will convey your Letters to me, and return my Answers.—This is the only Way I can find out to keep Hope alive, and the Day you neglect the Opportunity I give you, the most terrible of all the Passions will take entire possession of my Thoughts, and Madness, or some horrid kind of Death, be the Portion[2] of

The Wretched
ELISMONDA.

---

[1] So little insight as to be seduced by her cunning.
[2] Destiny.

LETTER XVII.

Theano *to* Elismonda.
In Answer to the foregoing one.

SURE it is in the Power of *Elismonda* alone at once to pain and please, to make even Despair look lovely, and while she kills, transports!—What but the Divine Softness of your last Letter could enable me to support the cruel Misfortune it brings me News of?—Could any Thing but your partaking it alleviate my Sorrow at so sad a Deprivation of those Joys I have been so profusely blest with?—Oh, my Soul's only Comfort! that I endure this Alteration in my Fortune, with any tolerable Degree of Patience, is among the Wonders of the Power you have over me.—Though separated from all, for which I wish to live, I yet will live in Hope of better Days.—The Continuance of your Affection affords too real a Heaven in this World to admit a Desire to exchange it for another. No, *Armida*'s Malice shall not so far triumph over me, as to deprive me totally of *Elismonda*, nor my Charmer of a Lover, whose Constancy, Ardency and Tenderness, Earth cannot equalize.—Conscious then of my unshaken Faith, and that I have given all imaginable Proofs of it, how ought I to chide your Want of Confidence.—Methinks you should know it is impossible for *Theano* to let slip any happy Moment which should present him with the Means of reminding his dearest, his for-ever ador'd *Elismonda* of her Vows, and the ravishing Assurances she has given him never to be but his.—Never do I quit your Presence without the most passionate Regret.—Never do I approach you without the Raptures of a first Enjoyment.— No Business, no Diversion, or Amusement had ever the Power to drive you from my Thoughts, even for the smallest Particle of divided Time.—Sleeping, or waking, your Idea is ever before me.—And all my Hopes, my Fears, my Wishes, are for you, and the dear Interest of our mutual Love.—Can a few Days of Absence then have any Effect over a Faith so firm, a Tenderness so rooted? No, were it (which Heaven forbid) to last as long as Life, to Death I should adore with equal Fervency, still flattering my fond Heart with the Belief that in another World I should enjoy those Blessings which are deny'd me here, and live, and love to all Eternity.—But say, my dearest! Have I nothing, beside the present Want of your Conversation, to fear from this unhappy Separation?—Will not the Arts of *Armida* prevail to my Undoing, when I no more am present to convince you by a thousand nameless Endearments how truly I am yours? Oh how successful does witty Malice often prove! And how many Instances does History and daily Experience give us of Love ill-treated, and Tenderness abused, meerly by the base Designings of Persons envious of Joys themselves deserv'd not to partake.—Were I not perfectly acquainted with your Divine Penetration, how dreadful would this Reflection be! but I think you see too much into my Soul to give Occasion for it, and I will no more suspect my Fate or you, the sweet Disposer of it.—I wait with an unspeakable Impatience, a Line from you, which, I hope, will inform me when I may expect to renew that Happiness the curst *Armida* has interrupted: And in Pity to the Agonies this Absence inflicts, afford some fresh Assurances, that nothing shall persuade you ever to retract those Promises you have made

The Most Faithful, and

Most Passionate,

THEANO.

LETTER XVIII.

ELISMONDA *to* THEANO.

CONSOLE your self, my Dear *Theano*, if it be true, indeed, that you stand in Need of it for being, for a short Time, depriv'd of *Elismonda*: Soon will she be restor'd to you with added Passion and redoubled Tenderness: The Effect this Absence has produc'd in me, is to make me know more perfectly, than ever I could before, the Pleasures of your Presence, and endears you to me by a Kind of Obligation, for which I want a Name.—I cannot express what 'tis I now feel for you, and how greatly the Proofs of your Constancy has touch'd my Soul.—*Reason* now takes the Part of *Inclination*, and justifies my Choice.—I have now that infinite Satisfaction of knowing that I love not, because the most agreeable Person that Nature ever framed attracted my unwary Eyes, and captivated my

Heart; but because I have found a Man in whom no Deceit can harbour; a Man who has a Mind incapable of any Notions but those inspired by Virtue and by Honour, and who has in him so much of the Divine Essence, as to render him immutable; and can know no Variation in his Desires or Aim.—How blest I think my self, Words wou'd but meanly show; in your dear Arms alone my Soul can be explain'd.—The cruel Enemy of our mutual Wishes is to Morrow happily engag'd in a Business where my Presence is not desired. I will take that Opportunity of visiting *Clarinda*, where, if you meet me, as if by Accident, we will adjourn to some Place where I may freely show the God of my Desires,

I am all his,

ELISMONDA.

LETTER XIX.

ELISMONDA *to* THEANO,
on her having fail'd to meet him.

NEVER did I pass a Night in more Disquiet than the preceeding one.—I imagin'd that all the Professions of Love I had made you would now seem feign'd, and that you would hereafter account *Elismonda* among the Number of the false ones; but Oh! my Dear, if the Disappointment be really as cruel to you, as the past Demonstrations of your Love make me believe, by your own Agonies you may judge of mine, and without my telling you so, be assured that my Choice had no part in detaining me from your Embraces.—Heaven knows with what a pleas'd, yet impatient Expectance I past the Hours till the Time of *Armida*'s intended Departure. But Oh God! The long-wish'd Hour no sooner arrived, than all on a sudden, she fell into the Spleen,[1] fancy'd herself sick, undrest, and went to Bed: Though I knew her Distemper[2] was only in Imagination, had I attempted to leave her, the Neglect would have put her on an Enquiry into the Cause, she wou'd presently have thought it proceeded from *Theano*, and

---

[1] Became irritable.
[2] Illness.

had certainly sent a Spy after me.—I had no Person I could entrust with a Billet to you, else had sent to *Clarinda's* to prevent your waiting there, as I doubt not but you did, for my coming.—Oh, my dearest! to miss the Blessing of your Society is wretchedness enough, add not to my Misfortune by any unjust Suspicions of my Love or Truth.—I hope and expect a few Days more will put an End to the Constraint I am under, and convince you that you are Master of the whole Soul of

Your Devoted
ELISMONDA.

LETTER XX.

ELISMONDA *to* THEANO.
Writ immediately after the former;
on hearing he had not been at the Place appointed.

I AM extremely sorry that the News of how little Consequence the Justification of my Love is to you, did not sooner reach my Ears.—A few Minutes had spar'd my officious[1] Tenderness the Pains of Writing, or you the Trouble of Reading, an Excuse for what was rather an Obligation, than the contrary.—How fond, how weak, is our believing Sex when once that destructive Passion, Love, has taken Possession of our Hearts! How wretched did I make myself in the Thoughts of the imaginary Disappointment I was compell'd to give you, while you, forgetful, perhaps, of the Assignation, or indifferent what Opinion I might have of your Neglect, was trifling away the Hours of my Disquiet in Company more agreeable than mine.—Ungrateful Man! Is this the Love, the Constancy, the Honour you profess'd? Have you, with the softer Wishes, thrown off all Complaisance,[2] all Civility and common Respect, that you treat me in this manner? But why, alass! Do I reproach you for a Fault of which I am myself the Cause? In gratifying the one, I forfeited my Title to the others, to expect those Marks of Esteem which once were *Elismonda's* Due, would be too

---

[1] Dutiful.
[2] Politeness.

presuming and vain in the Slave of your looser Pleasures.—
Miserably blinded that I was, not to see this Truth till it was too
late.—When first charmed with the Prospect of your imagined
Tenderness, I stood unheedful on a Precipice, a dreadful Depth
behind me, which one false Step has plung'd me in, never to rise
again. This, therefore, shall be the last of my Upbraidings, or
Complaints: To Heaven I commit the Care of my Revenge for your
Perfidiousness;[1] and as I have sinned against Virtue, and myself, yield
to endure all that Remorse can inflict.—Terribly poignant[2] as are
the Agonies of my present State, I submit to them with the more
patience, because I cannot doubt but that they will soon take from
the World,

The ruin'd,
ELISMONDA.

LETTER XXI.

THEANO *to the Causelessly-offended* ELISMONDA.

HOW different from all her Sex is *Elismonda!* others, deceived
by their own Vanity, believe much more than our utmost flattery
can profess: But the Charmer of my Soul has a Humility which
will not suffer her to do justice to her own Merits, and renders it
impossible to make her assured that the Heart that once has felt her
Power can never cease to do so.—Yet in Spite of all your
Diffidence, I despair not of obliging you, hereafter, to acknowledge
that you are beloved with an unalterable Fervency. This Triumph,
I am certain, is reserv'd for the happy *Theano*.—And in Confidence
of that Blessing I read your Letter with no other Emotions than
were occasion'd by my Concern for the Pain it gave the dear
Writer.—Recollect, Sweet Distruster! how terrible a Storm arriv'd
with that Hour in which you intended to visit *Clarinda*. Did not
the angry Heavens seem all on fire? were not half Mankind shock'd
and appall'd to hear the Thunders roar, and see the bellying Clouds
pour down such Cataracts[3] of Rain as threatned us with a second

---

[1]   Deceitfulness.
[2]   Emotionally painful.
[3]   Waterfalls.

Deluge? and cou'd I expect, or indeed, desire my *Elismonda* should expose her soft and tender Frame to the wild Fury of so merciless a Season, against which neither a Coach nor Chair[1] was a sufficient Defence? All Endeavours to represent what 'twas I felt would be in vain, I thought the very Elements conspired against my Hopes, and utter'd, in my passion, Things which can be render'd excusable by nothing but the Cause.—So little was I able to brook the Disappointment with any Shew[2] of Moderation, that I thought it entirely inconsistent with Prudence to go to *Clarinda's*, where I should have been asked a thousand impertinent Questions concerning my ill Humour. Conscious however of the Force of Love, and how trifling any Dangers would appear to me which afforded a Probability of bringing me to my charming *Elismonda*, I was sometimes tempted by my fond Wishes to believe that the same Degree of tender Passion might influence her to dare even the Horrors of that Tempest to bless the longing Arms of her *Theano*.—I contriv'd, therefore, to send a Person who I was certain, was unknown to *Armida*, or any of her Family, to enquire if you were at Home, and being informed you were; took more Delight in indulging Contemplation with your dear Idea alone in my Chamber, than I could have done in any Company where I expected not to see you.—Wound me then no more with causeless Doubts of my Love, or my Sincerity, I am fully satisfied within myself that never Man felt more of both, and if any Thing could allow a Possibility of making you less dear, it would be your being guilty of an Injustice of this Kind.—I cannot bear the Pain it gives yourself; nor, as conscious Virtue is rarely without some Share of Pride, can ill brook to be deprived of a Title I so much glory in, that of being the most *Constant*, as well as most *Passionate* of all who ever called themselves Lovers.—I depend on the ravishing assurance your first Kind Billet this Morning gave me, of seeing you soon in a Place where we shall be eas'd of this cruel Constraint, and I have leave to prove, by Demonstrations more convincing than Words, how infinitely my Soul adores you.—Farewel, thou Life of my Desires.—Let nothing hinder me from the Blessing which even

---

[1] A large carriage or a one-seated vehicle for hire, carried on poles.
[2] That is, show.

this distant Conversation affords, and once more establish in your
mind a good opinion of

Your Entirely Devoted
and Unchangeable
THEANO.

LETTER XXII.

ELISMONDA *to* THEANO
in Answer to the Preceeding one.

TOO much Acquaintance have you with my Soul, not to
know that it admits with Pleasure every Thing in your Favour.—
Dreadful, as were the Pangs of your suppos'd Ingratitude, the Joy
of finding there is a Possibility that you are not guilty, fills me with
a Joy which more than compensates for my past Endurings.—I
love you, my dear *Theano!* with a Delicacy which is not to be
describ'd, nor is it in my Power to be satisfied with those Returns
which might make another Woman happy.—Ambitious that I
am, and too presuming.—What do the blest Above enjoy but a
perfect Harmony of Mind, Pleasures uninterrupted and the pure
Intelligence of each others Souls! yet I vainly aim to meet a parallel Felicity on Earth.—'Tis true, while in your loved Society, no
Mixture of Suspicion, or intervening Fears, disturb the soft
Delight; but alass! I own myself too Weak to endure the Shocks
of Absence.—A Thousand dread Ideas then take Possession of my
Soul.—Even now, this very Moment, how know I, but Chance
may present some Charmer to your View more worthy of you
than *Elismonda*, and that, if attracted by so great a Temptation, you
should even be able to resist it, and maintain the Faith you have
vowed, the Continuance of your Devoirs[1] to me would be the
Effect of *Honour*, not of *Inclination*; a Justice which you could not
swerve from, tho' you wished to do it.—Oh if so fatal an Accident
should ever happen, how miserable must I be!—To break off with
you, I must at the same Time break the Strings which hold my
throbbing Heart, and to continue a Correspondence with you,

---

[1] Acts of respect.

after knowing you thought me undeserving of it, would be a Meanness of Spirit which would render me contemptible even to myself.—Heavens, what a wide Sea of Perplexities do we launch into, when once we embark in Love! Hopes and Fears, immortal Transports, or distracting Horrors, divide our Hours, and lift us to the Skies, or sink us down to Hell; Tranquility is for ever fled, and the Position of our very Souls is changed.—Yet, let me never know Indifference more.—There is a Pleasure even in the Pains I suffer for *Theano*, which I cannot wish to part with for dull Insensibility and stupid Ease.—But why do I go about to discribe the Passion I have for you? You know, alass! more of my Extravagancies than I am able to express, and had need be possess'd of an equal Share yourself to pardon them in

Your

ELISMONDA.

P.S. *I cannot positively appoint the Day of our Meeting, but am flatter'd with the Hope, it will be in a few Days. A Billet before shall inform you of the Time and Place. Adieu my only and everlasting Dear.*

LETTER XXIII.

THEANO *to* ELISMONDA,
On being oblig'd to go into the Country.

HOW great an Enemy to *Love* is *Fortune*? no sooner do we begin to taste the Blessings of the *One*, but immediately the other with some curst Accident intervenes, and snatches us from the Scene of Joy.—Freed from *Armida's* jealous Envy, all your Suspicions of my Faith removed, with what a Heavenly serenity did I reflect on my rewarded Passion.—But alass! a new Misfortune falls upon me, and again subjects me to the Pains of Absence, and all the nameless Ills which are the irremedible Consequences of it.—I must leave you, *Elismonda*, for a long Age, for a whole Month, and have nothing to console me in so sad a Separation, but the Hope that the Affair I go to fix will put it in my Power to be eternally with you when I return. By this I doubt not but you guess I am about to dispose of my Concern in ***, the Management of which by Agency, you have heard me complain, has been so prejudicial to me: A thousand Times has the intricate Accounts I have received of it spread a Dulness over my Soul which scarce your dear Society was able to dissipate: Long have I desired to put an End to it in Person, but never could resolve to deprive myself of the Happiness your Conversation yields, but there is now an absolute Necessity, I must go, or consent to be imposed on in such a Manner as would merit your Contempt. I shall this Evening more fully relate the Particulars, when I expect to receive from you all that can ease the present Perturbations of

Your ever Faithful
THEANO.

LETTER XXIV.

THEANO *to* ELISMONDA.

THO I saw you but last Night, and then thought I had omitted nothing which might convince you of the Fervency of my Affection and secure the Continuance of yours, yet do I find already that I have utter'd but half the Meanings of my Soul, a Thousand tender Things crowd one upon another, and reproach me that the little I have said injures my Passion by the poor Description: Would Time permit another soft Adieu, Methinks, I could now, much better, represent how infinitely Dear you are to me.——Could pour out my abundant Fondness in Terms, which would lay my Heart as open as my Visage,[1] and shew the mighty Influence you have there.——But 'twill not be allowed, the Coach is ready, my Friends wait for me, every Thing is prepar'd for my Departure, and I but stole this Moment to remind you of your Vows, and to wish you more Happiness than can be found (when absent from you) by the

Ever Passionately-devoted
THEANO.

---

[1] Face.

LETTER XXV.

THEANO *to* ELISMONDA,
From the first Post-Town.

I SHOULD be strangely unworthy the Blessings I receive, could I consent to take any Refreshment till I had first return'd my Thanks to that Goddess, whose bright and loved Idea accompanies me in my Journey, smooths the most rugged Way, softens my Cares, warms me in the midst of wintry Storms, and defends me from a Sensibility of all those Fatigues complain'd of by the Companions of my Travels.—Oh *Elismonda!* if it be true that you, indeed, know what it is to Love like me, you need not be told that, such a Passion is every thing to the Mind possest of it. He who is *happy* in that Wish, is capable of no *Pain*: He, who is the *Contrary*, can feel no *Ease*: The severest Darts of ill Fortune strive in vain to wound the *one*; the most benevolent Planets would fail to satisfy the *other*.— While, by your divine Goodness I continue among the Number of the Blest in Love, no Cares, no Sorrows will have the Power to move me, my only Aim is *Elismonda*, and I have *all* in Her!—The repeated and impertinent Calls of my less spiritually employed Companions, remind me that Supper is on the Table, and compel me to defer till to Morrow, when I expect to reach *****, any farther Declarations how much I am, and ever must be,

> *My most Loved, most Ador'd*
> ELISMONDA's,
> *Constantly Zealous Votary*
> THEANO.

LETTER XXVI.

THEANO *to* ELISMONDA.
From *****.

THE Satisfaction I receive in being safely arrived at *****, is vastly heighten'd by the Belief you will participate in it, and that I am in a Place where I may hope speedily to be blest with hearing from you: Tho' to my Mind's Eye you are ever present, yet are the intellectual Conversations which the Spirit feasts me with too immaterial to be long subsisted on; I tell myself I am still as Happy as ever in your dear Affections, that you see nothing in Man which can obliterate the Memory of *Theano*, and give Ear to no Suggestion to his Prejudice.—But, alass! how soon may ever varying Imagination shift the Scene, and represent you, repentant of the Favours you have so profusely showr'd upon me, unkind, and seeking some Pretence to break off an Acquaintance you no longer think deserving your Regard.—Oh, save me from so dreadful an Apprehension! Write to me with all that soft Indulgence which first assured me of your Love, and omit nothing to strengthen the Weakness of my Faith in the Continuance of it.—What I already Feel, in this short Time, convinces me that I shall stand in need of your utmost Tenderness to enable me to support an Absence of eight and Twenty Days.—Oh, God! how many tedious Hours compose that space of Time! how would it be possible to beguile them without your kind assistance! But to shew you how studious I am for Happiness, I divide them into Weeks, one Day of which, I shall set apart for the Expectation of receiving a Letter from you; the next, for indulging the dear Delight of Reading it a thousand and a thousand Times; the third, for answering it; the fourth, for reflecting on what I have wrote, and forming an Idea to myself how obliging a Welcome you afford the Professions of my inviolable Integrity; then, return to the Hope of your Reply, and so on, till the long Age is expired. Take Care, therefore, my dearest *Elismonda!* and be punctual in writing, for should you neglect one Post, you break the whole Machine my industrious Love has form'd, for Hope, or Ease, to rest upon, and jealous Doubts, accompanied with a numberless Train of Inquietudes, will take Possession of my Brain, deform my Reason, and render me scarce to be known for

> *Your tenderly Affectionate*
> THEANO.

LETTER XXVII.

Elismonda *to* Theano.

AS I never was ambitious of Beauty but to please my dear *Theano*, so I was also content with that little share of Wit, Nature has allowed me, till I found the want I had of it, whenever I went about to express my Passion for him. I received your three obliging Letters, but with Rapture, 'tis impossible to make you sensible, unless Rhetorick were as easy to be learn'd as Love; and, with that Infinity of the one you have inspir'd, you had likewise instructed me in the other.—No Words but such as yours, charming Master of my Soul! are fit to set forth the extatick Bliss I feel in those precious Testimonies of your Constancy. Scarce can I think your Absence a Misfortune, since the Consequence of it is so glorious for me, and so honourable for you. The Thoughts of your Return, and our happy Meeting again, fills me with Ideas too ravishing to admit Allay, and the Grief to find you not with me now, is lost in the Joy that you will soon be so.— Like you, I count the Days, but 'tis those that are over, and receive new Pleasure every Night in the Reflection that I have still one less to pass in Expectation.—Instead of amusing myself with any Thing that might make me forget you, I take no Delight but in remembring you: Recollection presenting me with ten thousand nameless Softnesses your dear Society blest me with, I enjoy them over again in Theory,[1] and flatter myself that an exhaustless Store are still behind.—Oh *Theano*! If all who profess themselves Lovers, were. such as we are, the most Severe and Wise would cease to disapprove their Passion; the Name of Love would no longer be contemptible, nor our weak Sex be reduced to endure the unequal Conflict between Prejudice and Inclination. Impute not the Confidence I have in you, I beseech you, to any Vanity of my own Merit: No, were I Mistress of all that's excellent in Woman-kind, 'twould be too little to engage the Continuance of your Affection were you not more than Man, at least such as Man ordinarily is, but your dear Soul bears all your Maker's Image, and retains the Immutability of that Divine Source whence 'tis derived.—What once appear'd worthy of your Affection, will always do so, 'tis as impossible for you to become ungrateful as it would be for me to live after the Knowledge you were so.—I will therefore, lay no Injunctions on you to remember, or prefer me to the more deserving Objects

---

[1]   Loosely, imagination.

which may happen to fall in your Way.—You have sworn you
will, and that is sufficient to assure the

Fortunate and Depending
ELISMONDA.

LETTER XXVIII.

THEANO *to* ELISMONDA.
From ******.

KNOWING, as I do, the Excellence of your Nature, it is
impossible to suspect you guilty of Deceit; I set it down as a heavenly Truth, that I am blest in your Affection, and cannot, my
charming Heroine! sufficiently admire your Fortitude in sustaining a Tryal so severe as Absence: Fain would I, excited by your
Example, regulate my Impatiencies, and content myself with ideal
Joys till a Possibility of more substantial ones arriv'd. More than
half the cruel Time already is expired, and I confess I have enough
in the dear Assurances of your Love to make me pass the rest in a
pleas'd Expectation, yet still a restlessness of Desire creeps in upon
me, and will not suffer me to taste any true Felicity, till I have all
my *Elismonda* in my Arms, when engag'd on the most important
and serious Affairs, the Remembrance how far I am removed from
you comes cross my Thoughts, and will not suffer me either to
speak, or reply to what is said to me, with any Connection.—Oh!
how little capable is a real Lover of ought but Love!—how insupportable are any other Cares!—And how vainly do we endeavour
to forget our Passion, tho' but for a Moment!—Measuring of
Land, debating on the Bounds of it, giving Instructions to Lawyers,
and all the dull Formalities which attend business of that Kind, are,
methinks, beneath the Man whom *Elismonda* favours: It seems my
Duty, as I am sure it is my Inclination, to give up my whole Soul
to her, and it is with an unspeakable Reluctance, I deprive her of
the minutest Part, your consent, nay, your Commands, were
absolutely necessary to make me do myself Justice, in a Matter
wherein I had been so greatly wrong'd; and my Obedience to
them, infinitely more than any Interest of my own, obliges me to
assume the Man of Business as much as I am able.—Would to

Heaven the Task were over, and I now about to receive the sweet Recompence of my long Anxieties! my Heart beats high, and every swelling Vein throbs with tumultuous Joy at the very Imagination; what then will be my Raptures when I again behold you, and am permitted to revel in those immense Delights your yielding Charms affords! Oh that I could retain the Thought till I indeed were blest with the Reality! But 'twill not be, Fields, Woods, Rivers, the Distance of a hundred tedious Miles, divide me from that Heaven of Felicity, and remind me that 'tis yet a long Season, a Season of twelve Days, and as many cruel Nights, before I can be happy.—Pardon, my Dearest! the Wildness of my burning Passion, and know that, in our Sex especially, there is no Medium in Affection. I depend so much on your divine Promise, that I will not repeat my earnest Adjurations[1] that you should constantly write to me: Your Letters being the only Cordials[2] for a Soul languishing like mine. Farewel, my only, my everlasting Charmer! A Legion of Guardian Spirits, all Friends to Love and Truth, attend about you, and preserve you for

Your tenderly Devoted,
and most Passionate
THEANO.

LETTER XXIX.

ELISMONDA *to* THEANO.

NOTHING can be more true, than that the greatest Boasters have the least of what they pretend to.—I but deceived myself when I imagined, that I had Courage enough to sustain the Shocks of Absence, one Word, and that too spoke without Design, has had the Power to overthrow all the Resolution I believed too fix'd. Hapning to be at *Miranda's* the other Day, that Lady who, you know, is not ignorant of our Acquaintance, though she is of our Loves, said carelessly she doubted not but you would bring a Wife to Town with you. I forced myself to smile, and turned the

---

[1] Entreaties.
[2] Stimulants.

Discourse fearing the Continuance of it would have discovered me to be more interested in it than I would have her imagine. But, Oh Heaven! how many distracted Ideas did this Supposition of hers, raise in me.—The Person with whom your Concern in ***** is, I remembred to have heard has a Sister, whom, if Report does not greatly flatter, is a very lovely Woman, many other Gentlemen of the County would questionless be proud of your Allyance, and the bare Possibility that some one of the numerous Offers might be made you, would be acceptable, gave me Horrors which I am little able to express, much less endure for any long Time.—Variety has Charms for almost all your Sex, and when it presents it self joined with the prevailing Motives of Interest,[1] how can the already enjoyed *Elismonda* hope to defend you from their Insinuations? Tell me, my *Theano*! is my Love and Truth a sufficient Bulwark from the united Temptations of Wealth, Grandeur, and untasted Beauty? If I am indeed so blest, once more assure me of it, and though the Time of your Return is near arrived, anticipate the Joy of seeing you, by confirming what you have so often sworn, that you would bring to *London* the same Sentiments of me, with which you were possest at leaving it.—I would not give myself Liberty to think there is a Possibility you can be false, confine me, therefore, from doing you an Injustice of that Kind, by a kind and speedy Relief from all those Apprehensions, which, in Spite of all your Vows, and my own Endeavours to repel them, will sometimes invade the Heart of

Your undiscribably passionate,
ELISMONDA.

LETTER XXX.

THEANO *to* ELISMONDA
From *****.

PARDON me, my Dearest, when, according to the wonted[2] Sincerity of my Soul, I confess to you that I am not displeas'd to

---

[1] Profit.
[2] Customary.

know you recede a little from that Strength of Resolution you endeavour'd to maintain: not only because this Taste of Jealousy more assures me of your Love, but also, because you will, with greater Facility, be brought to pity what I endure in this tormenting Absence. Tho' conscious Truth, and an undiminish'd Ardency of Affection assures me, no Man can more deserve the Blessing of your Love than *Theano*, yet as there are many who may pretend the same, with greater Advantages than I can boast, in other Requisites[1] to please the Fair, how reasonable do my Doubts sometimes appear!—No more, then, blame those Apprehensions which my Demerit renders just, since you, so divinely stored with every Charm to captivate Mankind, are capable of suspecting your own Power.—But this uncertainty will, I hope, on both sides, be shortly at an End, and I shall again enjoy the unutterable Felicity of giving and receiving every tender Demonstration of a mutual and inviolable Passion.—My troublesome Affair is just on the Point of being concluded, I depend that to morrow will ease me of that inveterate Enemy of my softer Wishes, Business.—Then dearest *Elismonda*! if I delay an Hour, a Moment, hastning to your Arms, believe me the basest, falsest, and most ungrateful of my Sex, instead of

Your Passionately faithful

And ever Zealously devoted

THEANO.

P.S. *Tho I flatter myself that I shall begin my Journey towards you the Day after to morrow: Let not that prevent your writing; because if any unforeseen Accident should delay the wish'd for Expedition, I shall have nothing to console me, if by it I am also depriv'd of the Blessing of hearing from you: If I set out therefore, as I hope to do, I will leave a Servant behind to receive and bring your Letter after me to ***, when I will not fail to write to you.—Farewell, my Soul's best and dearest Part. Think justly of my Regard, and you will always continue to love me.*

---

[1] Particulars, respects.

LETTER XXXI.

HOW benignant[1] a Duty is Love to Hearts truly affected with his Influence! How vastly do the Pleasures he affords compensate for the Pains! Our very Sufferings are Blessings, and serve but to endear, and more refine ensuing Joys! Tho' I am half confident a Passion, such as ours, would never know Decay, were we to be together for a long Eternity, yet does this Interruption make us more sensible how little we should be able to live without each other, and by trying the Purity and Strength of our Affection, yield still new Reasons for our mutual Esteem.—Oh *Theano!* How justly dear are you to the Soul of *Elismonda*, and how greatly do I glory in testifying myself not unworthy the Place you vouchsafe me in yours!—Felicitous[2] Reflection! Blissful Harmony of Minds! We love without having any thing wherewith to accuse ourselves for doing so, and to how high a Degree soever our Passion rises, are certain it can never exceed the Bounds of Justice. If there be any thing in the Pre-existence of Souls, ours were, surely, Lovers from the Beginning, and shall continue so through all the Worlds we shall hereafter pass.—The Bent of our Desires so much the same, it seems, methinks, as if one Will actuated both, and we are two Persons only because we could no otherwise be pair'd. Oh with what Ardency do I long to be re-united to myself again! And with what Transports does my Bosom swell in the assured Hope of it! *Theano* is all the World to me, nor have I Ears or Eyes for any other Object; Haste then to restore me, for in thee is the whole Comfort, Light, and Life of

ELISMONDA.

---

[1] Benevolent.
[2] Happy.

LETTER XXXII.

WHAT could happen to contradict my Wishes has! Sir *Thomas* was taken suddenly ill, which prevented his coming to *****, and obliged us to go to his House: Two Days longer than I expected, therefore, have I been detain'd; and how happy was it for me that I entreated you to write, nothing but your dear Letter could have made me support that unlook'd-for Disappointment with any tolerable Degree of Resignation, but all my Cares are now over, and I have the boundless Happiness to tell the lovely Inspirer of my every Wish, that within an Hour I shall take Horse, in order to come to *London.* I chuse to return that way, because I could no other avoid the Company of those Gentlemen who accompanied me hither, and I flatter myself that Tenderness you so divinely express for me, will prevail on you to meet me the last Stage, which I expect to be at on Saturday. My Spirits are too much hurried, between the rapturous Idea of our Meeting, and my Impatience for that Blessing, to be able to answer your heavenly Letter as I ought, but think all that your own soft Soul can conceive, or your inchanting Tongue can utter in the most tender Moments, and believe that, and more, if it be possible, is, and will be ever, the Reflections of his most transporting *Elismonda's*

Eternally adoring
THEANO.

LETTER XXXIII.

THEANO *to* ELISMONDA,
From the first post Town. [1]

THE cruel Distance is now shortned twenty Miles, and before Sun-set I hope to be as many more nearer my *Elismonda.*—How delightful does this second Journey seem, and how irksome was the former. The rugged Roads are smooth'd, the Stages shortned,

---

[1] Town with a postoffice.

the Hills and Precipices are no longer frightful, every Thing, methinks, looks gay and lovely as I approach the Residence of my Soul's Charmer.—What Fatigue can be felt by him who goes to *Elismonda*.—That enchanting Thought makes me all Spirit, and incapable of regarding what concerns my grosser Part.—Oh I could dwell for ever on the extatick Theme, but the Moments are too precious to be past in Contemplations.—This comes but to repeat my earnest Entreaty of seeing you on Saturday at *** where about six you may expect to find

The Impatient
THEANO.

LETTER XXXIV.

THEANO *to* ELISMONDA
From the second Post Town.

NEVER did I experience a Disappointment more perplexing than this I now send you an Account of. The many Charming Assurances you have given me of your Affection made me certain of your Compliance with my Request of meeting me at *** and I indulged the Idea of that Blessing with Raptures, such as I flatter myself you sympathiz'd enough with, not to need any Description of. But Oh my *Elismonda!* the very eager Haste I made to you, deprives me of you a Day longer than I hoped.—I overtook *Cleander* in his Journey to *London*, and there is now no Possibility of quitting his Company till we both arrive there: Never, before, was the Presence of that worthy Friend unwelcome, but the Disquiet with which I now endure it, is not a small Proof how infinitely preferable your Charms are to all other Things the World calls dear or valuable.—Scarce can I behave to him with that Regard which his good Qualities, my long Experience of them, and the Alliance between us, claim from me.—He wonders at the unusual Uneasiness he perceives me in, asks me a thousand Questions concerning my Affairs, will not be perswaded but that something has gone wrong at *****, and endeavours to bring me into a better Humour by all the Pleasantries of Wit, and that unceasing Gaiety he is Master of.—But alass! he knows not I am no longer the

Theano that I was, that I am now all *Elismonda's*, and that every Thing which attempts to divert me from the Thoughts of her, or interrupts me in that sweet Employment, are no more than so many impertinent Intrusions, and *distract*, instead of *restoring* my Harmony of Mind.—But if, as I hope, and you divinely express, we have but one Soul, the Part I left behind with you, will sufficiently inform you of the Pain I feel in being depriv'd of the Happiness of seeing you at ***, and the Pleasure which fills my Breast when I reflect that on Sunday next I shall be in *London*, and in the dear Arms of her who is the only and everlasting Blessing of her

Most faithful
THEANO.

LETTER XXXV.

THEANO *to* ELISMONDA,
On his Arrival.

I HAVE now, Thanks to my Benignantly conducting Stars, reach'd *London*, let me know by a line if no cross Accident prevents my being this Night in Possession of a Happiness I have so long languish'd for.—I have with much ado got rid of *Cleander*, who would fain have perswaded me to accompany him Home, and I attend alone, full of transporting Expectations, the dear Mandate which shall summons me to the Heaven of *Elismonda's* Embraces.—Oh how I could dwell on the delightful Subject, but am now past the unsubstantial Joys which *Theory* affords, and burn with the most fierce Impatience for the *Reality*.—The Moments are too precious to be wasted in Contemplations; be therefore, my Angel, as brief in *granting* as I am in *requesting* an Admission to those Extacies, which, as they are in the Power of no other Woman to bestow, could be tasted by no Man in so superlative a Degree as by

The happy, and the adoring
THEANO.

LETTER XXXVI.

ELISMONDA *to* THEANO.
In answer to the former.

A Thousand, and a thousand Welcomes to the dear Inspirer of *Elismonda's* Wishes, and Source of all her Joys.—Oh fain would I discribe the Extacy I feel at your Approach, but 'tis not in the Power of Words.—Hasten then to my fond longing Arms, for 'tis in the mute Rhetorick of Love I can alone testify how passionately, how tenderly I am

My dear,

My *Transporting* Theano's

ELISMONDA.

P.S. *I have been denied to all Company this whole Day, in Expectation of my Soul's Treasure; delay not, therefore, a Moment to bless me.*

LETTER XXXVII.

DORIMENUS *to* ERMINIA,
On Loving at first sight.

IF Beauty be properly compar'd to Lightning, why should the sudden Influence of yours be doubted? They must be Charms of an inferior Nature, to those the divine *Erminia* is possest of, which require Time to steal into the Heart, and you are guilty of an Injury to yourself, which I could not pardon in any other, to suppose that there is a Necessity for you to be seen more than once, to make you be ador'd. I grant that you have Perfections too numerous to be discover'd at one View, and that no Imagination is extensive enough to take in all your Wonders without being perfectly acquainted with them, yet give me leave to affirm, by the Experience of my own Heart, that, tho' frequent Conversations may more secure your Conquest, you inspire as much with one Transient View as a Soul is capable of receiving.—Oh, why *Erminia!* are you the only Person of all the World who is Blind to your own Loveliness?—do you never look into a Glass?—or does the unfaithful Mirror represent you different from what you are?— No, no, you too well know your Beauty's Power, and but feign an

Ignorance of it to excuse that cruel Reserve, with which you have hitherto behaved to all Mankind. I confess the first Professions of our Sex may sometimes be justly enough suspected, only the Effects of Gallantry.[1] Nor will I alarm your Modesty by any farther Repetitions, how infinitely your Perfections exceed all that yet ever bore the Name of Charming, I only entreat to be permitted to give you more substantial Evidences of my Passion than Words can do.—My Constancy, my firm attachment to your Will, my everlasting Study to please and serve your every Wish, will, I doubt not, hereafter convince you of my Sincerity, and attone for the deficiency of other Merits. Till then I only beg to be receiv'd among the number of those who Visit you, and that you will allow me the Glory of Subscribing myself

The most adorable Erminia'*s*
Truly devoted Slave
DORIMENUS.

LETTER XXXVIII.

ROSANDER *to* AMYTHEA,
On being rejected by her for having lov'd before.

THE severe repulse you give my Passion, for having been devoted to a former Object, is not more cruel to me, than unjust to yourself. A young and unexperienc'd Heart is set on Fire by the least spark of Beauty, we immediately *like*, and call, nay, also imagine what we feel at that Time, *Love:* but alass, how widely different are all those wandring Flames, from the solid glow of serious Inclination. What I have been possest of for another, only serves to convince me of this Truth, and had I really ador'd with as much Fervency as you accuse me of, it still would but more testify the superiority of your Charms which triumph over it. But I am told, you say, that I receded not from my former Passion, but because either I found the Gratification of it an impossibility, or having obtain'd my utmost Wish, was become cloy'd with the Enjoyment of it. Assure yourself, Lovely *Amythea!* that both these Suppositions

---

[1] Polite attentiveness.

are equally groundless, and in the highest degree injurious to me; I am neither Coward enough to desist the Prosecution of any thing I desire for the sake of Difficulty, nor base enough to make the ruin of any Woman my Aim, I made my Addresses to *Bellimante*, because she appear'd the most deserving Lady I then was acquainted with, but since the Wonders of your Form and Mind presented themselves to my transported View, the Beauties, the Merits of your whole Sex besides are lost amidst their Blaze.—My Passion for you therefore is inspir'd, assisted, and must be continued by my Reason, which I must entirely be depriv'd of before I can cease to admire, what is in reality so much deserving Admiration, nor can my transferring those Affections to you, which I before had vow'd to another, be term'd Inconstancy, or by any disinterested[1] Judge be deemed as Criminal. Errors in Religion when rectified claim our Applause: 'Till now I was ignorant of the *true* Divinity, and to have worshipped a *false* one has been rather my *misfortune* than my *fault*; forgive it, I beseech you, O most Adorable *Amythea!* and content yourself with believing that I would not refuse Martyrdom to testify the sincerity of my Conversion, without putting it to the *proof*, since by it you wou'd be depriv'd of

The most Faithful of his Sex,
ROSANDER.

LETTER XXXIX.

AGARIO *to* MIRANDA,
On her confessing a Passion for Him, yet refusing to Marry him.

WHO but *Miranda* ever had the Art to mingle Heaven and Hell? to fill the Breast at once with Joys almost too great for Sense to bear, and Horrors adequate? To tell me as you do, that you approve my Person, that my Character, Principles and Humour[2] are such as you wou'd wish to find in the Man you should make choice on, and that nothing is so dear to you as the Proofs I give you of my Affection, yet at the same time refuse to

---

[1] Not motivated by desire for profit.
[2] Temperament.

make me yours by the most honourable Tye that Love can form, is somewhat so incongruous as cannot be accounted for. Ah, *Miranda!* if in reality you were truly sensible of that Passion you profess, the dull considerations of Interest, and the vain Censure of an ill-judging World, would have little Effect on you. What if Fortune sheds her Favours on us with a niggard[1] Hand, Love can abundantly supply all our Wants, and, under the Protection of that Bounteous Divinity, we may be shelter'd from every Storm of Fate. To those united by a sincere Affection all things are easy, they have that happy Art of converting into Felicity, what to others would be Wretchedness, because placing their *summum bonum*[2] in each other, they find it there, and esteem nothing a Misfortune that occasions not Separation. Few indeed are so sublime in their desires, and I remember to have heard a very ingenuous Person say, that to *Love,* and be *lov'd* in such a manner, was, he believed, too much of *Heaven* to be experienc'd on *Earth.* The Devil, that subtil Maligner of the Joys we are capacitated to possess, inspires us with Notions, which render us Enemies to ourselves. State, Grandeur, or at least Convenience are the general Motives that instigate both Sexes to Marriage, and if by chance two meet on other Terms, they are look'd upon by the rest of Mankind not as they are, Prodigies[3] of good Sense and Honour, but as unthinking Wretches, mad-brain'd Fools that know not what they do. Prejudice of Education goes a great way in propagating this Opinion; our Fathers told us so, and we imagine ourselves under an Obligation to believe as they did. But, dear *Miranda,* you have too great a share of Reason yourself to depend on that of others; exert it, and I ask no more. Examine if you have any thing to apprehend in giving yourself to a Man, of whose Love and Honour you confess to have receiv'd undeniable Proofs. If I, on the maturest deliberation, can resolve to run all Hazards with you, endure all the Hardships of a narrow Fortune, you may assure yourself I shall take care to ease the load of them on your side as much as possible, and does not that Generosity

---

[1] Stingy.
[2] Literally, highest good; the usage here is irregular, although its meaning is clear.
[3] Exemplary instances.

of Soul, that delicacy which in other Affairs is so conspicuous in you, teach you to reflect that you ought to forgo the *Superfluities* of Life for him, who with you cou'd feel no Ills in *Poverty*, nor without you, no felicity in *Wealth?* But if even this is too little to influence you, believe my Love and Life are so wound up together, that without the Gratification of the one, the other cannot last, and resolve not utterly to destroy him who adores you with an unextinguishable Affection,

AGARIO.

P.S. *I intend to wait on you this Evening, and have some distant hope of finding you in a more favourable Disposition; Nay, may almost venture to assure myself of it, if any part of that Tenderness you have so often made Professions of be real.—Farewell, my dearest Angel. Reflect seriously on what I've said, and be assur'd that when I protest to live no longer than I am permitted to expect the Reward of my Passion, I do it with the same Sincerity and Resolution which you have observ'd in me, on concerns of infinitely less Consequence to my Eternal Happiness.—I desire no answer in Writing, chusing rather to hold an Argument with your Eyes than Pen. Be alone, if possible, and about four expect the impatient* Agario.

LETTER XL.

JULIA *to* ANTIPHONE.
On being about to be compell'd by her Parents to marry another.

IF I had follow'd the Dictates of my Inclination, I shou'd rather have chose to inform you by word of Mouth, of the cruel necessity there is for us to part, than to have wrote it. But as I have believ'd you Love, and know the impatience that Passion inspires, in Persons of your Sex, I could not trust myself to the Danger of your Complaints.—Take then, the sad Truth at once, for the Confusion of my Thoughts will not suffer me to say much.—My Parents, who prefer Wealth to Merit, and imagine that by making me *Great* they make me *Happy*, have commanded me, in spite of all my Tears and Prayers, to give my Hand to *Orosinus:* Judge if my Heart has any share in this Testimony of my Obedience, and not upbraid but pity me. 'Tis true, I have a thousand times confest that you alone were capable of influencing me with any soft Emotions, and as often have given you all the Assurances in my Power that I would be only yours; but alass! you knew I was not Mistress of myself, and ought not to have too much depended on what my Passion induced me to promise. Fortune ever is averse to Love, but this may serve to Console you, that it is not the effect of my Choice.—No, *Antiphone*, believe the disappointment of our mutual Wishes is infinitely more terrible to me, than it can possibly be to you, not only because my Soul's more Tender, and endued with a less portion of Fortitude, but also, because you have only a single Woe to combat with; But I am destin'd to a double Misery of quitting all I love, and devoting myself to the Object of my Hate.—Oh! what a shock to Nature, to lye in loath'd Embraces.—To aid detested Raptures, and by tyranick Duty be compell'd to take Delight in my own Wretchedness.—How shall I support it?—How disguise my fix'd Aversion? Could the unutterable Passion which my Soul feels for you ever be extinguish'd, *Orosinus* would be still rather my Scorn than Love; but as the remembrance of your Worth, your Tenderness, your Constancy, your thousand Perfections, will, to my Lifes end, be ever present to me, how greatly must that remembrance heighten my disgust! 'Tis knowing *Heaven*, to be doom'd to *Hell*.—'Tis not in the Power of Duty, Virtue, or Advice, to comfort me under a Calamity no words can give a Name to, nor Thought, unfeeling it, conceive.—Your sight, your Conversation was once my only Blessing, now would it be my greatest Curse in rendring me criminal, as well as miserable.—Avoid me, therefore, I conjure you, write to me, see me, speak to me no more! lest, as now, I should declare the Fondness of my distracted Heart, and falsify the Vows I am constrain'd to make.—'Tis Guilt enough, even before the fatal knot is tyed, to acknowledge what I do: Let *Good Nature* teach you to Pity, and *Religion* to Pray for me; for as I am, there is not a Wretch on Earth so lost, so abandon'd by her Reason.—As for what you will suffer on my score, *Philosophy* will, I hope, enable you to sustain, and *Time* to put a Period to it; for I desire not to be loved when all Returns are hopeless.—No, that would be to hate you, Heaven forbid that you should feel any part of those tormenting Pangs, which rend my Breast, and make Life a Burthen.—Among the various perplexities I am in, that of resolving to be for ever separated from you, without even the melancholy Consolation of a last Adieu, is not the least Difficult to be born, yet dare I not allow myself to take it, for the Reasons I have already told you; nor will I admit of any Answer to this, unless you can prevail on yourself to write nothing that may add to my Distraction; I mean, not offer by vain Arguments to perswade me contrary to that indispensable Obedience owing to those who gave me Being.—As all I am is theirs, they doubtless have a right to dispose me either to Happiness or Misery; and since they have decreed the latter, *Resignation* must be my *Practice*, and *Patience* my *Study*.—Would to Heaven there were a Possibility of attaining it, 'tis all I have now to implore, or hope for myself.—But for you, if there be any Blessings in the Almighty's Store-house, superior to what was ever showr'd on Man, may you be distinguish'd in the Enjoyment of them, and in their unintermitting course pass all your Days, that Death may seem but a Translation from one Heaven to another.—Farewell, think with Compassion, but not Grief on the Sufferings of

The lost,

The despairing,

JULIA.

LETTER XLI.

ANTIPHONE *to* JULIA.

In answer to the foregoing.

TO tell you I receiv'd yours, is enough to make you sensible of the Position of my Heart, at least if you are capable of feeling any part of that Passion you have so abundantly made Professions of. In vain, Oh too much lov'd, ador'd! You think to sooth my Anguish by setting forth your own, you *make* your Misfortune, if it be one, mine is *constrain'd*, and to be unhappy thro' *Choice* is a different thing from being so by *Necessity*.—No Law, either Humane or Divine, obliges us to resign ourselves to the Will of our Parents, when they would impose injustice on us, and what can be more so than to give away what is not our own? By their Consent, and your Inclination, I once was Master of your Vows.—

You were mine.—They had no longer a Power to dispose of you.—A Gift once given ought never to be resum'd, and if out of my extream regard for you, I forbear demanding that Satisfaction of your Father, which such an injury requires, I will yet force the Invader of my Right, the haughty *Orosinus*, to confess the Error he has been guilty of, and quit his Claim.—No, *Julia*, no, 'tis thro' my Blood alone he shall obtain a Passage to your Arms.—To waste the Time in idle, and weak complainings, would defeat both my Love and my Revenge.—'Tis not *Words*, but *Deeds*, shall speak how much I prize, how greatly I am wrong'd.— You see I am punctual to your Commands, in attempting not to dissuade you from that implicite regard you seem resolved to pay to the injunctions of your cruel Parents, it lies in me to vindicate my Pretensions, and prove myself not unworthy the blessing they once made me hope.—Before the expiration of 12 Hours you will know more.—'Till when adieu my Eternally-lov'd, but too scrupulous Charmer.—Be assured that in Life or Death I can be

Only Yours,

ANTIPHONE.

LETTER XLII.

JULIA *to* ANTIPHONE.
Written immediately after the reception of his.

COULD I have thought there was an ill in Fate to encrease the number of my Woes, or if there were, that *Antiphone* would inflict it? How dreadful are the Idea's you raise in me! Sometimes, methinks, I see you pale and bleeding, cursing with your last gasp the Fatal Passion that led you to Destruction.—At others, imagine I hear the News of *Orosinus's* Death, slain by your own Hand, and you compelled to appear a convicted Criminal at the Seat of Judgment.—Tormented Fancy now presents you to my View only as murther'd, or a Murderer.—I cannot bear it, shield me from these apprehensions, if either Love or Pity have any share in your enraged Soul.—Let me see you this Evening at *Clarissa's*, I consent to another Interview, provided a line from you assures me you will attempt no Violence till after that Time.

My Messenger has orders to wait your Answer: Detain him not, I conjure you; for every Moment of uncertainty brings with it a fresh Agony to

The Wretched

JULIA.

LETTER XLIII.

ANTIPHONE *to* JULIA,
In answer to hers.

AS I hoped not for the condescension you now offer, my surprize is equal to my Satisfaction; but would not have you believe it has so much Effect on me, as to put a Period to, tho' it may suspend my just Resentment; which latter, I assure you, shall be, on your Desire, accomplished: And, to shorten as much as possible your Disquiets on that score, I haste to tell you, that I will not fail to attend you at the appointed Place about Eight, and that, tho' abandoned by you, am as ever,

Your most Constant,

And zealously-devoted Adorer,

ANTIPHONE.

LETTER XLIV.

BELLIZA *to* PHILEMON,
On perceiving a Decay of his Affection.

ALL things, they say, are liable to Change, but certainly there is in nothing so much as in the Affairs of Love,[1] there was a Time (Oh never will that time return) when I wrote, and you received my Letters with the utmost Rapture, now no more remains of our past Endearments than a remorseful Remembrance on my side, and a boastful Pride on yours. You have indeed good Nature enough to endeavour to keep from me the worst of my Misfortune, and by a forced Civility would make me believe, that

---

[1] Presumably a printer's error resulted in the omission of material at this point.

tho' you love me less than you have done, you have not trans-planted your Affections to another Object.—Oh *Philemon!* there are no Eyes so penetrating as a Lover's; I see into your Soul, and all dissimulation[1] is in vain.—When you tell me that you regret being so often absent, I easily perceive that your inclination is at War with your Gratitude that you present yourself at all before me.—When seemingly out of Humour and disgusted with the World, I perceive I am the most disagreeable thing in it, and tho' you feign a Melancholy at taking leave, your Eyes, in spite of you, inform me you do it with a secret Pleasure, 'tis alass! all I am now capable of affording you. Ease yourself therefore of a Constraint which must needs be troublesome to you, and is only an affront to my Understanding to imagine I am deceived by: Generously confess the Inconstancy of your Sex, and lay the fault on Fate or Nature, or whatever else you please, provided it be not imputed to my want of Merit; for tho' I am sensible of my Deficiencies that way, I doubtless am not less worthy than when I was more beloved, and I would not have the Man I have so much esteemed, appear guilty of so little discernment, as not to be able to discover what is, or is not deserving.—I have still so good an Opinion of you, that I believe my Unhappiness is not the Effect of your Choice. You would continue to love me were it in your Power, and that 'tis only the Apprehensions how wretched I must be in the knowledge of this Truth, makes you endeavour to conceal it; but all this while you forget that you expose me to an Evil equally pernicious.—How despicable must I appear in the Eyes of the World, when look'd on as the only Person who is ignorant of what so nearly concerns me.—While under this suppos'd deception, my Credulity[2] is the wonder of my Neighbours, the pity of my Friends, and the derision[3] of my Enemies.—I can no longer endure to make so wretched a Figure.—No, I chuse rather to be thought miserable than a Fool, and shall take it now as the great-est Favour you can do me, to openly abandon me.—Oh God! that I should live to make you this Request, yet so much am I worn

---

1 Hypocrisy.
2 Gullibility.
3 Mockery.

out with silent Grief, that even Rage would be an Ease, and I should find some Pleasure amidst my Pain, when it was known for whom I was forsaken.—I confess the very thought on't ought to make you as Contemptible to me, as my too much Tenderness has render'd me to you.—But Men can find Charms even in Deformity itself, when *Novelty* invites, nor would an Angel, when enjoy'd, retain ought to create Desire. My unworthy Rival, tho' liberal enough of her Favours to others, is yet cruel to you, she either sees not those Perfections in you I have done, or is to be purchas'd by other means than Merit; 'tis therefore highly probable she may long have the Glory of your Addresses, and you may languish in fruitless Expectation for a considerable Time.—This will be sufficient for my Revenge, nor indeed could the most Implacable wish more, than that you might know the Pangs of unrewarded Love, and for an Object, which must make your Passion at perpetual Enmity with your Reason, and subject you to the just ridicule of all who are acquainted with it.—But whatever Disquiets you may endure from your own Reflections, I shall forbear to add to them, by dwelling any longer on this Subject. All I have to say is, that since, depriv'd of your *Heart*, I have too much Delicacy, as well as too much sincere Affection to content myself with any other part, and have resolv'd to tear myself for ever from you: saying with *Octavia* in the Play, *I cannot have you all, and scorn to take you* half.[1] If, therefore, you would have me think of you with a common Esteem, forbear for the future all shows of Tenderness, avow your Dislike, and shun all Conversation with the

Unfortunate
BELLIZA.

LETTER XLV.

BRILLIANTE *to* LOCUTIO,
In Answer to a Letter of advice she had received from him.

I SUPPOSE, my dear *Locutio!* you expect a Reply from me peculiarly adapted to every Paragraph of yours, but I must be

---

[1] See John Dryden, *All for Love* (1678), IV. i. 427–28.

strangely changed indeed when I afford Time for order in any thing, especially on a Subject of this Nature.—I have heard much talk of *Seneca's* Morals,[1] but if they contain any thing more dull, more formal, or more mortifying to the pleasures of Life, than what you have wrote, I dare venture to renounce for ever all Opera's, Masquerades, Assemblies,[2] or whatever else makes Youth and Beauty a Blessing, and be confined to hear the sound of Love from no other Mouth than yours.—Do not infer from this that one grain of the Affection I have profest for you is abated; No, I assure you there are none of my Admirers I value the Thousandth part that I do you, yet will not humour your Caprice so far as to discard one of them at your Request.—But now, I think on it, instead of having too little Tenderness myself, I ought to accuse your want of it, in pretending to debar me from every thing I take delight in.—Is it not the first Principle of Love to study the Happiness of the Person we adore? Yet you pretend the most violent Passion for me, and at the same Time would make me Wretched!—Let any disinterested Person be Judge which of us is in the Right.—Besides, I will make it appear, that it is impossible for me to Live, if immur'd[3] in the manner you propose, there is no Recipe for the Spleen so effectual as variety of Conversation, no Cordial so reviving to a Woman of a nice Constitution as a new Lover.—The perpetual hurry of receiving and answering *Billet Doux*,[4] the pleasing Terror we are in, least the Rival Slaves should proceed to Violences against each other, and the pains we are frequently oblig'd to take to Reconcile them, keep the Spirits awake, and rouze Lethargick[5] Wit.—To be admir'd, and address'd,

---

1   The *Epistolae morales* of Lucius Annaeus Seneca (*c.*4 BC–AD 65). A popular volume of selections in English was published in 1678; the thirteenth edition appeared in 1729.

2   Italian opera flourished in England, as did serious and comic opera in English, due in large part to the influences of George Frideric Handel (1685–1759), patronized by the monarchy from 1713, and John Gay (1685–1732), whose *Beggar's Opera* (1728) initiated the rage for 'ballad opera'. Masquerades, or private masked balls, were a popular and somewhat 'daring' form of entertainment. Assemblies were simply social gatherings; the 'tea-table' that provides the setting for another work in this collection constitutes one example.

3   Confined.

4   Love letters.

5   Sluggish.

are essential to make us look well; it gives a new Life to the Eyes, clears the Complexion, spreads a Vivacity over all the Features, and makes us more worthy the Love of him, who in reality we have an inclination for. In fine, I should immediately fall sick, and, in all probability, dye, if I were confin'd to one Town, one set of Company, one Fashion, or one Lover.—Torment me then no more with antiquated Sentences, leave *Religion* to the *Priest*, *Morality* to the *Philosopher*, a *grave Behaviour* to those who want the Power to indulge *Gaiety*, and the care of my Reputation to myself.—I meddle not with your Conduct, and desire you will look on mine with the same indifference; of one thing you may be assur'd, that all you can say will never prevail on me to alter it, for these 20 Years at least. But if you continue your Affection for me till that time, 'tis possible you may then find me what you wish,

BRILLIANTE.

P.S. *I doubt not but you will be sufficiently nettled at this Obstinacy, as you term it, and, to make you some amends, will put off a Party of Pleasure in which I had promis'd to make one, and devote this Evening wholly to you.—Farewell, come about Five, but leave all your ill Humour behind.*

LETTER XLVI.

LOCUTIO *to* BRILLIANTE,
In answer to the foregoing.

AS you confess it an impossibility to think seriously on any thing, I must own myself guilty of an equal Indiscretion to attempt making you do so.—The Tenderness I have for you has rendred me indeed but too officious.—I shall endeavour to correct the Error, but I must then forbear to see you, or listen to any accounts given me of your Vanity, and only compassionate[1] at a distance those Misfortunes which my Knowledge of your Temper gives me an assurance are unavoidable.—Enjoy, Madam! those Felicities you mention while they continue to be such, I will not seek to deprive you of them, either this Evening or your

---

[1] Feel compassion for.

whole Life; to the end of mine I shall not cease to Love you, but must have so much regard to my Character, as not to blend it with a Person's who professes to despise all that the World can say of her. I therefore take my everlasting Leave, wishing that to prevent your Ruin, some Guardian Spirit may inspire you with those just Remonstrances, which you cannot be prevail'd on to regard from

The sincere and affectionate,

LOCUTIO.

LETTER XLVII.

THEOLINDA *to* HERSILIUS,
On Sincerity.

AS neither *Love* nor *Friendship* can justly be call'd such where *Sincerity* is wanting, so can neither long subsist where once that charming Quality is suspected: 'tis that which chiefly makes the Felicity of a particular Conversation. How infinite the Pleasure when we reflect, that we have another self, can talk to the beloved Object as to our own Heart, are certain when *absent* to command the same Affection, the same warmth and zealous Tenderness, as when *present*, and that the Thought of us is a suffi-cient Defence against all Temptations to our Prejudice.—I speak not this, my Dear *Hersilius*, that I have any doubt of yours; No, were you adorn'd, if possible, with more Perfections than you are, cou'd I suppose you guilty of the least Deceit, I would sooner rip open my fond Breast, than suffer your Idea to harbour there.—I pity, but in my Soul contemn those Women who are always Dubious, and yet always Love.—'Tis certain, that whoever has once been influenc'd by a real Passion, cannot immediately abandon it; but, methinks, continued Anxieties should in Time make us assume Courage enough to dare the worst at once, and chuse rather to forgo the illusive Blessing, than accept it mingled with so substantial a Curse.—The jealous have but moments of Delight for years of Pain.—Defend me from that Misery, good Heaven, whatever ills beside are destin'd for me.—I have hith-erto been blest in a perfect Confidence, Oh may I eternally be so! I am assur'd that my Faithful, my Charming *Hersilius*, burns with Equal Impatience for an Interview, meets me with the same Joy, and takes leave with a regret not inferior to mine.—That the Remembrance of me secures his Constancy in Absence, and makes my Presence doubly Transporting.—And that it is a Thing utterly impossible for him to be false to me, even tho' he should be tempted by an Angel's Form.—'Tis this that makes you so Valuable to my Soul, and justifies the Passion I have for you by my Reason.—Love is stiled Divine, because it is immutable, and those who are its Votaries are distinguish'd by their *Constancy*.— The most base Desires may wear the same Appearance in their beginnings, but Time alone proves the *Sincerity*, that is the Love; I am certain that the longer we continue our Conversation, the more it will Endear me to you, else would it now were at an End; for as the Poet justly says,

All other Debts may compensation find,
But Love is strict, and will be paid in kind.[1]

As therefore I have given my self entirely to you, and to the end of my Life shall persevere in the same unchangeable Fidelity, I expect, nay depend that it will be return'd by you. Adieu! thou dearest Treasure of my Soul, be ever Happy, ever True, and I shall not fail of being so,

THEOLINDA.

LETTER XLVIII.

SIMONIDES *to* AMARANTHA,
On Reconciliation.

HEAVEN forbid that Souls so truly united as ours are, shou'd ever be at Variance more.—For tho' the Torments I felt while separated from my better Part, are more than compensated by the Joys of Reconciliation, yet I have been told that frequent Jarrs of this Nature weaken by degrees the Passion, and make the

---

[1]   Dryden, *Aureng-Zebe* (1676), II. i. 307–8.

amorous God grow weary of his Residence.—Let us therefore resolve for the future mutually to forgive each other whatever Faults we either are, or shall be guilty of.—'Tis an impossibility for me to commit any in prejudice of my Affection and Vows, and I believe you will have the same regard to yours; all others are of the pardonable kind, and to resent them is perverting that Happiness we might enjoy in the assurance of rewarded Love. 'Tis certain indeed that after a Cloud the Sun appears more bright; but who would chuse Winter for the sake of longing for the return of Spring?—I think myself as blest in the Possession of my charming *Amarantha* as Mortal can be, I know sufficiently her value and need not the apprehensions of losing her, to teach me how much I ought to prize her; let me therefore henceforth experience only the Joys she dispenses, and all the curst Attendants of Spleen and Vapours[1] be far remov'd from our Heaven of Felicity.—Believe me, you will also find your Account in it, and taste a double Satisfaction in always affording it to

Your ever Faithful,
SIMONIDES.

LETTER XLIX.

CLEOPHIL *to* SAPHIRA.
Upbraiding her for breach of Promise.

IS it thus, ungrateful Charmer! you repay my long and constant Services? Is all I have done for you too little to engage even that which is owing to the whole World, nay to your own Honour? If the insinuations of that false Friend, *Jenetta*, are more prevailing with you, than the Proofs I have given you of my Sincerity and Affection, why did you give me so many Assurances you would see her no more? This is a Behaviour which joins Deceit to Ingratitude, and may make me but too justly suspect your Fidelity in Things of greater Consequence.—You are sensible I endeavoured to break off all Conversation between you and that unworthy Woman, for no other reason than that the Advices

---

[1] Nervous disorder, usually indicating what we now call depression.

she gives, and you have so much to the prejudice of your Interest and Character adhered to, might not at last bring on your utter Ruin.—This is a Truth which you seem'd to be convinced of, and yet you still visit her, write to her, and in every thing continue to treat her as a Person you infinitely regard.—Tell me, *Saphira*, is it to your Weakness and Irresolution, or to a premeditated intention of deluding my too easy Nature, this Conduct is owing?— Fain would I believe it the former inexcusable as it is, because I should then not doubt being beloved, tho' not esteemed by you; but the latter would forfeit all pretensions to that Passion, and make me know all you have said on that score, as little to be depended on as your Contempt of *Jenetta*. If there be any thing to be alledg'd in your Vindication, I beg you will not defer acquainting me with it; for I would fain think you as little guilty as possible, being in spite of all you do,

> *Your passionately-affectionate,*
> *and ever-faithful,*
> CLEOPHIL.

LETTER L.

AMANDA *to* LOTHARIO,
On his taking all Opportunities to quit her Company.

HOW great a Riddle is your late Behaviour; you profess to love me with the utmost Tenderness; yet by every Look and Action testify the most violent disgust! What Wretches do you chuse to pass your Time with, while I am languishing for a sight of you! What Pretences do you make to find fault with all I do, even when I am most endeavouring to oblige you! How great a Pleasure do you take in exerting that Power, which my too fond Love has given you over me! And how little do you share in either my Sufferings or Rejoycings! tho' the first are occasion'd only by your unkindness, and the latter a stranger to my Soul; but when (Oh very seldom does that time arrive) I flatter myself, that, in spite of all appearances you still Love me.—Why do you delight in giving me a continual Torment? Would it not be less cruel to confess I no longer am thought worthy a place in your Affections,

than to keep me on the rack of suspence? Ungrateful and ungen-
erous Man! too much have you triumph'd over me without
adding Insults to the Agonies I endure from a too late
Repentance.—By Heaven it looks like studied Malice, to scorn
the Slave you have in Bonds, yet keep her so, you have indeed
given me a sufficient Cause to endeavour for Liberty, but when,
thro' the assistance of my Reason, I am just ready to obtain it, you
throw the Lure of kindness out, and bring me back to my former
unworthy Subjection.—I know you will impute this Complaint
(as you always do) to the Suggestions of my Jealousy, 'Tis true, the
Extravagance of my unbounded Passion has made me sometimes
doubtful of my own Merit to engage long a Person of yours; what
we extremely prize we always are in dread to lose, and as that was
only a Fault of too much Love, you easily might pardon, if possest
of any part of it yourself: The famous *Dryden*[1] says,

The Faults of Love, by Love are justify'd.

But without you are as void of Reason as you are of
Tenderness: You must confess what I now regret is not the insti-
gations of a Passion you so much condemn, because it is not only
Persons of my own Sex that deprive me of you, but any, even the
most trifling of your own: You court all Company but mine, and
are uneasy in no other.—Oh God! when I begin once to reflect,
so many Proofs of your Unkindness crowd on my tortur'd Mind,
that I could wish for Madness, Stupidity or any Thing that would
ease me of the pain of Thought.—'Tis insupportable!—Why
have I been flattered with the Reputation of being Good-
humour'd, Witty, or Agreeable? The only Man to whom I would
appear so, in his Behaviour, shows he thinks me perverse and
peevish in my Temper, an Idiot in my Understanding, and odious
in my Person.—Wou'd this had ever been his Opinion, I had not
then, by a fictitious Tenderness, been deceiv'd into a real one, nor

---

[1] Haywood drew heavily on the work of the former poet laureate John Dryden
(1631–1700) throughout her career. The subsequent line is from 'Sigismonda and
Guiscardo', l. 281, in *Fables Ancient and Modern* (1700); the poem is a loose translation
of Boccaccio, *Decameron*, IV. i.

had my Tranquility been exchanged for Disquiet.—The Perfections of your Mind and Form had then made no Impression on me to the prejudice of my repose; I cou'd have admired them without Loving.—A bare Civility was all I should have paid, or expected to receive; but as you made me believe I was capable of inspiring you with the most tender Sentiments, I gave up my whole Soul to you, and thought myself blest in avowing you were its Master. I took a pride in testifying how intirely I was yours, and the Confidence that you were mine, and only mine.—Oh could those Days return, I wou'd with Pleasure submit to all other Ills Fate has in store to plague unhappy Mortals; but they are past, I must indulge no more those former flattering Dreams of Happiness, all that remains of them is the Remembrance which serves only to heighten my distress, by comparing what I have been, with what I am.—But I doubt not if troubling you with this long Epistle be not an addition to the number of those other Faults which you accuse me of; be therefore so kind to answer this, either in Person or by Writing, and I will endeavour to forbear for the future any Importunities of this Nature; but for Heavens Sake deal now sincerely with me, reveal your Soul with the same Freedom I do mine, and fix the too long uncertain Doom of

The most perplexed and miserable,
Tho' ever Faithful,
AMANDA.

LETTER LI.

LOTHARIO *to* AMANDA,
Confessing an Abatement of his former Passion.

I RECEIV'D Yours, my still much loved *Amanda*, and have perus'd it with Emotions, such as would engage your Pity, were you sensible of them.—It was the distraction of my Thoughts which alone hindred me from Writing sooner, I could not presently resolve in what manner I should answer your indeed too just Complaint.—To wound your tender Soul with the Knowledge of the unhappy Truth, is terrible to me; yet as I am an Enemy to Insincerity, and you so strenuously press me to reveal myself, I have at last judged it more generous to comply with your Request.—Yes, *Amanda*, I own your Penetration.—I am but too guilty, and will no longer disguise it, nor attempt to delude the Confidence I have abused.—The Violence of that Passion I profest, and in reality once felt for you, is in Enjoyment extinguish'd.—No more I languish for your Presence.—No more dissolve with Pleasure at your sight.—My once burning Wishes are now cool as Ice, and I can press that Bosom, be enfolded in those Arms, and feel the melting touches of those Lips whence Love and Wit perpetually are flowing, without remembring that I am a Man.—Those Extasies your lavish Kindness so abundantly bestow'd, are now no more. Oh pardon the fault of Nature, and believe that in exchange for those Transports, my Soul is filled with the utmost Gratitude, that I acknowledge all your Charms, as much as when I most dyed for the possession of them, and would return your Constancy in soft Desires, with the same Fervour, to a long Eternity, were it in my Power; but since it is not, I wish nothing with so much Eagerness as that it were possible you might convert Love to Friendship, in that pure and elevated Passion I could pass Ages with you, and still remain unsatiated.—Tower then above the rank of vulgar[1] Lovers, forget your Sex, and confess that to be thus United infinitely exceeds the transitory Joys which Sense affords.—Be assur'd, Oh most deserving *Amanda!* that I have an infinite Esteem for your good Qualities, the kindest and most grateful sense of the Favours you have conferred on me, and the softest Compassion for the sufferings my late Behaviour has occasion'd you, and certainly to think on you in this manner merits not your Hate.—When I reflect how blest I have been in the Condescensions you were pleas'd to make, I endeavour by calling back the past, to taste the same again; but Oh it will not be, and I am as unfortunate in having lost my sense of Pleasure, as you are in being depriv'd of the Gratification of it.—Let us therefore pity one another, and try to make up in Friendship what we have lost in Love.—I dare not meet the Reproaches of your Eyes, after a Confession so rare for one of my

---

[1] Ordinary.

Sex to make, or one of yours to forgive; but let your Pen inform me the situation of your Heart, and be not too severe to him, who is still, tho' in a different manner,

Sincerely yours,

LOTHARIO.

P.S. The Impatience I am in to know your Answer, obliges me to order my Servant not to leave you till he has obtain'd one.

LETTER LII.

AMANDA *to* LOTHARIO,
In Answer to the foregoing.

EXCUSE me that I gave you the trouble of sending your Messenger a second time, if it was difficult for you to answer the Complainings of my unhappy Passion, how much more so must it be to me to determine in what manner I shall receive the Confirmation of my Eternal Ruin, and your Perfidiousness.— Were there a Possibility that the *Spiritual* part of Love could subsist, when the *Sensual* one is extinct, with how much Pleasure should I accept the Friendship you offer; but alass, where you carry your Desires, there also will be your Affection, nor indeed is Love, in your Sex, any other than a Desire of Enjoyment.—In your Friendships, I confess, you are more sublime, we have had Examples of *Men* who have done Wonders, when instigated by that generous Passion; but I never heard of any who remembred the Professions he had made of it to a Woman, after he had forgot to like her as such.—I hope, as you are perfectly acquainted with my Humour, you will do me so much Justice as not to impute the regret I express at losing you as a Lover to a vicious Inclination; no, had we began on the score of Friendship, all my Wishes had been center'd in it, nor should I have imagined there was any thing superior; but having flatter'd myself that the Tenderness you felt for me, was something beyond either Love or Friendship singly, because it seem'd compos'd of both in the most elevated Degree, hard it is indeed to fall from that ravishing height of Passion to a dull formal Civility, which is all you now call Friendship.—Cou'd I believe, that, with your Love to me, all desires for my whole Sex wou'd be at an End, I cou'd content myself, nay, be happy in some measure, in the Imagination, that all the Regard remaining in you for Womankind was still for me; but while I reflect that you are Young, Gay, and Vigorous, have a Heart susceptible of Beauty, and that the first new and agreeable Face will make an impression on it, I cannot but be miserable.— Can I behold your Languishments for another Object? Can I hear you sounding forth my Rival's Praises? Can I promote your Happiness with her, which are the Duties of Friendship?—No, I shou'd run mad, and perhaps be enforc'd by my Desperation to be guilty of some Act wou'd plunge us all in Horror.—Rather, for ever shun my Sight, fly all Conversation with me, and as much as possible keep from my Knowledge all Accounts which may awaken my Love or Jealousy.—Be assured I shall endeavour to think of you no more, but can never be brought to think of you in the manner you now desire.—Can Indifference succeed a Passion such as mine? Can the Sight of you inspire ought but the extreamest Love, and, when mingled with an equal Indignation, what dreadful Effects may it not produce?—I therefore take my everlasting Leave! You shall no more be persecuted with the Reproaches nor Complaints of

The most forlorn,

Most wretched, and

Most undone,

AMANDA.

P.S. In the Confusion of my Thoughts, while Writing, I had forgot to thank you for the Acknowledgment you make, tho' late, of the Truth; insupportable as my present Circumstance is, it is yet to be preferr'd to the Tortures of Suspence, and I chuse rather not to have any hope, than to retain so doubtful a one. Once more Farewell for Ever.

LETTER LIII.

CLEOMIRA *to* BEAUMONT,
Accusing him for attempting her Virtue.

IS it thus, Ungrateful *Beaumont!* you repay an Affection so pure and disinterested as mine? Does the generous Confidence I reposed[1] in you, deserve to be abus'd by Insincerity and false Reasoning? Is there a Necessity I must be Vile, because I Love? Or because I have confest it, that I must be weak enough to be deceived by such weak Arguments as base Desires can furnish?— No, no, mistaken Man! My Passion is of another Nature, the Esteem I profest for you was built on the Belief of yours for me, nor had I own'd it, without the highest Opinion of your Virtue.—How vainly do you endeavour to make me think your late Attempt was occasion'd only by the Violence of a too ardent Love, Oh, blaspheme not that divine Flame, by disguising an Inclination so impure and ignoble as yours is with a Shew of it: Call it rather Hate; for what more justly can be term'd so, than an Intention to betray and ruin! 'Tis thus the Lyon loves the Prey he is about to devour.— 'Tis thus a Tyrant loves the Country he depopulates.—Nothing, methinks, is more absurd than to pretend the endeavour to gratify an inordinate Appetite, is any other than Self-love; yet how wretchedly are Women, who allow not themselves leisure for Reflection, frequently deceiv'd in this Point, tho' it be the nicest and most dangerous one in their whole Conduct.—'Tis the Knowledge of this unhappy Truth, which no doubt encourag'd your Design, but I pity your want of Penetration, which inform'd you not, that I was not among the number of those liable to be beguil'd by such Pretences, since I cannot accuse myself of any indiscretion in Behaviour to occasion it.—I hope, however, you are by this Time too sensible of the Error you have committed to be guilty of it a second time, on which Condition I consent to receive you as before, but tho' with the same Freedom as ever, I confess an infinite Regard for you, and find Charms in your Person and Conversation, which none of your Sex beside can boast; shou'd you persevere in the dishonourable Enterprize you have begun, I never would see you more, teach myself to think on you with the utmost Detestation, and as the most treacherous and dangerous Enemy of

CLEOMIRA.

P.S. Visit me not, nor write, till you have made a Resolution to treat me in the manner you ought to do, and I both merit and enjoin.[2]

---

[1] Placed.
[2] Loosely, insist upon.

LETTER LIV.

CELADON *to* FLORINDA,
On Despair.

I HAD no sooner left my ador'd and for ever lov'd *Florinda* last night, than I went to visit poor *Myrtillo*, whom for several Days I had not seen; but never did I behold a Man so chang'd: His once gay and lively Disposition is now converted into a peevish Sullenness, his Thoughts seem full of Horror, and all that formerly afforded Pleasure is now an addition to his Pain. From our Childhood we have been link'd in the strictest Bonds of Amity,[1] a mutual inclination to each other, our Desires were so near a kin, that the one could not be sensible of a Joy, nor an Anxiety, but the other must partake it; yet is my Presence become irksome, and the Advice I offer'd for the mitigation of his trouble, rejected with a kind of churlish Contempt.—But because I doubt not but you are impatient to be acquainted with the Cause of so strange a Transformation, know that he feels, what your Divine Goodness has preserv'd me from, the Hell of Despair.—The inconstant, and perfidious *Anareta*, after all the Tenderness she exprest for him, is married to *Dametus*, and has forbad him ever to see her more.— How terrible, my dear *Florinda!* are the Pangs of ill-requited Love, and how ought I to bless the charming kindness by which I live, and enjoy a more than mortal Happiness!—Despair is a Passion which only the damned and slighted Lovers can experience.— 'Tis the very Poyson of the Soul, and turns all our Contentments into Bitterness, making us loath whatever is Good, and indulge Mischiefs, Horrors, and Desolations.—Those so accurst, wish to be yet more so, if possible, and take a sort of Pride in being Prodigies of Misery, refusing all Comfort, and seeking still fresh cause of Anguish.—The very Thought of it is dreadful; but in my lovely *Florinda's* Arms I'll banish it, and lose the Memory of every thing but the present Bliss.—I will only dispatch two or three impertinent Letters I am obliged to write to some Friends in the

---

[1]   Friendship.

Country, and fly to the source of all my Joys.—'Till then, my Soul's Charmer; and ever believe me

Your most Faithful,
CELADON.

LETTER LV.

The unfortunate Lysetta *to the neglectful,
but still most dearly belov'd* Lyonides.
On having been debauch'd by him with a Promise of Marriage.

HOW terrible is the reverse of my Condition! I am now compelled by your Unkindness, and the miserable Circumstance I have brought myself into, to become a Petitioner to him who was my Slave, and sue for a Happiness which I was once, with the utmost submission, entreated to bestow.—How often, Oh *Lyonides,* have you swore, that to have me for a Wife was the ultimate of all your Wishes; that you never cou'd taste the Joys of Life, till you possest me as such; and would prefer Death to any other choice?—Why are you now so chang'd?—Is either my Beauty or my Wealth impair'd since I appeared so worthy your Regard? Have I been guilty of any Fault should render me less charming in your Eyes, but that which an excess of Love, and readiness to oblige you, caus'd me to commit?—Did you not use ten Thousand Arguments to prove, that the Ceremony of Marriage was the least Essential part; made as many Vows that you considered me with no other View than that of Wife; and that I should be made so in the Eyes of the World as soon as your Father's Funeral Obsequies were over? Yet Months since that are past, and I am still no more than Mistress.—For Heavens sake reflect in what Condition I am, and save me from the shame of being a Mother without a Husband.—Or if, ungrateful, no Consideration of my Love or Ruin is of force to move you, at least be not unjust to that dear Part of yourself, which nothing but the performance of your Promise to me can defend from the Contempt of an opprobrious[1] World: He must as soon as Born,

---

[1] Censorious, critical.

be branded with the mark of Scorn, bred up in mean Obscurity, and capacitated to inherit only his Mother's Infamy.—How cruel, how shocking is that Thought! Can you have Nature, Humanity, or Honour, and sustain it?—Oh image to yourself that scene of Woe, imagine the Time of my Delivery being arriv'd, you behold a Woman, your equal in Birth and Fortune, and, what is more, a Woman you have sworn Eternally to Love, in racks of Mind more exquisite, more terrible than all the Body can sustain, even in that dreadful Moment, to which the pains of Hell are justly compar'd; her Kindred, dishonour'd by her Conduct, flying the guilty Chamber, and, with the most bitter Taunts, refusing their Assistance; none but some disinterested Servant, or slight Acquaintance near, to Condole or Comfort her; the hapless Innocent unlov'd, unregarded, scarce pitied by any but his wretched Mother, with ominous Cries bespeaks the Sorrows he is doom'd to share.—Oh *Lyonides!* Can you think on this without resolving to defend from it those two, who of all the World ought to be most dear to you?—No, you cannot: You will not, I am certain, sully the Lustre of so many Perfections as you are possest of with Perjury and Ingratitude, the foulest Crimes Man can be guilty of.—But do not any longer defer obeying the Dictates of your Honour; my Pregnancy, alass! will soon grow perceivable, and all you can then do will be too late to conceal the Errors of ungovernable Passion.—I know not if it be not already suspected, a Consciousness at least makes me interpret every Word and Look as a Reproach, and gives such Wounds to my Modesty, as frequently renders me liable to betray the Truth by an over Endeavour to conceal it.—Once more therefore I conjure you, if not for Love, for Pity's sake, haste to repair the Ills you have already caused, and preserve from the future

Your too passionately devoted

and most Faithful,

LYSETTA.

P.S. *If it be true, that the present hurry of your Affairs will not permit you to see me as frequently as usual, you might at least borrow so much time from Sleep as to write to me. Adieu.*

LETTER LVI.

URANIA *to* FAVONIUS,
On Insensibility.

HOW vainly, my unkind and too much valued *Favonius!* do you endeavour to make me contented with my Condition, by pretending yourself insensible of the force of Love, and that all you are capable of feeling of that Passion is in my Favour! You must convince me you want delicacy of Soul, are dull and stupid, before I can believe you are not form'd to taste the same Extreams of Pain and Pleasure that you give; a great Genius never appear'd in the World, without giving Proofs of a transcendent Tenderness; the Gods of *Love* and *Wit* are always Friends, and mutually assist each other; 'tis impossible for a Fool to be much in Love, or for a Man of a fine and elevated Wit to avoid being so.—Be assur'd, *Favonius*, you will one Day experience this Truth, and that you are thus long in ignorance of it, is because you have not yet met with a proper Object to inform you.—But when that Time arrives, then will you own your Error; then learn to pity the *Pangs* which soft Desires create when *unrequited*; then envy the *Felicity* of a *rewarded* Flame; and confess you have felt for me no more than bare Esteem, or at most but Friendship mingled with that inclination which the difference of Sex excites.—'Tis the certainty of this makes me wretched: So dearly do I prize you, I cou'd be blest, even to an Extacy, with the regard you now profess for me, Cold and Languid[1] as it is, were not some *other* destin'd to enjoy those Ardors I, alass! want merit to inspire.—Oh that you had in you less the Materials for a vigorous Passion, or I more Charms to kindle them! 'Tis not because for two Years I have been Mistress of your Faith, that I can hope to be ever so, you may be Mine in the manner you now are for a much longer time, yet I at last may lose you, and one unlucky Moment destroy the Constancy of Ages; nor is it because I know you have convers'd with a great variety of the most *Lovely*, and most *Witty* of our Sex, that I can imagine you are Proof against the Temptations of *all*; 'tis not always *Merit* that engages the

---

[1] Weak.

Heart, and I have sometimes seen those who have the greatest share of it themselves, regard not the want of it in the Persons they make choice on: To the *aukward*, the *silly*, and the *unloving*, Fortune and Fancy frequently afford what is denied to *Beauty*, *good Sense*, and *Tenderness*.—Heavens! it would be impossible for me to resign you, with any tolerable Patience, even to the most deserving; but shou'd a Creature unworthy your Affection boast the Glory of engrossing it, I shou'd run Mad.—*Pride* would enhance the Agonies of *Despair*, and I should *Hate* without being able to cease *Loving*.—Oh may my happy Rival, therefore, have all the Charms that Nature can bestow; may every perfection of Form and Mind justify your Change, and compel me to restrain Reproach.—Yet may I first be folded in my Shrowd, and die in the Belief I am not absolutely scorn'd, nor abandon'd by you.— But I forget that I offend you by dwelling on this Theme; you have already chid my too Prophetick Fears, I will not therefore anticipate my Misfortune, nor render myself yet less agreeable to you, by indulging a Melancholy which you will not allow I have any Grounds for. I expect to see you to Night, and resolve if possible to banish every thing from my Thoughts, but the transporting Joys your Presence never fails to give

The most tenderly Affectionate,

URANIA.

LETTER LVII.

ORONTES *to* DEANIRA,
Entreating her to give him a Meeting.

IN vain, Oh most adorable *Deanira*, do you go about to flatter me with a Belief I am not indifferent to you, while you continue so cruel a distrust.—Can one *Love* what one *esteems* not? Or can one *Esteem* what one has no *Dependance* on?—How can you profess a *Regard* for me, and at the same time testify so ill an *Opinion* of me?—I must, indeed, be strangely unworthy your *Affection*, were I capable of abusing your *Confidence* in the manner you seem to suspect.—I have a thousand Times sworn, and now again confirm it, that my whole Reason for desiring a private interview was to disburthen[1] my Soul of its weight of Tenderness, and endeavour to inspire you, if possible, with softer Ideas than I fear you have yet been capable of conceiving; I never see you without Witnesses of our Conferences, and my Pen is but a poor Interpreter of the Language of my Heart.—Were you but half sensible how truly I am Devoted to you, and how much in your Power it is to inspire, new form, and bound my every Wish, you would not need to fear any thing from me you would have cause to regret, or be offended at.—I Entreat therefore, I Conjure you not to refuse this only Proof that can convince me, you have sincerely any kind Thoughts of

> *Your most passionate,*
> *And truly devoted,*
> ORONTES.

LETTER LVIII.

FIDELIA *to* LEANDER,
On Secrecy in Love.

WELL does my dear discerning *Leander* observe, that those Women who boast the Affections of their Admirers, have a greater share of *Vanity* than *Love:* The Pleasure, methinks, of knowing oneself beloved by him we Love, is too great to need any addition from the Congratulations of others. It would afford me little satisfaction to have the World believe me of the utmost Consequence to your Happiness, if Conscious I had not in reality the power of contributing to it, nor does it in the least affect me, to hear another given to you for a Mistress, while I have so many Reasons to assure myself your Heart is only mine.—'Tis this Blest Security which absolves the Extravagance of my Passion for you, I cannot do too much to prove it, and if I am capable of feeling any discontent arising from our Conversation, 'tis only when I reflect how much my *Inclination* is bounded by my *Inability.*—I want to testify the sincerity of my Soul by some Action beyond all that ever Woman did, or can by any Words be

---

[1]   That is, unburden; relieve.

exprest.—A Faithful Friend, or Constant Mistress, are Characters too mean for my ambitious Love.—Had I a Wealth immense, a Beauty unparallel'd, a Reputation unblemish'd by the Tongue of scandal, the Sacrifice of them would be deficient to my capacious[1] Wish.—I long for Worlds to offer you; and even then should think it all too little.—This is indeed to Love, and those who imagine they do so, without being possest of such Sentiments, but affect the Passion, and deceive themselves, and those they call the Objects of it. A Woman who plumes herself in the publick Assiduities of her Lover, makes her chief Aim the gratification of her Pride; *Dryden* justly says,

> *With Noise and Pomp, and in a crowd some woo;*
> *But true Felicity consists in two.*[2]

Let your Complaisance, therefore, and exterior Civilities be directed where Birth or Fortune seem to challenge it, or where your own Interest shall render it Prudence, 'tis in your Heart alone I wish to Reign; I shall not envy the *Admiration* you may pay to my whole Sex, while convinc'd 'tis me you only *Love*, I beg then that you will do the fervor of my Passion the justice to allow it is not blended with the least mixture of Vanity or Ostentation,[3] and that it is to the purest and most disinterested Tenderness you are indebted for my subscribing myself,

With the most sacred Truth,
Your Eternally-devoted,
FIDELIA.

LETTER LIX.

AMALTHEA *to* PERIANDER.
On having rashly vow'd to see him no more.

I RECEIV'D yours, wherein you express a very just surprize that I left *Semandra*'s the moment you came in.—'Twas a

---

[1] Loosely, immense.
[2] The lines are not in fact by Dryden.
[3] Pretentiousness.

Behaviour which I am now convinc'd you had no Reason to expect from *Amalthea*; and, Oh my for-ever Dear *Periander*, I must confess I was deceiv'd into a forgetfulness of every thing but Rage, and that curst Passion mingled with Despair drove me to Resolutions for which I am and must, while Life endures, be severely punish'd.—I was told, Oh forgive, if it be possible, my wretched Credulity, that, false to all your Vows, and ungrateful to my Love, you had transferr'd your Affection to *Amasia*, that you had visited her several times in private, and, what most of all was stabbing to my Soul, that you had made a Merit of forsaking me;—This, heightn'd with all the aggravating Circumstances that inventive Malice could furnish, did your false Friend, the base designing *Ironius*, inform, and swear to me was Truth.—As I knew him Partner of your Secrets, I suspected not the imposition, and, prompted by the sudden Emotions of my jealous Indignation, that moment knelt and utter'd Imprecations too dreadful to incur the Effect of, if I ever consented to see or speak to you more. Yes, *Periander*, I confess, that it is now out of my Power to continue a Conversation with you, without renouncing all I have to hope from Heaven or fear from Hell.—Oh to what sad Extreams does madding[1] Passion sometimes transport the Soul! and how immediately did I repent the Error of my wild Impatience! I had no sooner taken the Fatal Oath, than *Violetta* came to Visit me; among other Things she told me, that *Amasia* had been at a Friend's House in the Country for five Weeks, in all which time I knew you had never been out of Town: This news struck me with Horror and Remorse; but, resolving to be fully convinc'd, I sent to the Lodgings of my suppos'd Rival, and found *Violetta*'s intelligence just; I afterward recollected the various particulars *Ironius* had related concerning your Conduct, so far unlike the manner in which I could imagine you would act in such a Case, that I no longer doubted if I had not been deceiv'd by Him.—All I can say would poorly represent the Agonies I felt, at the Consciousness that my *own*, and *only my own* Folly had depriv'd me of a Treasure I would have dyed to keep.— Oh pity, rather than condemn the wretched Circumstance to

---

[1] That is, maddening, threatening to one's sanity.

which I have reduc'd myself; and as you have said you loved *Amalthea* for her own sake alone, endeavour not to make me become perjur'd; it would greatly add to the Disquiets I labour under, to have reason to believe you had so ill an Opinion of me, as to imagine I dare Violate the solemn, tho' rash Promises I made to Heaven.——Fly my Presence, as I for ever must do yours, I am tyed up from every thing but Writing to you; that distant way of conveying to each other the meanings of our Souls is not forbid.——If that will afford you any Pleasure, I consent to share it with you, and will farther assure you, that, since I must avoid you, I will live a Recluse from all your Sex.——Content yourself, therefore, my much wrong'd *Periander,* with the Theory of Love; and by the Assiduities of your Pen, console me for the loss of those I am not permitted any longer to receive.——I dread, yet am impatient for your Answer, till when, and Ever am,

My only valued Periander's
most Faithfully affectionate,
tho' unfortunate,
because guilty,
AMALTHEA.

LETTER LX.

ISMENA *to* HORATIO,
On the Pleasures of Conjugal[1] Affection.

IN this constrain'd Absence, you bid me, my dear *Horatio!* set forth that felicity I enjoy in the assurance that you are now irrevocably mine, and that a perfect Knowledge of your Soul makes me depend entirely on you. Alass! how unequal am I to the Task! and how impossible is it for me to describe what is beyond all description! To think one has another self, another dearer part which participates of all our pains and joys, or rather feels the greater part of them, as being more concerned for the interest of the beloved object than its own, and to be confident that this is not only for a Time, a sudden start of fondness, but for ever; fills

---

[1] Having to do with marriage.

the Mind with Ideas so ravishing and delicate, as can ill be represented by the force of Words.—A tender Friendship, even between Persons of the same Sex, has in it such Pleasures and Conveniencies, as the greatest Men have thought nothing too much to purchase, and has been the Theme of the most elevate Genius's; but how much more delightful must it be, when to the solidity of Friendship the warmth of Love is added, when the still growing Passion heightens every Transport, when all the Senses come in for their part, and Soul and Body join to make the Bliss compleat.—Marriage has in it all we can conceive of Heaven, when the Persons so united have but one Will to actuate them both, one Principle to direct them, and one Interest to follow.— With such the word *Duty* is of no force, they make it their Study to please each other, not so much because they ought to do so, as because it is a pleasure to themselves; as the faculties of the Mind take a delight in gratifying each other, so does the tender *Husband* and endearing *Wife*.—'Tis a matter of indifference to this happy Pair what's doing in the World, for, finding in each other all they wish or want, they have no need to look abroad for variety of Entertainments, and if sometimes one is, as it were, obliged to be employed in something the other does not immediately partake, it does but afford an opportunity of testifying an open sincerity in communicating it, and a new Theme for Conversation on it; as the Mind revolves within itself the different Objects which the sense takes in, so do they jointly whatever has fallen within the observation of either when apart.—'Tis thus my most deservedly dear *Horatio*, that we have lived since the happy Moment that the sacred Ceremony, and mutual Inclination, made us one; and where an Affection is founded on a sympathy of Humours, confirm'd by Reason, and made strong by Time and Constancy, it never can fail to give Joys which are as impossible for my weak Pen to express, as it is for those joyn'd by any other Motives than such as I have mention'd to taste; but which I am not the least diffident will always be the portion of,

My unspeakably-belov'd Horatio's
Most passionately-tender,
And faithfully-devoted Wife,
ISMENA.

LETTER LXI.

SABINA *to* FILLAMOUR,
Declaring a Passion for him.

I AM certain that I do not wrong the Truth when I assure you, that this is the last of a thousand Letters I have wrote, to inform you of something which I would give the World, were I Mistress of it, that you knew; yet would rather die than be the discoverer of, if there were a possibility for you to be sensible of it by any other less shameful means.—Oh cou'd you have been witness of what I suffer'd e're I began to write, and also when finding no Words of force to represent the Agonies I felt, I committed to the Flames those Testimonies of my Weakness, you would not accuse me of Immodesty that I now at last declare the Civilities I treated you with, spring from a warmer Source than that of Friendship.—Yes, too agreeable *Fillamour!* I have found it impossible to know your worth without considering it with something more than Admiration.—Heaven adorn'd not your Form and Mind with such unmatch'd Perfections, to inspire a moderate liking, in a Soul so penetrating, and capable of distinguishing as mine.—And as I find nothing but you worthy of my Love, must regard you with that Passion which is called so.— Custom, indeed, has rendred it undecent for a Person of my Sex to make a Confession of this kind, till a long Courtship and a Million of Services, have given her an opportunity to disguise her secret Languishments with the pretence of Gratitude; and what I endure, thro' the Reproaches of my Pride and Bashfulness, in breaking thro' it, is not to be described.—Yet are not those Remonstrances the most terrible that assault me. I have a stronger Passion still, which is my too just Fear, that it is only because you discerned nothing in me worthy of your Tenderness, I am constrain'd to make the first Address.—But when I consider, that, to a generous Heart, Love, and such a Love as mine, may make up for abundance of deficiencies, I am not without some Consolation.—Let me know your real Thoughts of me, I conjure you, but let it be done by your Pen, I cannot presently resolve to stand the shock of seeing you, after a declaration such as this, 'tis only the assurance of your favourable reception of it, can make me forgive myself, or put an end to the present struggles in the Soul of her, who, to what Fate soever you condemn her, can never be but

Yours,

SABINA.

LETTER LXII.

FLORIDANTE *to* CLOTILDA,
On Levity.[1]

HOW much in Vain, Oh too lovely, unless more prudent, *Clotilda*, do you attempt to enchant me with a Belief I have the secret to please you, when your good Opinion, like a Feather, is to be tossed and puffed about by every blast of Wind: When you receive a Copy of Verses from *Alcimon*, you appear transported with his Wit, all Mankind beside are stupid to him, and this Trophy of your Conquest is expos'd with praise to all who come near you, till a tender Serenade under your Window by *Endimion*, charms you with a new delight. He gives place but to *Laertes*, who takes your Senses with a magnificent Ball and Collation:[2] even old *Mythras* can render you forgetful of the whole World for a set of China, and *Hermon* dazzle the Eye of Reason with a Diamond Bodkin:[3] My plain and honest Love comes sometimes in for a share with them; I know you have at least so much regard for me, as to desire I may continue among the train of your Admirers; but whether I owe this Condescension to Love or Vanity, I scarce dare ask myself the Question: I am much afraid, if I consult my Judgment, it will give it for the latter. Women of your Taste, *Clotilda*, have but little Notion of true Passion, they are too much taken up with themselves to study long what will be pleasing to another, and imagine their Beauty's a sufficient Sanction for their Faults. This Belief may perhaps hold good while you continue as a Mistress, but be assured it will render you an unhappy Wife; a Man when he becomes a Husband can of all Things the least

---

[1] Lack of seriousness.
[2] Light meal.
[3] Long hair-pin.

endure a Coquette Behaviour, because he is certain to wear the brand of dishonour on his Brow, even tho' the Lady should be innocent in Fact.—Consider, therefore, my Dear *Clotilda*, that you have long enough indulged this Humour, and having experienc'd a vast Vicissitude of Changes from one Folly to another, now change once for all from Folly to Discretion: Make some one Man happy in your settled Affection, and quit the train of Fops,[1] which are of no farther Service to you than to feed a present Vanity, which is the worst weakness of the Mind. As my Pretensions to you were always accompanied with the strictest Honour, I am ready to make them good whenever you consent, and believe I shall prove, notwithstanding my blunt way of Courtship, as tender a *Husband* as you have found me

A Faithful Lover,
FLORIDANTE.

---

[1] Frivolous and preening men.

Appendix A: Haywood on Female Conduct

1. *A Present for a Servant-Maid* (1743)

[*A Present for a Servant-Maid* appeared anonymously in 1743 and was instantly popular; it was issued in multiple editions during Haywood's lifetime and inspired several copycat publications.

In this work, a female narrator dispenses advice to young servants. Haywood's interest in the reformation and education of women is evident here, as it is in her more numerous works pitched to higher-class audiences. Many of her strictures on comportment among female servants, for example, anticipate the advice that she would dispense to women of loftier social status in works such as *The Female Spectator*. Haywood's advice cuts across lines of gender as well as those of class, most notably by implicating men as sexual predators. Characteristically, however, her counsel about chastity cuts both ways, warning those who might be seduced while admonishing their seducers. This sort of double discourse recalls the 'persecuted maiden' scenarios that Haywood subverts in amatory writings such as *Fantomina*.

The following sections include commentary on the welfare of young women new to the metropolis, the importance of remaining conscious of one's 'place', the dangers of public entertainments, and the necessity of guarding one's virginity.]

DEAR GIRLS,

I Think there cannot be a greater Service done to the Commonwealth, (of which you are a numerous Body) than to lay down some general Rules for your Behaviour, which, if observed, will make your Condition as happy to yourselves as it is necessary to others. Nothing can be more melancholy, than to hear continual Complaints for Faults which a very little Reflection would render it almost as easy for you to avoid as to commit; most of the Mistakes laid to your Charge proceeding at first only from a certain Indolence and Inactivity of the Mind, but if not rectified in time, become habitual and difficult to be thrown off.

As the first Step therefore towards being happy in Service, you should never enter into a Place[1] but with a View of *staying in it*; to

---

[1]   Accept a job.

which End I think it highly necessary, that (as no Mistress worth serving will take you without a Character)[1] you should also make some Enquiry into the Place before you suffer yourself to be hired. There are some Houses which appear well by *Day*, that it would be little safe for a modest Maid to sleep in at *Night:* I do not mean those Coffee-houses, Bagnio's, &c. which some Parts of the Town, particularly *Covent-Garden*,[2] abounds with; for in those the very Aspect of the Persons who keep them are sufficient to shew[3] what manner of Trade they follow; but Houses which have no public Shew of Business, are richly furnished, and where the Mistress has an Air of the strictest Modesty, and perhaps affects a double Purity of Behaviour: Yet under such Roofs, and under the Sanction of such Women as I have described, are too frequently acted such Scenes of Debauchery as would startle even the Owners of some common Brothels. Great Regard is therefore to be had to the Character of the Persons who recommend you, and the Manner in which you heard of the Place; for those Sort of People have commonly their Emissaries[4] at Inns, watching the coming in of the Waggons, and, if they find any pretty Girls who come to Town to go to Service, presently hire them in the Name of some Person of Condition, and by this means the innocent young Creature, while she thanks *God* for her good Fortune, in being so immediately provided for, is ensnared into the Service of the *Devil.* Here Temptations of all Kinds are offered her; she is not treated as a Servant but a Guest; her Country Habit[5] is immediately stripp'd off, and a gay modish one put on in the Stead; and then the design'd Victim, willing or unwilling, is exposed to Sale to the first leud Supporter of her Mistress's Grandeur that comes to the House: If she refuses the shameful Business for which she was hired, and prefers the Preservation of her Virtue to all the Promises can be made her, which way can she escape? She is immediately confined, close watched, threatened, and at last forced to Compliance. Then by a continued Prostitution withered in her Bloom, she becomes despised, no longer affords any Advantage to the Wretch who betrayed her, and is turned out to Infamy and Beggary, perhaps too with the most loathsome of

---

1   Letter of reference.
2   Covent Garden, in northwest London, was known for its brothels ('Bagnio's') and other sites of temptation.
3   That is, show.
4   Spies.
5   Outfit.

all Diseases,[1] which ends her miserable Days in an Hospital or Work-house,[2] in case she can be admitted, tho' some have not had even that Favour, but found their Death-bed on a Dunghill.

Nor are these Artifices confined to Country Girls alone, those cunning wicked ones have their Spies in every Corner of the Town, who lie in wait to intrap the Innocent and Unwary; it behoves you therefore to know very well, for what, and to whom you hire your-self, and be satisfied, at least, that it is for honest Purposes, and that the Persons you serve are People of Reputation ....

Apeing the Fashion.] The second of these [i.e., 'small Errors' that 'frequently lead on to greater'] ... is the Ambition of imitating your Betters in point of Dress, and fancying that tho' you cannot have such rich Cloaths, it becomes you to put them on in the same Manner: Whereas nothing looks so handsome in a Servant as a decent Plainness. Ribbands,[3] Ruffles, Necklaces, Fans, Hoop-Petticoats, and all those Superfluities in Dress, give you but a tawdry[4] Air, and cost you that Money, which, perhaps, you may hereafter have Occasion for. This Folly is indeed so epidemic among you, that few of you but lay out all you get in these imagin'd Ornaments of your Person: The greatest Pleasure you take is in being called *Madam* by such as do not know you; and you fear nothing so much as being taken for what you are: I wish you would seriously consider how very preposterous all this is. Enquire of your Mothers and Grandmothers how the Servants of their Times were drest, and you will be told that it was not by laying out their Wages in these Fopperies[5] they got good Husbands, but by the Reputation of their Honesty, Industry, and Frugality, in saving what they got in Service. Besides, can you believe any Mistress can be pleased to find, that she no sooner puts on a new thing, than her Maid immediately jumps into something as like it as she can? Do you think it is possible for her to approve, that the Time she pays and feeds her for, and expects should be employ'd in her Business, shall be trifled away in curling her own Hair, pinching her Caps, tying up her Knots,[6] and setting her self forth, as tho' she had no other thing to do, but to prepare for being look'd at? This very Failing, without the Help of any

---

1   Syphilis.
2   Home for the poor and the unemployed.
3   That is, ribbons.
4   Cheap, pretentious.
5   Frills.
6   Pleating or otherwise preparing her head-wear and arranging ribbons for her hair.

other, I take to be the Cause that so very few of you are able to continue long in a Place, and have so little Money to support yourselves when out. Yet this, my dear Girls, bad as it is, is not the worst; there is an Evil behind that is much more to be dreaded, and may be said to be an almost unavoidable Consequence, and that is, your Honesty is likely to be call'd in question: People will be apt to examine, how much you gave for such or such a thing, compare your Profits with your Purchases, and if the Calculation of the Expence amounts to a Scruple more than they can account for your receiving, will presently place it to the Score of those you live with, and say, you owe your Finery to your Fraud: If innocent, your Character inevitably suffers; and, if guilty, you pay dearly for the Crime your Vanity has ensnared you into, by a sooner or later sad Remorse ....

Publick Shews.] But these two Virtues [i.e, 'Industry and Frugality'] ill agree with an immoderate Love of Pleasure, and this Town at present abounds with such Variety of Allurements, that a young Heart cannot be too much upon its Guard: It is those expensive ones, I mean, which drain your Purse as well as waste your Time: Such as *Plays*, the *Wells*, and *Gardens*,[1] and other publick Shews and Entertainments; Places which it becomes no body to be seen often at, and more especially young Women in your Station. All Things that are invented merely for the Gratification of Luxury,[2] and are of no other Service than temporary Delight, ought to be shunned by those who have their Bread to get: Nor is it any Excuse for you that a Friend gives you Tickets, and it costs you nothing; it costs you at least what is more precious than Money, your Time; not only what you pass in seeing the Entertainments, but what the Idea and Memory of them will take up. They are a kind of delicious Poison to the Mind, which pleasingly intoxicates and destroys all Relish for any thing beside: If you could content yourselves with one Sight and no more, of any, or even all these Shews; or could you answer that they would engross your Thoughts no longer than while you were Spectators, the Curiosity might be excusable: But it rarely happens that you have this Command over yourselves; the Music, the Dances, the gay Clothes, and Scenes make too strong an Impression on the

---

[1] Popular spots like Epsom Wells, Tunbridge Wells, and Lambeth Wells offered medicinal waters as well as gambling, concerts, and other entertainments. Formal gardens like Vauxhall and, from its inception in 1742, Ranelagh, featured music, dancing, dining, and fireworks.

[2] Undisciplined appetite.

Senses, not to leave such Traces behind as are entirely inconsistent either with good Housewifery, or the Duties of your Place. Avoid, therefore, such dangerous Amusements; and that it may be the more easy for you to do so, refrain the Society of those who either belong to them, or are accustomed to frequent them ....

Chastity.] I come now to warn you against all those Dangers which may threaten that Branch of Honesty which concerns your own Persons, and is distinguished by the Name of *Chastity.* If you follow the Advice I have already given you, concerning going as frequently as you can to hear Sermons, and reading the Holy Scripture, and other good Books, I need not be at the Pains to inform you how great the Sin is of yielding to any unlawful Sollicitations; but if you even look no farther than this World, you will find enough to deter you from giving the least Encouragement to any Addresses of that Nature, tho' accompanied with the most soothing and flattering Pretences: Every Street affords you Instances of poor unhappy Creatures, who once were innocent, till seduc'd by the deceitful Promises of their Undoers; and then ungratefully thrown off, they become incapable of getting their Bread in any honest Way, and so by Degrees are abandoned to the lowest Degree of Infamy. The Lessons I have given you concerning the Manner of passing your Time, your Temperance, your Fidelity, the Obligations you lie under to those you serve, if duly observed, will also be no inconsiderable Defence against the Snares laid for you on this Score; but I would have you not only be strictly *virtuous* in rejecting all the Temptations offer'd you, but likewise prudent in the *Manner* of doing it. There may be some Circumstances in which you will have Occasion to vary your Denials, according to the different Characters of the Persons who sollicit you: I shall begin with one which happens but too frequently, and that is, when the Temptation proceeds from your Master.

Temptations from your Master.] Being so much under his Command, and obliged to attend him at any Hour, and at any Place he is pleased to call you, will lay you under Difficulties to avoid his Importunities, which it must be confessed are not easy to surmount; yet a steady Resolution will enable you; and as a vigorous Resistance is less to be expected in your Station, your persevering may, perhaps, in Time, oblige him to desist, and acknowledge you have more Reason than himself: It is a Duty, however, owing to yourself to endeavour it.

Behaviour to him, if a single Man.] If he happens to be a single Man, and is consequently under less Restraint, be as careful as you can,

Opportunities will not be wanting to prosecute his Aim; and as you cannot avoid hearing what he says, must humbly, and in the most modest Terms you can, remonstrate to him the Sin and Shame he would involve you in; and omit nothing to make him sensible how cruel it is to go about to betray a Person whom it is his Duty to protect; add that nothing shall ever prevail on you to forfeit your Virtue; and take Care that all your Looks and Gestures correspond with what you say: Let no wanton Smile, or light coquet Air give him room to suspect you are not so much displeased with the Inclination he has for you as you wou'd seem; for if he once imagines you deny but for the sake of Form, it will the more enflame him, and render him more pressing than ever. Let your Answers, therefore, be delivered with the greatest Sedateness; shew that you are truly sorry, and more ashamed than vain, that he finds any thing in you to like: How great will be your Glory, if, by your Behaviour, you convert the base Design he had upon you, into an Esteem for your Virtue! Greater Advantages will accrue to you from the Friendship he will afterwards have for you, than you would ever have obtained from the Gratification of his wild Desires, even tho' he should continue an Affection for you much longer than is common in such Intrigues. But if you fail in this laudable Ambition, if he persists in his Importunities, and you have Reason to fear he will make Use of other Means than Persuasions to satisfy his brutal[1] Appetite, (as what may not Lust seconded by Power attempt, and there is no answering for the Honour of some Men on such Occasions) you have nothing to do, but, on the first Symptom that appears of such a Design, to go directly out of his House: He will not insist on your forfeiting a Month's Wages for his own Sake, for fear you should declare the Cause of your quitting his Service; and if he should be even so harden'd in Vice, as to have no Regard for his Character in this Point, it is much better you should lose a Month's Wages, than continue a Moment longer in the Power of such a one.

If a married Man.] Greater Caution is still to be observ'd, if he is a married Man: As soon as he gives you the least Intimation of his Design, either by Word or Action, you ought to keep as much as possible out of his Way, in order to prevent his declaring himself more plainly; and if, in spite of all your Care, he find an Opportunity of telling you his Mind, you must remonstrate the Wrong he would

---

[1] Animal-like.

do his Wife, and how much he demeans both himself and her by making such an Offer to his own Servant. If this is ineffectual, and he continues to persecute you still, watching you wherever you go, both abroad and at home, and is so troublesome in his Importunities, that you cannot do your Business quietly and regularly, your only Way then is to give Warning; but be very careful not to let your Mistress know the Motive of it: That is a Point too tender to be touch'd upon even in the most distant Manner, much less plainly told: Such a Discovery would not only give her an infinite Uneasiness, (for in such Cases the Innocent suffer for the Crimes of the guilty) but turn the Inclination your Master had for you into the extremest Hatred. He may endeavour to clear himself by throwing the Odium[1] on you, for those who are unjust in one Thing, will be so in others; and you cannot expect, that he who does not scruple to wrong his Wife, and indeed his own Soul, will make any to take away your Reputation, when he imagines his own will be secured by it. He may pretend you threw yourself in his Way when he was in Liquor, or that having taken Notice of some Indecencies in your Carriage, and suspecting you were a loose Creature, he had only talked a little idly to you, as a Trial how you would behave; and that it was because he did not persist as you expected, and offer you Money, that you had made the Discovery, partly out of Malice, and partly to give yourself an Air of Virtue. But tho' he should not be altogether so unjust and cruel, nor alledge any thing of this kind against you, it would be a Thing which you never ought to forgive yourself for, if by any imprudent Hint you gave Occasion for a Breach of that Amity[2] and Confidence which is the greatest Blessing of the married State, and when once dissolved, continual Jarring[3] and mutual Discontent are the unfailing Consequence.

Temptations from your Master's Son.] But there is yet a greater Trial of your Virtue than these I have mentioned, which you may probably meet with; and that is when your young Master happens to take a Fancy to you, flatters your Vanity with Praises of your Beauty; your Avarice with Presents; perhaps, if his Circumstances countenance such a Proposal, the Offer of a Settlement for Life, and, it may be, even a Promise of marrying you as soon as he shall be at his own

---

[1] Loosely, blame.
[2] Friendship.
[3] Domestic discord.

Disposal. This last Bait has seduced some who have been Proof against all the others: It behoves you therefore to be extremely on your Guard against it, and not flatter yourselves, that because such Matches have sometimes happened, it will be your Fortune: Examples of this kind are very rare, and as seldom happy. Suppose he should even keep his Word, which it is much more than a thousand to one he never intended, what you would suffer from the Ill-usage of his Friends, and 'tis likely from his own Remorse for what he has done, would make you wish, in the greatest Bitterness of Heart, that it were possible for you to loose the indissoluble Knot, which binds you to a Man who no longer loves you, and return to your first humble Station. Such a Disparity of Birth, of Circumstances, and Education can produce no lasting Harmony; and where you see any such Couples paired, all the Comfort they enjoy are mere Outside-Shew; and tho' they may wear a Face of Contentment, to blind the Eyes of the World, and keep them from prying into the Merits of their Choice, their Bosoms are full of Disquiet and Repining.[1] Suffer not, therefore, your Hearts, much less your Innocence, to be tempted with a Prospect wherein the *best* that can arrive is bad enough. What then must be the *worst!* Eternal Ruin; every Misery you endure rendered more severe by the Stings of Disappointment, and a too late Repentance.

Gentlemen Lodgers.] If it be your Chance to live where they take in Lodgers or Boarders, especially such Gentlemen as do not keep Servants of their own to sit up for them, you may be subjected to some Inconvenience, when they stay out till after the Family are gone to Bed, come home in Liquor, or without being so, take this Opportunity of making Offers to you. If the Attempt goes no farther than Words, get out of their Way as fast as you can, and shew that tho' you are a Servant, you have a Spirit above bargaining for your Virtue: But if they once proceed to Rudeness, acquaint your Mistress with it, who, if a Woman of Reputation, will resent it as an Affront to herself, and rather lose her Lodger, than permit any Indecency in her House. But if you give any Ear at first to the Sollicitations made you, or accept of any Presents given on that Score, even tho' you neither make nor intend any Return, you will be accounted a Jilt,[2] used ill by the Person you impose upon, and

---

[1] Discontent.

[2] Loosely, 'tease'.

if it comes to your Mistress's Knowledge, infallibly lose your Place, with the same Disgrace as tho' you had yielded to the Act of Shame.

[Source: Eliza Haywood, *A Present for a Servant-Maid*, in *Miscellaneous Writings, 1725–43*, ed. Alexander Pettit, set 1, vol. i of *Selected Works of Eliza Haywood* (London: Pickering & Chatto, 2000) 213–14, 226–27, 238–39, 241–44.]

2. *The Female Spectator* (1744–46)

[*The Female Spectator* was a commercial success, earning a central place in Haywood's canon and in the history of the English period-ical. Haywood's professed goal—that 'Ladies would take example' from the stories and letters—affiliates the work with the mainstream of advice literature. But the miscellaneousness of *The Female Spectator* discourages generic pigeonholing: its twenty-four books encompass a multitude of topics, from literature to popular culture to science, religion, and philosophy. Tales of love and betrayal reminiscent of Haywood's early erotic fiction are interspersed among entries containing serious moral reflections. The effect is often startling, producing a sense of formal and thematic disjunction.

The selection below purports to teach young women about the dangers of premature marriage but in fact illustrates the effects of passion more broadly. Martesia recalls the heroine of *Fantomina* in that sexual passion catapults both women beyond acceptable social bound-aries. Haywood discards the terminal ambiguity of the earlier work, however, favoring an ending in which the heroine is clearly ruined. Modern readers may also want to consider this narrative alongside the 'novel' of Beraldus and Celemena in *The Tea-Table*, above.]

To be well convinc'd of the Sincerity of the Man they are about to marry, is a Maxim, with great Justice, always recommended to a young Lady; but I say it is no less material for her future Happiness, as well as that of her intended Partner, that she should be well assured of her own Heart, and examine, with the utmost Care, whether it be real Tenderness, or a bare Liking she at present feels for him; and as this is not to be done all at once, I cannot approve of hasty Marriages, or before Persons are of sufficient Years to be suppos'd capable of knowing their own Minds.

COULD Fourteen have the Power of judging of itself, or for itself, who that knew the beautiful *Martesia* at that Age, but would have depended on her Conduct!—*Martesia*, descended of the most illustrious Race, possess'd of all that Dignity of Sentiment[1] befitting her high Birth, endued by Nature with a surprizing Wit, Judgment, and Penetration, and improved by every Aid of Education.—*Martesia*, the Wonder and Delight of all who saw or heard her, gave the admiring World the greatest Expectations that she would one Day be no less celebrated for all those Virtues which render amiable the conjugal[2] State, than she at that Time was for every other Perfection that do Honour to the Sex.

YET how, alas, did all these charming Hopes vanish into Air! Many noble Youths, her Equals in Birth and Fortune, watch'd her Increase of Years for declaring a Passion, which they fear'd as yet would be rejected by those who had the Disposal of her; but what their Respect and Timidity forbad them to attempt, a more daring and unsuspected Rival ventured at, and succeeded in.—Her unexperienced Heart approved his Person, and was pleased with the Protestations he made her of it.—In fine, the Novelty of being address'd in that Manner gave a double Grace to all he said, and she never thought herself so happy as in his Conversation. His frequent Visits at length were taken Notice of; he was deny'd the Privilege of seeing her, and she was no longer permitted to go out without being accompanied by some Person who was to be a Spy upon her Actions.—She had a great Spirit, impatient of Controul, and this Restraint serv'd only to heighten the Inclination she before had to favour him:—She indulg'd the most romantick Ideas of his Merit and his Love:—Her own flowing Fancy invented a thousand melancholy and tender Soliloquies,[3] and set them down as made by him in this Separation: It is not, indeed, to be doubted, but that he was very much mortified at the Impediment he found in the Prosecution of his Courtship, but whether he took this Method of disburthening[4] his Affliction, neither she nor any body else could be assured. It cannot, however, be denied, but that he pursued Means much more efficacious[5] for the Attainment of his Wishes. By Bribes, Promises, and Entreaties he prevailed on a Person who came

---

1 Loosely, refinement.
2 Married.
3 Private utterances.
4 That is, unburdening; relieving.
5 Effective.

frequently to the House to convey his Letters to her, and bring back her Answers.—This Correspondence was, perhaps, of greater Service to him, than had the Freedom of their Interviews not been prevented:—She consented to be his, and to make good her Word, ventur'd her Life, by descending from a two Pair of Stairs Window,[1] by the Help of Quilt, Blankets, and other Things fasten'd to it, at the Dead of Night.—His Coach and Six[2] waited to receive her at the End of the Street, and convey'd her to his Country Seat,[3] which reaching soon after Break of Day, his Chaplain made them too fast for any Authority to separate.

As he was of an antient honourable Family, and his Estate very considerable, her Friends in a short Time were reconciled to what was now irremediable, and they were look'd upon as an extreme happy Pair.—But soon, too soon the fleeting Pleasures fled, and in their Room Anguish and Bitterness of Heart succeeded.

MARTESIA, in a Visit she made to a Lady of her intimate Acquaintance, unfortunately happen'd to meet the young *Clitander*, he was just return'd from his Travels, had a handsome Person, an Infinity of Gaiety, and a certain Something in his Air and Deportment[4] which had been destructive to the Peace and Reputation of many of our Sex.—He was naturally of an amorous Disposition, and being so, felt all the Force of Charms, which had some Effect even on the most Cold and Temperate.—Embolden'd by former Successes, the Knowledge *Martesia* was another's did not hinder him from declaring to her the Passion she had inspired him with.—She found a secret Satisfaction in hearing him, which she was yet too young to consider the Dangers of, and therefore endeavour'd not to suppress 'till it became too powerful for her to have done so, even had she attempted it with all her Might; but the Truth is, she now experienced in *reality* a Flame she had but *imagin'd* herself possess'd of for him who was now her Husband, and was too much averse to the giving herself Pain to combat with an Inclination which seem'd to her fraught only with Delights.

THE House, where their Acquaintance first began, was now the Scene of their future Meetings:—The Mistress of it was too great a

---

1 Second-floor window.
2 Large carriage, drawn by six horses.
3 Residence.
4 Conduct.

Friend to Gallantry[1] herself to be any Interruption to the Happiness they enjoy'd in entertaining each other without Witnesses.—How weak is Virtue when Love and Opportunity combine!—Tho' no Woman could have more refin'd and delicate Notions than *Martesia*, yet all were ineffectual against the Sollicitations of her adored *Clitander*.—One fatal Moment destroy'd at once all her own exalted Ideas of Honour and Reputation, and the Principles early instill'd into her Mind by her virtuous Preceptors.

THE Consequence of this Amour was a total Neglect of Husband, House, and Family.—Herself abandon'd, all other Duties were so too.—So manifest a Change was visible to all that knew her, but most to her Husband, as most interested in it.—He truly loved, and had believed himself truly beloved by her.—Loth he was to think his Misfortune real, and endeavour'd to find some other Motive for the Aversion she now express'd for staying at home, or going to any of those Places where they had been accustom'd to visit together; but she either knew not to dissemble, or took so little Pains to do it, that he was, in spite of himself, convinc'd all that Affection she so lately had profess'd, and given him Testimonies of, was now no more.—He examined all his Actions, and could find nothing in any of them that could give occasion for so sad a Reverse.—He complain'd to her one Day, in the tenderest Terms, of the small Portion she had of late allow'd him of her Conversation:—Entreated, that if by any Inadvertency he had offended her, she would acquaint him with his Fault, which he assured her he would take Care never to repeat.—Ask'd if there was any thing in her Settlement or Jointure[2] she could wish to have alter'd, and assur'd her she need but let him know her Commands to be instantly obey'd.

To all this she reply'd with the most stabbing Indifference.— That she knew not what he meant.—That as she had accus'd him with nothing, he had no Reason to think she was dissatisfy'd.—But that People could not be always in the same Humour, and desired he would not give himself nor her the Trouble of making any farther Interrogatories.[3]

HE must have been as insensible, as he is known to be the contrary, had such a Behaviour not open'd his Eyes; he no longer

---

1   Romantic intrigue.
2   A settlement is the portion of an estate settled on a wife upon her marriage; a join-
    ture is the portion reserved for her after the decease of the husband.
3   Enquiries.

doubted of his Fate, and resolving, if possible, to find out the Author of it, he caused her Chair[1] to be watch'd wherever she went, and took such effectual Methods as soon inform'd him of the Truth.

IN the first Emotions of his Rage he was for sending a Challenge[2] to this Destroyer of his Happiness; but in his cooler Moments he rejected that Design as too injurious to the Reputation of *Martesia*, who was still dear to him, and whom he flatter'd himself with being able one Day to reclaim.

IT is certain he put in Practice every tender Stratagem that Love and Wit could furnish him with for that Purpose; but she appearing so far from being moved at any thing he either said or did, that, on the contrary, her Behaviour was every Day more cold; he at last began to expostulate with her, gave some Hints that her late Conduct was not unknown to him, and that tho' he was willing to forgive what was past, yet as a Husband, it was not consistent with his Character to bear any future Insults of that Nature. This put her beyond all Patience.—She reproach'd him in the bitterest Terms for daring to harbour the least Suspicion of her Virtue, and censuring her innocent Amusements as Crimes;[3] and perhaps was glad of this Opportunity of testifying her Remorse for having ever listen'd to his Vows, and cursing before his Face the Hour that join'd their Hands.

THEY now lived so ill a Life together, that not having sufficient Proofs for a Divorce, he parted Beds, and tho' they continued in one House, behaved to each other as Strangers; never eat at the same Table but when Company was there, and then only to avoid the Questions that would naturally have been ask'd had it been otherwise; neither of them being desirous the World should know any thing of their Disagreement.

BUT while they continued to treat each other in a Manner so little conformable to their first Hopes, or their Vows pledg'd at the holy Altar, *Martesia* became pregnant: This gave the first Alarm to that Indolence of Nature she hitherto had testify'd; her Husband would now have it in his Power to sue out a Divorce, and tho' she would have rejoic'd to have been separated from him on any other Terms, yet she could not support the Thoughts of being totally depriv'd of all Reputation in the World.—She was not ignorant of

---

[1] One-seated vehicle for hire, carried on poles.
[2] Invitation to duel.
[3] Morally odious acts.

the Censures she incurr'd, but had Pride and Spirit enough to enable her to despise whatever was said of her, while it was not back'd by Proof; but the glaring one she was now about to give struck Shame and Confusion to her Soul.—She left no Means untry'd to procure an Abortion; but failing in that, she had no other Resource than to that Friend who was the sole Confidante of her unhappy Passion, who comforted her as well as she could, and assur'd her, that when the Hour approach'd she need have no more to do than to come directly to her House, where every thing should be prepar'd for the Reception of a Woman in her Condition.

To conceal the Alteration in her Shape, she pretended Indisposition, saw little Company, and wore only loose Gowns.— At length the so much dreaded Moment came upon her at the dead of Night, and in the midst of all that Rack[1] of Nature; made yet more horrible by the Agonies of her Mind, she rose, rung for her Woman, and telling her she had a frightful Dream concerning that Lady, whom she knew she had the greatest Value for of any Person upon Earth, order'd her to get a Chair, for she could not be easy unless she went and saw her herself. The Woman was strangely surpriz'd, but her Lady was always absolute in her Commands.—A Chair was brought, and without any other Company or Attendance than her own distracted Thoughts, she was convey'd to the only Asylum[2] where she thought her Shame might find a Shelter.

A MIDWIFE being prepar'd before, she was safely deliver'd of a Daughter, who expir'd almost as soon as born; and to prevent as much as possible all Suspicion of the Truth, she made herself be carried home the next Morning, where she went to Bed, and lay several Days under Pretence of having sprain'd her Ancle.

BUT not all the Precautions she had taken were effectual enough to prevent some People from guessing and whispering what had happen'd.—Those whose Nearness in Blood gave them a Privilege of speaking their Minds, spar'd not to tell her all that was said of her; and those who dar'd not take that Liberty, shew'd by their distant Looks and reserv'd Behaviour, whenever she came in Presence, how little they approv'd her Conduct.—She was too discerning not to see into their Thoughts, nor was her innate Pride of any Service to keep up her Spirits on this Occasion.—To add to her Discontents,

---

[1] Torment.
[2] Sanctuary.

Clitander grew every Day more cool in his Respects, and she soon after learn'd he was on the Point of Marriage with one far inferior to herself in every Charm both of Mind and Person.—In fine, finding herself deserted by her Relations, and the greatest Part of her Acquaintance, without Love, without Respect, and reduced to the Pity of those, who, perhaps, had nothing but a greater Share of Circumspection to boast of, she took a Resolution to quit *England* for ever, and having settled her Affairs with her Husband, who by this Time had enter'd into other Amusements, and 'tis probable was very well satisfy'd to be eased of the Constraint her Presence gave him, readily agreed to remit her the Sum agreed between them, to be paid yearly to whatever Part of the World she chose to reside in, she then took leave of a Country of which she had been the Idol, and which now seem'd to her as too unjust in not being blind to what she desired should be concealed.

BEHOLD her now in a voluntary Banishment from Friends and Country, and roaming round the World in fruitless Search of that Tranquility she could not have fail'd enjoying at home in the Bosom of a Consort[1] equally belov'd as loving.—Unhappy charming Lady, born and endu'd with every Quality to attract universal Love and Admiration, yet by one inadvertent Step undone and lost to every thing the World holds dear, and only more conspicuously wretched by having been conspicuously amiable.

[Source: Eliza Haywood, *The Female Spectator*, bk. 1, in *The Female Spectator, Volumes 1 and 2*, ed. Kathryn R. King and Alexander Pettit, set 2, vol. ii of *Selected Works of Eliza Haywood* (London: Pickering & Chatto, 2001) 22–27.]

---

[1] Companion.

Appendix B: Eighteenth-Century Pornography: Jean Barrin(?), Venus in the Cloister; or, The Nun in Her Smock (1724)

[In October 1724, Edmund Curll printed a translation of *Vénus dans le cloître, ou la religieuse en chemise* (1683), a pornographic work probably written by Jean Barrin and certainly translated by Robert Samber. Curll was jailed for much of the period 1725–28 as a consequence of the publication.

The following excerpt illustrates themes in *Venus in the Cloister* that are common in the erotica of the period: the sexual enthusiasm of young women in European nunneries, the tendency of nunneries and monasteries to be havens of transgressive sexuality, and the eagerness of the Catholic clergy to debauch their charges. Haywood perhaps means to invoke these illiberal commonplaces at the end of *Fantomina*, when she informs the reader that the heroine will be dispatched 'to a Monastery in *France*'. The excerpt also dwells on the particulars of the young female body, considers the allure of cross-class promiscuity, and glances at the eros of disguise. In these ways, too, *Venus in the Cloister* resembles *Fantomina*.

Venus in the Cloister comprises five dialogues between the twenty-year-old nun Angelica and the younger Agnes, a newcomer to the nunnery. The excerpt is from the fourth dialogue. Angelica has just informed Agnes that another nun, Eugenia, has left the nunnery. Samber's notes are drawn from various points in the text.]

Agnes. But tell me, What did *Eugenia* say was the Reason of her quitting the Habit?

Angel. Only what we would all quit it for, a handsome young Fellow and one of a good Family.

Agnes. His Name?

Angel. 'Tis young *Frederick*, eldest Son to the *Sieur de Vitford*, you do not know him; I would draw you his Picture, but, to tell you the Truth, I had rather draw one of our own Sex.

Agnes. Why so? Is there so vast a Difference between the Men and us?

Angel. Most certainly, a very remarkable one; and which thou art very well acquainted with; or the *Abbé* and *Feuillant*[1] have spent their Time but very dryly in their Instructions.

*Agnes.*You make me laugh. But since you will not give me the Pourtrait of a Man, give me that of Sister *Eugenia*; for it is a good While since I saw her, and I cannot tell whether if I saw her, I should know her.

*Angel.*With all my Heart, my Dear: Thou must know then that she is very tall, and treads extremely well; she is Mistress of a fine Body, and her Flesh is white and delicate, plump, yet as soft as Velvet; she is neither Fat nor Lean; her Breasts regularly divided, round, and not too prominent; she is, however, full chested, and very slender in the Waste; her Face delicately smooth, lovely black large Eyes, her Hair black as Jet, and the loveliest Complexion in the World, her Arms round, her Hands of a moderate Length, but small, her Hips handsomely rising, her Legs beautifully straight, supported with two little Feet, which makes her, altogether, a compleat Beauty. But besides all these Beauties Nature has bestowed upon her, she is Mistress of all those fine Qualities of the Mind, which make a young Lady infinitely agreeable and charming.

*Agnes.*You may very well say, I do not know her, neither should I if she be thus accomplished as you say, for that little that I remember of her, pointed her out quite the Reverse.

Angel. She is indeed much alter'd; I told you I did not know her myself, at first, but you know fine Cloathes and Carriage make a vast Alteration, besides Conversation with the *Beau Monde*,[2] for she has been, it seems, two Months out of the Convent,[3] gives a different polish to what we meet with generally in Religious Houses.

---

[1] Earlier, Angelica had arranged sexual encounters for Agnes with these men. '*Abbé* ... does not signify an Abbot, or superiour of a Monastery of Men, but one who holds some Sinecure, of which there are a great many in *France*, and abundance of them not in Priests-Orders, and as great Libertines and Debauchees as one could wish. They ... wear fine Bands, and most of them very sparkish in their Dress: Take Snuff, go to Plays and Operas, play at Cards, and talk Love to the Ladies' (Samber's note). The *feuillants* were members of the Order of Cîteaux, which was affiliated with the *couvent des Feuillants*, or convent of Feuillants, in Paris. 'They wear fine white Stuff, they are called *Feuillants*, from *Feuille* a Leaf, because they carry in their Arms a Branch with Leaves' (Samber's note).

[2] Fashionable sector of society.

[3] 'Convent is the same as Cloister, and is applicable to those of Men and Women' (Samber's note). The terms are not in fact synonymous but were often used as if they were.

Agnes. There is something in that; but, since you say she is to be married to young *Frederick*, pray inform me, Is not this Gentleman the same Person I told you I saw once at *Paris*, at an Entertainment which the Count *Arnobio*, a *Florentine*, gave to the Gentlemen and Ladies on the Grand Duke's Birth-Day?

Angel. The very same; and I am as glad of *Eugenia's* good Fortune as if I were to participate of their first Enjoyments.

Agnes. And I am as glad of the Visit she paid you: It may find subject matter for Discourse.

Angel. That Girl has a great deal of Wit, and knows more than you think of; and tho' thou may'st, I do not wonder at her quitting the Cloister,[1] her Constitution is as amorous as thy own. It is not long since an Affair happened to convince me of this. Thou must know then, that *Frederick* taking the Benefit of our Enclosures[2] being open, got very early into the Convent, disguised like a Workman, and watching his Opportunity, conveyed himself into *Eugenia's* Cell,[3] after her breaking her *Novice-ship*,[4] where he found her stark naked, the Weather being very hot; she knew him, and turning about with a Smile, asked him what he wanted? He answered only, my Dear, my Life, my Soul! and could say no more. After these Words, she put on her Smock[5] and came up to him. He immediately put his Hand you may guess where. She, all surprized, asked, if he was not ashamed to treat her after this Manner? All this signified nothing, he embraced her closely in his Arms, and in a languishing Tone, cryed, Kiss me, my Soul, which she had no sooner done, but he threw her upon the Mattress, and run over her Breast and Stomach, and other more secret Parts, with a thousand Kisses, and then proceeded on to Pleasures more particular, which made her, if she was not so before, a perfect Woman.

Agnes. And how came you to know all this?

---

[1] Nunnery.

[2] 'When there are any Buildings to raise, or Reparations made in Nunneries, the Enclosure … must be open for the Workmen, and anybody may then go in' (Samber's note).

[3] Single-person room in a nunnery or monastery.

[4] The syntax was presumably garbled in translation or in printing, but the point seems to be that Eugenia has completed her noviceship, or novitiate, the period before the formal taking of vows. See Samber's note: '… the Probationers, who are to try for a Twelve-Month whether they like the State of a Nun, and during that Time are called *Novices*.'

[5] Camisole.

Angel. I'll tell thee: I thought I saw one of the Workmen enter her Cell, and tripping softly along the Dormitory,[1] made up to her Door, which having a large Chink between the Boards, I saw what I tell you. The first Thing I beheld, was *Eugenia* all naked, with *Frederick* sitting by her, holding in his Hand —— which extremely surprized me, imagining to myself that she could never enjoy the Excess of Pleasure I afterwards found she did.

Said I to myself, Lord! what Pain must poor *Eugenia* undergo? How is it possible he should not tear her to Pieces? These were my Thoughts, but I suppose he treated her very gently on Account of her Youth, for she was but bare[2] Fifteen. While I was thus busied in my Thoughts, I heard *Frederick* say, *Eugenia*, my Dear, turn upon your Back, which after she had done, he got up and put his —— into her —— for my Part I was quite frightened when I heard her cry out as if she were in excessive Pain, this gave me, as thou may'st well imagine, a great deal of Uneasiness, for I did not dare to come in for fear of surprizing of them, which might have had perhaps but very ill Consequences. However, a Moment after I saw her move her Legs and embrace her Lover with both her Arms after such an extraordinary Manner as sufficiently expressed the utmost Satisfaction.

Frederick was no less pleas'd with this Encounter. Ha! said he, What Pleasure does thou give me? In short, after endeavouring to exceed each other in the amorous Combat, they softly sighed, and then for some small Space reposed as in an Extasy. And to shew[3] thee what Love *Eugenia* had for her Lover, I must tell thee, that notwithstanding this pleasing Trance, she could not help now and then giving him many a Kiss, nay, I think she kissed him all over, and spoke to him the kindest Things in the World, which sufficiently convinc'd me what Excess of Joy she then received. This raised a Desire in me to taste the same Love Potion, and indeed I even grew distracted[4] with strong unknown Longings and Desires; I could not help thinking of it all Night, and slept not a Moment till the Morning, and by a lucky Accident Fortune, who favoured my Desires, gave me some Consolation. It was the Son of the Count *Don Grassio*, who by chance cast his Eyes upon me, and began to

---

[1]   '[A] *Dormitory* … is that Gallery in Cloisters on each Side of which are the Cells, or little Chambers, of the Religious [i.e., nuns and monks] of both Sexes' (Samber's note).

[2]   That is, barely.

[3]   That is, show.

[4]   Deranged.

fall in Love with me: Every Time I saw him, it was impossible for me not to make a mutual Return. We began both by amorous Looks, Salutes[1] of the Body, then of the Mouth, and after that by sweetest and most particular Testimonies of Love and Friendship. But what gave me some Uneasiness was, that in the height of our Expectations I was obliged to change my Apartment, which gave me the utmost Chagrin; however, this did not hinder him from secretly conveying to my Hands a Letter, in which he assured me that he burned with Excess of Love for me, beseeching me to have Pity on his Sufferings by making suitable Returns to his Flame and Passion. Thou mayst imagine with what Pleasure I read this Letter; I thought I should have fainted away for Joy, and thought of nothing but possessing my dearest *Don Grassio*, and to this End I returned for Answer, that he should come as soon as possible, that I would grant him every Thing that he could desire from a young Woman who loved him more than her own Life; and that he would certainly find me in that Apartment where we first engaged. He no sooner had my Letter but he flew like Lightning, and in the Disguise of a Mason, for that Stratagem[2] I learned from *Eugenia*, came to that Place where we were to give each other full Proofs of our Affections. It was very happy that he met with Sister *Magdalene*, thou know'st that good-natured Lay-Sister, who is my very good Friend and Confidant, from whom I learned what extreme Desire he had to come to the Height of our Wishes, she shewed him up into the old Room through the back Stairs, and placed him in an obscure Hole[3] where we used to put our Wood in, for the Infirmary; which done, she came to me with a great deal of Joy, and told me where she had concealed *Don Grassio*, and that he attended with the utmost Impatience, for my Commands. This Stratagem of poor Sister *Magdalene* was better than I could have hoped for; with her then I went into the Wood-house, where poor *Magdalene* stood Centinel, and *Don Grassio* immediately, without any Ceremony, embraced me after such an amorous Manner as gave me just grounds to believe that I should soon be the most happy Creature living. My Modesty, combating with my Passion, made me receive his first Caresses with some Reluctance and inward Shame, but a

---

[1] Gestures of greeting, often, specifically, kisses.
[2] Trick.
[3] Dingy room; basement.

little after I returned them in so sensible a Manner as he did not expect. Upon which, throwing off his Coat, he gently laid me upon it on the Floor and kissed me a thousand Times, nor were his Hands without Employ. I receiv'd all this like a true Child of *Venus*, and we repeated it more than once, but with a Pleasure still more exquisite. He bestowed on me such Kisses as would raise Jealousy even in the Gods! Ah! how full of Tenderness are those Embraces! how agreeable and delicious his Touches! Let, said he in a trembling Tone, Oh let me put my Mouth between thy Bubbies, and let this my Hand cover this Mountain sacred to Love and *Venus*, and with this other repose on thy Lovely Thighs.

Agnes. And were you often thus happy? Tell me, *Angelica*, and hide nothing from one who loves you as her Soul.

Angel. The next Morning we renewed the Battle after the same Manner, though he sweetly told me that our Pleasures would be yet imperfect if I did not contribute a Remedy: But, said I, you have no Manner of Reason to complain against me of any Crime that proceeds only from Ignorance, for I am naturally more inclined to be compassionate than cruel, and insensible in relation to the Pains or Pleasures of other People, and especially of those I love, I beseech you then to pardon my Simplicity;[1] I hope in Time I shall learn how to be provided with every thing that may make us enjoy our Pleasures with the greatest Satisfaction. Having said this, I was going for some Books that treated on these Subjects, and might fully instruct me in my Duty, but he held me by my Petticoat and desired me to stay and return to our Caresses, and to shew each other the Excess of our mutual Passion before we parted; upon this, he laid me down once more, and after swearing that he loved me more than his own Life, and making on each Side Protestations of eternal Friendship, we returned to what ended in each others excessive Satisfaction.

Agnes. And certainly this contented you: Was not your Curiosity fully satisfied to have lost, as I conclude you did from what you say, your Virginity? But tell me, *Angelica*, did not *Don Grassio* run a Risque of falling ill by so much Exercise?

Angel. I'll tell thee: Sister *Magdalene*, the next Day, being sent to the Market, accidentally met with *Catherine*, *Don Grassio*'s Maid, who told her the ill Luck which had befallen her Master, who told me with a great deal of Chagrin and Sorrow, that *Don Grassio* had

---

[1]   Lack of sophistication.

got a violent Fever, which had reduced him to the last Extremity. Thou must easily imagine how much this News afflicted me as well as poor *Magdalene*, to whom I afterwards understood he had been also somewhat lavish of his Favours. She went about her own Affairs, and I was in the greatest Concern in the World, believing I should never be able to retrieve that Loss, for I was told he ran a great Risque of losing his Life, which indeed too truly some Days after happened, to my no small Affliction.

Agnes. Poor *Angelica!* and so you lost your Play-Thing.

Angel. I did so; but it was not long before Fortune provided me with another full as agreeable.

Agnes. And who was this, I beseech you?

Angel. No less a Man than *Pierrot*, our young Gardiner.

Agnes. For Shame, *Angelica*, how could you submit to the vile Embraces of such a Fellow?

Angel. Poor Fool, thou dost not consider that Love makes no Distinctions, neither shouldst thou judge Things by the External. I tell thee, *Agnes*, under that mean Garb is something more agreeable than under the richest Drapery; besides, he is fresh, of lovely ruddy Complexion, full of Vigour in his Actions, and there lies an excessive Charm, simple, artless,[1] and undisguised.

Agnes. Well, you are a mad Creature, but tell me from the Beginning how this Adventure happened.

Angel. Thou must know then, that my Lady sent me one Day to carry her Orders to *Pierrot*, concerning the planting of some Roses; when I came to the farther End of the Garden behind the high *Espalier* Hedge of Hornbeam,[2] I saw *Pierrot* musing, as it were in a brown Study,[3] and then starting of a sudden sent out a loud Sigh, and flew immediately into the little House where he lies and keeps his Tools.[4] I followed, moved by a certain Curiosity to see the Cause of this sudden Flight, when coming to the Door, which he only put to, and had forgot to fasten, I saw him throw himself upon the Bed, and handle his Play-Thing with a very deep Sigh or two. Alas, poor Boy! said I to myself, he is without a Woman, as I am without my *Don Grassio*. I perceived, that since he had no other Conveniency,

---

[1] Sincere, simple.

[2] Row of hardwood saplings, affixed to training stakes.

[3] Daydreaming.

[4] 'Tool' and the corresponding French word, *outil*, are slang terms for 'penis'; the English usage dates at least to 1640.

that he was resolved to make Use of what Nature had given him. What! thought I, shall I stand thus, and see that thrown away which may be better elsewhere bestowed; no, no, no if he has any Occasion, I'll go and content him after a more agreeable manner.

Agnes. And you say he is young and handsome?

Angel. To a Wonder, he is no more than one and twenty, of a middling Stature, his Hair of light Brown, and the finest in the World, his Eyes very amorous and languishing, his Face unexceptionable, his Lips softer than the softest Velvet, and his Legs admirably turned; but then he kisses, *Agnes,* Oh! I cannot express what ——

Agnes. No more of your Raptures, but continue your Narration.

Angel. Well, to go on regularly, after I had seen what I told you at the Door, all trembling as I was, I resolved to knock, but Love exceeded my Fear, and made me enter boldly without waiting his coming to let me in.

Agnes. Indeed, I think you were very forward to one you have so little Knowledge of.

Angel. You are mistaken: I have been acquainted with *Pierrot* these two Years; there have passed indeed some little Liberties between us, but we never came to the grand Point. The poor Boy, in the Condition he was in, was more surprized than I; as not doubting but I had been an Eye-Witness to all the Postures and Gesticulations[1] with which Love had inspired him. I could not help smiling to see how unmoveable he sate, not being capable to move a Finger. I came up to the Bed-side, smiling, and he taking my Hand with his Left-Hand, (for his Right-Hand was not quite disengaged) Ah! *Angelica,* said he, my Love, my Heart, what do we do? And then drawing me to him, threw me on the Bed, and viewed my Breasts with Eyes so soft and languishing, that I no Ways doubted of the Consequence; upon which I leaped up, and went to secure the Door, and stop up all the Holes: Then coming back, with somewhat the Air of a Prude, said to *Pierrot,* I took this Precaution to say something in particular to thee.—Upon which, interrupting me, he was going to put his Hand —— Ha! *Pierrot,* said I, what would'st thou do? Take away thy Hand there. But alas! *Agnes,* all was in vain, the poor Boy, and i'my Conscience, I believe it was the first Time by the Aukwardness of his Manner, fell suddenly into a Kind of fainting, which when I

---

[1] Bodily movements.

perceived, I was frightened, by an involuntary Discharge of his Ammunition before he reached the Counterscarp,[1] his Vigour lost.

Agnes. Terrible Disappointment, indeed, poor *Pierrot.*

Angel. Say, rather, poor *Angelica.* However, this did not last long, the Champion rallied his Forces, and pushed so furiously in the Attack, that he gained the Fort entirely, tho' with the Effusion of much Blood.

Agnes. All this I could the better bear with, but with a nasty Gardiner Fellow, fogh! I'll no more of it.

Angel. I have done, and will change the Subject. Know then, that some Time ago I received a Visit in the Parlour[2] from the *Sieur Rodolphe*, accompanied with a young Person of Quality, whose Name was *Alicia*, who was indeed richly dressed in every Respect as beautiful as an Angel. It is impossible to describe her Charms. She sung several fine Songs with those agreeable Rollings of her Eyes, that inspired Love into us both, especially *Rodolphe*, who took this Opportunity to enter into a particular friendship with her, begging of her in the most engaging Terms in the World, that she would suffer him to do himself the Honour of sometimes seeing her, hoping that this would not be refused him, as believing it would be a Thing neither disagreeable to her Father's Inclinations, nor her own. He continued his Discourse, by telling her, how charming her Conversation was to him, and that if he dared, he could take, some Day, the Liberty to wait upon her at her Father's Country Seat; in short, he said to her abundance of other agreeable and tender Things, which I make no doubt had the desired Effect, for he sometime after paid her a Visit, at that Place which he might well have called the *Palace of Pleasure*, not so much on Account of its Regularity of Structure, but because in the Presence of his *Alicia* he enjoyed a thousand unspeakable Pleasures, but dared not farther advance for Fear of her Father, whom he dreaded; but flattered himself, nevertheless, that by some little Artifices and Address,[3] to arrive at the Port of his Happiness.

---

[1]   Literally applied to military fortifications: the outer (i.e., safer) wall of a ditch, a desirable strategic position.

[2]   'Parlour, is a Room (of which there are several in every *Nunnery*) into which the *Nuns* come to talk with Strangers: It is divided in the Middle by an Iron Grate, and contrived so, that those in one *Parlour* cannot hear what is said in another. Strangers come into it through a Gallery, having first received a Key from the Mother Porteress' (Samber's[?] note).

[3]   Cunning and persuasion.

Agnes. But had he no Amorous Dalliance with her, did he not entertain her with no little Liberties, not talk to her of particular Pleasures? I am afraid, *Angelica*, that you will not tell me all.

Angel. I see very well thy Malice; I shall talk to thee another Time of that Affair; every Thing in its Season. I shall now only tell thee, that I heartily pray, that all the Powers Above, who are sensible of his Passion, to be favourable to *Rodolphe* in his Amorous Enterprise.

Agnes. I see *Rodolphe* is one of your good Friends, you wish him so well. I will not tell you what my Thoughts are of *Rodolphe* and you. I shall only say, that I believe he has communicated to you a little of Love's *Elixer Proprietatis*.[1]

Angel. I believe in talking th[u]s to me, thou hast only a Mind to make thyself merry. But hear what happened to poor *Alicia* afterwards, which I had from her own Mouth.

One Day, above the rest, *Alicia* went with her Father to visit a certain Capucin[2] of this City, called *Pere Theodore*, (or Father *Theodore*) whose Blessing she begged, and whom thou wilt have a perfect Idea of, when I shall have told thee, that he is one of those who affect an Austerity of Life, and a particular Severity: Thou must know, that every Thing preaches up these Fathers, I believe thou understandest these Terms. Mortification,[3] Penance, and their long Beards,[4] which they let grow and nourish with so much Care, which make their Faces look dry and meagre, render the Minds of the People as so many Mirrours of Sanctity. Well, my Child, said he to *Alicia*, you have here a Father, who will spare nothing to make you as perfect as you ought to be. You are to be married in a little Time, as I am informed, to *Rodolphe*. You must therefore cleanse your Soul from all manner of Impurity, to render you worthy of Celestial Grace, which cannot enter into one that is sullied with the least Ordure.[5] You must know, continued he, that if you are pure, the Children produced by this Marriage, and which you shall bring into the World, shall help to supply, one Day, the Places of the fallen

---

[1]   The construction joins Arabic ('elixer', or drug) and Latin elements and is meant to suggest an aphrodisiac; the meaning, loosely, is 'an elixer of a nature all its own' or 'love's own elixer'.

[2]   That is, Capuchin, friar of the Franciscan order.

[3]   The deadening of the senses through the infliction of bodily pain.

[4]   'The *Capucins* after they have taken their *Vows* of *Profession* never shave or cut their Beards, which makes some of them have terrible long ones' (Samber's note).

[5]   (Moral) filth.

Angels; but on the contrary, if you have any evil Quality, they will be infected and go into the Way of Perdition to increase the Number of those miserable Wretches. It is you must cleanse, my Child, said he, either of these two Conditions, there is no middle State between.

Alicia was so ashamed she knew not how to speak. Speak, speak, said he. I desire, said she, to be purified, and that my Children may be good. There was along with Father *Theodore* a certain Reverend Father Jesuit, who, having for some Time heard this Conversation, went away; which *Alicia* was not sorry at, as having then more Courage to discourse with *Theodore*, to whom, after he entered the Confession-Chair which stood in a dark Corner of the Church, for there it seems was this Entertainment, she confessed all her Sins, even to the least Circumstance of what had passed between herself and *Rodolphe*, her Father staying at some Distance.

When the good Father heard how far she had already advanced in these Love-Affairs, he fell into a violent Heat,[1] and gave her a severe Reprimand, after having told her, she must have all these Kinds of Affections in the utmost Horror. Then coming towards her Father, gave him a little Bundle of Cords, which he pulled out of his Sleeve with these Words: Go, said he, and do not spare your Daughter, give her an Example your own self, and be not too indulgent. After this, they took their Leave of Father *Theodore*, and went home.

Agnes. Do you not wonder, *Angelica*, how these People abuse our Simplicity? I doubt not but *Alicia*, as well as her Father, believed these Words, as if they proceeded from the Mouth of an Evangelist.[2]

Angel. Very probably. However, as soon as they came home, her Father calling her up into her Chamber, shut the Door, and giving her the Bundle of Cords, bid her, with a Smile, untangle them, which she did, and found it to be a Scourge, or Discipline,[3] made up of fine little Cords, knotted with an Infinity of little Knots at some little Distances from each other. Ha! my Child, said he, it is with this Instrument of Piety, as the good Fathers call it, that you must dispose of yourself for the Marriage State, which you desire to enter into, this must serve to purify your Continence.[4] This good Father, continued he, hath commanded us both to make Use of it:

---

[1] Passion.

[2] Narrowly (as here), one of the authors of the Gospels: Matthew, Mark, Luke, or John.

[3] 'A Discipline, is a sort of Cat of Nine Tails with which they [the nuns] whip themselves in Monasteries' (Samber's note).

[4] An irregular usage, here connoting sexual appetite.

I will begin, said he, and you shall follow; but do not let the Vigour with which I treat my Body frighten you; be not afraid, and only think, as well as I do, that during this Holy Exercise, my Mind tastes such Pleasures as I am not able to express.

Agnes. Without doubt *Alicia* trembled to hear her Father talk after this Manner.

Angel. No; and I wonder that she had so much Strength as to undergo so rude[1] and painful an Exercise as she did.

Agnes. There is nothing in Reality more constant and courageous than a young Woman when she is resolved to be so; in this Case she will outdo herself to support, with an admirable Firmness of Mind, those Sufferings which would vanquish the most courageous Man in the World: I make no doubt but it was the Love of *Rodolphe* that inspired her to suffer such rude Treatment; but go on with your Relation, I beseech you.

Angel. Just in the very Instant, *Alicia* and her Father were going to begin, *Alicia*'s Aunt came into the Room. This Aunt, who is a mighty *Bigot*,[2] would take her Brother's Place, telling him, It was not usual for Men to act after this Manner, and that for her Part, it was a great Honour for her to put herself into the Room[3] of another, to execute the Orders of good Father *Theodore*, which she immediately did, by unclothing herself to her Smock, which she pulled up over her Shoulders; after this she kneeled down, taking into her Hand the Discipline, Look, Niece, and see how you must use this Instrument of Penance, and learn to undergo it by the Example I am going to give you: Scarce had she finished these Words when some one knocked at the Door, Oh! said *Alicia*'s Father, this must be the good Father *Theodore*, who is come, no doubt, to assist at this Holy Exercise: He told her, he would not fail of being here, if he could but get Leave of his Superior to come out of the Convent. He knocked a second Time: It is he, said *Alicia*'s Father to her, go open the Door quickly: What! Sir, said she, would you have him see my Aunt thus naked? You do not know, said her Father, that this holy Man knows your Aunt to the very Bottom of her Interiour, and that we must conceal nothing from him. Her Aunt, however, pulled down her Smock, while *Alicia* went to open the Door, when immediately

---

[1] Violent.

[2] Religious zealot.

[3] Place.

Father *Theodore* came in and commended the Aunt for the good Example she gave her Niece; after which he made a Discourse upon that Subject, but with so much Force and Energy, that it had almost made *Alicia* prevent him, by desiring to treat her with greater Vigour, than she might do herself.

Agnes. Lord! Is it possible? Was she such a Fool? So silly, and so much a Bigot!

Angel. Had'st thou then been there, thou would'st not have resisted, but have suffered thyself in like Manner to be persuaded. He proved to them, that Virginity, without Mortification and Penance, had no Manner of Merit; that it was a dry and barren Virtue; and, unless accompanied with some voluntary Chastisement, there was nothing more base and despicable. They certainly, continued he, ought to be ashamed and blush, who shew themselves naked before Men, in order to prostitute themselves to their Concupiscence,[1] but on the contrary, others are praise-worthy who do so only out of a Principle of Piety and Penance, and for a holy Zeal to purify their Souls. If you consider the Action of the former, said he, continuing his Discourse, you find nothing in it but what is infamous;[2] and if you cast your Eyes upon the other, you will observe that it contains in it every Thing that is really honest: One can only satisfy Men, the other charms, if I may use the Expression, the very Gods. But above all, said he, these Kinds of Correction are of great Use, when they are duly taken; they are like a divine Fountain, the miraculous Waters of which have the Virtue to cleanse the Female Sex from all Impurities they might have contracted; they have no other Way to purge themselves but in suffering with Firmness of Mind and Patience, the Penance that is impos'd upon them, from having tasted, with Sensuality, forbidden Pleasures. In short, he told them, that by this Method their Souls were cleansed from an Infinity of Sins that Shame and Modesty might have often hindered them from revealing in Confession ....

Agnes. Alas! poor Thing, she would have been more agreeably entertained with her dear *Rodolphe*; and I make no Doubt, but had she known where he was, or he her, they had been together and made Use of her Time.

Angel. He surmised something, and Fortune was so favourable to him, that at the very Instant her Aunt had left her Father's House, by

---

[1] Sexual desire.
[2] Vile.

the Assistance of the Maid, who told her also, that her Master was gone Abroad to Supper, he came into *Alicia*'s Chamber, whom he found upon the Bed. *Alicia* knew who he was, but pretended being asleep, he flung his Arms about her Neck, and kissed her a thousand Times, handling amorously several Parts of her Body. When she who could no longer bear these sweet Caresses with a Transport,[1] took him hold by —— Ah! Lord, I cannot name it! and then—you may imagine what followed. For my Part—But hark, I hear somebody coming along the Dormitory, let us separate till to Morrow.

Agnes. It is fit we should, 'tis now near Supper-time; but you are a terrible Gossip, and love to prattle[2] to your Soul; nor indeed can I be anywise angry with you for affording me so many Hours agreeable Conversation. Adieu.

Angel. Adieu, dear *Agnes*, kiss me, my Soul! Adieu, my Life, Adieu.

[Source: Jean Barrin(?), *Venus in the Cloister; or, The Nun in Her Smock*, trans. Robert Samber (1724), in *Edmund Curll and Grub-Street Highlights*, ed. Kevin L. Cope, vol. ii of *Eighteenth-Century British Erotica* (London: Pickering & Chatto, 2002), pp. 303–31.]

---

[1]   Ecstasy. An error may have obscured the meaning here: perhaps 'with' was meant to read 'without'; perhaps a dropped comma after 'Caresses' is the culprit.

[2]   Chatter.

Appendix C: A Source for Reflections on the Various Effects of Love: Nahum Tate, A Present for the Ladies: Being an Historical Account of Several Illustrious Persons of the Female Sex *(1692; 2nd ed., 1693)*

[In *A Present for the Ladies*, Nahum Tate, poet laureate of England from 1692 to 1715, enters into the lively debate about the moral, intellectual, and professional merits of women. The following excerpt specifies Tate's argument and initiates the roll-call of historical and quasi-historical women that will occupy him throughout the work. Haywood references *A Present for the Ladies* once in *Reflections on the Various Effects of Love* and, as the notes in this edition indicate, draws from it on a number of occasions therein. The lineage becomes more extensive when Haywood discusses Pauline, wife of the Roman philosopher Seneca. Her account is partly drawn from Tate's, and Pauline is one of the three women whom the French essayist Michel de Montaigne had praised in a work that Tate acknowledges elsewhere in his treatise (see p. 277 n.1, below). Haywood thus joins a cross-gendered tradition of celebratory feminist historiography. Montaigne and Tate, however, anticipate the Victorian doctrine of 'separate spheres', with its attendant praise for the moral excellence of the domestic woman. Haywood does not. Rather, her emphasis is on sexual passion, particularly female, and the dangers of ignoring it. The tale of the Persian Monarch, which appears in the following excerpt and which resurfaces in *Reflections on the Various Effects of Love*, constitutes one useful illustration of this difference.]

THE PREFACE.

'Tis a sort of Knight-Errantry[1] to draw a Pen in Defence of the Female Sex, and taken for a kind of Challenge by most of Ours. We have with such confidence laid claim to all the nobler Faculties, that the World is half perswaded we have Right for the Pretence. Some

---

[1]   Chivalry, with the implication of irrational or Quixotic behavior.

few amongst us have generously expos'd the Cheat, and with the fortune of all Reformers been accounted Hereticks to Mankind for their pains. Yet such I have ventur'd to Copy in this little Treatise, and thought it no Sacriledge in the Ladies defence to take down from their own Temple the consecrated Weapons of their former Champions. At least, I must seem as pardonable a Plagiary[1] as any of their modern Satyrists, harmless Creatures in themselves, and only indebted to others for their Venom.

'Tis the hard Fortune of Ladies to create Enemies by their Repulses, and to become subjects of slander, because they will not be guilty. The few Examples, cited in this Treatise, (out of infinite numbers in History) sufficiently justifie their vertuous Accomplishments and Qualifications upon all accounts. And even the Imperfections we charge upon them will be found in greater measure to lye at our own doors.

We tax them with Inconstancy, whereas they are seldom or never seen to change, without just grounds, when they have once condescended to dispose of their Hearts. Which is so far from being reputed a Crime in our selves that it is almost scandalous for a Man to be thought a Constant Lover.

Neither is this wholly to be imputed to the Degeneracy of the present corrupted Age, since it was practis'd by several Men of the first Rank, in former Times: for was not *Theseus* as inconstant to *Ariadne*, as the effeminate *Paris* to *Oenone?*[2] Was it not the Ingratitude of Heroes that more than half furnisht *Ovid* with Subjects for his Epistles?[3]

Reservedness and a just Value for their own Worth we too often misconstrue for Pride in them. A worthy Esteem for her own Dignity is perhaps one of the most useful Precepts[4] that can be read to a young Lady in the School of *Vertue*. The constant Practice of the World convinces us, that no Merit can support its necessary Character, that

---

1   Plagiarist.

2   Ariadne, daughter of Minos, King of Crete, helped Theseus kill the man-eating Minotaur; Theseus honored his promise to take Ariadne away from Crete but abandoned her on the island of Naxos. Paris, son of the Priam, King of Troy, was abandoned at birth and raised by shepherds on Mount Ida, where he wed Oenone. Reunited with the royal family, he deserted his humble wife and ran off with Helen, wife of Menelaus, thereby initiating the Trojan War.

3   Ovid's *Heroides*, published around the time of the birth of Christ, purports to be a series of letters from legendary heroines to their lovers and husbands.

4   Instructions concerning moral conduct.

has not learnt to put some reasonable value upon it self. Yet experience tells us, as often as any laudable occasion requires their Compassion or Assistance, the Angels themselves are scarcely more ready to forget their Stations and condescend to Offices of *Charity*.

If they appear with the Ornaments of Dress, it is no more than their Sex's Priviledge, who were made for Natures greatest *Triumph*. Lustre and Value is inherent to Diamonds and precious Gems, yet who can find fault to see them set in *Gold?*

If by *Pride* we mean *Vanity of Mind*, let us fix the Instances in what we please, and I am afraid that our Sex will appear more guilty of that frailty than theirs. Perhaps it is not the smallest Instance of our Vanity to flatter our selves, that we are able to flatter them. Can the Female Register present us with any thing so vain as *Xerxes*, who imagin'd to scourge the Sea into calmness?[1] or like *Nero*, to enter on a common Stage and supplicate the Applause of his Subjects, (to say nothing of his setting the Imperial City on fire, to heighten his diversion, while he play'd the Destruction of *Troy*)?[2] so prodigal as *Alexander*, who, according to *Plutarch*, spent twelve Millions upon *Hephestion's* Tomb, when it was doubted if the current Cash of the World would answer so prodigious a Sum? Was it not his own Vanity, that caus'd him to set up for the Son of *Jupiter Ammon*; and the Temperance of his Mother *Olympias*, that checkt his foolish Ambition, and desired him not to make *Juno* jealous?[3] can the extravagance of *Cleopatra* her self compare with *Heliogabulus*, who filled his Fish-ponds with Rose-water, and suppli'd his Lamps with Balsam of *Arabia?*[4]

There is yet another Weakness wherewith we are wont to charge them, and that is, in point of *Secrecy*. The worthy keeping of a Secret

---

1   The Persian king Xerxes, at war with Greece in *c.*480 BC and enraged that the stormy Hellespont had destroyed one of his bridges, ordered his men to lash, yoke, and brand the sea.

2   The emperor Nero (AD 37–68) is said to have sung the martial song 'The Destruction of Troy' while Rome endured a fire that he himself may have ignited.

3   Alexander the Great, son of Olympias and Philip II of Macedonia, spent lavishly in honor of his friend and lover Hephaestion, who died in 324 BC. The oracle Jupiter (or Zeus) Ammon advised Alexander that Hephaestion should be worshiped as a hero. Juno (or Hera) was Jupiter's wife. Tate's primary source is Plutarch (AD *c.*50–*c.*125), *The Lives of the Noble Grecians and Romans*, 'Alexander'.

4   Heliogabalus (correctly Elagabalus), Roman emperor from AD 218 to AD 222, was reviled for his showy behavior. Cleopatra (69–30 BC), Queen of Egypt, was mistress to Julius Caesar and then to Mark Antony; she too was known for public shows of 'extravagance'.

entrusted to us, is certainly one of the noblest Talents whereof Humane Nature is capable; and if Women were not Mistresses of this Heroical Quality, the Fable of the *Syrens* would be made true, and the Sex would be only so many Charming Treacheries.[1] But certainly they have all the reason and justice in the World to dispute this Matter with us, which if it were to be fairly decided by Precedents, the Ballance would undoubtedly turn on their side.

'Tis reported indeed of a *Roman* Lady, the Wife of *Fulvius* the intimate Favourite of *Augustus*, that she committed the indiscretion of divulging a Secret, that in the consequence must prove fatal to the Life of her Husband: However, we are assur'd by the same Authors, that she was no sooner sensible of her Error, but she endeavour'd to expiate it by her own voluntary Death.[2]

We must first justifie the Conspiracy of *Cataline*, before we can well blame *Curius* his Mistress for the Discovery she made.[3]

But where the Cause is honourable, and the Service and Safety of one's Country concern'd, there is nothing more celebrated in History than *Female Fidelity*. Where have we any thing parallel to *Epicarnis* the *Roman* Lady, whom all the Threats of *Nero* could never compel to discover the Accomplices in the Plot with which she was made acquainted: He could by no means make her speak against the purpose she had taken of keeping a Secret of that importance. The sight of Torments shook the Resolution of the *Undertakers*, but she prevented the Executioners, and made the Tyrant confess, that she had more *Constancy* and *Discretion* than the very *Men* that form'd the Design, had *Weakness* and *Irresolution*.[4]

'Tis then a necessary Consequence, That Women are capable of *Friendship*. He that will not allow, that this Vertue is understood and practis'd by them in the most perfect degree, must never have read

---

[1] The Sirens, part bird and part woman, sang lovely songs to attract sailors to their island, where the men died.

[2] The reference is obscure but perhaps concerns Augustus Caesar's close friend Maecenas, who in 23 BC revealed a state secret to his wife (and Augustus's mistress), Terentia, concerning a conspiracy against Augustus.

[3] Catiline conspired against the consul Cicero, perhaps with the covert support of Julius Caesar. Curius was one of the conspirators; his mistress, Fulvia, may have informed Cicero of the conspiracy. ('*Curius* his Mistress' is a possessive form meaning 'Curius's mistress'.)

[4] The low-born Epicaris was privy to a plot against the Roman emperor Nero; she killed herself after being tortured but refused to reveal the names of the conspirators.

the Names of *Orinda* and *Leucasia*.[1] 'Tis but seldom they can have occasion of exercising this Vertue without scandal, beyond the sphere of their own *Sex*. A most eminent Divine of our Church, and Friend of the forementioned *Orinda*, to whom he address'd his most excellent Treatise of *the Measures and Offices of Friendship*,[2] He tells us, *'tis disputable whether have been more Illustrious in their Friendships, Men or Women*. He further adds, *that vertuous Women are the Beauties of Society and the Prettinesses of Friendships; and when we consider, that few persons in the World have all those Excellencies by which Friendship can be useful and illustrious, we may as well allow Women as Men to be Friends, since they have all those Qualifications that can be necessary and essential to Friendships: And we shall do too much honour to the Female Sex if we reject them from Friendships because they are not perfect; for if to Friendships we admit* imperfect *Men, (no Man being perfect) he that rejects Women, finds fault with them because they are not more perfect than Men, which either does secretly affirm, that they* ought *and can be* perfect, *or else it openly accuses Men of* Injustice *and* Partiality.

If any other Imperfections should be objected against the Sex than what is here mention'd, I make no question they will be found more justifiable upon every such account than *Ours*. However, I thought this short Apology requisite to precede the ensuing *History* of their *Vertues*. For which Historical Way of Vindication, two Reasons offer'd themselves, both as it seem'd the most proper Method of doing Justice to the fair Sex, *Examples* being *Demonstrations* in the Case: And that their Cause would thus receive least prejudice by any Defects of mine in Style or Language. For, proceeding upon the Testimonies of History, there was little more left for me to do than barely to *Translate* or *Transcribe*. Plainness of Expression being most natural in matter of Evidence, and Truth uncapable of receiving advantage by any Colours of *Rhetorick* or *Fancy*.[3]

Lastly, In Defence both of this Undertaking and the Method pursu'd in the following Treatise, I have follow'd, as well as I could,

---

1   The 'Matchless Orinda', as she was called, is Katherine Philips (1631–64); many of her poems on friendship and other subjects were written for Anne Owen, 'Lucasia' in her verse.

2   Jeremy Taylor's *Discourse on the Nature and Offices of Friendship in a Letter to the Most Ingenious and Excellent M[rs] K[atherine] P[hilips]* first appeared in 1657. The third edition (1662) bears the title that Tate reproduces; see pp. 96, 98–99 for the subsequent quotations.

3   Imagination, invention.

the Direction of *Montaigne* in his *Essays*, in his Chapter of *three Illustrious Examples of Female Vertue*.[1]

These are (says He) *my* Three Stories, *which I find as Divertive*[2] *and Tragick as any of those we make out of our* own Heads, *wherewith to entertain the People. I wonder that they who are addicted to such Relations, do not rather cull out a thousand fine Stories which are to be found in very good* Authors, *that would save them the trouble of* Inventing, *but be more* useful *and* diverting. *He that would make a* Collection *of them would need to add nothing of his own, but the* Connexion *only, as it were the Sodder of another Metal, &c.*

I shall therefore pretend to be no more than a *Collector* in this Essay, (the Method and Connexion excepted) and if I have not always made choice of the best Examples the respective Subjects would afford, yet I have at least taken such as are capable of affording some Entertainment. I shall reckon, that I have done enough by way of *Original*, if the three *Additional Characters* may endure Reading after the Historical Instances. 'Tis my comfort, that the Female Sex can no more be dishonour'd by my imperfect *Oblation*,[3] than it can stand in need of our *Panegyricks* to support their Reputation; being in this particular like the *Divine Nature* describ'd by *Lucretius*,[4]

Ipsa suis pollens opibus nil indiga nostri.

Enricht with their *own Excellence*, they shine,
Nor want our *Worship* to become *Divine.*

---

1   For the subsequent quotation, see Michel Eyquem de Montaigne (1533–92), 'Of Three Good Women', in vol. 2 of *The Essays of Michael Seigneur de Montaigne*, trans. Charles Cotton (1686) 666. The women are Romans who died self-sacrificing deaths: an unnamed neighbor of the letter-writer Pliny the Younger; Arria, wife of the consul Cecinna Petus; and Paulina, wife of the philosopher Seneca. Some of Tate's remarks on these women elsewhere in his treatise borrow from Montaigne's account. Haywood discusses Paulina in *Reflections on the Various Effects of Love.*
2   That is, diverting; entertaining.
3   Offering.
4   The subsequent quotation, from Lucretius (*c.*99–55 BC [?]), *De rerum natura*, ii. 650, concerns what appears in a modern translation as 'the very nature of divinity': 'itself mighty by its own resources, needing us not at all' (W.H.D. Rouse, trans.).

THE CONTENTS OR Principal Matters, Illustrated by *Examples in the ensuing Treatise.*

AN Historical Vindication of the FEMALE SEX.

If Art[1] were necessary in the Charming Sex's Defence, I should have declin'd the Undertaking; but since there is no more requir'd for their Advantage, than setting Things in a true Light, I shall commit their Cause to impartial Sincerity and their own Merit: which will sufficiently furnish us from its own rich stock, without traversing the Fairy Regions of Invention.

Since we are apt to reproach them up as high as *Eve*, I know not why we should not appeal to the Creation for their Dignity and Preeminence. We there find our first Father Created like a Commoner in the open Field, amongst the Brutes of the Earth, and form'd of the self-same Mold: the Woman of more delicate Composition, and framed of a Rib taken from the Man; from whence, according to the force of the Original Language, the Creator is said to have *made* Man, but to have *built* Woman. The divine Artifice was first exercis'd upon the Elements and inanimate Productions, after these upon inferiour Animals, who were succeeded by the Man, and He by the Woman,

---

[1] Artifice, invention.

who was the Consummation of the Works of God. The Man was put into the Garden, where the Woman made her first Appearance like a queen in her Native Palace, when all things were fitted for her Entertainment. Since when by a particular Priviledge of Nature, she carries in her looks an Air of Paradise. If she occasion'd the Expulsion of the Man from his happy Seat, she brought all the Beauty of *Eden* in her own Person. We find *Adam* complaining of Paradise without his *Eve*, but never after Exile, of his *Eve* without Paradise.

This Soveraignty of Beauty is a Prerogative born with the Sex, and the only thing whereof we have at no time been able to divest them. The Moroseness of the Philosopher, the Speculation of the Recluse, the business of the Statesman, nor the Fatigues of the Warriour, have render'd them insensible of its Charms. By the prevalency of this resistless Spell, they have baffled the Resolution of the wise, and disarm'd the Resentments of the most furious. By this Triumph of Nature they have effected what was despair'd by the Art and strength of Man. In the lowest Ebb of Fortune they have wrought those Wonders, and brought to pass those Revolutions, that have astonisht Mankind, and left them silent Admirers of the Performance. It was by the Force of her Beauty, that *Abigail* prevented the incensed *David* from extirpating her Family, a devoted Sacrifice to Destruction, for the churlishness and indiscretion of her Husband.[1] 'Twas the Intercession of Beautiful *Esther* that reversed the deplorable Condition of her Countrymen.[2] *Judith* by the same Harmless Magick preserved her Nation from Ruin.[3] Nothing on Earth could compare with the Extent of *Job's* Afflictions but his Piety: His Sufferings and Submission were equally without Precedent; but after all, as the greatest Earthly Reward that Providence could find for his unparallel'd Patience, it blest him with Daughters surpassing all other Women in Beauty.[4] For the Truth of this Topick I dare appeal to every Man that has Eyes and a Heart. If Mankind were consulted, we should scarce find one

---

[1] In 1 Samuel 25.3–42, the wealthy Nabal mistreats King David's servant. David vows to destroy Nabal and his family; Nabal's wise and beautiful wife, Abigail, successfully intercedes.

[2] In Esther 2.1–8.14, the beautiful and virtuous Queen Esther and her cousin Mordecai thwart Haman's plan to kill the Jews.

[3] In Judith 10.11–15.13, the beautiful widow Judith saves the Israelites when she entices and then decapitates King Nebuchadnezzar's general Holofernes, who had besieged her town.

[4] Job's beautiful daughters were Jemimah, Keziah, and Keren-happuch.

Individual of so cold and Saturnine[1] a Temper, who has not seen some Face that charm'd him.

Let us hearken to the Sentiments of Nature, that is always true in her first and unprejudic'd Decisions.

It is reported of a Persian Monarch, who for many years had no Issue, and being desirous to have an Heir of his own Body, upon his earnest Supplication to the Gods, he obtain'd his Wishes in the Birth of a Son. So unexpected a Favour made him more than ordinarily solicitous for the Education of the Child, and his future Fortunes; wherefore he sent to the Astrologers for an exact Calculation of his Nativity. They return'd him Answer, That if the Infant saw Sun or Moon at any time within the space of Ten Years, he would most certainly be deprived of sight. The King thereupon caused a Cell to be cut for him in a deep Rock, recommending him to the Care of a Learned Tutor to instruct him in the liberal Arts. The Time being expired, and He permitted to come into open Day, they brought before him a Dog, a Horse, a Lyon, with several others the most beautiful of Creatures, whereof he had been told, but knew not how to distinguish them. He shewed some Complacency in the sight of them, but without any Transport, and asking their respective Names, he passed them over. They likewise shewed him Silver, Gold and Gemms, which he survey'd with as little Regard. The King at length commanded certain beautiful Virgins, and richly attir'd, to be brought into his Presence, whom the Prince no sooner beheld, but with a strange Alacrity in his Countenance, and Ecstasy of Spirit, he demanded what kind of Creatures they were, by what Names they were called, and to what use Created. His Tutor jestingly reply'd, *These be those evil Spirits of whom I have so often told you, the great Seducers of Mankind.* To which the Prince warmly made Answer, *If you have better Angels make much of them, good Tutor; but leave me to be attended by these pretty Devils.* If this Relation be not true in Fact, it is certainly so in Nature; and whensoever the same Circumstances shall happen, I will answer for the same Event.

[Source: Nahum Tate, *A Present for the Ladies: Being an Historical Account of Several Illustrious Persons of the Female Sex*, 2nd ed (1693) A2r–B3v, 1–7.]

---

[1] Sluggish, gloomy.

Bibliography

I. Critical Edition

Selected Works of Eliza Haywood. Ed. Alexander Pettit, et al. 6 vols. London: Pickering & Chatto, 2000–2001.

II. Editions of the Principal Works in This Volume

Fantomina. British Literature, 1640–1789:An Anthology. 2nd ed. Ed. Robert DeMaria, Jr. Oxford: Blackwell, 2001. 602–16.

Fantomina. Masquerade Novels of Eliza Haywood. Delmar, NY: Scholars' Facsimiles & Reprints, 1986.

Fantomina. Norton Anthology of Literature by Women: Traditions in English. 2nd ed. Ed. Sandra M. Gilbert and Susan Gubar. New York: Norton, 1996. 205–24.

Fantomina. Popular Fiction by Women, 1660–1730: An Anthology. Ed. Paula R. Backscheider and John J. Richetti. New York: Oxford UP, 1996. 227–48.

Love-Letters on All Occasions. Miscellaneous Writings, 1725–43. Ed. Alexander Pettit. *Selected Works of Eliza Haywood,* set 1, vol. 1. London: Pickering & Chatto, 2000. 123–204.

Reflections on the Various Effects of Love. Miscellaneous Writings, 1725–43. Ed. Alexander Pettit. *Selected Works of Eliza Haywood,* set 1, vol. 1. London: Pickering & Chatto, 2000. 73–122.

The Tea-Table. Miscellaneous Writings, 1725–43. Ed. Alexander Pettit. *Selected Works of Eliza Haywood,* set 1, vol. 1. London: Pickering & Chatto, 2000. 1–34.

III. Primary and Secondary Bibliographies

Backscheider, Paula R., Felicity Nussbaum, and Philip B. Anderson. 'Eliza Haywood'. *An Annotated Bibliography of Twentieth-Century Critical Studies of Women and Literature, 1660–1800.* Ed. Backscheider, Nussbaum, and Anderson. *Garland Reference Library of the Humanities,* vol. 64. New York: Garland, 1977. 159–61.

Barash, Carol L. 'Eliza Fowler Haywood'. *An Encyclopedia of British Women Writers.* Ed. Paul Schlueter and June Schlueter. *Garland*

Reference Library of the Humanities, vol. 818. New York: Garland, 1988. 223–25.

Blouch, Christine. 'Eliza Haywood: An Annotated Critical Bibliography'. *Eighteenth-Century Anglo-American Women Novelists: A Critical Reference Guide*. Ed. Doreen Saar and Mary Anne Schofield. New York: G.K. Hall, 1996. 263–300.

Spedding, Patrick. *A Bibliography of Eliza Haywood*. London: Pickering & Chatto, forthcoming.

IV. Biographical Studies

Beasley, Jerry C. 'Eliza Haywood'. *British Novelists, 1660–1800*. Ed. Martin C. Battestin. *Dictionary of Literary Biography*, vol. 39, part 1. Detroit: Gale, 1985. 251–59.

Blouch, Christine. 'Eliza Haywood'. *Miscellaneous Writings, 1725–43*. Ed. Alexander Pettit. *Selected Works of Eliza Haywood*, set 1, vol. 1. London: Pickering & Chatto, 2000. xxi–lxxxii.

———. 'Eliza Haywood and the Romance of Obscurity'. *SEL: Studies in English Literature* 31 (1991): 535–52.

Firmager, Gabrielle M. 'Eliza Haywood: Some Further Light on Her Background?' *Notes and Queries* n.s. 38 (1991): 181–83.

Fletcher, Edward G. 'The Date of Eliza Haywood's Death'. *Notes and Queries* 166 (1934): 385.

Ingrassia, Catherine. 'Additional Information about Eliza Haywood's 1749 Arrest for Seditious Libel'. *Notes and Queries* n.s. 44 (1997): 202–4.

Moore, C.A. 'A Note on the Biography of Mrs. Eliza Haywood'. *Modern Language Notes* 33 (1918): 248–50.

Whicher, George Frisbie. *The Life and Romances of Mrs. Eliza Haywood*. New York: Columbia UP, 1915.

V. Introductory Studies of Haywood (selected)

Backscheider, Paula R. Introduction. *Selected Fiction and Drama of Eliza Haywood*. Ed. Backscheider. New York: Oxford UP, 1999. xiii–xliv.

Beasley, Jerry C. Introduction. *'The Injur'd Husband: or, The Mistaken Resentment' and 'Lasselia: or, The Self-Abandon'd'*. Ed. Beasley. Lexington: UP of Kentucky, 1999. ix–xxxiii.

Schofield, Mary Anne. *Eliza Haywood*. Boston: Twayne, 1985.

———. *Quiet Rebellion: The Fictional Heroines of Eliza Fowler Haywood*. Washington DC: UP of America, 1982.

Tobin, Beth Fowkes. Introduction. *The History of Miss Betsy Thoughtless*. Ed. Tobin. New York: Oxford UP, 1997. ix–xxxv.

VI. Critical Essays on the Principal Works in This Volume

Craft, Catherine A. 'Reworking Male Models: Aphra Behn's *Fair Vow Breaker*, Eliza Haywood's *Fantomina*, and Charlotte Lennox's *Female Quixote*'. *Modern Language Review* 86 (1991): 821–38.

Croskery, Margaret Case. 'Masquing Desire: The Politics of Passion in Eliza Haywood's *Fantomina*'. *The Passionate Fictions of Eliza Haywood: Essays on Her Life and Work*. Ed. Kirsten T. Saxton and Rebecca P. Bocchicchio. Lexington: UP of Kentucky, 2000. 69–94.

Ingrassia, Catherine. 'Fashioning Female Authorship in Eliza Haywood's *The Tea-Table*'. *Journal of Narrative Technique* 28 (1998): 287–304.

Nelson, T.G.A. 'Stooping to Conquer in Goldsmith, Haywood, and Wycherley'. *Essays in Criticism* 46 (1996): 319–39.

Pettit, Alexander. 'Eliza Haywood's *Tea-Table* and the Decentering of Moral Argument'. *Papers on Language and Literature* 38 (2002): 244–69.

———. 'The Function of Food in Eliza Haywood's Rhetoric of Restraint'. *Sustaining Literature: Essays in Commemoration of the Life and Work of Simon Varey*. Ed. Gregory Clingham. Lewisburg, PA: Bucknell UP, forthcoming.

———. 'Our Fictions and Eliza Haywood's Fictions'. *Talking Forward, Talking Back: Critical Dialogues with the Enlightenment*. Ed. Rüdiger Ahrens and Kevin L. Cope. New York: AMS, 2002. 144–66.

Thompson, Helen. 'Plotting Materialism: W. Charleton's *The Ephesian Matron*, E. Haywood's *Fantomina*, and Feminine Consistency'. *Eighteenth-Century Studies* 35 (2002): 195–214.

From the Publisher

A name never says it all, but the word "Broadview" expresses a good deal of the philosophy behind our company. We are open to a broad range of academic approaches and political viewpoints. We pay attention to the broad impact book publishing and book printing has in the wider world; for some years now we have used 100% recycled paper for most titles. Our publishing program is internationally oriented and broad-ranging. Our individual titles often appeal to a broad readership too; many are of interest as much to general readers as to academics and students.

Founded in 1985, Broadview remains a fully independent company owned by its shareholders—not an imprint or subsidiary of a larger multinational.

For the most accurate information on our books (including information on pricing, editions, and formats) please visit our website at www.broadviewpress.com. Our print books and ebooks are also available for sale on our site.

broadview press
www.broadviewpress.com

MIX
Paper from
responsible sources
FSC® C013916

The interior of this book is printed on 100% recycled paper.